Praise for
SHRINKING THE HEROES

Originally published as
From the Notebooks of Doctor Brain

WINNER
Carl Brandon Society, Kindred Award 2007

SPECIAL CITATION (Runner-Up)
Philip K. Dick Prize 2007

CHARLES SAUNDERS, author of *Imaro:* "Pure satire . . . laugh-out-loud comedy. Superhero parodies have been done before. So have dysfunctional super-beings, ranging from Spider-Man and the Fantastic Four to *Watchmen*. But nobody has done it as well as the Minister. If Richard Pryor had ever written science fiction, he might have come up with something like *Shrinking the Heroes* .... Minister Faust is shaping up to become a one-man New Wave in the SF genre."

PUBLISHERS WEEKLY (STARRED REVIEW): "Sharp satire of caped crusaders hides a deeper critique of individual treatment versus social injustice .... uncomfortable parallels to real-world urban tragedies in the novel's 'July 16 Attacks.'"

ENTERTAINMENT WEEKLY: "Entertaining . . . saavy."

ROBERT SAWYER, Author of *Wake:* "Minister Faust does it again: an outlandish, outrageous tour de force by the most innovative prose stylist in the field, bar none."

ST. LOUIS POST-DISPATCH: "Brilliantly complex ... dead-on satire of our times."

BOOKLIST: "[An] excellent superhero comedy as well as an unsettling satire."

BOOKPAGE: "One of the most entertaining books to cross your path this year."

SCIFI.COM: "[Minister Faust's] insane fecundity and jazzy verbal dexterity, his sheer brio and exuberance... reminds me of Ishmael Reed or Steve Aylett... plenty of moments in this novel where I laughed out loud."

EDEN ROBINSON, author of *Monkey Beach:* "Gleefully surreal approach to storylines, wonderful wordplay and offbeat, faster-than-speeding-bullet wit... a marvellous read."

COREY REDEKOP, author of *Shelf Monkey:* "Faust's novel stands equal to such classics [as *Watchmen* and *Dark Knight*]."

SFSITE.COM: "A whirlwind of jokes, satire, obscure pop references, devastating cultural analysis and prose poetry that never lets up from beginning to end .... This is political and cultural satire of the highest sort, and Faust is earning a place among the masters of the craft."

CHERYL MORGAN'S BEST OF 2007: "A modern-day Watchmen written by a Canadian Lenny Henry with a passion for race politics."

BLOG T.O. SUNDAY BOOK REVIEW: "A major accomplishment that is laugh out loud funny . . . This is the most revolutionary work of SF since William Gibson's *Neuromancer*. Faust has invented a whole new genre of writing and rendered it in some of best prose in any genre. He's basically given birth to the future. And it's one good looking baby.

"Ostensibly, the book is a self-help book for superheroes written by their psychiatrist. But once you look beyond the humour you find a novel about America and September 11, an actual self-help book that works on the political and personal level, and a careful examination of our cultural myths and gods. It's funny, insightful and very serious . . . . I'm confident in saying that this is the best SF book of the 2007—maybe the best book of the year."

THEOCENTRIC: "Hilarious.... Faust's writing style is absolutely a blast."

RENO GAZETTE-JOURNAL: "A hilarious new voice.... One of the most compelling reads I've experienced.... One of the most layered, complicated narratives I've come across, and the ending is particularly chilling."

THE PINOCCHIO THEORY: "Had me laughing from the first page to the last. But the book is also a mind-boggling, multi-levelled allegory of racism and corporate fascism in America today. The novel's brilliance has much to do with its exuberant linguistic and conceptual inventiveness. Faust gleefully rings the changes on all sorts of pop culture sensations and scandals, with superheroes as the celebrity targets of paparazzi and gutter journalists. The lives of the superheroes abound in episodes of drug addiction, hidden sexual fetishes, nervous breakdowns, and bitter family disputes — not to mention miscegenation, still a matter of shock and bewilderment, shame, hysterical confusion, and disavowed fantasies in our supposedly 'post-racial' society. In its offhanded and slyly ironic way, the book both delivers a hilarious roller-coaster ride filled with comic book thrills and chills, and reminds us about what is really scary."

THE GATEWAY: "...scathing social commentary and political satire [on] the nature of modern journalism and politics, to drugs, racism and vapid, shallow celebrities .... Excellent."

THE EDMONTON SUN: "Wildly imaginative."

THE GATEWAY: "...scathing social commentary and political satire [on] the nature of modern journalism and politics, to drugs, racism and vapid, shallow celebrities.... Excellent."

THE EDMONTON JOURNAL: "Tough political message underlies comedy about a Doctor Phil for the superhuman... highly entertaining and sneakily politically provocative."

STATIC MULTIMEDIA.COM: "... a hilarious, sure-fire page turner."

SUNQIST BLOG: "The best book of the year... incredibly important...."

STRANGE HORIZONS: "Hilarious and pointed.... Like all the best satirists (Swift comes to mind).... Cutting commentary... true art."

SF READER.COM: "A well-paced suspense novel packed with twists and bluffs, together with an intelligent satire on post-9/11 Western society.... Wonderfully written... a multi-layered and satisfying read."

SAKURA OF DOOM: "Brilliant."

Praise for
THE ALCHEMISTS OF KUSH

ISHMAEL REED, author of *Mumbo Jumbo:* "It was only a matter of time before the hip hop culture would invade the literary world. With *The Alchemists of Kush,* Minister Faust is leading the invasion. His novel is possibly the first hip hop epic. Hip hop has a short attention span on most occasions. *The Alchemists of Kush* gives it gravitas."

CHARLES R. SAUNDERS, author of *Imaro:* "Minister Faust's first two books broke new ground in the SF field. His latest, *The Alchemists of Kush*, not only breaks new ground; with the story-telling skills of a modern jali, the Minister creates new vistas of history, mythology, erudition, uplift, tragedy, triumph, and contemporary community activism. Once you start the first page of this book, you won't be able to put it down until you've finished the last one."

SPARKLE HAYTER, author of *What's a Girl Gotta Do?:* "I started *The Alchemists of Kush* and kept reading until I finished. Minister Faust has the most electrifying and true voice I've read in years. *The Alchemists of Kush* is brilliant."

KENNETH T. WILLIAMS, playwright of *Thunderstick:* "I loved the story, the mythology, and the characters. I found myself locked into it for hours at a time and couldn't put it down. Rich in detail . . . A great book."

WAYNE ARTHURSON, author of *Fall from Grace:* "A hell of a story. A hell of a book. A hell of a style. A frenetic novel and voice—very enjoyable. Minister Faust knows how to write about male relationships, brotherhoods, and getting into the hearts of men, and about boys turning into men. The Alchemists of Kush is a triumph, not just for Minister Faust, but for Edmonton and the community of Kush."

SALADIN QUANAAH ALLAH, author of *Tales of an Urban Sufi,* MC on *Brothers from Another Planet:* "Inspired by a true story and set against an urban backdrop of African immigrant communities in present day Edmonton, Minister Faust weaves a masterful tale around the sacred Book of the Golden Falcon, ten Hermetical scrolls that expound upon the cross pollination of cultural themes and social considerations shared by Original People throughout the African Diaspora.

"*The Alchemists of Kush* is more than a story; it's a philosophical elixir of Kemetic (Egyptian) folklore, African traditions, urban Sufism, hip hop culture, and Five Percenter pedagogy designed to transmute the challenges of colonialism, assimilation, juvenile delinquency, and moral decay into a universal solvent. Through an array of colourful characters facing unique struggles towards advancing a common cause, Minister Faust boldly takes his readers on an alchemical journey of Self Knowledge, Self Determination, and Community Action, a transformative terrain of true & living 'gold'!"

ARLO MAVERICK, MC/producer, Politic Live: "*The Alchemists of Kush* is both a powerful and vital contribution to Canadian literature that looks at contemporary Edmonton from an African-Canadian perspective. The characters reflect the true diversity of African-Canadians living in Edmonton. Hopefully this is the beginning of more great novels from people in Edmonton that look like us that tell stories about us."

JAY TURNER, game writer on Dragon Age, Mass Effect 2: "You don't read this book; you hear it. You absorb it, and you learn it. Minister Faust writes with impeccable rhythm and percussive language, describing each scene on a bassbeat of emotion. His words move like a camera through a movie scene, showing you what's most important and leaving out the chaff.... The author could have written this book on a turntable as easily as a keyboard, and the message would have been just as clear. Conflicts, beliefs, culture, and fears ... reflected against the backdrop of a violent myth of slavery, escape, murder, and transformation.... Pulsing, thundering, and yet gentle and charming way.... Fully recommended.

MARK KOZUB, author of *The Uptown Browns*, founding father of The Raving Poets: "*The Alchemists of Kush* is its own kind of alchemy: ancient past, gritty present, mythic fantasy, social activism, it's how Minister Faust blends it all that gives the book its rare power. Reflecting the brilliance of his earlier novels, Minister Faust again strikes the perfect balance between eloquence and entertainment. Within the first twenty pages, I could (and did) imagine *The Alchemists of Kush* on the big screen. It's got that epic sweep to it. More importantly, I kept reading (and reading, and reading) because Minister Faust knows it's all about creating characters you'll love. I wept at the end."

MILTON JOHN DAVIS, author of *Meji*, co-editor of *Griots: A Sword and Soul Anthology*: "Minister Faust presents a fierce piece of fiction in a way that only he can. I was entertained, educated and fascinated with his alchemy. The Alchemists of Kush has to be one of the best books I've read this year."

MARI SASANO, writer and journalist: "Minister Faust's *The Alchemists of Kush* is an inspiration—bringing voice to an area of E-town and a diverse cultural community that are too easily overshadowed by crime stories. Minister Faust also creates a mythic metastory that runs parallel to the authentic characters and vivid settings, balancing the abstract with the heart-wrenchingly specific. No one will fail to be moved by the struggles of the divine, but it's the recognition of the heroism in the mundane that will change the world."

ANDREA HAIRSTON, author of *Mindscape:* "In *The Alchemists of Kush,* Minister Faust risks telling stories that threaten the empire-builders, that encourage us all to become agents of action. Such a novel demands a truthful response. I've been thinking we need prayers for right now. Advertising jingles and gangsta rhymes split our souls, jangle our spirits a thousand times a day. Minister Faust is a technician of the sacred, getting the geometry, the dance of our humanity into his words. Buy The Alchemists of Kush for yourself and a friend. Read it and then give it away. Give it away a lot."

LESTER K. SPENCE, author of *Stare Into the Darkness: The Limits of Hip Hop and Black Politics:* "The first modern Pan-Africanist coming-of-age story, bringing together the traditional components of the Hero's Tale with a rich understanding of Ancient Egypt and contemporary realities for diasporal youth. The characters jump off of the page as Minister Faust, one of the best black male writers of my generation, deftly moves back and forth between Ancient KMT and contemporary Edmonton."

NATHAN CROWDER, author of *Cobalt City Blues:* "The Alchemists of Kush blew my expectations clean out of the water. The importance of faith has been fresh in my mind recently. And as the novel is, at its heart, about a spiritual awakening, it felt perfectly timed that I discovered it when I did. The twin stories and characters had me drawn in immediately, and it didn't hurt that there was ample name dropping of favourite musical artists (Gil Scott-Heron among them) and comic book characters (Static and King Peacock). The characters are rich, their battles hard fought and heartbreaking. And the resulting affirmation of love, community, pride, responsibility, and family makes this the caliber of book I would love to see as required reading …. Highly recommended."

Praise for
THE COYOTE KINGS
Book One: Space-Age Bachelor Pad

2004 FINALIST:

The Philip K. Dick Award
The Locus Best First Novel Award
The Compton-Crook Award

A TOP TEN BOOK OF 2004 FOR:

January Magazine, Fiction
Barnes & Noble, SF&F
Amazon.com, SF&F
SF Site, SF&F, Editor's Choice

A LOCUS NOTABLE BOOK

ERNEST DICKERSON, director, *The Walking Dead, The Wire, Dexter, Demon Knight, Never Die Alone:* "Minister Faust is Samuel Delaney, Harlan Ellison and Ishmael Reed all rolled into one. His writing is biting, insightful and hugely entertaining."

THE NEW YORK TIMES: "A jumpy, hold-nothing-back style.... Faust anatomizes [the Edmonton setting] with the same loving care Joyce brought to early-20th-century Dublin.... fresh and stylish entertainment."

KIRKUS REVIEWS and ***THE HOLLYWOOD REPORTER:*** "Like Kevin Smith as if he'd grown up in an African immigrant neighbourhood-just as comic- and pop culture-obsessed but with a dose of righteous ethnic minority fury."

ROBERT J. SAWYER, author of *Hominids*: "A stylistic tour de force. The characters are unforgettable, the slang infectious, and the whole thing is just incredibly charming."

RICHARD MORGAN, author of *Market Forces:* "Outstanding, like nothing I've ever read in the genre . . . in fact Minister Faust has pretty much invented his own genre. Full of surprises, caring and heartfelt. I'm kind of envious of what he's done here. Really edgy unpleasantness . . . up there with the best of them."

CHARLES SAUNDERS, author of *Imaro:* "A few pages in, I was hooked – not only by the quality of the prose, but also by its sheer audacity.... In the Minister's hands, Edmonton becomes as lively and lethal as New York and Los Angeles put together.... A brilliant first novel..... Minister Faust... is shaping up to become a one-man New Wave in the SF genre."

NALO HOPKINSON, author of *Brown Girl in the Ring* and *Midnight Robber:* "Off the freakin hook. Funky... with heart, style, humour, and attitude to spare."

TANANARIVE DUE, author of *The Good House* and *The Living Blood:* "Incredibly imaginative and bulging with pop culture and political references, this is a trip unlike anything you've ever read. Endlessly entertaining."

STEVEN BARNES, author of *Lion's Blood* and *Zulu Heart:* "Minister Faust has a voice that has to be experienced to be believed. Once you read Coyote Kings, you'll never forget it."

SHEREE THOMAS, editor of *Dark Matter:* "Outrageously hilarious and horrifying by turns.... Sharply satiric intelligence and immense imagination... an exciting new voice in the field."

COREY REDEKOP, author of *Shelf Monkey:* "Alive with vitality and verve, a jumping jive of energy juice that never stops moving. I loved every moment of it."

BOOKLIST [Starred Review]: "Interwoven narratives and fascinating characters with strong voices...make for a fantastic contemporary adventure."

THE NATIONAL POST; THE OTTAWA CITIZEN; CANWEST NEWS SERVICES and CITIZEN NEWS SERVICES: "The most exciting Canadian debut in decades."

PUBLISHERS WEEKLY: "The dense writing, the ponderings on the nature of reality and a complex plot that all comes together at the end... will remind some readers of Neal Stephenson [and] represents a sharp-edged new voice in the genre."

Narmer's Palette
Edmonton, Alberta

Jacket and interior design by Gentle Robot.

Print: ISBN 978-0-9877039-0-3
Amazon-Kindle Edition: ISBN 978-0-9869024-8-2

Version 2.2

First Narmer's Palette Books Print Edition: September 2013

SHRINKING THE HEROES

Originally published as *From the Notebooks of Doctor Brain*

WINNER
Carl Brandon Society Kindred Award 2007

SPECIAL CITATION (Runner-Up)
Philip K. Dick Prize 2007

A novel by

Minister Faust

For my very own
Mary-Jane Watson,
my beloved wife,
Michelle

UNMASKED!

WHEN BEING A SUPERHERO CAN'T SAVE YOU FROM YOURSELF

SELF HELP FOR TODAY'S HYPERHOMINIDS

By

Doctor Brain

Advance Praise for

UNMASKED!
When Being a Superhero
Can't Save You From Yourself

About the Author

Dr. Eva Brain-Silverman lives and works at the Hyper-Potentiality Clinic inside the refurbished Mount Palomax Observatory in Los Ditkos. She has been helping hyper-hominids for over twenty years, and is the author of such best-sellers as:

Seven Habits of Highly Defective Teams

Why Do Bad Villains "Happen" to Good Heroes?

Evil Geniuses Who Hate Humanity and the Women Who Love Them

Sacred Identity: Reclaiming the Demi-God in You

Secrets from Menton's Brain: Using Two Lefts to Make Yourself Right

Being Super-Mom in Today's Multiverse

Side-Kicked! When the Alpha-Hero Treats You Like Omega

Bulletproof, Schmulletproof

Secret Origins, Starring: Your Miserable Life

PREFACE

HEY! YOU IN THE CAPE!

Why Are You Reading this Book?

You can wrap a steel I-beam around your neck with your bare hands and wear it like a tie. You can swim so quickly that you can go back in time to offer Columbus correct directions to India. You can climb the outside of a building, regurgitate the ton of paper you've eaten, and weave a beautiful multilevel hive while not paying a cent in downtown rent.

But are you happy?

There was an innocent time not so long ago when most people assumed that the flamboyant adventurers whose stories emblazoned the front pages of our newspapers and whose exploits ricocheted across the six o'clock news must really have had it all: fame, good looks, public adulation, and seemingly godlike powers.

But as our society has matured, many of the greatest heroes of our time have come to the numbing epiphany that invincibility and immortality simply aren't enough. The war of *Götterdämmerung* was finally concluded in victory, the worst ultra-menaces were locked inside the maximum-security force fields of Asteroid Zed, and the rest of the misguided offenders are being cared for by the finest psychiatric facilities for the atomically insane.

But while super-lawbreakers are being profiled in movies of the week, fêted for their (sometimes literally) ghost-written autobiographies, and cared for to the price of millions of tax dollars, who will care for *you?*

Who will care for you, the brave men and women who put away the menacing malefactors? Who will care for you, the courageous crusaders who risked your headquarters, your magic bracelets and diadems, your proprietary technology, your connection with your sub-dimensional xeno-souls, and even your lives? Who will care for you, who jeopardised every relationship you were forced to put on hold or which you allowed to wither while you were fighting to preserve our freedom?

Far too often, the sad answer has been . . . *no one.*

You men and women who kept our world safe from the likes of the Infinity Farmer and his Time Tractor, from X-Stacy and the Ravers, or from the technopurges of Robot-Stalin, have too often defined yourselves solely by the existence of your foes. But what are you supposed to do now that those foes are gone, and the ungrateful world no longer applauds from the safety of its decorative balconies?

What are you supposed to do now that you're trapped in a safe world of your own making, a world which offers you no challenge, no rôle, no identity, and no external enemies?

Yes, the supervillains of old are gone. But there's a new group of them around today. And they're psychic. No, not psychic like Sarah Bellum, Menton the Destroyer, or the specially-relative Einstein Baboons.

Nor have these villains crafted poisons such as green glowing crystals hidden inside lead strong boxes, or poisonous prions murdering you one DNA-helix at a time. Instead these poisons are locked inside your head and your heart, revealing themselves as depression, paranoia, rage, guilt, performance anxiety, psionic decay, dimension-shifting, impotence, im-omnipotence, or any number of other impairments of the soul.

Perhaps now you're forced to recognise that hyper-hominidism is equal part curse to the blessing of your glory days.

But if you've been suffering due to HH, the time to suffer without help is no more.

MEET YOUR MENTOR

My name is Dr. Eva Brain-Silverman, but to thousands of super-powered individuals like you I'm simply known as Doctor Brain. For twenty years at my Hyper-Potentiality Clinic in the refurbished Mount Palomax Observatory in sunny Los Ditkos, I've been helping the extraordinarily-abled to adjust to a life beyond heroics, and to feel alive again even when there are no more neutron bombs to defuse inside the UN building.

The book you're holding in your hands is the summation of two decades of advice I've dispensed as balm to heroes across North America at lectures, seminars and clinical sessions.

But it's more than that. It's also the case study of the most spectacular group session of my career, whose destructive dysfunction culminated in the diabolical July 16th Attacks which are even now reshaping our world.

When first contacted by the Board of Directors of the Fantastic Order Of Justice to assist its six most contentious and confused members in conquering their intercommunal conflicts, I leapt at the opportunity to assist. Which heroes among Earth's foremost fighting force for freedom, I wondered, were so bent on antagonising each other and destroying themselves that their own leadership was threatening to terminate them unless they solved their problems in group therapy?

To my astonishment, my line-up was a list of legends *among* legends:

- **Omnipotent Man,** AKA Wally Watchtower, seventy-one year old refugee from the destroyed planet Argon, and Earth's mightiest man,
- **The Flying Squirrel,** AKA Festus Piltdown III, seventy year old billionaire industrialist and scourge of the criminal underworld,
- **Iron Lass,** AKA Hnossi Icegaard, the immortal Norse warrior-goddess and the planet's leading martial strategist,
- **The Brotherfly,** AKA André "P-Fly" Parker, twenty-six year old wall-crawling, wise-cracking, blue-bottled ladies' man,
- **Power Grrrl,** AKA Syndi Tycho, the nineteen year old dynamic diva and pop music sensation, and
- **The X-Man,** AKA Philip Kareem Edgerton, the thirty-four year old detective supreme and militant rabble-rouser from the squalid ghettoes of Los Ditkos.

While numbering only six, these individuals bore afflictions galore: **SID** (Secret Identity Diffusion), **NPD** (Narcissistic Personality Disorder), **SC** (Saviour Complex), **ODI-CFFB** (Obsessive Defensive-Ideation and Compulsive Fight-or-Flight Behaviour), **IC** (Icon Trap), **Mortiquaeroticism** (death-seeking urges), and **RNPN** (Racialised Narcissistic Projection Neurosis), among others.

Added into this miasma of mental maladies were group dysfunctions: **Rudolfism** and the **Uranus Complex.** And pervading all their disturbances, the leading malaise of our times among hyper-hominids: **MILD** (Mission-Identity Loss Disturbance), also known as **PHSD** (Post-Heroic Stress Disorder).

MY MISSION ... AND YOURS

By examining the three-week travail-to-triumph odyssey of the most extraordinary assembly of patients—or as I prefer to say, "sanity supplicants"—I have ever treated, you will put yourself on a trajectory out of the magma-pits of mediocrity and into the metropolis of mental health.

Unmasked! When Being a Superhero Can't Save You From Yourself will give you back the ultravision you once had—but stronger, so that you can perceive not only threats like MicroCrip and his Nanogangstas, but the *ennui* that destabilises the super-ego ions of your self-respect.

Reading this book is the first step in re-arming yourself with the ultrapower necessary to rescue the only innocent person you've so far failed to save: *yourself!*

PART ONE:

VERY
BAD
CONDITION

CHAPTER ONE

Operation: Cooperation!

THERE'S NO "I" IN TEAM,
BUT YOU CAN'T SPELL "TEAMWORK"
WITHOUT "ME AT WORK"

FRIDAY, JUNE 30, 1:43 P.M.

"Omnipotent Man," shouted Iron Lass, "help me knock zis monster off balance!"

Her cloak exploding like coal dust and transforming itself into huge black wings, the Valkyrie streaked into the sky with Omnipotent Man trailing her as a red, blue and white flash.

The rest of the team scrambled in the badlands sands, narrowly escaping being crushed. With ever-increasing speed, the mile-high metallic wheel of mayhem rolled its juggernaut path north-west towards the ten million people of Los Ditkos.

"What *is* that thing?" screamed Power Grrrl.

Buzzing above us and almost silhouetted by the flaming sunset, the Brotherfly whooped, "Muss be Codzilla's hoola-hoop!"

"Don't either of you know a kot-tam thing? That's Cyclo-Tron!" yelled the X-Man, gaping at the terror-wheel rolling its long arc to merge onto the Interstate towards its target. From this distance, Cyclo-Tron's twirling lights resembled an ultra-massive Ferris wheel, but only for a carnival of destruction in which the cotton candy is made of pink insulation and the corn-dogs have sticks of dynamite inside them. "Nearly destroyed Houston in '78," yelled X-Man, "until—"

"—until Captain Alamo and the Confederate Wrecking Crew turned it into the world's largest spare parts yard," said the Flying Squirrel, focusing his Squirreloscope on the retreating spectacle of Iron Lass and Omnipotent Man failing to knock over the unicycled behemoth. "Well, X-Man? We need a vehicle!"

The X-Man closed his eyes. Brotherfly wrapped his arms and legs around Power Grrrl to fly her away, scraping the ground occasionally with her legs from bearing the additional weight.

Slowly, carefully, the X-Man enunciated the word *au-to-mo-bile*.

A geometry of shadows—onyx curves, lines and planes—congealed in front of me, composing themselves into the finned sleekness of a shining 1955 Ford Fairlane. X-Man and his elder jumped inside, rocketing down the cracked and splintered highway.

Clicking forward several miles, I found Iron Lass and Omnipotent Man swirling like chaff in a dust devil, desperately dodging deathbeams from the sinister spokes of the Cyclo-Tron. The wheel's blinding neon rays slashed mile-long smoking scars into the badlands, leaving the rubble reeking of sulfur. Omnipotent Man was virtually invulnerable, but airborne, Iron Lass lacked the protection of her impregnable wings, and was ignitable as a chicken breast marinated in ethanol.

Witnessing Cyclo-Tron nearly incinerate the Brotherfly and Power Grrrl, Iron Lass swooped down to where they were flying mere inches above the badlands floor of cactus and purple sage. "Get her out uff here, you verdammt ik-noramus!" she yelled.

"Like, we have every *right* to be here?" shouted Power Grrrl, clinging to the Brotherfly's midsection like a baby possum on its mother's belly. Even while furious, she intoned her statements like questions, as if expressing uncertainty or seeking the permission of some unknown agency.

"You cannot do any goot here, Broderfly!" yelled Iron Lass. "Get aheadt to Los Ditkos—get ze civilians out of ze way!"

"But damn, Lass," said the Brotherfly, "you c'n fly faster than I can, specially with this li'l girly-girl weighin me down!"

"Omnipotent Man unt I vill slow Cyclo-Tron down—now you get her *out* uff here!"

Off flew the two youngest members, Iron Lass shouting to her partner to follow her lead. Zooming miles ahead on the highway and then hovering low, she swung her black long-sword Darkalfheimsdottir towards the road. Muspells-fire belched from her blade, turning a hundred-yard stretch into a hundred-foot-deep flaming crater.

Streaking back another mile, the valourous Valkyrie dragged her white Grendelsmuter short-sword with her, the entire distance crackling into ice in her wake. "Vally, rip it up!"

Sweeping low like a stealth bomber, Omnipotent Man dug his arms beneath the skin of the road, ripping it into the air like grass-clippings.

Cyclo-Tron rolled right through their speed bump, slowing slightly, but not stopping.

Iron Lass: "Odin damn it!"

Omnipotent Man: "Hnossi, I unnerstand y'upset, but there's never any need for that kinda language, even if y'are invokin yer heathenish blasphemy agin—"

"Vally, for ze love of fuckink Loki, just do sumsingk!"

"Roger that, Iron Lass, ma'am," he said, streaking off.

Clicking over to Route 22 on the outskirts of Los Ditkos, I found the Brotherfly and Power Grrrl struggling to evacuate a Squirrel Burger drive-in franchise.

"Yo, my peeps," yelled the Brotherfly, crawling along the ceiling and yelling down towards the customers, "you gots to get your Squirrelly Fries and Nut Shakes on an turn yo highways to bye-ways, cuz danger is biz-anging on the door and briz-anging hell with it, kwawm sayin?"

Apparently none did know what he was saying, for staring back at him were nothing but blank eyes, while mouths kept chewing and seam-popping polyestered legs remained motionless beneath the bright pink furry tables.

"I got this one, Brotherfly!" said Power Grrrl. "Hear ye, hear me," she called out, disco lights streaming out of her bustier, a dance track thumping out of her Power Pumps. She sang:

"You got to get the move on, your groove on!
It's time for PG's smooth song, the lube song!
And o-o-o-O-O-uh-uh-UH-UH-UH-"

she intoned, rippling in her trademarked R&B/gospel trill,

"—can you think! slink! and JINK like ME?"

In a Squirrel Burger blink, sixty diners of all ages, body-shapes, races, and genders simply . . . disappeared.

Replacing them instantly, in the same chairs and the same poses, were three-score uniformed Power Grrrls, "booty-shaking" their way behind the original as she dance-beat them to safety outside and away.

A moment later, a grey-haired man in plaid slacks with an eagle-shaped "Elvis" belt buckle shuffled his way out of the restroom, zipping up his fly. Swooping down on him, the Brotherfly plucked him up and out of the restaurant an instant before Cyclo-Tron flattened the diner into an inch-high greasy crust of flaming rubble and burning food products.

BURNING BRIDGES

Checking my display, I clicked myself over to the fringes of mainland Los Ditkos where the X-Man and Flying Squirrel were speeding at a hundred and sixty miles an hour over fractured highway right behind the thundering Cyclo-Tron.

Lacking any real opposition, the hurricane wheel had ceased firing its particle beams—otherwise X-Man and Flying Squirrel would have been reduced to nothing but costumed puffs of smoke.

"Omnipotent Man, Iron Lass!" shouted the X-Man into his comm. "What in the hell're you two doing in south-east Los Ditkos? We've gotta stop this thing *out here!*"

"Wellsir," crackled back the voice of Omnipotent Man, "we can't let this here monster-osity cross the Centurion Bridge over to Bird Island. If downtown Los Ditkos were destroyed, th'whole free ennerprise system of the state could be at stake!"

"So you're gonna bring down that big metal bastard in *my* neighbourhood? *So what* if all the coloureds buy it, so long as you can save Ivory-Town?"

"Son," snapped the Squirrel, "this isn't the time for your Zulu god-damned nationalism, do you hear me? For once in your life listen to people who know what they're actually doing and let them bring down this giant steel cocksucker like they know how to!"

"Old man, we can clear the path to Centurion Bridge and destroy the bridge to drown this motherfucker in the river, we can destroy Cyclo-Tron here while we still can, or I can personally rip you to pieces and fry you into hot wings. Now either shut your caviar-hole or help me blast this freak—or better yet both!"

"And how do you suggest we do that, Rochester?"

"What's its power source?"

Even behind the mask, the Flying Squirrel's eyes glinted. "Get me as close as you can to that super-colliding son-of-a-bitch!"

As if he were piloting a ship in a tsunami, X-Man ripped at the steering wheel, hurtling inside in the ditch while keeping pace with the giant wheel's hub, all the while dodging the storm of crushed cars, spinning street lamps, and flying trees pouring down on them. Dialling his comm, the Flying Squirrel waited for his connection and then unleashed thirty seconds of fury at the person on the opposite end.

Instantly Cyclo-Tron's lights went black. Slowly, the peak of its rotation dipped left, and the device fell straight for the Ford Fairlane.

X-Man cranked hard to the right, arcing 180 degrees east. Behind him, the entire mile-high apparatus that was Cyclo-Tron plummeted. From that height, the distance to fall was so great that the descent appeared to be in slow-motion, until the wheel clapped the earth with a sound like God backfiring His own Humvee, turning every window within four miles of the shock wave into a mutilating hurricane of slivered glass.

"I can't *believe* you pathetic bunch of cripples!" snapped the Flying Squirrel, ripping off his Event Helmet, unstrapping himself from the Event Chair, and storming out of the Id-Smasher® before I could call him back.

I tapped my panel, releasing all my sanity-supplicants from their Event Chairs. Each one detached him or herself, stretching and groaning, before exiting the techno-pinnacle of my analytical career. At over three stories tall, the neuro-dimensional Id-Smasher® was a glittering titanium tower of nine hundred terabits of cognintegrated processing power. I held back a moment, admiring the technology which interlaced the psychespheres of my patients via the long, slender transduction rods through its two black processing bulbs.

"Looks just like a giant shrimp, Doc," said the Brotherfly, observing me observing. "Come to thank of it, I'm hongry for some take-out now that we up outta there! Brotherfly be sayin' *'ka-pow!'*—or should it be *'kung*-pow?' *Bzzzt!* Somebody, anybody, can I get a witness?"

Laughing at his own joke, he looked around for reinforcement, holding out a hand palm-up for slapping reinforcement. He received none.

"Thank you for sharing, André," I offered.

"Now could somebody fill me in on suh'm?" said Omnipotent Man, rubbing off a dried trail of drool from the side of his mouth. "How exactly did we brang down ol' Cyclo-Tron, anyway? Cuz I think I mighta missed how thet happened."

Festus shook his head. "Since you people couldn't destroy it, I went after its power source."

X-Man snorted. "Only because I *told* you to!"

The Flying Squirrel rippled an eyebrow in my direction, then said, "When we were driving alongside that mangler, I called Senator Grapht. For the ignorant among you, Grapht is the head of the Defense Appropriations Committee which funds the DOD and therefore kept Cyclo-Tron operational. I had Grapht yank its funding." He harrumphed, fluttering his cape-flaps. "Hell of a simulation you've got there, Doctor, to've actually arranged a simulated Senator for me to talk to. Do you have a J. Edgar in some other section of that program, too?"

"I'm glad you approve, Festus. The program improvises according to the essential logic of any gambit you take and responds accordingly."

"Hmph. Anyway," he said, "that's how it's *supposed* to be done. Analyse the situation first. That's what Hawk King taught us—those of us who bothered to learn. Forget brute-force idiocy. That's for amateurs. We're the professionals."

I waved everyone along. "Now, if you'd all like to get dressed, we'll pick up in the Group Dynamics Verbalarium."

BACK TO BASE,
AND BACK TO "BASE SICKS"

All teams, super or otherwise, function and dysfunction like all families do: with inter-generational misunderstanding, birth-order clusters of privilege and disfavour, brutal grudges, pathological co-dependencies, tragically "scripted" behaviour loops, toxic levels of neglect and abuse, and phony displays of affection and loyalty.

This catalogue of psychological cancers forms what I call the "base sicks"—the bombed-out foundation of every human being which is the source of all adult misery and the terror of every "inner child." Because these base sicks are buried at the deepest-level programming of any group's origin, they're as invisible to the individuals they're poisoning as a rainbow is to Dog Man.

IT'S EASIER TO CHANGE ONE'S UNIFORM THAN
ONE'S MIND-SET

Emerging from the changing room, Power Grrrl stumbled, falling into me. I helped her along while she regained her "reality legs," noting the extraordinary change in her appearance. Gone was the black and silver Sensosilk Event-Tunic, replaced by one of her more restrained uniforms: a dazzle of sequins, a lace vest with garters, and thigh-high leather boots whose skyscraper heels had no doubt contributed to her tumble.

"Like, Eva," she asked me, "could we have like *died* or something in that simulation? Because I am totally not cool with that?"

Behind us, Iron Lass ground her teeth so loudly that for a moment I thought she was chewing ice.

"No, Syndi, not to worry," I said, intercepting the Valkyrie's objection. "The multiple waivers you signed cleared me of any liability in the unlikely event of your mental incapacitation, grievous bodily harm, or life-cessation, but while you could experience the illusion of pain inside the Id-Smasher®, your bodies couldn't be killed, even if your somatic simulations could be."

"It's precisely that kind of cowardice," grumbled the man waiting for us inside the Verbalarium, "that's destroyed this organisation."

Sitting already in the ring of chairs, the Flying Squirrel almost glowed from the sunlight streaming onto him. The fur of his world-famous mask was gleaming with its oversized animal ears, snub nose, long white whiskers, and giant, pink-rimmed black eyes. With his Olympic build, tight skin, and laser-like stare, he looked more like the young Brian Dennehy portrayed him in the 1976 feature *Flying Squirrel and Chip Monk* than the seventy-year-old he was. But no one could mistake the power throbbing inside his clawed and furry gloves for that of anyone else.

"Cowardice. Contempt for chain of command. Lack of discipline," sneered the Flying Squirrel. "And a hundred other maladies of character forming a lethal cocktail that has shaken, not stirred, everything that Hawk King spent decades building. If he'd seen how you invalids performed in there today—"

"O-*ka*-ay, we get it?" said Power Grrrl, snapping her bubble gum. "You *know* Hawk King, you like *worked* with Hawk King, you used to fetch *coffee* for Hawk King—I got it the like *first* thousand times?"

"Aw, man, Squirrelly," said André. "Brotherfly say Girly-Grrl just put the *bzzzt!* on you—"

"Quiet, you," said Festus Piltdown III. He paused to scrub Power Grrrl with his glance. "And as for *you*, your juvenile blandishments which reduce every statement to an interrogative don't erase the simple fact that your performance was sub-farcical!"

"Oh, now jess tether yer ponies a sec, Festy," said Omnipotent Man, making a "whoah" gesture with his hands. "I'ont think we was all s'bad in there. We set 'er up, an you an th'X-Man knocked 'er down. That's the hokey-pokey, right?" He grinned and winked at the ravenish woman in the winged helmet. Iron Lass's ivory faced flushed. He sang, *"Now we turn ourselves around . . . thet's what it's all about!"*

"Ah, poor, pathetic, possum-fried Wally," said the Flying Squirrel, shaking his head minutely. "Would you be giving that moonshine-and-stained-overalls assessment if Hawk King were here? Did you happen to notice that your so-called *settin' 'er up* amounted to a virtually-zero rôle in the mission's success?"

The X-Man spat, *"'Success'?"*

All faces turned to Kareem Edgerton, HKA the X-Man, before flitting towards my hand, which I kept poised above my whistle like a gunfighter fingering his Colt.

Kareem leaned back in his seat, letting out a breath while reconsidering his tone. "If today's 'combat' had been real, there would've been a hundred thousand people lined up outside of hospitals looking like bleeding pin-cushions from the flying glass. 'Success'?" he said, catching his voice just as it spiked. He glanced toward my whistle, looked down, loosened his fists, and stage-whispered, "You call that success . . . I'd hate to see failure."

THE UTILITY OF
AGGRESSION-AVERSION THERAPY

Festus Piltdown said, "If you'd been in this business as long as I have, Edgerton, you'd know that sometimes tough decisions, executive decisions, are required when the professionals take on the hard jobs no one else is qualified for—"

"Professionals?" said the X-Man, extravagantly sweeping invisible lint from his black blazer and pants. "Mr. Squirrel here said 'professionals' like that's something to be proud of. But there're professional *killers*, too. And *those* two," he said, wagging his chin across the circle, first to Omnipotent Man and then to Iron Lass, "were willing to *professionally* liquidate everyone in Langston-Douglas to protect the borough of Bird Island. Don't the people in Stun-Glas have the right to life, liberty, and the pursuit of not being blown to kot-tam hell?"

I moved my whistle towards my lips.

"Excuse me, Doc," said Kareem. "'Blown to golly-gee-whiz-gol-dang heck.' Or was it just that not enough *professionals* live over in mainland Los Ditkos?"

Hnossi Icegaard shifted in her chair, gripping her skull as if to keep it from splitting along its sutures. "It vuss only a simulation, Kareem," she sighed, adjusting her gleaming silver-gold breastplate and blackfeather cloak. "No actual human beinks vut haff been harmedt. Just like in ze moofies."

"So why not—!" Kareem stopped, lowered his volume and tempo. "Why not . . . just let Cyclo-Tron hit the island, then? Like the Squirrel said, when we were inside the simulation we all believed it was real. And yet you and Wally had no hesitation to sacrifice how many of *us* to save how few of *you?*"

"Oh, Kareem!" snapped Power Grrrl. "That's, like, not even—"

"That didn't take long, did it?" said Festus. "Have we gone to simulated Las Vegas now? Because once again Kareem is playing his race cards!"

"You know, in my experience," said Kareem, caging his fingers and drawing out his words, "the *jokers* . . . who talk the most about 'playing the race card' . . . are the people who own all the *diamonds* . . . who've picked up the *clubs* . . . to beat down the *spades* . . . because they've got *no heart.*"

The Brotherfly laughed, slapping his knees in exaggerated delight. "You gots to admit, Squirrelly-man, Kareem just put the *bzzzt!* on y'all!"

Kareem switched his gaze to Omnipotent Man and Iron Lass. "Five times more people live on the mainland than on the island. I even told you two to clear a path for Cyclo-Tron to get onto Centurion Bridge so we could sink it there. Did you even consider moving into position?"

"For all you know, Kareem, even if ve'd destroyt ze bridch, Cyclo-Tron vut haff continuedt rollink out of ze vaater. Dit you sink about zat?"

"I notice you dodged my question, Hnossi: did you even consider taking out the bridge or not? Or did that just never even enter into your equation?"

"Now, X-Man, hold up there a minute," said Wally. "Yore saying it's like we *wannid* t'harm the citizens of Langston-Douglas, or like we jess din't care whether they got smoked. But now, what if Bird Island got flattened, and then th'entire economy crashed? Then all the mummies an daddies in Langston-Douglas woulda lost their jobs! Well then how they supposta pay their mortgages? You really want alla them folks t'lose their homes?"

"Wallace, have you ever even set foot in Stun-Glas? You think the people there have mortgages? You think half the people there even have jobs?"

"Now jess round up yer rangers a spell, Kareem. I been to mainland Los Ditkos all kindsa times. Jess last week I got a ball off the roof at one of those midnight basketball dealies. Very nice fellas playin, too. And don't be bad-mouthing those folks by saying they don't have jobs, no sir. I saw lots a fine automobiles there with some very shiny, expensive-looking hubcaps, an that means hard-working folks, car loans an auto dealerships fulla happy employees. Gracious jiminny, th'folks down there even try t'dress like superheroes—evra-one wearing all-red or all-blue—"

"This monolithic level of ignorance about life in Stun-Glas," said Kareem, imploring the ceiling itself, "is exactly why the F*O*O*J lost its HUD contract to police the neighbourhood in the first place, and why the L*A*B picked it up and protected our homes, reduced crime to almost nothing and earned the loyalty of the people there—"

"Maybe, Kareem," said Festus, "if your L*A*B wasn't such a bunch of spear-sharpening, whitey-boiling racists, they would've kept in HUD's favour. But then they wouldn't be the League of Angry Blackmen anymore, would they?"

"You hear that, Doc? Where's your whistle now? Festus, those sheets you ride around in at night—they made of satin, or silk?"

"I don't have to take that from you, Edgerton!"

I blew my Mind Whistle™, and the bickering ceased as quickly as the migraines sucked everyone's hands to their skulls.

"Ladies and gentlemen, we went over the rules yesterday," I reminded them, while resentment skittered across my group's faces like silverfish across a dinner plate.

"I'd thought we might go a few weeks at least before the whistle first had to be used, but . . . well. While controlled venting is a necessary part of the therapeutic process, aimless unleashing of anti-happiness merely blasts psychemotional shrapnel into the vulnerable underbelly of our healing community. Your real task inside the Id-Smasher® wasn't tactical training, of course, but to prepare you for post-simulation self-observation of how you are de-capacitating the life-potentials you seek.

"Your Board of Directors—pardon me, your F*O*O*J Leadership Administrative Committee—was quite specific with me, and with all of you. Unless you six can resolve the problems that are making you, and I quote, 'contentious in the extreme, dysfunctional, and impossible to work with,' end quote, the F*L*A*C will terminate your employment *with* and membership *in* the F*O*O*J."

I let the weight of my words rest like rhetorical cement blocks upon their psychemotional fingernails. Each hero was still wincing from the beneficial operant-conditioning of the Mind Whistle™.

"Now, while some of you are unconcerned at the prospect of losing your benefits and pension, either due to your personal fortune," I said, nodding to the Flying Squirrel, "or due to your immortality," I continued, nodding to the Iron Lass, "I assume the real threat is that of dishonourable discharge from the Fantastic Order Of Justice.

"And while such scandal might be a temporary boost in the 'no press is bad press' mode, dishonourable discharge from the F*O*O*J could severely damage a young heroine's outside commercial endorsements," I said, nodding to Power Grrrl, "distance oneself from the command of dedicated soldiers," I said, nodding again to Iron Lass, "or from a community of friends and admirers," I said to the young black man with the floppy transparent wings, blue-bottled bug-eye goggles, and hairy antennae.

I finished by nodding to the thirty-four year old black man in his conservative black suit-and-tie. "And it would annihilate an ambitious man's career aspirations."

Everyone finally took their chairs to join Festus Piltdown III in the circle, leaving the X-Man as the last man standing, since he'd been jockeying to avoid sitting near either Power Grrrl or Festus. Finally he sat on the opposite side of the circle from his implacable adversary, the Squirrel.

Perhaps ironically (for those untrained in psychoanalysis), the quietest of the group stood out the most. He'd made neither fuss nor folly during the just-concluded mini-fracas, and he sat serenely resplendent in his blue suit, golden epaulets, red necktie, and cape. Were I not a highly perceptive practitioner of the healing arts of psychotherapy, I might have believed this man had no worries at all, with his massive brawn and his hands folded in his lap so immaculately they appeared to've been carved by Michelangelo himself.

But I *did* know better. For Omnipotent Man was as wracked with self-destructive pain as any of his comrades beside him.

EVERY SUPER-STRENGTH IS ALSO A SUPER-WEAKNESS

As you just saw, conflict on a hyper-hominid team is virtually inevitable. That's because careers self-select for personality type. The irony, of course, is that success during the workday can mean severe interpersonal and psychological dysfunction at night.

Take Clifford David Stinson, HKA the Tectonic Man. His heroism demanded his willingness, indeed his eagerness, to smash anything, anywhere at any time. But during domestic disputes, he also smashed several of his own homes and vehicles as well as those of his neighbours in Los Ditkos's upscale Royal Arch district. In 1988 he so flattened Bucksome Hills that City Council had to rename it Spinster Flats.

Eventually Clifford Stinson's personal failings became professional ones. In 1983, when the Gasteroids threatened to infest the intestinal tracts of the entire population of Crystal City, Arizona, Stinson reduced its City Hall, Jewel Museum, and forty percent of its downtown to shards. No one doubted that smashing has its place—but never in Crystal City.

Similarly, Magna's magnetic-seduction was powerful enough to sway even the Iron Eunuch and the Cobalt Castrati. But her over-reliance on her erotopathic powers to the exclusion of all her others tossed her off the peak of a celebrated career and into a sewer of sexual addiction, face-down in the lap of the *capes*, the niche-porn market of ex-heroines and heroes.

The chief social advantage of the *Götterdämmerung* was its demand from all citizens, and certainly from the college of heroes, for self-sacrifice—that is, the development of the super-ego. But lacking an over-riding threat, many in our society, including its former champions, developed over-active ids. Such was the case with nearly everyone in my team.

WHO'S THAT WHISPERING FROM YOUR SHOULDERS?

Selfish desire and highest ideal—in the cartoons, they're represented by a miniature devil and a miniature angel perching on our shoulders. In rare cases, these voices are literal, as with the tiny wizard Mage Mogdobnag and Lord Lizaard on the opposite epaulets of Noble Man.

But for most of us, these "voices" are expressions of our id and super-ego, our respective sub- and super-cognitive urges towards selfish, violent gratification, and altruistic self-actualisation.

Our id isn't evil. Its self-interest fuels our self-preservation and individual advancement. The id's social defect is its incapacity to value the needs of others. And while the super-ego's lofty goals might seem almost saintly, if left unmoderated, a super-ego-controlled individual could starve to death from refusal to harm animals or plants, or be so possessed by her idealism as to slip out of our reality and into the Platon Dimension of pure Ideals.

That's where the ego comes in. The ego balances selfishness and selflessness. But because the super-will of most heroes comes from the interaction between super-ids and super-super-egos, destabilisation occurs when one capacity becomes strong enough to overwhelm the other completely. Unfortunately for several members of my team, a post-*Götterdämmerung* world has starved their super-egos, letting their ids grow unchecked, like black-dripping toadstools on a yellowing psychemotional lawn.

FAILING CHECKS AND BALANCES
AMONG SUPER POWERS

"Now, ladies and gentlemen," I said, resuming our afternoon session, "I'd prefer not to blow my Mind Whistle™ again. But I should remind you that you are here in no small part to learn to get along with each other. To that end, we're going to continue our session with debrief on your combat simulation."

Against their chorus of groans, I raised my whistle to my lips. Instantly the protest ended, the operant conditioning having already begun.

My gaze flew across their sea of stormy expressions, finding a single calm island upon which to land.

"Wally," I asked, "whereas the rest of our team is having a veritable shouting-match of body language, you seem quite relaxed. Tell me about that."

Omnipotent Man, who at age seventy-one seemed an Adonis-like forty, almost glowed with unperterbedness. "Wellsir, ma'am, I felt like we done a purty good job in the simulation. And my compliments on how truly real t'all seemed! When I was in there I couldn'even 'member I was in your computerisated jingamathing—m'heart was drummin, m'pits was trickling—"

"That's why it's called," said the Flying Squirrel between gritted teeth, glancing once towards my whistle, *"a simulation,* Wally. It wouldn't work if you remained aware it was phony."

"Well I know all that, Festus—"

Flying Squirrel: "—which is a symbol of something, I'm sure."

Omnipotent Man: "But still. Gol-dang impressive, y'know?"

I probed further. "So you feel you were successful, then?"

"Yessir, ma'am! Finished the mission, didn'we?"

"So, mission accomplished, then? And all is well?"

"Uh . . . yes? Or . . . wait a sec, now . . . you're usin some kinda *irony beam* on me or suh'm, right? Am I right, Doc?"

A distressed *clink* rang out. We all turned to see that Festus had slammed his cappuccino cup (where he'd gotten hot cappuccino, or a cup, was unclear, but I guessed from his famed Utilitarianism Belt).

"Festus," I asked the Howitzer of a man, "despite your simmering soup-pot of rage which has just bubbled over onto your behavioural stove, you haven't walked out. Why not?"

He silently levelled his eyes on me like twin turrets.

"As one of the country's wealthiest men," I probed, "you're at the head of a corporate empire of mass media, defense contracts, surveillance technology, and fast food. You've led a distinguished career as one of the nation's finest investigators—"

"The World's Greatest Detective®," growled the black-haired septuagenarian. "Period."

The Brotherfly: "Damn, Squirrelly. Takes balls to be trademarkin y'self as the world's greatest dick, knawm sayn? *Bzzzt!*"

Everyone ignored André while he laughed. "C'mon, y'all! All y'all can't be that uptight, can ya? Who gon leave a brother hangin like that? Syndi-girl, snap me a *bzzzt!* from them bad-girls!"

Syndi smirked, shook her fortified cleavage in tardy acknowledgement of his jape. "That's what I'm talkin bout! *Bzzzt!*"

"Kot-tam, André," snapped Kareem, "would you please, for just five minutes, Q.C.?"

"Whuzzat, Exxy?"

"Quit *cooning!*"

"Festus," I re-focussed, "you're obviously dis-eased with the therapeutic process, and you've never been one to follow orders meekly. So why haven't you simply defied the F*L*A*C and marched out the door?"

Festus Piltdown III sat back in his chair, crossed his gloved fore-arms across the flying squirrel silhouette emblazoned on the tunic across his massive chest.

The X-Man: *"I* can tell you why, Doc."

"Kareem, ze *Doktor* dit not ask you."

"And *he* didn't answer her, Hnossi!"

"Gawd, Kareem, would you, like, shut up?" said Syndi, stamping her boots *one-two* and putting one hand on her hip-strung Backlash. "You want her blowing her like whistle-thingy again?"

Finally Omnipotent Man put up his hand.

"See now, ma'am-doctor, maybe Festy's a might modest, but as y'all probably know, he's fixin to run in th'upcoming election as Director of Operations. You knew that, din'tcha?"

"I think I recall having heard it somewhere, Wally, but as I don't follow politics, it must've slipped my mind."

"Wellsir, an as y'can pro'ly guess, if the F*L*A*C shows ol Festy out through the F*O*O*J saloon flappers, he caint run for D.O.O. Then his dreams're hooched, knowuttamean?"

"I, uh . . . I think so, Wally."

"An Wally pro'ly figures, an I agree with im, that he's earned this gol-dang job. He was in the F*O*O*J almost since the beginning! He's served almost ev'ra other p'sition on the F*L*A*C—Director of Personnel, of Finance, of Investigation—he was even Chair once. So y'can unnerstan if the F*L*A*C sendin im to your wood shed an threat'nin to turn im loose altogether has got his fur up an hackled."

I asked Festus how he felt about Wally's remarks.

He glared back at me with all the glowering, terrifying, predatory intimidation of his mammalian namesake.

ON THE RECEIVING END OF F*L*A*C

For a group of men and women who had devoted their lives to saving others, my six psychemotional journeyers were stunningly incapable of saving themselves. That many of them despised each other was obvious to anyone; that each one despised him- or herself was unknown to all of them.

And that is why the F*O*O*J's F*L*A*C had ordered them into my care and analysis, since the infighting and dysfunctionality generated by their mutual- and self-loathing threatened to vapourise their organisation at a time when the F*O*O*J was particularly vulnerable: election time. Three of the six Directorships were up for grabs, and for the first time since the F*O*O*J's inception, so was the post of Director of Operations.

In theory the most powerful position on the F*O*O*J Leadership Administrative Committee, the D.O.O. was responsible for setting long-range mission goals, determining strategy and vetting tactics, outlining long-term needs for staff- and materiel-acquisition, and, potentially, reforming the obese F*O*O*J bureaucracy. The retirement of Colonel Strom Flintlock from his grandfathered, unelected position meant that the F*O*O*J was poised for potentially massive change. And while many people had assumed that Festus Piltdown III, HKA the Flying Squirrel, was destined for the D.O.O. post which was the *de facto* commander-in-chieftancy of the F*O*O*J, there was a surprise buried beneath the election field like a landmine in a miniature golf course.

If the F*O*O*J had been a vehicle for national and even global change, the F*L*A*C was the front axis of that vehicle's wheels. So the candidate—or candidates—in our therapeutic sessions were in desperate need of a good greasing.

BACK ISSUES: THE ORIGINS OF THE F*O*O*J

Forged during America's now-mythical Golden Age of Heroism to counter the threats of rum-running, communism, juvenile delinquency, and marijuana, the (then) Fraternal Order of Justice was Earth's foremost and finest fighting force of fury. Delivering the decisive blow against the German war machine following the Soviet invasion of Berlin, the F*O*O*J became a planetary icon for justice and freedom. Its founding members' names are synonymous with glory: Omnipotent Man, Iron Lass, Liberty Belle, Gil Gamoid and the N-Kid, Captain Manifest Destiny, and their brilliant, mysterious, mystical mentor, the incredible Hawk King.

Returning to America and the expansive East Coast metropolis of Seagull City, the F*O*O*J moved into its first legendary headquarters, the Mando Mansion, and began recruiting among the nation's growing ranks of costumed avengers.

Thus began the F*O*O*J's "Silver Age," shining with new and glorious stars—Siren, Flying Squirrel and Chip Monk, the Evolutionist—defending our country and our planet against some of the worst scourges imaginable: Nemesaur, the Leninoids, Codzilla, Black Mamba, Standing Buffalo, Cosmicus and the Hordes of Entropy . . . truly an unlimited series.

But in the goggled eyes of some, the atomic-powered America of the Silver Age was mutating into something unrecognisable. Gone were the neat pleats and fedoras of the founding era of the F*O*O*J. Now rock-and-roll, the Civil Rights and women's movements, miniskirts, hippies, and drugs were bubbling out of the gutters and recolouring the splash pages of our country.

Like most institutions, the conservative F*O*O*J resisted any change until change was forced upon it, mandated not only by the pervasive influence of altered American mores, but by legal action. Gone was the adjective "Fraternal" because of the Siren's embittering lawsuit; the word was replaced by the adjective "Fantastic," so the F*O*O*J's heralding acronym could be preserved.

Other changes—some with far more sweeping outcomes—were on the way. Warlock War II saw the magical relocation of Seagull City to the West Coast and its integration into the city of Los Ditkos. The War's destruction of Mando Mansion led Festus Piltdown III to construct a replacement F*O*O*J headquarters, the glittering gold-silver Fortress of Freedom which remains the leading tourist attraction of downtown Bird Island in Los Ditkos.

Perhaps most contentiously, as a recipient of federal security contracts under President Nixon, the organisation could not by the early 1970s continue to receive such funding if it remained all-white. Racial integration of the F*O*O*J introduced America to such now-classic crime-fighters as the Spook and La Cucaracha.

Colossal figures were undergoing colossal change.

THE BITTER AFTER-TASTE
IN THE CHALICE OF VICTORY

But there's only so much change any organisation can take before its primary-coloured tunic begins washing out and splitting at the seams.

Integration, popular demands that the F*O*O*J apply itself to new threats such as environmental devastation and domestic abuse, and increasing public concern about due process and the legal loophole-ism that allowed superheroes to operate, meant that the very legitimacy of the F*O*O*J's mission—if not existence—was in question.

But no one, least of all the F*O*O*J's founders, could have dreamed of the devastating impact that America's and the world's two major victories would have: the almost simultaneous collapse of communism, and victory in the *Götterdämmerung*, the global war against supervillains.

Suddenly, for over two hundred active F*O*O*Jsters, several hundred affiliates, and the public they were sworn to protect (and whose taxes funded them), the F*O*O*J no longer had any reason to exist.

Fortunately for the F*O*O*J, drugs continued to plague America's cities, but the battle against this epidemic lacked sufficient drama to inspire a generation and the media, and initiated as many awkward questions as it answered.

Possessing a lugubriously legendary legacy impossible to leap above, but no longer possessing a substantial-enough organising objective (or, "mythic narrative"), the F*O*O*J's workplace dysfunction soon became a matter of public record. Bickering among heroes transformed itself into publicised personal attacks and escalated into lawsuits, public brawling which shattered whole city blocks, and finally criminal charges against legendary heroes in front of a mortified America.

Released: Jack Zenith's sensational *Two Masks of a "Hero,"* the era-shattering tell-all and the very first investigative book on the F*O*O*J with a credible inside source—Clifford David Stinson, HKA the Tectonic Man.

Revealed: Decades-old internal conflicts, lurid allegations of harassment, assault, and perversion, cases of heroes gambling on the outcomes of their own super-battles, countless tales of substance abuse, power-fixation, and dimension-shifting, and most shocking of all, the outing of dozens of secret identities.

Reduced: Dozens of heroes who had traipsed across our globe like gods above the Trojan War were revealed as the lawyers, scientists, industrial magnates, romance novelists, major imprint editors, husbands, wives, and robots they actually were.

For a world weary and wary of secrecy among the powerful, *Two Masks of a "Hero"* was an electro-magnet for the alloy of public scrutiny and popular outrage. Demands exploded for the full disclosure of F*O*O*J mission records and especially its financial accounts. On the advice of managers, attorneys, and P.R. agents, some heroes pre-emptively revealed their own identities in order to shape perception about themselves and their careers and thereby limit the damage from on-going and future investigations.

The shattering of the old paradigm was loud enough to cause permanent damage to the ears of some heroes. And just as the ear is the centre of balance, the psychological disequilibrium that followed cast many costumed crusaders upon the grimy, vomit-streaked barroom floors of their careers and personal lives. Golden Age icons and F*O*O*J-founders such as Gil Gamoid and sidekick the N-Kid, implicated in a heinous conspiracy and revealed at trial to be suffering from paranoid schizophrenia, were sent to languish in the psychic detention facilities of Asteroid Zed. And while rumours of sightings persisted, since 1975 the immeasurably masterful Hawk King had withdrawn to his mysterious Blue Pyramid, accepting only a rare audience for his cosmic counsel.

If Golden Age greats such as Gil Gamoid and the N-Kid could disintegrate, and if visionary founders such as Hawk King could abandon the world of men, then surely the epoch of the invincibles was as done as that of the dinosaurs.

The resulting shockwave through the hero community saw not only the inferno of more published tell-alls, but a tornado of resignations, divorces, self-exile, and even suicide. And so the new generation of 1980s and 90s crime-fighters, the so-called "Digital Age" warriors, was all dressed up . . . but with no place to go.

America not only didn't need heroes any more—it no longer believed they existed.

HYPERPOTENTIALITY IS FIRST AND LAST A STATE OF MIND

Such a private and public crisis of confidence was the case as the F*O*O*J stared into the new millennium.

Lacking a substantial external threat around which to create a new mission, while teeming with internal contradictions which threatened its cohesion, the Fantastic Order of Justice found itself facing an emergency that could only be resolved by looking within, especially for two generations of its most conflicted members.

Adding into this instability was the imminent power-vacuum of an on-coming election. And except for the fanatical conspirators involved, no one could have guessed how that election would lead directly to the July 16th Attacks.

Facing this complex interconnection of social, political and psychemotional chaos, none of which could be resolved by teleportation, spirit-gems, kraton beams, or an old-fashioned "dust-up," I charged my six sanity-supplicants with a new mission. That mission was to come to terms with the very ordinary, very fragile defining human experience: fundamental emptiness and limitless fear of meaninglessness, or what I call the crisis of infinite dearths. If your own identity is mission-rooted, and your mission is now complete, how could you not be as confused as to who you really are?

Directed to me by the winds of their own confusion, my patients arrived at my Hyper-Potentiality Clinic yoked to wagon-loads of psychemotionally dysfunctional produce. Other than this group's toxic mutual antagonism, chief among the disruptive behaviours reported to me by the F*L*A*C were:

- *the questionable competence and unrealistically unflappable optimism of Omnipotent Man,*
- *the bullying, aggression, and rage of the Flying Squirrel,*
- *the micro-management devolving into nano-management by Iron Lass,*

- *the social inappropriateness bordering on sexual harassment of the Brotherfly,*
- *the narcissism and self-absorption of Power Grrrl, and*
- *the insubordination and racial antagonism of, and unapproved investigations by, the X-Man.*

Even during those first sessions, I had recognised an encyclopaedia of psycho-social crises besetting the group—unmanaged anger and guilt, sexual confusion, the Uranus Complex, Secret Identity Diffusion, and the Saviour Complex chief among them.

Clearly, ahead of us lay a Trojan struggle to resolve the problems of such great powers. But of course, with great power, there must also come great psychoanalysis.

And just as it was my task to help the F*O*O*Jsters accurately envisage their own contra-efficiencies, so is it your mission to recognise your own. Periodically throughout this book I'll be asking you to use a journal to record your answer to the generation-appropriate question I posed to my "Big Six" throughout our explosive time together. Keep your responses brief (ten words of less), and then reflect on how your responses change depending on the varying exercises and processing you're experiencing each time.

For Golden and Silver Age heroes: What will it mean for your life, and your view of yourself, if the glory days never return?

> **Omnipotent Man:** "I'm good. America's good. And being good is great."
>
> **Flying Squirrel:** "Given these pathetic invalids, America needs me more than ever."
>
> **Iron Lass:** "Never was it glory, but ever justice that I sought."

For Digital Age heroes: How will you face knowing that you will never exceed, or even equal, the accomplishments of your predecessors?

> **The Brotherfly:** "Brotherfly be fine. Always has been. He's a survivor."
>
> **Power Grrrl:** "*They* never looked inside *them*selves. I won't make that mistake."
>
> **X-Man:** "Who are *they* to be equal to? *Deserve* victory. Period."

GAZING INTO THE DUSK

Mere demi-moments into our reconvened session in the Verbalarium, I was summoned by my secretary to take a call. Knowing that only a true emergency could have motivated Ms. Olsen to have disturbed the sanctity of a session, I took a call from the Spectacle, the F*O*O*J's Director of

Investigations.

I listened to the Spectacle, and the world as I knew it shattered.

And while none could have then known, the information conveyed in that call led directly to the abomination of the July 16th Attacks.

Exerting every erg of professionalism at my command, I re-entered the discussion chamber with a visage of calm detachment.

As I continued around the circle, the Brotherfly glanced up at me anxiously. For the first time since I'd met him, his face and posture betrayed an emotion other than flip playfulness or hyperscrotal lust. Perhaps his legendary "fly-feel" was tingling, hinting to him the horror of what I was about to reveal.

"My friends," I said finally, clearing my throat. "I have . . . some very difficult news . . . to share with you."

"What, Doc?" asked the Brotherfly.

"The man . . . the hero . . . you knew as the incredible Hawk King . . . is dead."

Everyone stood, their faces focused on mine.

Jaws unlatched, relatched.

"Vut?" said Iron Lass, at last. "You caun't be—*Fräu Doktor*, zat's impossible—Hawk Kink *caun't*—"

"Now ma'am-doctor, you musta gotten yer facts wrong on that one, cuz evrabody knows that ol Hawk King can't—"

"Miss Brain, I do believe you're flipped your substandard lid. Master Hawk King is an Egyptian deity. *Dying*, by definition, is one of the few deeds beyond his potential—"

"How?" yelled X-Man, standing, the sole voice of non-denial. "How, kot-tammit?"

"The call came directly from the F*O*O*J," I explained. "Major Ursa had an audience scheduled at the Hour of the Ninth Gate last night . . . but the *Ka*-Sentinels at the Blue Pyramid never showed up to let her inside the retaining wall—"

"Ze Kink never missed an appointment," said Iron Lass. "Not in over fifty yearss, for any reason—"

"When there was still no response by 10 a.m. today, Major Ursa and the Spectacle led a team back to Sunhawk Island. The gate was open, the *Ka*-Sentinels were in a state of stupefaction . . . the Pyramid portal was open . . . .

"They found Hawk King lying on his back inside his Duat Chamber, gripping his crook and flail."

They sat silently, but their eyes were screaming.

"The Spectacle's preliminary call," I concluded, "is natural causes."

"'Natural causes'?" spat the X-Man. "Closest thing to invincible, closest thing to omniscient, and suddenly, just like that, dead by 'natural causes'?"

While the rest of us stood impotently, Kareem lowered himself back into his chair, his face ripped by rage, and then suddenly, horribly blank.

And incongruously in that expressionless void, tears seeped from his eyes like pus from open sores.

"No way. No *way* was this natural causes," he muttered, staring at the seam where one wall crashed into the next. "Hawk King was *murdered*," he said. "And if someone could kill him, that means all of us, and the world . . . are in for some serious shit beyond anybody's reckoning."

INTO BATTLE: BUT WHERE—AND WHO— IS THE FOE?

Ironically, at the exact moment that global peace has triumphed, the gravest threat to superheroic mental health has become paranoia.

Although super-citizens now can bask in the summer sun of safety, the hypervigilance of their careers has cast them into a winter of ODI-CFFB: obsessive defensive-ideation/compulsive fight-or-flight behaviour, much in the way that a satyr or nymphomaniac, if placed in solitary confinement, may fall into chronic masturbation with attendant carpal tunnel syndrome.

The death of a loved one or a revered icon such as Hawk King is often a trigger for paranoia, but that paranoia speaks to a deeper drive than mere fear. Paranoia is a defiant charge to a cold, unfeeling cosmos: "Hear me! I exist! I'm important!" Because after all, if "someone" is actually orchestrating the chaos of the universe against you personally, then you actually do matter. When no one seems to care anymore, "enemies" give you the comforting illusion that at least someone does.

As we'll see throughout *Unmasked! When Being a Superhero Can't Save You From Yourself,* above all psychic threats, paranoia holds more destructive potential than even Cosmicus, the Digester of Worlds. As the old saying goes, paranoia can indeed "destroy ya."

CHAPTER TWO

Facing the Ultimate Arch-Enemy

Although as a hyper-hominid you've spent your entire career risking your life, there's only one task as difficult as facing the unresolved scandals and unsightly scars of your secret origin. And that is facing the deaths of others, especially of fellow heroes.

After all, you've spent your professional career beating the odds, continually cheating the grim reaper at his own gravestone card-table. But Death plays the ultimate trump card, and is the only arch-enemy guaranteed to cash in everyone else's chips.

STAGES OF GRIEF

SATURDAY, JULY 1, 9:30 A.M.

The morning after such an epoch-shattering event as the death of Hawk King, it would have been predictable for my team of sanity-seekers to skip out on therapy at my Hyper-Potentiality Clinic. That's because they, like everyone else, were falling up and down the escalator of the Nine Stages of the Brain-Silverman Grief Scale™ (Revised):

> *1. Confusion*
> *2. Obsession*
> *3. Lust for vengeance*
> *4. Self-pity*
> *5. Boundless contempt*
> *6. Reckless adventurism*
> *7. Depression*
> *8. Paranoia, and*
> *9. Hollow acceptance*

Regardless of each hero's sadness, the F*L*A*C's orders were emphatic: even at this moment of global mourning, any of my F*O*O*Jsters who failed to attend therapy and achieve measurable improvement would be summarily removed from the ranks of Earth's most celebrated super-team.

And thus, in the bright sunlit Saturday morning of the Anger Room, my heroes sat in a circle of morbid moroseness.

In their fumbling individual attempts to bear the psychemotional weight of their legendary mentor's death, each F*O*O*Jster shared something with the group to ease individual and collective sorrow, and offered with a few halting remarks met by sodden silence. In doing so, each one evoked aspects of his or her personality which had until that point remained hidden—tenderness, nostalgia, melancholy, compassion, and more—a stunning departure from the factionalising and fractious fracas-factory of the previous day.

Wally W. Watchtower brought with him a Pharaonic crown given to him by Hawk King, an inter-royal gift from an ancient Egyptian king to the surviving prince of the doomed planet Argon; Wally explained how that gesture, in late 1944, had helped him rise from confusion as a wandering, super-powered Jehovah's Witness farm boy from Kentucky, to his grand destiny as Omnipotent Man. The Flying Squirrel distributed free, advance copies of two books from PiltdownPerennial: a coffee-table book of the most famous photographs of the Egyptian deity, plus a small, black, cloth-bound volume of wisdom-quotations called *The Utterances of Hawk King*; even Festus Piltdown's perpetual gadfly the X-Man seemed impressed and moved by the gift.

André supplied a sumptuous collection of delicate confections he'd baked personally, from flans to *mille-feuille*, and while serving them to everyone uttered not a single *bzzzt!*; Syndi distributed advance CD singles of the dance-beat eulogy she'd rushed into production the previous night called "Hawk On (Long Live the King)". And during a moment of intense quiet, Iron Lass produced a gleaming silver ram's horn she'd brought from Aesgard more than a millennium before, from which she elicited a sound like Louis Armstrong on a muted trumpet, rendering in tear-trickling agony what she later informed me was Duke Ellington's "Solitude."

Only one of my sanity-supplicants came empty-handed: the X-Man. But even he would nonetheless later share something—a situationally inappropriate, but entirely predictable paranoid rant.

STAGES OF GRIEF: CONFUSION

"How do you all feel," I said, looking for anything to get our discussion started at last, "about . . . oh, the media coverage of Hawk King's passing?"

Finding no responses, I held up a couple of newspapers. The Los Ditkos *Sentinel-Spectator* carried the headline "Nation mourns founding

F*O*O*Jster." The Los Ditkos *Sun* announced "Hawk King: Dead at 7000+."
USA Today blared, "'Avian avenger' dead/'Natural causes' rules F*O*O*J
coroner."

Each front page displayed iconic photographs of Hawk King, two of
his classic portrait and the third a seated image in a golden, woven wicker
throne. From the portrait beamed his golden beak and gold-rimmed
black eyes, and his black feathered-face topped with golden Pharaonic
crown. In the seated image, his black body gleamed, bedecked in golden
Egyptian skirt and sandals; his hands clutched a golden crook and flail,
and his black-golden wings were spread as if to devour the seven winds.

I clicked on the television. PNN was broadcasting aerial shots of tens
of thousands of people gathered on the mall of the F*O*O*J's Fortress
of Freedom and at the gates for the ferries to Sunhawk Island and its
mysterious Blue Pyramid. At both places, mourners deposited offerings
of hand-made Egyptian mortuary *ushabtiu* figurines, pipe-cleaner and
tissue-paper lotus flowers, and small bottles of milk and beer. According
to the reporter, arrests for public drunkenness and lactose-intolerant
public vomiting had sky-rocketed.

"And the radio call-in shows," I said, further prompting them while
shutting off the TV, "are equally wrenched by misery."

To my group's silence I added, "Perhaps it would help if people
shared their own memories of Hawk King, their personal experiences
with him."

The Flying Squirrel sucked in a big preamble breath; since he tended
to dominate discussion, especially by name-dropping Hawk King and
verbally footnoting their own connection, I immediately asked Iron Lass,
the only person Festus Piltdown III seemed never to interrupt.

Her eyes shifted towards me dully, the glint from their cold metal
apparently rusted over. She was actually slouching—this, despite
routinely targeting me and her team-mates for comments about our
posture.

"Hawk Kink," she said at last, putting down a piece of André's *baklava*
onto a coaster, "vuss ze greatest of us all."

After a pause, I asked her to continue.

"Alzough, *ja*, I am a goddess, I felt, perhaps becoss he is an even olter
deity from a more ancient panseon . . . venever I vuss in his presence, I
could unterstaant vut mortals felt when zey met Odin, ze lort of Aesgard.
Hawk Kink inspiredt . . . . Ze only vurt I can sink uff . . . iss *awe*. I vuss
alvays in awe of him. He vuss a brilliant scientist, a brilliant alchemist, a
brilliant leader, *ja*, all of zat. But more. He vuss . . . ."

She stopped, looked down, cleared her throat.

Festus Piltdown sucked in another pre-elocutory breath, but Iron
Lass flashed a glare at him until he let it out, wordlessly.

"I vurked vis Hawk Kink for fifty years. I haff liffdt two sousand," she
said. "Zere vill never be anuzzer like him."

I waited for the pathos of Hnossi Icegaard's words to permeate everyone's thoughts.

When Festus looked ready to speak again, I asked Wally to share his feelings. At that moment he was leaning his head towards his shoulder, as if the weight of his grief exceeded the strength of his neck. His hair, flattened, lacked its usual gloss and front-row e-curl. When I'd called his name, he'd perked up momentarily, his ever-present, generally unrealistic optimism seemingly recharged. But just like that, the lightning in his expression grounded itself in the deep, dark rings beneath his eyes.

"Wellsir, ma'am-doctor," said Wally, "the King recruited me. Hnossi, too, an Liberty Belle, an, well, all of us in the original team—course evrabody knows he foundeded the F*O*O*J. Don't know . . . I mean . . . it's like, let's say if suh'm came up, an ya didn'know what to do about it, y'd just ask him, y'know? Djunnerstann what I'm sayin?"

He scanned the eyes of his two older colleagues, but neither returned his gaze.

And in words so childishly pathetic I will never be able to forget them, Wally W. Watchtower looked imploringly at his comrades, his hands upturned and empty upon his knees, and with voice cracking, asked, "And now . . . what're we sposta do if suh'm goes wrong . . . an we don'know how t'fix it?"

Saturday morning sunlight fell into Wally's eyes, twinkling wetly. Wally leaned over, picked up André's entire uncut apple strudel. As soon as he sank his teeth into it, the strudel began crumbling over his suit and cape. He blew on the dessert, crackling the entirety of it into a strudel-cicle, crunching chunks between his teeth in mournful mastication.

"Good fritter, Br'erfly," he said, looking at the floor and chewing. "I should show y'all m'recipe for fried peanut butter-banana-and-candybar samwidges."

By then, not even the younger heroes could look at him.

I asked Kareem to share his thoughts.

"Since there's no reason to believe Hawk King could have died of natural causes," he said without hesitation, his voice as raw as an abrasion, "we're dealing with a murder."

STAGES OF GRIEF: OBSESSION

All eyes clutched onto Kareem, like a loanshark's hand on the neck of an overdue lendee.

"The murder of the world's smartest man, by the very nature of such a crime," said the X-Man, "indicates threat on a scale we may never have seen before. Despite my persistent warnings, this organisation has been over-confident, stuffing its belly with its own myths. And we've been acting as if all our enemies were dead or locked up on Asteroid Zed, and that all the ones up there now have been rendered totally harmless—"

"This is not the time for your post-season quarterbacking, Edgerton!"

said the Flying Squirrel. "Difficult F*O*O*J decisions were being made on a daily basis by heroic men facing death for decades before you were even born. You're going to choose a time of planetary mourning for your astigmatic recriminations?"

"Look, Festus, unlike some people around here, *I* actually cared about Hawk King, which is why I'm putting my energy into investigating, not mourning. Now look at this."

Kareem closed his eyes, enunciated the word *suspects*, and a rotating rogues' gallery glistened blackly into shadow-shapes above us.

"These," said Kareem, pointing to the lower ring and the upper ring in turn, "are the Beta- and Alpha-level foes of the F*O*O*J who are still unaccounted-for. The Heavyweights," he said, gesturing to the lower ring.

Although the images were devoid of any colour save black, we could make out the forms as Kareem announced their names: the glinting man-lizard called the Crystal Crocodile, the oversized crushing hands of Key Grip and Best Boy, the robed and lightning-bolt-excreting Shockrates, and the obviously-shaped Specially-Relative Einstein Baboons.

"And from the Super-Heavyweights," said Kareem, pointing to the nuclear-armoured dictator Baron Von Drako, then to the horned head of the star-consuming titan Cosmicus and his herald the Gold Glider, then to the swirling miasma of horror called L-Raunzenu, then to the aardvark-faced sociopath Warmaster Set, and finally to the shambling mass called Ymir the Planet-Corpse.

"How is it possible," asked Kareem, while his audience gazed up at the rings of terrors orbiting above their heads, "for someone of Hawk King's power to have been killed? And how could he have failed to see such an attack coming in the first place?

"His *Ujat*—that's what you people call the Eye of Horus, what should be the Eye of Hru if you could bother to learn the Kemetic, Afro-Egyptian name—should've alerted him. So what we're looking at is someone with soular-invisibility, dimension-shifting, or counter-remote-viewing.

"On the Heavyweights list, it's possible Shockrates could've generated a strong enough electrical field to disrupt the Eye ... and the E-Baboons might've been able to use a string-dimensional tunnel to get inside the Blue Pyramid. But neither should've had the power to kill him.

"On the Super-Heavyweights list, Cosmicus seems unlikely—we would've detected his Nebula-Naught approaching, just like we would've seen Ymir's iceberg fleet if he'd reconstituted himself at the North Pole. Warmaster Set's vendetta is seven thousand years old ... but there's been no sighting of him or anyone else on that list since the *Götterdämmerung*. Of course, there's always the possibility of L-Raunzenu."

A monstrosity of pure terror described in *The Encyclopedia of F*O*O*J Adversaries, Vol. III (Revised)*, as "a cosmic culmination of a billion horrors, personified and transmogrified into a universal force of unstoppable, ravaging evil," L-Raunzenu, in the most literal way possible, was everyone's worst nightmare.

But despite media fireworks about the threat posed by L-Raunzenu, fewer Americans were killed by that entity during its entire existence than the number of people in the same time period who died from rattlesnake bites or choking on chicken bones. And the L-Raunzenu death toll was simply insignificant when compared to, say, the annual human and financial cost of alcohol- and tobacco-related illness and morbidity.

But, blinded by grief-induced obsession and paranoia, Kareem was oblivious to such basic logic.

"Of course," continued Kareem, "there's also the matter of those supervillains who *are* accounted for. Who are on Asteroid Zed right now. Menton—"

Everyone glared at him. He shut his mouth, realising the enormity of his breach of etiquette, as if he'd just thrown his grandmother's corpse on a barbecue and slathered it with Worcestershire sauce.

"Ve don't speak his name . . . so *idly*, Kareem," whispered Hnossi, narrowing her eyes. "Unt need I remind you zat he's been in a psionic-impotence helmet for five years?"

"I'm aware of that, Hnossi," he said slowly. "But Ment . . . the *Destroyer's* abilities were off the scale. Do we really know if a P-Imp hat could stop him?"

Iron Lass rolled her eyes at Kareem's abbreviation. He continued without regard for her disdain. "And on that exact same topic—"

Knowing where he was going, the older F*O*O*Jsters reacted instantly.

Hnossi: "Zere are certain lines zaat even *zey*—"

Wally: "Now, Kareem, I know what y'all're about t'say, but lemme tell you suh'm—"

Mr. Piltdown: "I don't care what they were alleged to have planned—even you can't seriously accuse them of striking out against our greatest—"

"They went bad. *Very* bad," said Kareem, too loudly. Then he whispered something inaudible.

Behind him, massive shadow-sculptures, like a miniature Mount Rushmore, oozed into existence. Even in black, the busts were unmistakable. On the left, the elder with thick neck, wild beard, wild eyes, and spike-teeth. And on the right, the junior with ram's horns and flowing mane. The two titans from the distant world of Ur-Prime orbiting the mysterious quasar Q-939.

"Yes, Gil Gamoid and the N-Kid were founding members of the F*O*O*J. Yes, they *were* great heroes. Once upon a *time*. But now they're locked up wearing P-Imp hats on Asteroid Zed *because they're paranoid schizophrenics who were conspiring to commit mass murder.*"

"Zey were fount not guilty—"

"On account of being criminally insane, Hnossi? You call that a defense?" he sneered. "Hell, I rarely grok brain-to-brain with you people, but on this issue . . . you not only floor me, you *basement* me. Those two 'heroes' were planning to *massacre* all of you! You Stone Agers aren't exactly the most forgiving freaks in the circus, so why all this sympathy for Gil Gamoid and the N-Kid?"

"Listen to me, Edgerton," growled Festus. "And this will be more complex and nuanced than your minstrel show ever apparently ever gets, so listen closely—"

"You hear that, Doc? Aren't you gonna censure him? Well if you're not reporting him to the F*L*A*C for that cracker-ass crack—"

"Listen, sonny, those two heroes—yes, heroes," said Festus, "were wounded terribly in the line of duty. Mentally poisoned, probably by the Destroyer—but possibly by L-Raunzenu. But even given the awesome extent of their mental damage, they would never, I'll say that again, *never* plot against our Founder."

"Even though both of them plotted to kill the rest of you?"

"Even if they did, which was never proven in court—"

"Come on! Hawk King recruited them into the original F*O*O*J, and he used the *Ujat* to uncover their plot! He built em up and he took em down. Don't you think that in their current state they might just want revenge?"

"Why now, Edgerton? Can you answer me that? Why would they or anyone else want to move on Hawk King *now?*"

"You're the self-proclaimed world's greatest detective. Why don't you tell me?"

"Damn, dawg," said the Brotherfly, *"fuck* this."

STAGES OF GRIEF: BOUNDLESS CONTEMPT

Even Hnossi Icegaard's lips parted at that outburst. Even more than Power Grrrl, André Parker, HKA the Brotherfly, was the most fun-loving, unflappable, and glibly superficial member of the group. Because no one could have expected his reaction or even his capacity for deep feelings, no one spoke—not even Kareem or Festus, at whom the intense psychemotional verbalisation was targeted.

"André?" I asked. "You just psychemotionally verbalised intensely, targeting Kareem and Mr. Piltdown. Can you tell me about that?"

"I mean, *bzzzt*, Doc," said André. "Look, I'ont know about them fools, but fuh real, the King was the shit, knawm sayn?"

"So . . . you disliked him, then?"

"Naw, Doc—'the shit,' see, that means 'good'—"

The Flying Squirrel: "Then for the love of Greenspan, could you simply god-damned *say* that?"

"Festus, please. André, continue," I said. "You were saying that in your view, Hawk King was 'the shit.'"

"Damn skippy, Doc," he said. "I was actually blessed to meet the King when I was just a shorty, like, back in '82? I was one of a twenny-fi school kids—our class won a contest for essay writin—'Why would you like to meet Hawk King?', you knawm sayn? I mean, he'd already been up in his self-imposed exile an shit for, like, seven years by then—ain'no kids getting to go t'see the King no how, but, like, *we* was, son. Just about to turn thirteen, an I get to meet the King!

"So us an Miss Jackson, we take the ferry over to Sunhawk Island, his *Ka*-Sentinels be guiding us through the gates, then up in there through that portal of the Blue Pyramid, down the shafts, up the shafts, right up into his Celestial Chamber . . . all them turquoise hieroglyphics on them black-silver walls, movin like they alive, like they talkin to each other an the stars.

"An he sittin there right in the middle, right on his Sapphire Star Throne, like a sunrise in space, knawm sayn? Golden beak, black body, hands holdin onto his maces an shit . . . but the eyes. Never forget them eyes. Whole room was hummin, vibratin, an them eyes, like radio transmitters beamin inside my spine.

"Changed my life, dawg, goin there. I still dream about it, every week since I was a kid for like thirteen-fourteen years, of havin the chance, the *blessin*, you knawm sayn? to go back. But . . . y'know, thangs don'always work out how we want."

He cleared his throat.

"Anyway, I made up my mind right then—" he said, crackling an electrical charge between his antennae for emphasis without even saying *bzzzt!*, "I was gon be a superhero. Man changed my life. I owe him. We all owe him.

"An now . . . he's dead. An my aunt, she's, she just—look, it's like, after my . . . my uncle died . . . the King was the one thing in the world she could count on that would always make things right, knawm sayn? But now she caint stop cryin. You hear me?"

He shook his head, then jutted his antennae in the directions of the Flying Squirrel and the X-Man.

"An these two fools is gon sit here ying-yangin bout some muhfuckin unknown, unknowable, invisible 'conspiracy'? King's body ain'even cold, funeral still three days away an them super-brains caint shut up outta respect for a coupla kot-tam *hours?* Tryin t'get my *grieve* on, here, knawm sayn? Should be honourin his life, not squawkin like vultures over who gets to gouge open the muhfuckin corpse!"

Kareem shifted forward, facing his younger team-mate.

"Listen . . . André." I'd never heard Kareem's voice contain such—I won't say gentleness, but—lack of antagonism for André, or for anybody else. "It's absolutely essential that right now, we—"

"No, you listen, dawg," said, André, standing up and shouldering his thick, lobed, translucent wings behind him. "The man aint no 'debate topic,' knawm sayn? People die. You got that, son? They just die. An aint nuthin you can do about it, not with all your theories an your Afro-ballistics an your muhfuckin *maāxeru* magic words, knawm sayn? So stop stickin an stabbin the man's body with your Detecto-Junior Crime-Kit an let im have some muhfuckin dignity, my 'brutha!'"

Kareem's jaw muscles bunched.

"André," he gritted, "we're all . . . tense . . . now. So I'm gonna let that—"

"Whatever-whatever, Mista Mystery. Right now whyonchu let us feel the sadness and regret we all gots to feel. Specially since y'all don'know the meaning of the words!"

At that, André unfurled his proboscis, snapping at the rotating rogues gallery, and three of the "Super Heavyweights" smashed into obsidian shards. Then he hopped over to the window and proceeded to *tap-tap-tap* his head again and again against the glass.

After Festus finally suggested wielding a can of Raid™ against the noise, André stopped, putting his hands and feet against the wall and with a splippetty-splabbatty sound, crawled up towards the ceiling and stuck himself, glowering down through his two complex and three simple eyes.

Kareem whispered, and the shadow-sculptures of Gil Gamoid, the N-Kid, and the remaining rotating supervillains and the shards of André's tongue casualties dispersed into dark mist and disappeared.

Wally excused himself to go to the rest room.

I suggested we move on. "Would others like to discuss their own experiences of Hawk King?"

Syndi snapped her gum, raised her hand half-way.

"Like, I didn't really know Hawk King? An like, hello-o, I get it: 'sad!' But does the whole city have to go spaz-mode? Like, last night I couldn't even get a table at Chez Guevara because they closed early? And I was gonna take my crew to Dance-Tronics, but, yeah, clo-osed!"

I asked her how she spent her night in lieu of her usual frolicking.

"I like stayed home, cut that Hawk King single, and answered fan mail."

"You—!" choked Iron Lass. "You awnser *fan mail* vile all uff Midgard cries out vis agony unt tears?"

"Like, no-o. I had my PA do it. I am so like stressed, you know? So I got Brianna to do me—you know, massage? But now, today, the stress is all back! Thank God for André's strawberry tarts—they're better than Prozac." She smiled at him sweetly. "Thanks, P-Dawg."

"Baby-doll, when ain'nuthin funny, eat what's sweet. That's my philosophy," said André. "Glad everybody like em. Cept Kreem, who ain'tried pastry-one. Shoulda made him suh'm with cherry, chocolate, an kiwi. Only red-black-and green for the great Marcus Garbage. My man wouldn'even *dream* of eatin no angel food cake, knawm sayn?"

Kareem reached for the plate, popped into his mouth a piece of crystallised ginger covered in nougat, and chewed defiantly.

"And yet, Syndi," I said, "despite listing rather trivial issues such as answering fan mail or being denied access to trendy restaurants, perhaps to imply that you're entirely unmoved by the death of Hawk King, you did 'cut that single,' as you put it, which means—"

"Which means she exploitet zis great beingk's passink to make a qvick morbid buck!"

"I think it means more than that, Hnossi, although perhaps Syndi wants us to think otherwise. How about that, Syndi?"

I looked between the two women, waiting for either of them to respond.

Facing their silence, I resolved to put the two together for a later session, to spelunk the depths of the psychemotional stalactites and stalagmites they perpetually aimed at each other. But at that moment I changed directions.

"You've been rather quiet, Festus," I asked. "How did you spend yesterday evening?"

I expected Festus to unleash a blistering denunciation of Syndi, but instead Festus Piltdown III delicately swept lady-finger crumbs from his tunic pants. "Like Hnossi," he said quietly, "I went to my post."

He irradiated everyone with his glare.

"The F*O*O*J Fortress. Scanning for threats. Doing my duty to our country. To our planet. When a champion of such magnitude falls, criminals become an opportunistic infection poised to contaminate us all."

"Festus vuzn't simply vaatching ze monitors in ze Situation Room, *Fräu Doktor,*" said Hnossi Icegaard, smoothing her raven mane. While speaking to all of us, she looked only at Mr. Piltdown, who stared at a part of the ceiling where the Brotherfly wasn't then crawling. Removed from our sight-line, the only indication André remained in the room came from a soft, high-pitched buzzing near the lamp.

"Festus spent last evenink unt all last night comfortink ze heroes unt heroines who'd assembult at ze Fortress, like a vize unt gentle faazer or feutal lort, offerink his shoulder or knee for zeir tears. Unt vile shelterink our soldiers vis his . . . his *moral* leadership, he spoke vis everyone, softly. Uff honour, unt diknity, unt true heroism, from a life devotet not to self, not to glory, not to personal revardt . . . but to justice." She sighed lengthily. "Unt sroughout all zis, vhere vere *you*, Kareem?"

Kareem stiffened in his chair, goggling at her.

"Where was *I*, Hnossi? I was in Stun-Glas! Walking the streets, talking to my people! *My* people, the ones *you* people always seem to forget about, the ones you were gonna let Cyclo-Tron crush! I was down with the people praying in the AME Church on the corner of Cowan and McDuffie, down with the folks stuffing fried mock-chicken an cornbread down their mouths at Dark Star, down at the Q*R*I*B with the League and patrolling Stun-Glas to keep people cooled out and safe! What I *wasn't* doing was pulling any fake-Churchill act, covertly campaigning for D.O.O. on the grave of a real hero!"

Mr. Piltdown: "Why you invidious, usurping, cork-faced hypocrite, accusing *me* of exploiting the death of our Leader!"

"Nothing stabs like truth, does it, Goebbels?"

"You are out uff line, Kareem!"

I held up my whistle until the combatants stood down emotionally, and then asked Festus to explain his claim that Kareem was being hypocritical.

"Miss Brain, I'll tell you this just once: whatever your mawkish, liberal, multicultural self-delusions, do *not* trust this individual. He's already launched his plot to exploit Hawk King's death by seeking the post of Director of Operations for the F*O*O*J."

All eyes fell on the X-Man.

His mouth opened silently.

STAGES OF GRIEF: RECKLESS ADVENTURISM

"Well, deny it, Edgerton," said Festus, "if you can!"

"Kareem, is zis true?" asked Iron Lass. "You're standink for election after beingk a F*O*O*J member for only two years? You don't sink zat's presumptuous?"

"Hnossi," chuckled Festus, "this fraud couldn't get himself elected head of a chain gang."

"You shoulda told that to Hawk King, Fester," said Kareem. "Because I'm submitting nomination papers signed by him!"

Silence settled on the room like fog.

And then came the lightning.

"You're a goddamned liar, Edgerton!" yelled the Flying Squirrel. "How *dare* you blaspheme the holy name of our departed mentor like that!"

The X-Man closed his eyes and whispered the word *pamphlets.* Instantly, rectangles of darkness congealed in each of our laps.

I had difficulty reading what Kareem had given us; the logogenic tracts were black only, with empty space where the letters went. I spread his literature out over the thighs of my pant-suit so the pamphlet's holes could be read in contrast (fortunately I'd worn beige that day).

Above a shadow cut-out image of the white-shirted and black-tied and -suited X-Man exhorting an implied, adoring crowd beyond the picture frame, were the block letters

Elect
X-MAN
Director of Operations
A Better F*O*O*J
FOR A BETTER WORLD

On the next panels of the material was Kareem's "Five-Point Platform for A New F*O*O*J":

1. Shift the F*O*O*J's investigative focus to corporate crime, now that the *Götterdämmerung* is over
2. Rewrite the Concord of Heroic Duty to prevent the F*O*O*J from intervening in the affairs of sovereign states
3. Defend and extend quality-of-life security for ordinary citizens—security from predatory corporations, landlords, polluters, *etc.*, not only in disaster relief but via crime prevention
4. Deploy F*O*O*J technology towards public service and job creation
5. Liaise with schools, community organisations, and other non-supergroups to promote safety, freedom, and public responsibility

"Damn, Kreem!" said the Brotherfly, fluttering down to snatch the pamphlet from Power Grrrl's lap, then laughing once he was stuck back on the ceiling. "You gots to be insane in the hind-brain if you think you gon win gainst Squirrelly-Man! He gots the money, the experience, the money! And did I mention the money?"

"I'm more concerned," I said to Kareem, "by your campaign literature's lack of attention to the very problems that brought you and your colleagues here in the first place. Nowhere in here do you acknowledge the importance of confronting the internal supervillains, such as the crisis of infinite dearths, id escalation, depression—"

Kareem rolled his eyes.

"Your delusion is truly tragic, Edgerton," said the Flying Squirrel, "even beyond this nonsense about Hawk King having 'endorsed' you. Even if, due to some thermodynamic miracle combined with an unforeseen alignment of the voodoo-gumbo-chicken bone-stars, you actually somehow got elected as D.O.O., you'd be nothing but a legless mule. Piloting the F*L*A*C means navigating the interpolitical high seas relationships of six highly willful—"

"Six positions, plus Chair," said Kareem, counting them off on his fingers. "Chair, Merry Mac, privately known as Mitchell Morgan McDonald, age sixty-three. Retiring. Director of Personnel, the Manipulator, PKA Emory Dogstale, age fifty-nine. Retiring. Director of Finance, the Downsizer, PKA P. Martin Klein, age fifty-eight. Retiring. Director of Operations, Colonel Strom Flintlock, age one hundred-seventy-three. Retiring.

"That's the old guard. They're gone.

"But there's a new crew up in this election, Festus. Gagarina Girl's vying for D-Personnel against your girl, Major Ursa, I believe—"

Festus spluttered. Kareem breezed on.

"—and she's got a better chance than either Earnest Beaver or Spoiler Man. Dynamiss is going take on your boy Dow-Man for D-Finance—"

"Neither of those nattering neophytes stands a chance against Team Squirrel!"

"Be that as it may," said Kareem, smirking, "three positions *aren't* up for election this round. The Spectacle's D-Investigation, age forty-three. Periodic Man's D-R&D. He's forty. Shockra's D-External Affairs. She's thirty-six. That's a young bunch, Festy. Digital-Age heroes looking for change, looking to deal a better hand than they were dealt. And even if neither Gagarina Girl nor Dynamiss wins, the three incumbents plus me'd make a majority on the F*L*A*C. Wouldn't even need the Chair to break ties. You and the rest of the old motherF*L*A*Ccers're history, Squirrel!"

Iron Lass: "Kareem! Langvicht!"

Everyone quivered in their chairs anxiously, clasping their hands about their ears in anticipation of my blowing the Mind Whistle™ either at Kareem's epithet or to circumvent the inevitable Flying Squirrel retaliation.

But apparently retaliation was not inevitable. Festus simply sat silently staring at Kareem, hurling neither invective nor his chair. Instead, he methodically crumpled and tore the logogenic Elect X-Man pamphlet into a primitive origami squirrel.

DISSECTING THE FLYING SQUIRREL

"Festus," I probed, seizing the moment, "shredding that tract isn't helping you to focus your psychemotional microscope upon the slide of your pain. What, precisely, do you feel—you personally, right now?"

"What do I 'feel'?" he sneered. He tore at the remains again, erecting two snubby ears on the paper squirrel's head. "Did you actually ask me what I 'feel'? I 'feel' I'm surrounded by morons!"

"Festus," I said, tapping my whistle. He grimaced and shoved his palms against his eyes, rubbing hard enough to make me wince. "I'm asking not for your assessment of the rest of the group, but of your psychemotional state. Try using an 'I-statement'."

"An 'I-statement'?" he snorted. "If I use an 'I-statement' you're just going to sic that goddamned dominatrix whistle of yours on me!"

"No, I'm giving you permission, because right now we're not in a free-for-all. You have the floor."

Festus glared. Grunted. Glowered.

Finally: "I feel frustrated. There. Have I satiated you?"

"That's good, Festus. Talk about that."

"It's good I'm frustrated?" he said. I raised an eyebrow at his playing dumb.

"I feel frustrated," he begrudged, "because I've devoted my entire adult life to this organisation, tending to it like a Shinto priest to a desktop grove of *bonsai*, cherishing it, protecting it . . . and now that I've arrived at the correct time, the appointed time, the *right* time for me to lead it . . . a, a goddamned dilettante lindy-hops his way in here with lies about a Hawk King endorsement and a sense of entitlement bigger than his afro and acts as if *he* has a right to lead! I *feel* nobody has the 'right' to lead. You *earn* that goddamned right by investing decades of service—

not milliseconds of presumption—earning interest and building capital of public confidence, collegial respect, and heroic loyalty, which I was intending to re-invest right now, in the traditions of our noble fraternity originally enacted by Hawk King."

Wally returned from the rest room. Perhaps because of the anxiety level in the Verbalarium, the air seemed almost to tingle. "Excellent, Festus," I reinforced. "You've done a fine job of—"

"I'm not done, Miss Brain. Bad enough to have our election turned into a midway freak show, but every day since the end of the *Götterdämmerung* to have to bear witness to what the slugs in the slime-trailing liberal media are saying about us—"

"*Bor*-ing," said Syndi. She got out of her chair, turned on her hip-speakers to the thump-whumping tune of her spring Top 40 hit "Boom! I Hit It Again," and activating her Power-Pumps, began high-speed rocket-skating/dancing around the room.

Festus: "Turn that goddamned jungle music off and sit down!"

Wagging my whistle, I warned Syndi to return to her chair, but I was reluctant to risk the whistle's over-use because my patients might habituate to its stimulus. Wally, snapping his fingers, conceded that he found the tune "kinda ketchy, though a might Jezebellish." I asked Festus to continue, but more loudly.

"—I feel humiliated!" he seethed above the bass line and drum snares, "violated because the papa-goddamn-*razzi* are trailing around a bunch of teeny-bopping costumed incompetents who're here because our F*L*A*C insists we have to change our image 'to suit the times', forcing us to incorporate mattress-back pop-tarts who're here because they want to be famous, not because they know or care one whit about protecting people or national security or what it means to have fought a war every day for the last forty-five goddamned years of your career while they're flitting away their May-fly existences preening and prancing around and having their highly publicised perverted little 'sexcapades' and publicly dragging the name of this organisation through a urinal, making a mockery out of what real heroes—men like Hawk King, women like Iron Lass—have sacrificed!

"*I*," he shouted, gripping his chair by the arms so hard his glide-flaps and whiskers shook, "*feel furious!*"

STAGES OF GRIEF: LUST FOR VENGEANCE

Festus Piltdown III panted and grimaced while blinking—I couldn't tell whether from exhaustion or embarrassment. Finally, after regaining his breath, he said simply, "That's it."

"Don't hold back, Squirrelly," yelled a voice from the ceiling. "You might still have some spleen or pancreas up in there left to spit up—"

"André, please. Let's positively reinforce Festus's commendable first foray into self-revelation."

"And that's another thing, Miss Brain," said the Flying Squirrel. "In *my* day, people didn't call their elders or their superiors by their first names. One said Mister-so-and-so and Miss-such-and-such. Would you go around calling Hawk King 'Hawk'? No. It's called respect. *Propriety.* And perhaps if we had a little more of that, our Fraternal Order wouldn't be swirling down the toilet right now."

"Can I say something, Eva?" Power Grrrl reverse-rocketed to a stop and raised her hand as if she were a school-girl.

"Only if you turn that music down, Syndi."

She wagged her hips, and the music ceased. "Why is it okay for Mister Piltdown to be sitting there judging us and insulting me? If he wants to be respected, doesn't he have to, like, treat the rest of us with some respect?"

"*Bzzzt* for me too, Girly!"

I openly fondled my whistle, but, lost in their escalating id-confrontation, my F*O*O*Jsters raged on obliviously. "Treat *you* with respect?" spat the Squirrel. "I'll treat you with respect when you goddamn start acting like you *deserve* some respect! What would Hawk King say if he could see—"

"Festus—Mr. Piltdown, please. Please. Look deeply. You spoke a moment ago about propriety. Don't we need to model the behaviour we wish to have others emulate? Focus on how *you* feel instead of what other people are doing. That way you can take ownership for your own feelings. Remember, you're a stockholder in the exchange of your own emotions, but *only* your own. You can't control other people."

The Squirrel crossed his arms, leaned back. "That's the goddamn problem. These children *need* controlling!"

Syndi wagged her hips and the music resumed. "I don't have to take that!"

I blew the whistle.

But nothing happened. As soon as my team realised that they were not paralysed by behaviour-modification migraines, they waded back into their swamp of invective. I raised my voice. "All right, now—which of you did this? Who used their powers on my whistle?"

They met my interrogative with stares of *faux*-innocence.

"I see. Presumably, had only one of you sabotaged my whistle, someone else would have revealed his or her name out of vindictiveness. Since no name is forthcoming, I have to assume all of you attempted to or succeeded at using your powers against my whistle. That's disappointing. And I'll have to report that to your F*L*A*C."

They raised a chorus of objections against me, but none was willing to lay the blame at another's feet. Either they were *all* guilty—a bad sign indeed—or they were protecting one of their confederates, which meant there might, indeed, be hope for reducing the toxicity of their interrelationships.

"Could somebody tell Sir-Shouts-A-Lot," said Syndi, exploiting the break in our proceedings, "that he's gonna hafta put more quarters in the meter if he keeps parking in front of the building called 'I'm Hawk King's bitch'?"

While my whistle was unfortunately useless, I let the flash of my pen above my notepad serve as warning enough. I expected Mr. Piltdown to leap into a rebuke, but surprisingly, Iron Lass spoke first.

"Insultink Festus iss vun sing, younk lady," said the goddess. Her eyes burned as they must have over her centuries of bringing the souls of the butchered to Valhalla. But at that moment they suggested she might do that butchering herself.

"I can tolerate many sings, even your persistent failure to show respect to me," said Iron Lass. "But speaking disrespectfully uff Hawk Kink . . . *zat* is an entirely different matter."

Power Grrrl drew her legs up in front of her on her chair, clutching them to her enhanced chest while she stared out the window towards the glittering Tachyon Tower in the distance.

Finally she glanced at Iron Lass, but only for a second.

"I was only, like, kidding," Syndi whispered. "Sorry."

The room was quiet.

"Don't you all see what's happening here?" said the X-Man. "This is all just a proxy power struggle! Cept without Hawk King, there's no ref, the gloves are off, and the brass knuckles are on!"

From the furry mask and snub ears: "How dare you incite a riot at a time like this, Edgerton!"

From the buzzing ceiling: "Kreem, dawg, you always stirrin shit, like a Nat Turner-plumber on a plugged-up Mandingo toilet!"

"André," spat Kareem, "I notice you aren't eating any of the cream-puffs you brought. Not into cannibalism?"

"Aw, fuck y'all!"

"André," I began, "regardless of my whistle's status, you know the rules about swearing—"

"You see this, Doc?" said Kareem. "Hawk King was the only thing left holding this screwfreak-museum together. Now that he's gone, the kot-tam F*O*O*J is gonna collapse at the precise moment there's someone out there powerful enough to whack *him?* Someone lit fire to the house while we're all asleep, an they're probably staked-out across the street for us to start runnin out so they can shoot us down one at a time!"

"Emotions," I said, standing to face the maelstrom, "are at critical energy, everyone. And I understand that. All of you held Hawk King in the kind of regard in which the public holds you. Right now you're vulnerable. You're afraid. You're passing through the nine stages of the Brain-Silverman Grief Scale™, Revised. And you're not here by choice, but under orders from the F*L*A*C to participate in these sessions. So I understand you're feeling especially pressured.

"Therefore it's time now to disengage, reflect, and resume later. You have some choices on how to spend our remaining hours today: in the Id-Smasher®," (a suggestion greeted by groaning) "with Direct-Writing time in the Neuro-Demonstrative Cerebiographer®," (more groaning, and louder) "or individual talk-sessions with me."

The groaning ceased instantly, as did Syndi's music.

While they mumbled their assent to choices #1 or 2, Iron Lass reminded everyone of their duties, including preparation for Monday's funeral for their fallen Founder.

What will it mean for your life, and for your view of yourself, if the glory days never return?

> **Omnipotent Man:** "I feel like a blinded horse with three busted legs."
> **Flying Squirrel:** "We'll defend this planet. It's what the King would've wanted."
> **Iron Lass:** "With the greatest of us gone . . . glory has no meaning."

How will you face knowing that you will never exceed, or even equal, the accomplishments of your predecessors?

> **The Brotherfly:** "We have no choice. It's live or be killed, right?"
> **Power Grrrl:** "Same old story. Elders abandon you. I'll get my own."
> **X-Man:** "A world without Hawk King . . . frightens me. Especially now."

FACING THE ULTIMATE ARCH-ENEMY

Nothing is more terrifying than facing the ultimate arch-enemy, Death, and its horrifying henchman, Grief. Maturity means recognising the inevitability not only of combatting these foes, but of defeat at their hands. Even if we live long enough to evade their grasp for a century (or in the case of Iron Lass, two millennia), our reward will merely be to see all of our loved ones cut down one after the other.

Because you are a hero, your identity is based on exceeding limitations; therefore, the awareness of such inescapable defeat is a mental kidney stone even you cannot pass during the urination of your psychemotional processing. Death is a barrier even *you* can't smash down, fly over, phase through, or disintegrate with your maser-vision. Consequently, dealing with death means invoking the most vile curse-word ever to contaminate the tongue of any champion: *surrender.*

But paradoxically, it is only in surrender that you can achieve victory, for without your acceptance of eventual vanquishing, you will perpetually be running away from reality. As Carl Jung said, avoidance of legitimate suffering is the root of all mental illness. And one truth you must suffer is that everything and everyone you love will eventually die.

Even gods.

No one wants to die feeling they failed to achieve their dreams, or that they failed to employ their powers to their full extent. So free yourself by recognising that you only *thought* you wanted those dreams, and that you didn't fail to live up to your power because you were never really as powerful as you'd made yourself believe . . . certainly, never possessing the power to cheat death permanently.

IDS, GODS AND DEATH

Rooted in every sentient being is the id-centered yearning to outshine others. The fate of anyone with the lust to be such a luminous being—or to employ the ancient name, a Lucifer—is clear.

Even for the most powerful and spectacular heroes, the quest to outshine all others will ultimately fail, and for everyone else beneath the paramountcy of power, the mission is a failure before its first sortie.

If all you want is simply to be the best at something, why not roll up the world's largest ball of string? If you want to be the best skater, why not break your competitor's ankles? You could be the world's most accomplished excretor, entering hotdog-eating championships after consuming a gross of Ex-Lax® tablets. Clearly such an aim—merely being "the best"—is empty on its own terms.

But even if victory were possible, it still couldn't provide meaning or genuine happiness, because saying "I want to be the best" is simply the polite way of saying "I want everyone else to be worse."

Selfishness is the very heart of your glory, the same impulse which caused the mid-1950s wave of superhero-on-superhero battles to prove who was bigger, stronger, or better. Yet not one of those battles to be the brightest produced anything of value (especially not for those heroes' insurance companies), and every last one of those champions and their comrades has already died or one day will. Even deities like Hawk King.

What you must do is decide how you want to live *now*. In fear? In rage? In competitive hamster-wheeling? Or in acceptance?

To avoid wasting your remaining time and relationships with ever-more destabilising distractions, all you need do is surrender. Surrender to this truth: that a life devoted to scaling the mountain of your own pride does not mean you can build a palace at the peak. Like everyone else, you'll still have to erect a sod-house on the flatlands of your own mere existence . . . which, too, will eventually crumble.

Visualising such an erection can be a powerful means to escape the awful anticipation of your own demise. If you've never employed visualisation before, go beyond the suggestions in *Unmasked! When Being a Superhero Can't Save You From Yourself,* and employ the approach I detailed in *Secrets from Menton's Brain: Using Two Lefts to Make Yourself Right* (also available on audiobook and holodisc). Your greatest power over emotions such as pride and fear is your imagination. So use it.

But as my F*O*O*Jsters are about to discover, the only path to escaping hubris and mortal terror is deicide.

CHAPTER THREE

Clash of the Icons

VOYAGE INTO THE IRON LASS'S BRAIN

Idols. Gods and goddesses. Icons.

They're the embodiment of any society's perspectives on the pinnacle of human achievement. Whether representing beauty, intelligence, strength, science, combat, industry, eroticism, or religion, icons serve as foci of mass attention and mass emulation.

But to the same extent, they serve as implements for mass infantilisation. When hyper-rôle models exist on a plane far higher than we can safely fly, our desperate attempts to touch the hems of their garments will eventually knock us down the staircase of humiliation and into the depths of abasement.

So what happens to one who both *is* an icon and *has* an icon, especially when his own icon fails? Can anyone survive the pincering punishment that is the iron mandibles of the Icon Trap?

ICON TO GENERATIONS

SUNDAY, JULY 2, 9:12 A.M.

She sat across from me, the only illumination inside the echoing darkness, radiant in her ravenfeather hair and flashing amethyst eyes. Given her composure, it was hard to believe that it had been only two days since she learned of the death of Hawk King. She'd exchanged her electrum-plated iron armour for an elegant black skirt and a mandarin-collared powder-blue cardigan, and her ubiquitous black-and-white feathered cloak was hung neatly elsewhere.

But if she was attempting to affect a *schule-fräu* appearance, it wasn't working; her six-foot-four feminine muscularity couldn't be contained by pleated wool. In the 1950s, more than one Hollywood scribe flattered Lauren Bacall by referencing the appearance of the deity seated before me. Half a century later, she still looked an athletic 39 when in fact, she'd seen two millennia. Yet by some accounts, she'd changed more during her 20th Century career than she had over the previous two thousand years.

This woman knew better than almost anyone what it meant to be an icon. Because for centuries, Iron Lass, PKA Dr. Hnossi Icegaard, UCLD professor of Military History, Political Economy, and German and Scandinavian Literature, was literally worshipped as Hnossi of Aesgard, daughter of Queen Frigg of the Norse gods.

Since our sessions began, I'd noted Hnossi's extreme reluctance to share her feelings, rather hoarding her words and thoughts in my presence as if they were a mound of Hostess Twinkies and I were a projectile bulimic. Hoping for better results today, I shifted into a new approach, as the two of us sat alone inside the temporal lobe of her brain.

"I'm sure that over the last forty-eight hours, Iron Lass, you've been reflecting mostly on Hawk King and your relationship with him, probably to the exclusion of pretty much anything else.

"But today, I'd like to touch on an outstanding issue at the core of why you're here—namely, why *are* you here?"

Purple lightning crackled overhead along a neural pathway, the synapses pulsating in echoing thunder like throbbing stars.

Hnossi Icegaard revealed nothing but a flicker in one eyebrow.

I remained undeterred.

"Frankly, Hnossi," I said as the cerebral thunder diminished into distant rumbles, "I'm surprised that the F*L*A*C required you of all the F*O*O*Jsters to attend our sessions."

Her eyes, like a cobra's, dilated and scoped on me as if I were a mongoose.

"After all," I continued, "on several occasions you've played the rôle of law-giver with your colleagues, *unto* them, if you will, maintaining order, decorum. Hardly a disruptive behaviour, it would seem."

Her chin tilted up, slowly shifting to the right; her eyes remained locked, like glinting safes.

"Does zis mean my presence is unnecessary, *Fräu Doktor*? Becoss if so—"

"It means your presence is highly *necessary*, Professor Icegaard. Necessary for your team-mates in providing limits, and necessary in providing a rôle model. Given all that, why in your opinion would the F*L*A*C suggest you're a disruptive influence in the F*O*O*J?"

She pursed her lips, maintained her stare at me. "You vud haff to ask zem."

"You've obviously had time to form your own analysis of the F*L*A*C and their decision."

She was silent. Behind her, the temporal lobe shimmered, but there was no lightning.

"So according to your analysis, what is the F*L*A*C's rationale for ordering you here? Where have they miscomprehended you and your work?"

"Ze F*L*A*C . . . unt ze FOOCH itself, fails to unterstant . . . ze significance uff self-discipline unt re-evaluation . . . durink difficult times . . . or uzzervise."

"And that refers to you how?"

"I haff providet guidance, *Doktor*. Guidance zey apparently belief is no lonker reqviredt. Alzough, perhaps now, sadly, in light of Hawk—"

"You're an icon, Professor," I said, changing directions again to prevent her clambering into her psychemotional bunker to escape the falling shells of my inquiry. "Not only as a Norse deity and as a twentieth century super-human, but in the academy . . . author of *Women Who Fly with the Valkyries, The Frigga Mystique,* and *The Buri Myth,* among others—"

"*Ja?*"

"You broke down doors, sometimes literally, to gain entrance to traditionally male domains. Dozens of female heroes entered the F*O*O*J because they were inspired by you, and they've sung your praises in interviews, books, and the motivational speaker circuit. And of course, the fact that you've been worshipped for centuries—"

"*Ja?*"

In the northern sky of her brain's emotional centre, blue lightning flashed; the thunder lagged by seconds. I motioned for her to stand and walk with me, which she did, and we headed off towards the nexus of her divine motor function.

"That's quite a burden," I said above the thunder finally rolling in, "having to live up to all that. Never being allowed to falter. To be vulnerable."

"Burtens are a part of life in zis vurlt. Hawk King . . . taught us all zat."

"A part of life, yes. You think they're the entirety?"

"I dit not say zat."

"A burden you've borne for twenty centuries. And now, even with the *Götterdämmerung* over, you're still having to hold yourself up as an example of what you can achieve if you have the will and honour, if you're devoted to what you consider 'right.' It must be . . . .

"Well, I won't tell you how it feels, but beholding a generation of younger heroes, younger women heroes, who comport themselves as if all the privileges and access they have *weren't* fought for and struggled for by the women who preceded them, most of whom never got to enjoy such opportunities . . . opportunities that they're . . . some would say . . . squandering? You must find that absolutely galling."

She drew in a huge breath through her nostrils, but even with her mouth closed I could hear her teeth grinding against each other as if she were chewing the ingot sweetbreads of the mythic iron goat Scyldscrotgnashhunt.

We were close.

ICONSTERNATION: IRON LIPS

I aimed my neuron-probe up into the cerebral "sky" of memory, the zone to which my Id-Smasher™ had mapped and routed the segments of Hnossi's actual flesh-and-ichor brain.

Inside her virtual cerebrum, the sky warbled at my neuron-probe's beam. I then tapped a sequence on my belt controls, stimulating the sensory-memory lobe, and around us IMAXed the remembered sights, smells, sounds and wind-rushing tactile impression of flying over snow-clutched Scandinavian mountain peaks. Neurally connected to her as I was, I felt the strain at my shoulders of wings surging through the stratosphere, felt the cold rushing across my body.

"Your other powers," I said, aiming my probe elsewhere, "include the ability to summon and command this vehicle, correct?"

Instantly we were standing in a bald, grey valley; a gleaming iron chariot appeared, connected to a train of tiger-sized iron cats. I clicked again: across the sky, we looked "down" at two massive projections of Hnossi's hands, into which materialized her two magic iron swords, one short, one long.

"Iron chariot; iron cats; iron swords. You can turn your wings into iron, you can occasionally turn your body into iron, you have gold- and silver-plated iron armour, your name is—"

"Your point, *Doktor*?"

"That's a lot of iron, Hnossi. You tell me. What's the point?"

"Mm, *ja*," she sneered. "Don't you sink zat's just a bit too . . . mm . . . precise, *Fräu Doktor*? Too purfectly pat unt pristine? Zat my carryink uff iron implements unt various transformations vis iron connote a hardness or hard-heartedtness uff my character, Freudianly suggestink furzer some sort uff pursonal or family dysfunction?"

"I didn't say a word about your family, Professor Icegaard."

She stiffened, blinking at me, looking like a sleeping cockatoo whose perch had suddenly collapsed beneath her.

"But the way you reacted to my question, Hnossi, is interesting. Have you found in your career or your mothering that shaming is an effective means of silencing people when they question you or your decisions?"

Her lips flattened like spatulas, her eyes nailed onto me like eviction notices. The giant projection of hands and swords flared and then turned to black smoke, while the entire sky erupted in flame.

The two of us stood crisping in the violent orange light of the inferno. But because I refused to look away from her face, Hnossi finally spoke.

"Vell, first uff all, you're mistaken ven you say—it's inaccurate to, totally incorrect to suggest zat I, zat I *shame* people, *Doktor*, vezzer professionally or personally. Unt even if, unt I punctuate *if*, vut I said to you vuss 'shaming,' zen zat's only becoss zat's vut you'd just been doingk to me!"

"Why are you choosing to think I was trying to shame you?"

"You, you just—you vere just tryink to somehow make me feel ashamedt uff my ferric powers! Vich I've been using for centuries in your vurlt, savink people like you, people who caun't take care of zemselfs!"

"So you admit that you did try to shame me as retaliation for what you perceived as me shaming you, and you just attempted to shame me again by saying people like me can't take care of themselves."

The firestorm emitted what I can only describe as a confused light, diminishing into vast, belching fields of smoke which I waved away with my hands. Hnossi removed her mandarin-collared powder blue cardigan, and from her back her wings emerged in a burst of snow and black ash. Standing, she flapped her vast, black falcon wings to clear our air.

"So in which ways, do you think," I said, coughing, "has this belief of yours that two wrongs make a right led to professional or personal problems for you?"

She stood agape, finally squeaking out, "I caun't belief your shoddy, scatter-shot, disjointed—you're not even listenink to me! I don't haff any professional or pursonal proplems!"

"Not even denial?"

"So if I defent myself against untrue accusations, I'm in denial?"

"You're divorced—"

An image glimmered behind her: her ex-husband in his cape, mask, wrestling tunic, and musky *machismo* smirk, the Mexican superhero Strong Man. "Yes I am, as are hundrets of millions of uzzer vimmen vis soughtless husbands in your vurlt—"

"You've been sent to therapy with me—"

An array of caricatures—dwarfish versions of the F*L*A*C officers—sprouted from the "floor" like toadstools. "Because an assembly of scaredt, jealous, foolish, myopic untermenschen on ze F*L*A*C is afraid of vut I represent unt how tiny zey feel ven zey're forced to evaluate zeir own lifes in comparison to—"

"You're estranged from your children, Hnossi."

Her mouth stopped. Shut.

A wall of hewn stone appeared behind her, soaring back left, right, and upwards, and with a thunder-smack concluded its construction as an impenetrable fortress.

From behind narrowed eyes, she said, "You don't know ennysing about my children."

"Tell me."

"I come from a culture, a generation, zat said private matters are private. Unt ve do not discuss our problems vis just vutever professional *gossip-junkie* happens to troll ze back alleys looking to . . . to 'score.'"

"But you just said you didn't *have* any personal problems."

Her eyes flared, her lips opening for a breath. But if she had a sentence waiting to fly, she never surrendered its passport. By then, Hnossi Icegaard was beginning to see that neither my office nor the Id-Smasher™ permitted the use of denial as an avoidance technique.

"Prove me wrong," I said. "If you don't have any personal problems, then tell me about your children, why your emotional-memory centre has metaphored a psychic fortress around any image of them, and why your not seeing them doesn't indicate or constitute a problem."

"Ve're not estrangedt! Ve see each uzzer all ze time!"

"When was the last time you had a meal together? Actual family time, sitting around the table for roasted wild boar, tankards of Jotun ale . . . recitations from the Poetic Edda?"

"Please spare me your painfully passetic attempts at cultural sensitivity, *Doktor.*"

"So. When was it? The last time?"

She looked to her left, looking "east," and the glittering Bifrost rainbow bridge raced up towards the mountain rising from the black plains of memory. At its peak glittered into existence the silver-golden meadhalls of Aesgard.

I ignored her attempt to hide in her "happy place."

"Married to, let's see," I said, clicking a projection of my IRON LASS file after Hnossi's prolonged refusal to speak, "married May 1962 to Hector 'Quetzalcoatl' El Santo, HKA, Strong Man." The life-sized smiling image of the caped-and-tunic-ed hero and Mexican screen idol re-appeared beside Hnossi. She moved closer to it as if automatically, then forced herself to step back and look away.

"Two children: Inga-Ilsabetta, born October 1962, and Baldur, nicknamed 'Lil Boulder,' born June 1964."

A tall girl and a shorter boy, both dark-haired, appeared at Strong Man's hips. Both looked up towards their father with smiles radiant as the sun.

"Separated from El Santo, 1974; children chose to live with father. El Santo eventually filed for divorce in 1981, which concluded the following year."

The family triad diminished into blackness and disappeared. I paused, looking at the woman staring at the fading footprints of shadows.

"Later that year, you drafted a paper entitled "Towards a Practical *Götterdämmerung*: A Logistical Analysis," ghost-rewritten and repackaged to the public as paperback bestseller *Time to Ragnarok!* It became the clarion call that initiated the War."

I glanced away from my file-projection to see Iron Lass's eyes attempting to carve me into individual slices of luncheon meat.

"The same year your husband tells you that your marriage is truly finished, you, essentially single-handedly, declare a global war that changes the planet. A war whose logistics *you* chart. A war you lead to victory."

"Zis is absurt," she said, her left hand glowing white, her right hand shadowing into black. "Vut ridiculous, patronising, reductionist nonsense, to claim an entire geo-political hyper-hominid conflict can be explainedt avay as merely *a vuman scornt?*"

"To go from leading your fellow Valkyries into battle for centuries, being literally worshipped as a deity of iron—to opening yourself up to simple, mortal love, meaning you'd've had to've made yourself soft and pliant and vulnerable to humans, even *bearing children* for a mortal man . . . and then after all of that, to be rejected? That's iconoclasm, Hnossi! The shattering of an icon . . . you!"

"So rather than being 'patronising' or 'reductionist,' I'm trying to get you to integrate everything you've gone through into a post-war logistical analysis of yourself."

Her eyes, aflame, dimmed; her body, rigid, melted by a degree. Her hands resumed their normal state, no swords having appeared in them.

"My muzzer," she finally muttered, "alvays sait to me, she sait, 'Brünhilde, you're too smart by half.'" She lowered her voice further. "She never rembert my name."

What will it mean for your life, and for your view of yourself, if the glory days never return?

> **Iron Lass:** "I never sought glory. Basic respect would suffice."

ICONDITIONAL LOVE

Blobs of day-glow colour oozed and swirled around me as if I were standing inside a giant lava lamp, and the air smelled like a mixture of bubble gum and the cosmetics department at a Target store.

"So, Syndi," I asked the only other person with me inside the Id-Smasher™'s neuroscape, "how do you feel about the F*L*A*C ordering you into counselling?"

"Like, as far as I'm concerned," said the young pop-star, once again and in quick succession yawning, stretching, snapping her virtual gum, and roving her eyes, "everybody should be in counselling."

Power Grrrl had manifested from her memories the leather sofa from my Verbalarium, and had draped herself across it, her back wedged

into one of its corners, one thigh hiked up over the sofa's arm, her hair
dazzled along the sofa's back as if she were awaiting her paparazzi.
Mentally-clad in black and silver leather dominatrix garb and swaying
her torso to the dance-beat seeping from her bustier-speakers, she was,
that day, unusually low-key.

"Tell me about that, Syndi. Why should 'everybody be in counselling'?"

"Isn't it obvious, Eva? These F*O*O*J-feebletons really need you, and
one day I'm sure they'll like thank you?" she said in her usual question-
intonation, smiling sugar all over me. "But just look at the world, you
know? Everyone's like crazy—all this negative energy they're beaming?
These F*O*O*J-fogies need to fix themselves before they start invading
everyone else's proximity, you know? Gawd!"

"So you think they're being hypocritical, Syndi?"

"Like, yeah!"

"Aren't superheroes *supposed* to be involved? Helping others?"

"How're you supposed to help people if you should really be under
round-the-clock observation on a coupla hundred meds?"

"You seem to get along fine with the Brotherfly."

"P-Fly? He's cool," she said, while behind her drifted an image of
the Brotherfly gazing at her adoringly. "He knows how to have fun. He's
not afraid to live, y'know? The others, like, need to get over themselves.
'Legendary heroes'? Right!"

"Not even Omnipotent Man?"

Brotherfly disappeared, replaced by an Omnipotent Man half his
correct size, and old beyond his years. "Just a sad old man who's like
totally lost in his own rep."

"The Flying Squirrel?"

Omnipotent Man disappeared, replaced by the image of an actual
flying squirrel wearing a black top hat sitting atop a pile of virtual money
and screeching. "Just an angry old tight-ass who can't deal."

"'Deal' with . . . ?"

"My orientation?"

"Yes. Let's discuss that in a moment. What about X-Man?"

She paused a moment with a look on her face suggesting she was
chewing a uniquely dreadful species of sushi. The top-hatted squirrel
was replaced, oddly, by an image of herself wearing a white shirt and
black suit-and-tie. The image appeared to be gasping for breath before
it disintegrated.

"Gawd," she said, "he's, like, the most uptight of all of them.
Everything's about race for him. He seriously needs your help, Eva. Like,
if he didn't have his job and his politics and his religion, he wouldn't even
have an identity!"

"And how about Iron Lass?"

She stopped her sofa-swaying, looking at me for the first time, while
above us towered a giant, rusting, iron-fleshed Iron Lass like a Norse

Statue of Liberty, glowering down from the clouds with such intense disappointment that the virtual ground beneath us split open.

Rolling her eyes, Syndi blew a bubble. Made it larger.

Larger still.

Popped it.

She sucked it back inside her mouth and chewed.

She rotated the twin volume knobs on each cup of her bustier. The thump-bump pumped louder, and only then did I recognise the song—one of her hits from the previous summer: "Thong Power."

"She's just a depressed, tired, worn-out, broken old woman, Eva," said Syndi, getting up from the couch and amble-dancing around the discothèque that had sprung up around us to shield us from the iron giantess. Syndi glanced at numerous mirrors and portraits of herself, then examined *objets d'art* and bookshelves her memory had manifested here from my office. She pulled books half-way out of their slots on my shelves, glancing at them before leaving them dangling.

"She's always daggering me with her eyes, always making these like snide remarks about how I dress, about my relationships with like Cathode Girl and Billi Biceps and Beast Mistress . . . saying I don't have any focus or purpose or direction . . . I mean, who does she think she is? My like mother?" She snorted. "I already *have* one of those, and she supports me every step of the way!"

Beside her, a full-sized Bianca appeared, a woman in her late forties, over-tanned and leather-skinned, wearing a bustier and white pants that would be called chic on a woman two decades younger.

"Yes, I remember after that open-mouthed kiss with Media Medea on the Golden Tunic Awards on ABC. There was a lot of controversy. Your mother backed you completely."

"Yeah," she beamed. "Bianca's cool."

"You call your mother by her first name?"

"Like, why not? We're not hung up with society's 'rules.' Plus she's like not only my best friend, she's my agent. She got me into the F*O*O*J, got me my Sony deal. If old Iron-Ass wants to be someone's mother, maybe she should start with her own kids?" My bookshelves disappeared, replaced by a floating array of gold and platinum records—hers, I assumed. "I hear neither of them even talk with her . . . I even heard one of her kids tried to like kill herself or something? Some rôle model. Iron Gash could like learn something from Bianca. Gawd! I hope you can help her out . . . for her kids' sake, if no one else's."

"I noticed, in the simulation against Cyclo-Tron, you and Iron Lass certainly seemed to clash. And you never speak to each other in front of me."

"Like, I just told you? She hates me."

"Well, Syndi, I've certainly never gotten the impression she—"

"No, she hates me, Eva, I'm telling you."

"Don't you think you might be exag—"

"She disapproves of me intensely, then! Happy now?"

"What's interesting to me is how much you too are alike."

She spun back around to face me.

"You have got to be like riffing."

"No, Syndi, I'm not 'riffing'. Look . . . you're both icons to women. You're both symbols of femininity and feminine power. From the 1940s through the 1980s, Hnossi inspired female superheroes and ordinary women to break into male-dominated professions and stand up for themselves, and now you're inspiring a generation of young straight and non-heterosexual women and girls to believe in themselves, to be proud. Surely you can see the connection."

"We're like totally different! She's all like 'Do it zis vay' and 'Diknity! Honour! Sacrifice!' It's all about trying to get everyone to be just like her!"

"But Syndi, what about your HEAT-ray?"

She gaped indignantly. "That's like totally not the same!"

"You used it in the Id-Smasher® simulation. You've used it in the small number of melees you've been in during your brief crime-fighting career, and you even use it in your concerts. Your . . . what's it called, now . . . Hyper-Emulation—"

"Acquisition Transmission ray, yeah, yeah—"

"Syndi, you turn people into duplicates of yourself. Literally. And literally under your control. Not to mention your highly successful line of *Power Grrrl's Grrrl Guides™: Power Grrrl's Grrrl Guide™ to Yoga, Power Grrrl's Grrrl Guide™ to Yoga Diamond-Hard Abs, Power Grrrl's Grrrl Guide™ to Yoga Buddhism,* the *Grrrl Guide™ to Yoga Writing the LSAT—*"

"So I know something about marketing. Is that a taboo or something? With all your books and videos, Eva, I'd think you of all people could appreciate that!" Suddenly the discothèque reformatted itself into what must've been a Barnes & Noble, guessing by the wafting smell of lattés.

Syndi wandered off, disappearing amid all the shelves of her own CDs, DVDs, *PG!* magazines and books. Just before I located her again, I finally found copies of something other than her work: a battered hardcover of Professor Icegaard's *Towards a Practical Götterdämmerung: A Logistical Analysis,* and a few copies of my own self-help series. They were in the deleted titles bin.

"Well, despite what you think, Syndi," I said, "I am impressed by how much you've accomplished—and not just for someone your age, but for anybody of any age. Your LSAT manual is apparently the most effective one on the market, and my own agent said your editor swears you wrote every word of it, even though you're only nineteen and you've never even been to Law school—"

"Of course I wrote it! I wrote all my books!" she said, climbing up a display case next to a standee of herself. "Why's that so hard to believe? People are like always underestimating me just because I express myself on my own terms!"

"So you don't see your manuals as an attempt to make other people live like you do?"

"I'm like *helping* them?" she said, vaulting from the display case onto the top of a decorative pillar. Miraculously despite her heels, she did not fall. She stood up straight. "That's not controlling them!"

"Yes, but don't you think Iron Lass sees her actions the same way?"

"I don't care what she thinks, Eva! Whose side are you on, anyway? I don't exactly feel supported here!"

"Syndi, my job isn't to be on anybody's side. It's to be on *everybody's* side."

"Gawd, what good are you then?"

"Syndi, did you ever think that using your HEAT-ray on others might be a violation of their rights?"

She chewed her gum furiously for several seconds, as if hoping her mastication might provide clarification. "Their *rights?*" she said finally. "What are you talking about? Because I included them in my *me*-ness?"

"People have a right to freedom, to individuality—"

"Eva," she said from atop her pedestal, "why wouldn't anybody want to be *me?*"

ICONQUEST? ID-DENTITY CRISIS AND THE POWER OF NARCISSISM

Part of the id's purpose is to assert its host personality onto the world to ensure its host's continued existence. *If I get enough,* says the id, *I will exist another day.*

But unlike what Gloria Gaynor sings in the classic disco song "I Will Survive," the id isn't satisfied with "enough," because enough is never enough. The id always needs more, or specifically, more than anybody else. So "enough" becomes "more than" which becomes "all." And even then, the id fears that all can be taken away, and therefore crushes the capacity of others to resist becomes paramount.

Narcissism is the id's assertion of itself, not just over its host, but over others as well. It is the illusion that one's own needs are not only more important than other people's needs, but that one's own needs *are* other people's needs.

Because Power Grrrl was a highly narcissistic personality, she could not understand that my rôle as therapist was to aid everyone from her team, and not to be her own personal ally or avenger. Nor could she understand that her paranormally over-developed id was the true power-source of her HEAT-ray, and that her use of it fundamentally abused the people whom she dominated.

Most of all, perhaps, Syndi's narcissism blinded her to her true reason for disliking Iron Lass: their similarity. Both iconic heroines sought to control others, believing such control was a boon, rather than a bane.

But while Iron Lass was overbearing, her attempts at control manifested through blame, guilting, and manipulation, all of which still provided some chance for resistance. Power Grrrl's HEAT-ray, however, provided no such chance for escape . . . a reality which led, indirectly but inescapably, to the July 16th massacres.

CLASH OF THE ICONS

"You come from a large family, Hnossi. And royalty, too, correct?"

Iron Lass's gaze flickered over to Power Grrrl before she looked back to answer me. She'd done that several times since we'd reconvened inside a neutral Id-Smasher™ mindscape both their brains had selected, a badlands grove of buttes at sunrise.

"*Ja-a-a-a . . . ?*" she said slowly.

Power Grrrl coughed into her hand, except it wasn't a cough—she'd barked the word *phony*, eliciting a glare from Hnossi.

"Syndi? Is there something you think we need to attend to?"

"Like, aren't we supposed to be honest here, Eva? Because I happen to know one or two things about this 'icon' over here, and they don't square with what she's been saying?"

Glaring back at the young woman, Hnossi's face looked as coldly cutting and metallic as the grill of a 1955 Pontiac. I asked the elder woman to respond, but when she said nothing, I pushed further. "Hnossi, am I missing something? You're Hnossi, daughter of Odin and Frigg, the royal family of—"

"Oh, Eva," sighed Syndi, "I thought you had a better B.S. detector—I can't believe you fell for Hnossi's 'royalty' shit."

"Vatch your langvidge!"

"Watch this," said Syndi, cupping her pudenda.

"*Ach,* Kvasir's bowl! Vhere's your vhistle now, *Fräu Doktor*? I shouldn't haff to stand here unt take zis—"

"Please, ladies—let's deal with this properly. Syndi? You said I fell for an un-truth. So what is the truth?"

"Like, there's more than one Frigg in the Norse pantheon, Eva. People always think that Frigg, the wife of Odin, is the other Frigg, also known as Freyja. And Iron Lassy there just lets em think that. Like, isn't that deceit or something? Doesn't that violate some sort of Aesir honour code-thingy or something?"

"So, Hnossi, you're not related to Frigg, wife of Odin?
Iron Lass: " . . . Nein."

"So why have you let people believe—"

"If people make zis mistake on zeir own, am I suppost to take all my time to correct zeir misconzeptions? I have a *life, Doktor*, of teachink claasses, gradink papers, providink guidance in ze FOOCH—"

"Lying . . . ."

"Syndi, please. All right, Hnossi. We can get back to family of origin later. Let's see, here . . . you became a Valkyrie, correct?"

"Ja."

"Why'd you join?"

Her eyes were like switchblades, swinging their glinting tips between Syndi and me. When she spoke, the indignation of her words grated like the fingernails of the damned on a blackboard in hell.

"I vaanted," she said, "to be part of sumsing devoted to ze greater goot. Vhere honour vut alvays vanquish self-indulchence. Vhere clarity uff vision decisively defeatedt ze false promises uff moral relativism."

Syndi rustled in the scrub grass, about to interrupt. I intervened.

"And you felt you weren't getting that at home?"

Syndi laughed, snidely enough to spoil yoghurt. "I bet that wasn't the only thing she wasn't getting at home."

"You're a disgraceful lout!" said Hnossi. She looked furious enough to knock down the buttes around us. "Everysing for you is sex, sex, sex! Do you have a sinkle uzzer sought in your het? I've devotet my entire life—"

Syndi mouthed the words along with Iron Lass: " . . . *to justice, honour, diknity!*"

"*Ja*, zat's right, little girl. Mock me all you vaant! But for centuries vimmen haff looked up to me as an example—unt now, sanks to people like you, I look arount unt find a generation of tarts more devotet to diamond tongue-stuts, unt engineerink media scantals, zan achieving power in politics, in ze vurkplace—"

"Your problem, Hnossi, is that you not only don't like men, you don't like women, either! You *liked* being the only woman in the F*O*O*J! How long was it after Liberty Lass like *died* that the F*O*O*J got its third heroine? Twenty-five years? And that was only after a lawsuit? What walls were you breaking down then? Oh, almost forgot—you were too busy getting ready to break down your marriage!"

"You know nussink about zis! You're a disgraceful, disrespectful— you'd be better off vis a little more Germaine Greer unt a lot less Camille Paglia, young lady!"

"And you'd be better off with a little less Ayn Rand and a little more Freyja! The real Freyja, like, your mother?"

"You're only in ze FOOCH to milk it for marketing, for 'synergy' tovards your next album, your next product line, your next *Grrrl Guide on Tantric Flute Playink* or vutever, or to launch a movie career! You haff no more devotion to zis organisation zan a tapevurm hass to a stomach! You need to straighten out your priorities! You need to chainch your life! You need to—"

"*You* need to remember you're *not my mother!*"

Both women fell silent.

A hot breeze blew through the neuroscape, tugging at each woman's hair, and the dust grew thick enough to choke on.

Syndi's simple statement of fact seemed to have sliced through the argument like a dull axe through a forehead. And it was the last sentence I could wrangle from either of them for the rest of the morning.

CHAPTER FOUR

Iconoclastic Means "I Can!"

ICONVERSION: ART FOR HEART'S SAKE

SUNDAY, JULY 2, 13:45 A.M.

"Your task," I told Hnossi, Syndi, Kareem and Mr. Piltdown inside the Aesthetics Laboratory of Hyper-Potentiality Clinic, "is to construct with the materials in this room a three-dimensional model of your own personal icon."

"Good god, 'doctor,'" said Mr. Piltdown, "is there any floor through which you cannot sink? The finest flame of the Age of Heroism has just been extinguished, and meanwhile you want us to pretend we're in grammar school so we can *drawr pitchers?*"

"Art therapy, Mr. Piltdown, is a highly reputable and effective means through which the subconscious mind can release its repressed fears, anxieties, grief, and yearnings. And during the psychemotional turbulence of having lost a figure of such importance to you all, to the country, to the world—"

"So the answer is *yes*, then," said the brawny septuagenarian billionaire. "This is pointless. And if I'm to be subjected to this pointless inanity, why aren't Wally and that dung-crawling tap-dancer here to be punished alongside us?"

"Festus, please," sighed Hnossi. "Let's just get zis over vis. Can ve just do zat?"

He paused, finally nodding to her. "For *your* sake, Hnossi."

"Sank you. Continue, *Fräu Doktor.*"

81

"Thank you, Hnossi. To answer your question, Mr. Piltdown, André isn't feeling well—"

"Either a hang-over, or a ho-over," muttered Kareem, possibly louder than he thought (or possibly not), "number seven-hundred and thirty-eight."

"—and Wally said he'd be here, so I'm sure he's just running behind."

Flying Squirrel: "Running *something*, I'd wager."

I looked to Mr. Piltdown, expecting him to elucidate. He said nothing.

I continued. "You have all afternoon. Look around the Aesthetics Laboratory. Use anything, from felts and crayons to swatches to minerals to industrial cast-offs, and employ whatever powers, skills, or talents you wish. All I want you to do is to evoke through art what moves you most about that person, group, or place that embodies your highest ideals. The point here, especially during this period of bereavement-processing, is to connect yourself with the power-source of your emotional-intellectual nexus.

"While you're working, I'll ask you some questions about what you're doing and why and how, and then at the end we'll have some conclusion-and-contemplation work. So, go to it!"

Power Grrrl raised her hand.

"Yes, Syndi?"

"Is there any of André's baking left from the other day?"

"No, Syndi."

"Like, could you call him and ask him to bring—"

"Just focus on ze *verdammt* assignment, *fräulein* 'Gurrrl'!"

"Whatever!"

ICONOGRAFFITTI

Because actual icons—the type held in museums—represent our most esteemed virtues, we might assume they must be constructed exclusively from genuinely precious materials such as marble, gold or achillium.

But during Europe's Middle Ages, a thriving trade in faked icons saw horse molars sold as the teeth of Saint Paul, stable splinters sold as shards of the True Cross, and bear's hair sold as clippings from the beard of Solomon. Clearly, the composition of an icon is irrelevant to its purpose—that being a focal point for our contemplation.

So if you're prevented from confronting your own inadequacies because you're prostrate in front of a golden calf that's been thrust upon you, or if you're stuck inside a narcissistic id-loop of worshipping yourself, then right now, put down *Unmasked! When Being a Superhero Can't Save You From Yourself*, and take whatever random materials you have in your apartment, headquarters, cavern, or hideout, and build an icon of your own.

When you're done, resume reading the chapter and follow along with my heroes. Write down your own answers to the questions I ask them, and take part in our final exercise. What you discover may put you much closer to freeing yourself from the cold clutches of your own psychic supervillains.

ICONSTRUCTION

My team quickly surveyed the room, each seeker securing the materials necessary to build his or her own icon, or in Mr. Piltdown's case, seizing the resources he thought others might require for their work.

I noticed that the dynamic detective was also depositing pamphlets around the room—red-white-and-blue glossies whose covers featured his own cowled scowl beneath the slogan *Return to Honour, Pride & Glory* and above the phrases *Elect FLYING SQUIRREL* and *Director, F*O*O*J Operations*. No one so much as glanced through one, not even Kareem, even though the tract was a direct challenge to him.

But while Mr. Piltdown tried to spark interest in Hnossi, to his obvious disappointment she was much more concerned with the three-yard wide broken slab of granite she was hefting from the industrial cast-offs section of the Aesthetics Lab and laying across the floor of her workbay. Syndi had dragged over a mannequin and gone back for armfuls of cloth scraps and cans of spray paint, while Mr. Piltdown began by flipping through a stack of magazines, constantly casting looks over his shoulders (whether from angry suspicion or embarrassment, I was not sure).

The X-Man, however, was standing at his workbay without tools, without materials, without scraps. His eyes were closed, and he remained motionless.

From behind me was a simultaneous rush of frost and heat—Iron Lass had manifested her white and black swords, alternately freezing and melting sections of her vast granite slab before shearing them away.

I noticed Mr. Piltdown had stopped entirely—not from gazing at Iron Lass but from focusing on the inside of a 1979 copy of *TIME* from which he'd been tearing out images and text.

He stood staring at a full-page photograph of a beautiful, slender-muscled, young Asian man in tight green shorts, a tight red leather vest, a short yellow cape, and a shiny black mask with stubby, furry gopher-style ears. His legal name, which had not been revealed when the article was written, was Tran Chi Hanh.

But back then he was known to the world as martial-arts ingénue and Flying Squirrel sidekick Chip Monk. North America's first born-Buddhist superhero, and its last.

"*You* were once *his* icon," I said as quietly as I could to Mr. Piltdown. "Before . . . before he left you."

He looked down at me, his eyes burning like piles of discarded hospital waste. "That was before he ended up in therapy," he hissed, "with the likes of you."

"Looking up to anyone as much as Tran did can be very destructive to one's ego-integrity—"

"The word 'therapist,' Miss Brain," snarled Mr. Piltdown. "You put a space after the third letter, and you get 'the rapist.' Chip fell into therapy, like any street junkie falls into smoking maki. That's what ruined him, not—"

"I can't imagine the burden you carry, Mr. Piltdown, of having to be an icon, always having to be perfect, never being able to make a mistake. Because the distance to the pinnacle that people believe you're perfect, it's to that same depth they'll be furious when they inevitably discover you're not."

"Tran's betrayal, Miss Brain," he said, "wasn't because of any perceived imperfection on my part. You brain-shredders! Devoting your lives to splitting up marriages, ruining families and organisations, digging up depravities that should be repressed and reanimating them in front of a crowd—"

"Perhaps the real problem, Mr. Piltdown, is being someone's icon inside any close or intimate relationship. It's inevitable that worship decays into contempt, because worship is ultimately about being trapped, being a slave."

"The only slavery I see here, Miss Brain, is your cultish, psychopathologising claptrap!"

He returned to his *TIME*, tearing the picture of Chip Monk down the middle and glancing at 1979 entertainment coverage of *Ragnarok Now!*, the Oscar-winning film about superheroes suffering from post-power stress disorder. "Tran Chi Hanh, the boy I raised as if he were my own son, betrayed me. Betrayed me because of a very sick and very evil little man."

He re-aimed his scorching glare at me, and then at everyone else, but no one was looking back or even listening. Had they heard him, they all would have instantly understood his reference—to the premier scandal of Reagan-era superheroics.

In 1980, after rumours of an ever-degenerating relationship between the Flying Squirrel and his sidekick, the Chip Monk resigned at his first, brief, and final press conference.

And then he disappeared for four years.

Surfacing in 1985 under his legal name and fresh out of law school, Tran began his new public identity as an intern at Human Citizen, the premier anti-superhero public interest law firm headed by the arch-nemesis of the Flying Squirrel—Jack Zenith, author of *Unsafe in Any Cape* and *Two Masks of a "Hero"*.

"'Betrayed' you?" said X-Man from his work bay, his eyes still closed. Apparently someone had been listening to Mr. Piltdown after all. "Interesting wording, Festus," he chuckled. "You sound like a lover scorned. Of course . . . that's exactly what everyone said actually happened, now isn't it?"

Festus was crossing the distance to X-Man's workbay and reaching for the weapons in his utility pouches before I could intervene. X-Man barked the word *Arms and armour!* and with the snap and stench of gunpowder he faced the Flying Squirrel in a battle-stance and wrapped in the gleaming black armour of a 15th Century Benin warrior, mace in one hand and lance in the other.

"You filthy-mouthed carpet-bagger!" said the Squirrel. "I'll beat the black off you!"

"I'm not your sidekick, Festy," Kareem laughed. "You won't be beating off anything around me!"

Suddenly there was a deafening *CRACK*, and a ten-foot high wall of blinding-white ice crisped into existence between the two would-be combatants.

"I vudn't touch zat, if I vere you, *Fräu Doktor*," said Iron Lass, her white short-sword *Grendelsmuter* pointing towards the barrier she'd just constructed. "Unt you needn't vorry about melting or mess, since ze vall's at least vun hundret dekrees below zero. When all zis nonsense is done, I'll turn it into steam unt be done vis it. Unt I suggest you get a new Mind-Vistle as soon as possible, *ja?*"

She turned back to her bickering fellow F*O*O*Jsters. "Now, shut up unt get back to vurk, you two, or I'll put you bose in briefs I'll make ze same vay I made zat vall."

ICONFLICT

"Tell you suh'm, Doc . . . gonna be some big changes when I get on that F*L*A*C," said the X-Man, standing in his work bay behind the ice wall.

After my warning to him and Mr. Piltdown that I'd immediately place a call to the F*L*A*C if there were ever again a hint of violence between them inside the Hyper-Potentiality Clinic, Kareem launched into a fifteen-minute lecture to me on why he should not be made to remain in therapy when he should instead have been investigating full-time the "suspicious" death of Hawk King.

But finally both his eyes and his mouth were shut, his armour was gone, and his body was perfectly still, back in its uniform of white shirt and black suit-and-tie.

I was very conscious how intensely dry my mouth was, probably because Iron Lass must've sucked all the moisture out of the room's air to make so much ice. Licking my lips to keep them from cracking, and wishing I had not only a psychemotional but an epidermal balm, I told Kareem, "You sound very confident about your chances of winning."

"It's not a matter of confidence, Doc. It's allies. It's strategy. It's diligence." He breathed in deeply, let it out in a long rasp as if from the bottom of his soles. *"Legs and feet."*

Like a prairie sky coning into twin tornados, dust and shadow condensed in front of me into two columns. Supple muscles puffed up like Ball Park Franks®, feet arching and toes curling inside golden sandals whose straps wrapped themselves like snakes around the calves of the disembodied legs.

Kareem opened his eyes, inspecting his work. "And it doesn't hurt being up against a Ku Klux Klown like the Flying Fart. He really thinks he can get more than two percent of the electorate onside? That old allosaurus is probably the most hated member of the F*O*O*J—and not just by the public, I'm talking about F*O*O*J members themselves, here."

"If he's no threat to your candidacy, why are you even talking about him?"

"Because even the *idea* of that filthy old fascist becoming the D.O.O. is offensive to me. Nothing but a northern cracker. A caviar cracker. A *canapé*. He's everything that's wrong with the F*O*O*J. He's—you know what this man is? The perfect metaphor for him is that ice wall right there. A cold, white barrier too tall to go over, and lethal to the touch."

He closed his eyes, tilted his head back slightly.

"Now, what we *should've* been doing, especially after the end of the War, is using the power of the F*O*O*J to clean this country up for real—and not going after freaks in tights, either, not that there're many of them on the outside of the F*O*O*J these days, anyway."

"But how do you think that—"

"Hold on a minute."

He concentrated, closed his eyes. *"Pelvis."*

Condensing into existence atop the two legs in three-dimensional block letters was the word *PELVIS*. It wobbled, fell to the floor, shattered.

The X-Man opened his eyes. "Damn it," he growled. *"Khaibtu kher."* The shards *popped!* into dust, and then even the dust disappeared. "Look, Doc, I've gotta *con*centrate on this—"

"Sounds to me like you were just about to say something rather important about what you feel is wrong with your organisation."

He sighed. "First of all, it's not 'my' organisation. The organisation is nothing but a bunch of mercenaries in rainbow lingerie. Decades of tax-payer money funnelled into DOD contracts for overseas ultra-violet ops or HUD contracts to 'stabilise' inner-cities? Which it has always failed to do? What is that?

"F*O*O*J headquarters are right here on the West Coast, but where was the F*O*O*J during the maki epidemic when the DIA and the Office of Naval Intelligence were shipping in coelacanth-weed to sell to Southern California gang-bangers to finance their terrorist army to overthrow the government of New Atlantis? Suddenly every black or Hispanic neighbourhood on the West Coast had a maki-house on every block and enough automatic weapons to fight a war!" he railed in a single, indignation-powered breath. "Where was the kot-tam leadership of the F*O*O*J during all that? I'll tell you where—Lying Squirrel was lunching with Kissinger and Reagan on how to destroy New Atlantis and Wally Watchtower was posing with Nancy on his lap on a CBS Christmas

Special telling kids to 'Just say no.' Meanwhile, you know what old Wally was just saying yes to?"

I waited for an answer, finally having to prompt Kareem with a "No, what?"

Kareem looked furtively around the room, his head hunkered turtle-like into his collar.

"Never mind," he snarled.

This was the first time I'd seen Kareem censor himself. Whatever he was hiding, he obviously had no plans to discuss it around these colleagues whose ratification votes he'd need to ascend to the F*L*A*C.

"Well," I said, "that's a, a fascinating *theory*, Kareem, but in terms of your *feelings*—"

"Jeez, Doc, you don't even try to hide when you're patronising me, do you? You ever talk like that to Festering Squirrel? 'Fascinating theory'?"

"Kareem, I assure you, I treat all my—"

"—all your coloured hero patients the same, yeah, I know. Look, don't you get it? It's not about 'theories' or 'feelings,' it's about what we can *do*. The F*O*O*J has patents on all kinds of technology, tech it licenses out to the government, to corporations. If all we did was take a cut of that and create some jobs, we could rebuild these inner cities we're being paid to protect—and failing to protect—from the maki gang wars our own government is responsible for having created!

"Instead," he said, gesturing to the space between his cupped hands as if he were holding donkey dung, "the F*O*O*J hands over its returns on licensing fees to a bunch of kot-tam parasitic investors! That's what the 'f' in F*O*O*J stands for, Doc. 'Financial.' And 'failure!' And 'fascist!' And completely fu—"

"Brilliant campaign slogan, Amos," said Mr. Piltdown from across the ice wall.

"As opposed to yours, Face-down? 'F*O*O*J ü b e r a l l e s ? ' "

"You're a disgrace to this entire organisation!"

"That's not what *Hawk King* thought," said the X-Man across the ice wall.

I could see it in Kareem's body language: he was making a decision. He made it, then stepped forward. "I'm gonna wait one week after the funeral—out of respect—and then I'm holding a press conference to announce the contents of a papyrus Hawk King wrote and gave to me."

Mr. Piltdown: "Hawk King never gave any papyrus to the likes of *you!*"

"I'm announcing," continued Kareem, "that what Hawk King wanted all along wasn't for the F*O*O*J to be some kind of kot-tam enforcer, the police-mafia in spandex, but to break down walls and build up halls, to shake the power*ful* and remake the power*less*. And when he got road-blocked, steam-rolled, and presidentially-knackered, he couldn't take it anymore, and *that's* why he went into exile!

"But he was ready to start all over again, smash the jail they built around him and be reborn with a new mission. And I'm going to reveal what *else* he said in his papyrus . . . which included that he was endorsing *me* as Director of Operations. And I'll hold up that papyrus for the world to read!"

All work in the room ceased.

"Edgerton, good goddamnit, you're nothing but a ghastly, ghoulish little con-man who's prostituting the corpse of our finest hero to foist your inadequacies upon Hawk King's finest creation! There's no papyrus—you're a fraud!"

"*I'm* a fraud? If that aint the fridge calling the stove 'white.' If Americans knew even ten percent of the truth about you, you'd be on *multiple* death rows right now, Fes-pus—"

"Well, Kareem," I cut in, "congratulations. You must be very happy."

"Happy? Happy that the King wanted me—*me*—to guide this group? Happy 'cause he left me an endorsement, which is the closest thing to God writing me a reference letter? Happy that I'm gonna lead this sad group into the twenty-first century and remake it into a hammer for justice?" he said in his rhetorical crescendo. "Kot-tam right I'm happy. I'm *slap-a-cracker* happy!"

"The King would never've endorsed you!" yelled Mr. Piltdown from over on his side of Hnossi's ice wall. "Not in ten million years! Not if you were the last biped on this planet! And you'll be laughing out of the other side of your watermelon-hole when I put a voting-day thrashing on you that'll make Hiroshima look like a campfire!"

I expected Kareem to materialise armour and weapons despite my warning, but instead he merely grinned triumphantly. "Alzheimer's," he stage-whispered to me, "has robbed America of its richest moron reactionary."

"I heard that!"

ICONDESCENSION

"Anyway," said Kareem, "what we need is more than just sweeping out the old guard fascists. We also need to clean out the new generation *fashionists*."

"Meaning?"

"Have a look," he said, thumb-pointing towards Power Grrrl and the mannequin she was working on, to which she'd affixed cloth scraps and wiring in a rough approximation of tassels, G-string, garters, and stockings.

Tension between these two had been obvious since the beginning of our sessions together. The X-Man did anything he could to avoid sitting next to Power Grrrl, and most of the time he wouldn't even look at her or acknowledge her remarks. Given the comments he'd aimed at the Flying Squirrel about Chip Monk, and about Power Grrrl's iconic status as the lesbian "it" girl, homophobia clearly informed at least part of Kareem's antipathy. A common cultural trait in the inner city, homophobic neurosis was obviously as strong a component of the X-Man's id-crisis as was his racial neurosis.

Such racial antagonism had publicly marked the X-Man's career from its inception. Prior to developing his full logogenic powers, Kareem had employed rudimentary pictogenesis in his burgeoning crime-fighting career, noteworthy for his corruption-crackdown on the moguls of African-American Network Television and the hip-hop/rap industry. Several years previously the prestigious *Los Ditkos Inspector* magazine carried a four-page feature on a younger Philip "Kareem" Edgerton, shortly after he'd switched his alias "Mac Rude" to "X-Man." As a rising star in the League of Angry Blackmen, which had drastically reduced crime in the Los Ditkos inner-city neighbourhood of Langston-Douglas, Kareem had been invited to speak before a $500 per plate dinner for the West Coast liberal philanthropic group, the Dream Foundation.

After disparaging the AANT executives in the crowd as well as hip-hop/rap artist-producers P. Bowels and the Nefarious N.I.G., Kareem, according to the *Inspector*, proceeded to tease, taunt, and ultimately terrorise the elite dinner audience with a self-righteous, condescending harangue that allegedly included him grabbing his crotch and inviting the crowd to sample "these nuts" after their soup. The *Inspector* concluded that such behaviour ultimately cost the L*A*B its HUD security contract for Langston-Douglas.

I asked Kareem, given his F*O*O*J political ambitions, how he expected to advance his career when his reputation was so rife with racialised rage.

"I've got a *right* to be hostile, Doc," said Kareem after a long silence in which he finally managed to logo-synthesise an actual pelvis above the two legs he'd formed earlier. "My people are being persecuted."

"Kareem, I read that *Inspector* article about the dinner you attended—"

"The *Inspector*'s a piece of crap, and ninety percent of what that punk wrote never even happened—"

"—and based on your behaviour at that dinner, it's clear that you *wanted* those people to dislike you. As if you were afraid of them."

"*Afraid?* What are you talking about, Doctor?"

"Afraid of their acceptance."

Dropping his jaw with *faux*-shock, he said, "Let me tell you about these people 'accepting' me, Doctor. That dinner, it was about half Day-Glo long-john types, a quarter media mucketty-mucks, and the rest wealthy superhero groupies. Some of that meringue mafia like to pretend to *like* people like me. It spit-shines their white liberal credentials. The rest don't even *bother* pretending.

"But you know who else was there? F*O*O*J punks like the Beaver Brothers, who were the number one source for that rat-gut reporter. And just two weeks ago I found out that Carroll Beaver's been spreading rumours about me. That I'm a sexist! *Me!* What kind of fecal fungus is that? You see how I treat Iron Lass. Is that sexist? And I never had anything but complete respect for the Supa Soul Sistas—"

"Yet you won't even acknowledge Syndi's presence, Kareem," I said. "And every time she speaks, you either roll your eyes, cross your arms in judgement, or get a look on your face like you're sipping from a bucket of something turgid."

"That," he said, immediately jabbing a finger towards me before catching himself, "that's an entirely different . . . and it's got nothing to do with gender, Doc."

"Is it because of her orientation?"

He rolled his eyes, crossed his arms, and got a look on his face as if he were sipping from a bucket of something turgid. "Trust me," he said, "it's got nothing to do with her 'orientation.'"

"Then tell me what it is about."

"This is all a joke!"

"What's all a joke?"

"*This!*" he said, sweeping the room with his chin. "Being in this laboratory, completely cut off from the real world . . . how's this high-tech chicken coop supposed to reveal anything about how we actually function out there? The real reason we're here isn't because of *our* fears, Doctor, it's because of *yours.* In here, you're safe. You're boss. You're in control. The way you like it.

"You claim you want to understand us, understand *me?* I'll believe that the day I see you walking the streets of Stun-Glas. And I should be out there investigating the murder—assassination—of the greatest hero of our times, instead of facing expulsion from the F*O*O*J for failing to attend this psycho-sycophantic suck-fest you've got us starched into!"

"Well-played, Kareem." I smiled, nodding at my young patient. "Very skillful."

"Meaning what?"

"Turning the conversation to someone else's supposed shortcomings and away from your antagonism towards Syndi."

"Look, Doctor. You want me to finish your assignment or not?"

Being one of the nation's most insightfully attuned psychoanalysts, I recognised when it was time to reel in a patient, and when it was time to release him. There'd always be time later for the net.

ICONFUSION

At the next work bay, after calling in my secretary for some lip-balm, I found Hnossi Icegaard listening to music on her Q-bot player. "I trust zere's no rule against zis?" she said, gesturing to her small silver cube.

"Not at all, Hnossi—this is art therapy, after all. Ella Fitzgerald, right?"

"*Ja.* She won ze Grammy for zis. 'Mack ze Knife.' Even zough she forgot ze vords, her improvisation vus genius . . . a true warrior of song."

She gestured with her short-sword to the granite slab she'd transformed into a stunningly elaborate scale-model replica of a walled fortress, complete with towers, armouries, mead halls, stables, and bridges: the mountain-peak home of the Norse war gods, Aesgard. I asked her to tell me about her icon.

Offering a description which differed somewhat from my recollection of the legends, she focused on the Hall of Valkyries, the fortress of the sisterhood to which she used to belong. Yet none of what she said was in the least personally revealing.

"You know, *Fräu Doktor*," she said confidentially, changing tone and direction, "alzough youngk Kareem can be undisciplinedt, you are too qvick to dismiss his legitimate concerns about Master Hawk Kink. I've spoken wis him at length about ze *primae facae* case he's been developink—"

Recognising her diversion for what it was, I realised it was time to reel Iron Lass in.

"I'll take that into consideration, Hnossi. But right now, I'm curious about something that came up in our dual session with Syndi. After that conversation, I did some further reading about your life . . . and your mother's."

She turned to me, and I was suddenly acutely aware of the power in the unsheathed swords clutched in her armoured hands.

"Unt vut," she said quietly, "haff you discovert, *Doktor* Brain?"

"Well . . . I . . . uh . . . I discovered that there is indeed quite a difference between Frigg, wife of Odin—the goddess-queen most people assume is your mother—and Frigg/Freyja, your actual mother." I cleared my throat, choosing my next words as carefully as I would the steps on a rickety bridge across a gorge.

"Whereas Frigg . . . wife of Odin . . . had an, an illustrious career as an Aesir warmaster and symbol of virtue . . . the other Frigg . . . your mother . . . was . . . she was . . . ."

"A whore," she stated. "Is zat ze vurt you vere lookink for, Eva?"

"It's, uh . . . the word you've chosen," I said, swallowing. "Tell me why."

She stared at me with her cold eyes of hot fury, a look that made me feel like a mouse crisping in a child's E-Z-Bake Oven®. The song on her Q-bot, meanwhile, changed to Patsy Cline's pathetically innocent rendition of "Tennessee Waltz." The juxtaposition only intensified my anxiety.

She continued staring at me, unblinking, unmoving, until the third verse in which Patsy lilted, *"Only you know how much . . . I have lost . . . ."*

I finally broke our gaze, flipping through my file until I found another angle to pursue.

"You're, um, highly lauded, not only among, uh, the public, but, ah, among F*O*O*J members, as a symbol of the very best in superheroism. Since the F*O*O*J's founding, you've enjoyed the highest consistent approval rating among civilians and heroes of anyone except for Hawk King and Omnipotent Man. Ball Buster said in a 1989 issue of *People* that if it weren't for you, she'd've committed suicide, and that she knew of at least two other heroines you'd gotten through similarly traumatic times."

"*Ja?*"

"You have enormous public regard, endless testimonials in your favour . . . . yet, in 1974, after your own daughter is hospitalised under mysterious circumstances, you separate from your husband, and your daughter and son choose to live with him."

I lowered my voice, kept my eyes on the contents of my file folder, forcing myself to take a step towards this sword-wielding woman with eyes of death.

"You've given of yourself to hundreds of thousands of people across the centuries, but the two people in the universe whom you would most logically want to regard you as their icon . . . rejected you. And your own icon . . . it isn't a person of flesh and blood or even divine ichor . . . but a group of cold stone buildings atop a mountain."

Her eyes were ominously huge, like twin amethyst bowling balls full of dynamite, threatening to drop and crush my skull and explode in my brain pan.

"My children, *Doktor*—"

"Sorry I'm late, ma'am-doctor," said Omnipotent Man too loudly, stumbling in and scanning the room to deduce what we were doing and why. The Arctic fury in Iron Lass's face melted into something softer, but far sadder. Wally tripped over his team-mates' work materials while finding a workbay of his own, laughing at himself self-consciously and whistling the theme to *Bonanza*.

"C'n I work over here, Doc? Sorry I'm late—rough night'n all. I'm sure y'all unnerstan—I aint th'o'ny one what's ever had one a them. Hey, Syndi, that's quite the . . . . Now, whatcha puttin on her—now, I aint sure that's an appropriate kinda . . . say, Doc, juss what're we doin, anyhow?"

I went over to Wally, explaining to him the task while observing his dishevelment: his hair was all a-shag, the bags beneath his eyes were big enough to carry hygiene products, and his body reeked of ozone. Re-examining earlier remarks about Wally by Mr. Piltdown and Kareem, I began to suspect a looming scandal which, during this time of crisis, the F*O*O*J and the country might not be able to withstand.

"So I can use anything in the room, ma'am?" he asked before I could inquire about his stench and his shabbiness, not to mention his tremendous tardiness.

"That's right, Wally, but first, I think we need to—"

"Wellsir, ma'am, gotta get started. Time is money, penny-saved, early worm gets two in the bush," he said, gripping the sides of the ice wall and ripping it up from the floor, hauling it off to his work bay and immediately carving it with his super-fast digits. And with the protective wall between Mr. Piltdown and Kareem gone, their conflict inflamed immediately to the verge of vengeance.

They'd both constructed images of the incredible Hawk King.

ICONFRONTATION

I expected a volley of insults, but each man was silent, stupefied with rage, each hero's contempt for the other intensified by a jealous, proprietary fury.

With both heroes motionless in their contest of wills, as if the one who moved first would prove himself the lesser worshipper, I was free to move and inspect their work, which the other F*O*O*Jsters did as well.

Kareem had employed his logogenic powers to sculpt a masterpiece, a six-and-a-half foot tall gleaming black hawk-headed man, adorned with Pharaonic double-crown and kilt, arms stretched forth, hands clutching crook and flail, and wings spread wide as if to encompass the world. One might easily imagine Egyptian peasants and priests prostrate before this statue. Everyone—except Mr. Piltdown, of course—was impressed.

The Flying Squirrel's work, while lacking the artistry, sophistication, or three-dimensional grandeur of Kareem's, was nonetheless fascinating. Since Mr. Piltdown could neither draw nor sculpt, he'd hewn a primitive collage from pictures, logos, and other text he'd torn from his stack of magazines. On a large sheet of Bristol board, a Frankenstein's monster of a Hawk King had been cobbled together from the body parts of various subjects; the figure stood in front of an undersized Blue Pyramid made from blue stretches of ads for automobiles, cleaning products, and perfumes. Radiating from Hawk King's crown like the sun's rays were corporate logos clipped into words and phrases such as "HeRo" and "GETting the JOB doNE Right" and "Master your WORK place" and "MISSion acCOMPlished."

"Fascinating work, gentlemen," I said. "Who'd like to tell me about his work first?"

The X-Man, without breaking his stare at his adversary, reached up and behind himself to his icon's face, which moved slightly. I noted with fascination that Kareem's icon featured limited articulation.

He rasped, "Care to look under the mask, Festy? Or you afraid what you'd find?"

"Well I'll be a pigeon's whiskers, Kreem, but that's a gosh-durn fine piece a work! Fine piece!"

The X-Man, eyes still chained to Flying Squirrel's, said, "Thanks, Wally. Glad you like it."

"Kareem," I said, "tell me about this detail here."

He didn't budge. "Which one?"

"This one where I'm pointing, right here."

Reluctantly breaking his glare, he scowled at me when he found me pointing at nothing and realised he'd been had.

"I just wanted you and Mr. Piltdown to break out of your testosterone-enflamed id-escalation. And now that you have, please take a few minutes to reflect on your icon so I can ask you about it."

"Hey, Doctor Brain, ma'am, look at mine! Look at what I done!"

Despite his late arrival, Wally had already transmuted Iron Lass's ice wall into an admirable ice sculpture, a ten-foot tall man with star-emblems across his jacket and DNA-brocade trimming his cape. The figure stood gazing towards the ceiling as if reading the mysteries enshrouding the ends of the universe.

"That's m'daddy, Jobuseen-Ya," said Wally, "th'late an greatest defender of th'late an greatest planet." He looked around for support, then offered, "Argon. Y'all knew I meant Argon, right?"

"Beautiful craftsmanship, Vally," said Hnossi. "Impressive vurk vis my ice. But, mm, perhaps you should freshen up your face, ja? Haff a coffee or sumsing? You're looking a tad . . . overvurked."

Iron Lass fooled no one. To the extent that Wally's icon was masterful, Wally himself was a sluice-floor hack-work: unshaven, straggle-haired, mud on his suit, rips in his cape, and the even-worse reek of ozone since his last trip to the rest room. "Tell me about your icon, Wally—"

"Eva, like, you haven't even looked at my icon yet?"

I was about to ask Syndi to wait her turn, but when I beheld what she'd built, I was both shocked, and shocked at myself for being shocked.

Syndi's mannequin-based icon, with its dominatrix-inspired attire, was an image of herself.

Having anticipated someone's possible failure to notice her icon's identity, Syndi had glued gold glitter into the forms of the letters P and G around the nipple spikes of the black breast cups of her monument to herself, and *Autographs Here* in the same gold glitter across the mannequin's buttocks and *Grrrls Do it Best* upon its crotch.

"And, like, I gave myself dreads," she said, pointing to the sections of rope festooned from the mannequin's skull, "cuz I've been thinking about like getting some?" She tilted her head with her trademarked coquettishness. "What do you think, Eva? They look good, don't they?"

The X-Man swore.

Syndi tilted her head the other direction. "Kareem, if you like use the word 'appropriation' even once, you can talk to my like autograph dispenser?"

With everyone's work complete, I moved them out of their workbays to their datapads on the table and had them type out why they'd made their icons, what these images meant to them, and what they'd learned from what they'd made. But as important as their answers were, my real purpose was to prime the pump for phase two.

"All right, everyone. You've completed your answers," I said. "Now it's time to destroy your icons."

ICONOCLASM MEANS "I CAN"

The F*O*O*Jsters stammered and sputtered into outrage, demanding to know why I would ask them to put such effort into their artwork if it existed only to be smashed. After reminding them that nothing real lasts, I told them one of my favourite Zen stories.

A monk had been walking through the jungle for several weeks on his way to a grand pagoda, when he encountered the Ganges. Where he found himself, the river was too deep and too wide to cross by walking or swimming, so he wandered downriver for half a day in search of a narrower, shallower point. The river grew only deeper and wider, and throughout his search, his unease grew that each step was taking him further from his destination, which he could see above the canopy in the sunset, glittering golden atop a mountain.

The monk finally realised that his only means across was to build a raft. Never having done so, he worked past sundown experimenting with construction methods, and then spent the entire night lashing together logs with vines, weaving a sail with fronds, and fashioning an oar.

When morning came, the monk tentatively ventured upon the river, not knowing whether he'd drown or be eaten by piranhas and crocodiles. But to his amazement he reached the other side of the Ganges in less than an hour, his unsurpassable barrier conquered easily.

Alighting upon the shore, he surveyed his work with pride. But he couldn't imagine abandoning the craft of his craft. So he gathered vines, hoisted his heavy raft upon his back and trudged through the jungle and up the mountain towards his pagoda.

"Why did the monk haul his raft with him?" I asked.

"Because he was obviously intending to sell the vehicle after he left the goddamned monastery. Or trade up, at least."

"Becoss he vanted neizer to litter nor to vaste."

"Cuz he had hisseff a nice lil ol boat, an he probably wannid to take er out fishin when he was done monkin for the day?"

"Because he didn't want anyone to like rip it off?"

"Because he was too blind, too self-delighted, or too afraid," said Kareem, "to accept that something useful had become a burden."

"Precisely, Kareem."

A small smile—not insincere—crawled onto the X-Man's lips, and I saw him then as he once must have been: the smartest student in the class. I tried to imagine him at a time before his awesome bitterness, when that smile would have been broader and more frequent, but it was difficult to picture.

And yet, despite myself in that moment, I found myself liking Philip Kareem Edgerton, and the impish twist of his lips suggested the feeling was slowly, surprisingly, becoming mutual.

"And the same is true of your icons," I continued, building from Kareem's solution to my wisdom-riddle, "not the artifices you've constructed this afternoon, but the ones that hold hegemony over your hearts and mastery over your minds.

"Especially during this id-crisis that's crippling your professional environment, it's critical for each of you to examine how you are exploiting your ideals and your idols to excuse yourself of your own dysfunctional behaviour."

The F*O*O*Jsters' arms were crossed, their faces dour. Except for Kareem's. Perhaps he chose to believe I wasn't including him in my description. Or perhaps it was something else entirely.

"Consider this, you men and women whom the world calls 'heroes.' By maintaining an icon, you are permanently placing yourself below someone or something which you consider to hold greater wisdom or intrinsic merit than you do. Icons, therefore, are 'virtual parents' situated inside your psyches, indefinitely infantilising you.

"If you want to terminate your internal id-loops and deactivate your interpersonal dysfunction, you need to escape your icon traps. And doing so is as simple as proving to yourself that you need no more false idols in your life. Ultimately idols can only fall down and crush you. You need to start taking care of yourselves, instead of being dependent on others or holding unrealistic opinions of your 'elders.' So go ahead. Smash your external icon. To do so isn't blasphemy. It's to be born again."

All five F*O*O*Jsters stood motionless, confused if not still upset.

"Like, does this even *apply* to me?" asked Syndi. "I mean, like I'm obviously not in this icon-trap-thingy like *them*, right?"

All but Wally rolled their eyes. I said, "No, Syndi, not *exactly* like the rest of them—"

"Good. Cuz I wanna keep mine."

"Wellsir, if she's keepin hers, Doctor, ma'am, c'n I keep mine?"

"It's made of ice, you clod. You're familiar with *melting?*"

"I c'n keep it frosted, Festy."

"Bickering, my friends," I said, "is a self-constructed off-ramp from the freeway to mental health."

"Fine," grunted the Flying Squirrel. "If the only way to escape the Sisyphusian nightmare of this 'therapy trap' and Miss Brain's meningococcal metaphors is to do as she said, let's be done with this rubbish and get the Sam Hill out of here. I don't have time for this hog-sputem—I've a eulogy to write for tomorrow."

And with that, Mr. Piltdown ripped his Bristol board Hawk King icon into two large pieces, then four medium ones, and then decreasingly into a flurry of Hawk-confetti. "You see? Painless. Done. Because it's meaningless anyway, Miss Brain."

An ear-splitting *CRACK* forced our gaze upon Iron Lass. Micro-Aesgard lay in rubble at her feet, her iron hand still in chop-pose before her and *ringing-inging-ing* like a temple gong.

"It is done, *Fräu Doktor*. Unt now, o unexpected cosmic bounty, I'm breassing sanctified air vis ze clean lunks of a mentally liberated purson. Oh, I feel so much freer unt better unt more joyful. Vunderbar. You truly are a miracle vurker, *ja*. Now can I go?"

"Doc, if it's all the same with you," said Wally, "can I juss let mine melt? Don't seem right to mush down m'daddy."

"Wally, you won't be 'mushing down' either your father or your love of him, because your father isn't controlling your life. Only your idealisation of him is."

"So can I, then?"

"No, Wally."

Hanging his head, his shoulders fallen, Wally looked like an intensely guilty gigantic child. He pulled up his dress shirt and lowered his trousers an inch, exposing his navel.

There was a blinding flash, and suddenly everyone's hair was drooping from the steam saturating the room. Although visibility was nearly nil through the ice-fog, Wally's icon-father was no more.

I found my next charge in the fog while Wally tucked in his shirt.

"Syndi?"

She pouted. She stamped.

When I insisted, she drooped her arms as if they weighed tons, and then started ripping the materials off her mannequin.

I found Kareem in his misted workbay, his back turned to me.

"*Khaibtu kher,*" he whispered.

With a sound like sifting sand, the X-Man's shining black idol fuzzed into black and silver smoke, faded to shadow, and was gone.

I touched Kareem's arm. He jerked away, still averting his face. I softly asked him the meaning of his magic words.

"'Shadows . . . shadows fall,'" he sniffed, before reaching a palm to his eye.

For Golden and Silver age heroes: What will it mean for your life, and your view of yourself, if the glory days never return?

> **Omnipotent Man:** "What's the point anymore?"
> **Flying Squirrel:** "The King would've wanted us to build a New Age."
> **Iron Lass:** "*Götterdämmerung* is the end of the *gods*, too. We're there."

For the Digital Age heroes: How will you face knowing that you will never exceed, or even equal, the accomplishments of your predecessors?

X-Man: "We have no choice . . . but to become *our own* kings."
Power Grrrl: "Who are *they* to be equal to?"

ICOMPOSTING: ENRICH YOUR MENTAL SOIL

Ironically, the very people who are icons to millions are often the most icon-worshipping of all. In many cases, such idolisation was the impetus for young heroes to challenge death on a daily basis. For hyper-hominids, idolisation led to emulation, emulation to over-identification, and over-identification with an elder "superior," paradoxically, to infantilisation.

No matter your intentions, when you wrap your super-ego inside the tunic of your icon, you're not wearing a cape. You're wearing a diaper.

Believing in anyone more than you believe in yourself causes you to suspend your own judgement which leads to counter-self-actualisation, or self-deactivation. And while Power Grrrl's exaltation of herself was certainly the cause (and effect) of many of her problems, that very exaltation freed her from the maleficent mandibles of the Icon Trap.

Most importantly, no one—and therefore no idol—is perfect. Inevitably you will discover your idol's imperfections. And when your idol falls, its final act will be to crush you.

ICONSCIOUSNESS: TIME TO TAKE OFF YOUR DIAPER

Adulthood means taking care of yourself—independence—not psychic dependence on others or clutching onto unrealistic opinions of your "elders." It's time to unchain yourself from your mentor. And while you might think that your idol is made of gold, it's really just made of garbage.

It's time to toss your idol into the composter. It might stink for a while, but at least it's transmuting into something useful . . . and fit to walk on.

But if you don't dispense with your empty idol, in all likelihood you'll be setting yourself up for the very chaos you are about to witness among the F*O*O*J.

PART TWO

MISSING NUMBER ONE

CHAPTER FIVE

Limited Series

IT'S IRONIC THAT FUNERALS ARE SAD

Funerals and superheroism are a natural combination. Each involves uniforms, oaths of allegiance, declarations of virtues, and connection to superhuman power under circumstances of high drama frequently performed to theme music.

But despite these abundant affiliations, hyper-hominids are notoriously psychemotionally mismatched with the requirements of funereal deportment. Consider the following cases:

- The pustulent eruption of grief from Tempest and Pyromanny at the laying-to-rest of Liberty Belle was a popped pimple on the face of the 1945 funeral scene, resulting in no less than a flash flood and an instant inferno (which thankfully cancelled out each other without loss of life, but not before transforming the contents of a nearby supermarket into a giant stew whose lingering aroma kept neighbourhood animals in a frenzy for months).
- The 1973 service for Doctor Patho saw the evacuation of forty square city blocks after her sidekick Dea Coli wept tears of pure anthrax which a sobbing Cumulus Maximus accidentally dispersed into the atmosphere.
- Hyper-hominid funerals have produced freezings, mutations, growth of vestigial organs, virgin births, impotence, chimpotence, shrimpotence, spontaneous macro-phagocytosis, and interdimensional neuro-flatulence.

As we saw in the previous chapter, because you as a hyper-hominid believe in the myth of your own invulnerability, facing death is even more difficult for you than it is for "mere mortals." Therefore no experience—

outside of death itself—is more traumatic (and dramatic) for you than the funeral. And that is because facing funerals means discarding your idols and becoming, for the first time, independent.

And, fundamentally, more alone.

INDEPENDENCE DAY

MONDAY, JULY 3, 8:00 A.M.

Despite the grief-stricken plans that the Pathetic Fallacy announced in the Los Ditkos *Sentinel-Spectator*, the weather at the sunrise funeral of Hawk King on Sunhawk Island could have dazzled a pharaoh. The disk of the sun glorified the horizon like a divine disco ball, drizzling gold along the eastern face of the distant Tachyon Tower, while the sky above us melted from orange to azure like a child's crayons left on a hot stove.

Media outlets from FOX and ABC to MutantTV and *CAPES* had been camped outside the wall of the Blue Pyramid Complex since the previous night, drinking from the stream of primary-coloured celebrities marching into the grounds since the dawn.

That day's costumes were the rarely-glimpsed dress uniforms and dress tunics reserved for funerals, replete with gold brocade, left-breast mission tags, ceremonial wands and sceptres, electrum-plated armour, and formal capes. Traditional bagpipes, taiko drums and throat-singers intoned the eschatological atmosphere amid the silent witness of obelisks, the giant *Ka*-Sentinels, and the radiance of the Blue Pyramid. Everything combined to say that we were truly at the end of an era, the exit of an epoch, the egress of an age.

Even before the service began, it was already clear that the gathering was the largest such funeral in history, exceeding even the final services of the *Götterdämmerung*. Silver Agers such as the Monolith, the Evolutionist, and Dynamiss were assembled, joined by Civil Rights-era stalwarts such as the Spook and La Cucaracha, and Digital Age up-and-comers such as the Beaver Brothers, the Cyberpunk, and Full Metal Asswhuppin. Even the oldest living F*O*O*Jster had arrived, the 168 year-old outgoing Director of Operations and Civil War veteran Colonel Strom Flintlock, floating in his hover-throne with his regalia of oxygen tanks and I.V.s like a modern-day Charlemagne. Only two people were in notable absence—two living founding F*O*O*Jsters, Gil Gamoid and the N-Kid, imprisoned on Asteroid Zed.

Smaller super-groups such as the Merry Men were there, including Dazzle Man, Fabulous Man, Original Fabulous Man, Simply Fabulous Man, Rainbow Man, and Man Boy. The Bold Bots 0001 through 0110 were orderly arranged and buffed to gleaming; the Blue Collars, the Supa Soul Sistas, the League of Angry Blackmen, the Asian Invaders and the Mohawk-Aztec-Mayan Brotherhood Organisation were joined by hundreds of unaffiliated heroes from Alpha Dog to Zed, the Living Phoneme.

Of course, the outpouring of mourning extended beyond the superheroic profession. Government and the international community were represented by President Bill Clinton, UN Secretary General Kofi Annan, and New Atlantis Comandante Uno Umboot Pinolawi among many others.

Suddenly everyone's quiet reverence was ripped apart by a media tornado at the entrance of two men: Tran Chi Hanh, FKA Chip Monk, flanking his replacement mentor and the head of Human Citizen, the unrelenting watchdog on the hyper-community, Jack Zenith.

A reporter who'd sneaked in disguised as a fire-engine with siren epaulets shoved a microphone into the face of the Flying Squirrel, demanding to know how he felt about Gil Gamoid and the N-Kid being prevented from attending Hawk King's funeral, while Jack Zenith, the Squirrel's sworn enemy, was allowed to walk in without even being jeered.

Mr. Piltdown growled, "It's a disgrace, a travesty," before hissing a canister of Squirrel Spray into the reporter's eyes and nose. The man hit the ground vomiting before being scooped up and outside the wall by the elongated arms of Extraneous Man.

No one had any clue that within minutes, two bombs would be detonated to rip apart the F*O*O*J as we knew it.

PAVANNE FOR A DEAD PRINCE

Never one for brevity, and id-charged by such highly public moments into grandiosity, Mr. Festus Piltdown began his address by thanking Liberty Belle and Captain Manifest Destiny, martyrs of the original F*O*O*J, and then spent the next forty-eight minutes citing every conceivable connection between himself and Hawk King.

" . . . which is why this city, this state, this country, this planet, yea, even dare I say, likely this very *galaxy*, joins me and us this morning in mourning a man-god of such magnitude, might, and magnificence.

"Because this honourable king of hawks embodied all that my gloved hands clutch at the epicentre of my heart: nobility, wisdom, determination, and unflinching defiance in the face of despots, demons, and the depraved defilers of all that is decent, right and good!"

Mr. Piltdown put his hand over his heart, just to the left of the black-on-bronze squirrel emblem of his dress uniform. Looking up towards the milky moon in the brilliant sky, his eyes glistened.

"And I promise you, sir, my comrade, my liege, my King, wherever you are . . . that I will follow you into whatsoe'er battle you so will for me, for now and ever after, that perpetually will I hold fast my shield and hold high my spear, and that I will never, ever slip from this crusade divine whose fire you ignited like the sun inside the space of my soul!"

Applause spattered up from the crowd from many of the younger heroes, unaccustomed as their generation was to the etiquette of such events. As Mr. Piltdown left the platform, he stooped to lay his hand on the Egyptian sarcophagus of Hawk King, and then straightened up to salute before sitting down in the front row.

I expected to see Kareem scowling, but the X-Man's face was a charcoal portrait of unreadability.

I was less surprised to see the Brotherfly looking as he did, tears leaking from beneath his Fly goggles. A week previous I could never have imagined that such an aimless, hyperactive, socially inappropriate, and vain young man could experience loss at such a depth. But from André's explosion in therapy two days before and his absence yesterday until now, he'd begun revealing himself as a more complex person than anyone could have deduced before.

WHEN THE GREATEST DEFENDERS ARE RENDERED DEFENCELESS

Throughout the morning's speeches, the anticipation in the crowd thickened like smog on a hot Los Ditkos day, awaiting the words of the man whose name was synonymous with hero.

"Afternoon, y'all," said Wally. "Or, I mean, g'mornin. This . . . this was a day . . . wellsir, a day I . . . I ain'never spectid t'see in, well . . . not in *my* lifetime, anyway."

Wally stood awkwardly at the podium, the eastern sun gilding one side of his face, the reflected light from the Pyramid blueing the other side of his visage. He tugged at his white collar, straightened his black tie, pulled at his black jacket and white cape, re-arranged his black epaulets, and hunched his shoulders in his famous manner, while the sole camera crew allowed inside—from Piltdown News Network—sent the image of the world's mightiest fidgetter to an estimated audience of three billion people.

"I never knew anybody like Mr. King. He was powerful smart. Powerful wise. Powerful-powerful. He recruited me. Taught me how t'use m'powers. Always kept my compass pointin north. An so for me, t'be, t'be *stand*in here in fronta y'all like this, without im . . . ." He looked down to the sarcophagus. "Well—"

He stopped to clear his throat into the microphone, a sound like a walrus yelp, clasping his right hand with his left and yanking at his fingers one at a time as if he could detach them.

All around me, I saw the people expecting to be comforted by Omnipotent Man's wisdom, and watched their faces shifting from morose to anxious, anxious to angry, and angry to confused.

"See, times like these, now," said Wally, hunching his shoulders ever more hunchedly, as if he were being transformed into a caped panda bear, "they tell a man, even when sometimes he i'n't inclined to be listnin, that suh'm . . . suh'm's . . . wrong. The Gooterdimmerang's done been over for years. The villains is all retired, beaten-down, locked up, or dead. An here we are . . . I mean, alla us . . . like a big ol slumber party messin around in our finest three-colour pee-jays . . . an meanwhile we jess found out—"

Wally's voice caught in his throat, like a mouse bisected in a trap.

He de-hunched his shoulders and took a breath, then let it out shudderingly.

" . . . jess found out . . . thet Daddy's dead."

Wally bowed his head to his raised cuff, dabbing his cheeks. Across from me, heroes such as Atomic Giraffe, Chloro Phyllis, and King's English immediately did the same.

"So . . . well . . . t'be honest, I jess don'know anymore. Who I'm sposta be. What the world thinks is *right* if fellers like ol Hawk King c'n jest up an die. Maybe th'world should figger its *own* way outta troubles from now on. Looks safe enough from where I'm sittin."

He took a quick breath, visibly making a decision.

"An so, ffective immediate-like, I am resignin as the world's mightiest man an retirin to private life."

Shock smashed through the crowd like a wrecking ball through a tea party.

"So, uh . . . thank y'all, 'Merica, planet Earth. Nice knowin yuh."

And with that, Omnipotent Man rose like a humanoid zeppelin above the anger and wailing, up, up, and away from Sunhawk Island.

Just before the second bomb exploded.

SUBLIMATING GRIEF DOESN'T MAKE IT BRIEF

"Brothers and sisters, ladies and gentlemen, friends . . . and enemies," said Kareem after the furor had died enough for him to take to the podium. "I greet you in the ancient manner of the splendour-power-and-triumph of the Forty-Two Chambers: *Dã'f xu, us, em maãxeru.*"

Members of the L*A*B and some of the Supa Soul Sistas intoned their response: *"Maa-ten neferu-f."*

"And I also greet you in the name of other great and fallen heroes, such as the Son of Nat Turner, killed by Kyklos the Imperial Grand Dragon in 1991, the Brother from the H.O.O.D., killed in a nightclub in 1992, and the man who was an inspiration to me and all of Stun-Glas, who inspired all of us who joined the L*A*B: Maximus Security," (scattering of applause, mm-*hm!*s and A-*men*s from the same area) "who was killed in Reagan's war against New Atlantis back in 1984." (Grumbling from other areas of the crowd, especially from the coterie around Mr. Piltdown.)

"This morning, I'd like to say a few words about the hero whose life we're here to honour, because just as I and many others are increasingly convinced—yes, that's right, I'm saying it—*convinced* that we aren't being told the truth about Hawk King's *death*, I know that practically nobody has been told the truth about Hawk King's *life.*"

Grumbling surged, joined by ejaculations of *Preach, brother!* and *Break it down.* X-Man waited for both grumbling and support to subside, then leaned into the silence to proceed.

"First, I'd like to acknowledge the League of Angry Blackmen who are here in full effect. Every Brother in the League, I'm sure, is taking this as hard as I am. Because after Maximus Security died, it was Hawk King who stepped up, who inspired every last one of us, to be what we are. Protectors. Defenders.

"Everybody here knows the official story. Hawk King was Hru, what those who don't know better call 'Horus,' the avenging son of Lord Usir of Kemet, who you call the 'Egyptian' saviour 'Osiris.' As Hawk King, he intervened seven thousand years ago in the world of men—and women, yes, sorry, Sisters—to wage his on-going battle on earth against his evil uncle, Warmaster Set, or out amongst the stars against the cosmic serpent Ãâpep, and to pursue the cosmic mysteries that consumed his incalculable intellect. And when he came back in 1937, he helped save Europe from the Nazis, and later on from threats such as the Specially-Relative Einstein Baboons, and Cosmicus, Digester of Worlds. He returned to his rôle in our realm as our greatest thinker, as our greatest teacher, and in the ancient sense of the word, as our Master.

"Now, everybody always thought Hawk King was Hawk King *only*, without any secret identity. But everybody was wrong."

The crowd fluttered and whispered at X-Man's implication of secrets about to be scattered, like a swarm of pigeons squawking in anticipation of ripped-up hoagie buns.

"As a celestial being," said Kareem, "Hawk King was physically powerful. But when he lived among us in his hidden rôle as a human, he did so in a frail body. Withered. Old. An agèd invalid in a motorised wheelchair who in the last few years of his life couldn't even talk. Had to have a voice-synthesising computer do it for him.

"The man inside Hawk King was a brilliant scientist and professor—an archaeologist, a cosmologist. Taught at Robeson College in Langston-Douglas for the last forty years. His name was Dr. Jacob George James 'Jackson' Rogers. He was my mentor.

"And Doctor Jackson Rogers, Hawk King, was an African."

Gasps and guffaws shot up like spontaneous sprinkler sprays on a golf green, with one man in the front row a geyser.

"How *dare* you!" shouted Mr. Piltdown, standing and aiming his finger at the X-Man as if it were an avenging foil.

"Hawk King wanted big changes," Kareem sped on, "huge changes in the F*O*O*J! He gave me all his final papyri—specific directions on how to overhaul the F*O*O*J and change the direction our planet's going—"

"Shut your *mouth,* you reprobate rascal! We are here to honour our greatest hero, not listen to your crack-induced baffle-gab—"

"—seeing what the F*O*O*J had become broke his *heart,* and he had a plan, a secret plan to completely revolutionise the group! One week from today I will reveal the contents of The Instructions of Hawk King, his final papyrus, detailing—"

"—*dare* you sully this *holy* day with your *self*ish, delusional election-*grand*standing and your bizarre, negroist *fan*tasies?"

"Don't be accusing *me* of electioneering, Mr. Two-Hour 'I Was Hawk King's Bestest Friend Ever' Eulogising Crypto-Fascist, who just so happens to *own* the only TV network allowed to shoot in here! And don'be doubting who Hawk King was, Pilly, 'cause I've got proof! Including the fact that Dr. Rogers went missing the day before Hawk King was found dead!"

Mr. Piltdown hustled onto the platform and towards the podium. The PNN cameras moved with him. "Get off there, now! You're *done,* Edgerton, you hear me?"

Kareem held up his hands, fingers splayed, saying something inaudible while the Flying Squirrel kept rushing towards him. X-Man leaned into the microphone, saying, "What, you gonna throw down right here in the middle of a—"

Mr. Piltdown's left fist slammed into Kareem's belly hard enough to double him over, whereupon his right fist smashed X-Man's face upward and back. Reeling from the uppercut, Kareem swung blindly, missing Mr. Piltdown's cheek by half a foot, but his second fist connected with the older man's throat. The PNN cameras caught it all.

All around me, men and women were scrambling into action, battle-lines gashed by race and/or generation. Members of the L*A*B, the Supa Soul Sistas, the Asian Invaders, MAMBO, and the Merry Men were deep-ending into the melee against F*O*O*Jsters such as the Beaver Brothers, the Newt, and the Evolutionist, followed by independent heroes such as Ivory Giant, Smithing Wesson, and the fifty-three year old Kid Kombat, Sr.

Folding chairs and chunks of burning sod ascended and descended like a convention of locusts; Messers Clinton, Annan, and Pinolawi were escorted out under guard throughout a chorus of swearing, screaming, and pleas for calm, with Jack Zenith leaving under the protection of his civilian-clothed protégé, the former Chip Monk.

Countless heroes waded into the dust-up, trying to separate the combatants. Extraneous Man and Cumulus Maximus formed a fog-and-flesh barrier while the sickle-and-hammer-caped Son of Soyuz flew left and right, biting people's bottoms, wagging his little tail furiously and barking at them to stop—

When suddenly the sky collapsed from an embolism.

Raging overhead, blotting out the sun, were what must have been millions of hawks, their screeching choir the sound of the world being buzz-sawed apart, their wings somehow transforming the remainders of the heavens into an awful anguished violet saturating the earth and everything else beneath them.

And then three bolts of lightning—amber, ruby, and emerald bolts of dazzling energy—pulverised the stage and the podium into smithereenlets.

All combatants jumped back from whomever they were pummelling or rolled away from whomever was pummelling them, crouching and quivering at the sight of the lightning which had struck and remained in place. The bolts snapped and twisted and finally congealed into the black-light forms of three titans: a giant with the face of a jackal, another with the face of a flamingo, and a female giant holding what looked like a massive feather.

The Jackal stooped, gently picking up the sarcophagus of Hawk King and cradling it like a baby. The Woman pointed her feather at the crowd like a lance, panning it across the crowd.

And then the Flamingo took each comrade by the hand, and the triumvirate transmuted itself back into lighting.

And disappeared.

PEACE IS NOT
SIMPLY THE ABSENCE OF WAR

Funerals are emotionally dynamic experiences, and even non-powered humans may find themselves reacting in ways that frustrate or embarrass themselves and others: excessive sobbing, laughter, panic attacks, and incontinence, among many other over-reactions, are common.

But for you in the super-powered community, careening through high-stakes careers and hobbled by over-active ids and the icon trap, outbursts and even violence at funerals are predictable occupational hazards.

To get a better understanding of how my sanity-supplicants were faring during this uniquely stressful time, I chose to observe them outside the clinical environment, seeking them out on their own turf where they'd be more able to process and safely/appropriately externalise/verbalise their psychemotional disturbances.

While a few of my patients retired post-funereally to the Fortress of Freedom, most made their way to a well-known eatery in midtown Bird Island, a cramped enclave on Bustle Avenue famous for its head-high smoked meat sandwiches and its heart attack-inducing cheesecake. Just as New York actors roosted at Sardi's, Los Ditkos hyper-hominids congregated at Soup 'n' Heroes, the old-fashioned two-story deli dwarfed by surrounding skyscrapers and owned by brothers Jan and "Stack" Leeby, who still squabbled daily over who invented which soup and which sandwich. And almost as famous as the deli's founders was its manager, the eye-patched and affable S. Bruce Pippen.

Sadly, Soup 'n' Heroes was no stranger to funereal receptions, and that day was crowded even more than usual. Its trademarked howling waiters merely whispered above the crowd's murmurs, while the diner's jukebox sat mutely unplayed. Draped beneath black cloth monogrammed with golden letters spelling *Hawk King*, the diner's mirrors reflected only shadows.

Despite my obvious capelessness, no one questioned my presence as I nudged my way through the over-capacity; I'd treated enough of these men, women, and cyborgs to have been accepted silently into their community.

REGRET: THE GHOST THAT HAUNTS THE LIVING

There were almost as many heroes on the walls as there were between them: framed and autographed black-and-whites from the Golden Age to the Glitter Age, including, controversially, shots of Gil Gamoid and the N-Kid. Despite complaints from some diners and even a few hyper-hominids, manager Bruce had always refused to take those down. Regardless of Gil's and the N-Kid's poisonous paranoia and murderous, malevolent madness, old-time hero-watchers still adored those two F*O*O*J pioneers from Ur-Prime, the mysterious planet orbiting the distant Quasar Q939.

The only sounds emanating from the assembled mourners were quiet clucking over the brawl, mixed with utterances of awe over the phantasmagoric apparition of Hawk King's divine relatives. But when the door opened and everyone beheld who entered, that soft conversing, crushed into immediate silence, seemed by comparison like the braying of a million of donkeys.

For how could anyone utter a word when the world's mightiest man ambled in after having announced his own self-imposed retirement and implied exile mere hours before?

Festus Piltdown III could.

"Well, well, well—if it isn't the world's mightiest quitter," he rumbled, not even in a mock-whisper. "To what do we mere mortals owe this anti-climactic farce of an honour?"

Despite his white dress cape with black trim and epaulets, Wally looked like a broken man, his shoulders hunched beyond even their usual enhunchment, like a show pony struggling beneath a morbidly obese rider.

"Jess wannid . . . to . . . I'ont know. Say g'bye t'folks? Proper-like. I didn'mean to have all that come out like it did at th'fun'ral."

Mr. Piltdown, perhaps in irony, made a sound very much like the word *harrumph*. "No, of course not. You certainly didn't intend to steal the funeral's spotlight any more than that *logos*-powered lawn jockey did." (Outside the therapeutic environment, it was clear that whatever inhibitions Mr. Piltdown might have had against unleashing his anticompassionate behaviour were negated.) "No, your grandstanding ... 'just happened,' is that right?"

"What? I didn'—"

"No, of course you 'diddin,'" sneered Mr. Piltdown. Reaching towards his boot, he removed his Squirrel Screen from its utility sheath. He unfurled it like a scroll, then plucked Wally's framed photo from the wall and hung the screen from the now-free nail. Pressing buttons concealed on his left long glove, Festus brought the screen to life and sifted among television channels.

Nearly every image was of Wally at the funeral dais uttering his resignation until finally cleaving skyward. The images were all identical. Evidently PNN had opted to sell the lucrative rights for the footage over maintaining the journalistic honour of an exclusive.

"Look, Festy, I never spected t'have m'speech all over th'TV like that—"

The image on Channel 101 switched to another event: Mr. Piltdown heckling Kareem before storming the platform; Mr. Piltdown racing towards Kareem who was yelling back "You'd better stand *down*, old man!"; the Flying Squirrel decking the X-Man, only to be throat-punched in return before the bursting melee of a thousand capes and tights.

"This is out*rageous*! How in the hell did—?" said Mr. Piltdown. "Filthy goddamned media *whores!* There was *another* camera smuggled in there?"

The image then switched to a howling pack of journalists outside the wall of the Blue Pyramid Complex.

CBS reporter: "With the impending F*O*O*J election and this special relationship you're claiming to have had with, uh, with Hawk King, not to mention the, the 'fracas' allegedly begun by the Flying Squirrel during the funeral, do you think either of you will be disciplined by the F*L*A*C, or do you think you're now a shoo-in for the post of Director of Operations?"

X-Man (grinning): "Well, Sheila, if there's one thing I learned today," (gingerly touching his belly) "it's that you can't ever know for sure what's gonna happen—"

Reporters: (laughter)

CBS Reporter: "What about this scroll, this papyrus you mentioned? What's it about?"

X-Man: "It was—The Instructions of Hawk King—it was Hawk King's final analysis of what's wrong with the planet and how to fix it before—"

Second reporter: "How will you be able to verify its authenticity?"

X-Man: "Trust me. Everyone'll see. Everyone'll know."

Third reporter: "Why are you waiting a week to reveal its contents?"

X-Man: "The country, the world, needs time to grieve. But as soon as the grieving's done, like ol Joe Hill said, we've got to organise—"

"Can you believe the *nerve* of that nattering negro nimrod?" said Mr. Piltdown to no one and everyone. "He's exploiting the death of our Leader to advance his own political career! He's a goddamned polyp inside the colon of propriety!"

> **CBS reporter:** "Following release of this violent amateur video smuggled out of this morning's funeral, an unscientific CBS phone-in poll found a majority of callers supporting the X-Man's Five Point Plan for F*O*O*J Renewal, favouring the so-called 'X-Slate' of candidates over the 'Squirrel Slate.' Results suggest that if the election were held today, a ratio of eight-to-one would support the X-Man over the Flying Squirrel for the post of Director of Operations—"

Stabbing the keypad on his glove and listening to his ear bud, Mr. Piltdown paused a moment before hissing into his wrist: "Yes, tell him—I don't goddamned *care* if he's meeting with the affiliates! I own the goddamned *network*! You tell Finchbeck to get up footage of those Egyptian goddamned gods exploding into the funeral—that's the most spectacular apparition ever recorded! It should've been leading the news every five—

"What do you *mean* the footage was blank? *All* of it? How can it all be . . . ? Fine, then just get up a poll—one of *our* polls—to answer this CBS swinewash before the beginning of the next commercial or the presidency of PNN will be open by the end of it!"

He stilettoed his finger onto his hang-up button, then switched his screen back to PNN.

PNN was broadcasting the same footage—some of it, anyway: Kareem hitting the Flying Squirrel, but minus the strike by Mr. Piltdown which initiated it. Mr. Piltdown clicked through a dozen other channels; on all those stations owned by Piltdown Corp, the X-Man was the aggressor.

"See, Festus?" said Wally, his eyes like dead bulbs. "They done forgot about ol'Omnip'tent Man an hour anna half later. I'm done. Yesterday's man. Y'all were worried bout nuthin."

Mr. Piltdown sneered again, turning his back on ever-more shoulder-hunched Wally. Behind him was the famous photograph of Omnipotent Man hovering beside Mount F*O*O*Jmore, where the last son of Argon had used his legendary chisel-vision to carve the giant busts of the F*O*O*J's founders following victory in the *Götterdämmerung*. Beneath their gazes, he'd hewn the phrase *ENDURING TRIUMPH*.

I called him over and drew his attention to the picture.

"This's been a tough day for you, Wally, hasn't it?"

"Yessir, ma'am-doctor."

"You know, Wally, looking at that famous photograph, reflecting upon all the pain and loss and the sense of lost-ness that you're feeling now, with your resignation in this age of peace you helped create . . . I wonder if the slogan you carved, if you can see how it might be ironic?"

He looked at the photograph, squinted."Whaddaya mean?"

"Well, 'enduring' doesn't only mean 'lasting.' It means 'getting through' or 'surviving despite.'"

He chewed his lip. "I . . . I'ont follow ya, ma'am."

"'Enduring'—see, it means . . . okay, that's fine, Wally. Look, where are you going now?"

"Back to An'ar'tica."

"Antarctica? Why Antarctica?"

"I'm retirin . . . so I'm gon retire to my Stronghold of Standing-On-My-Own-Two-Feetitude. T'live out my days. 'Merica don'need me no more."

"Wally, I think you're making a mistake, leaving like this before you've processed all your unresolved issues . . . but all I ask you to do is come see me at least once before you go, okay?" He looked doubtful. "Please, Wally. I'm worried about you."

He breathed in, his chest inflating to its full fridge-like volume and grandeur. But he was still looking at the floor.

"Kay, doc. But on'y for you." He tilted his head up, looked me in the eye. "Know why?"

"Tell me."

"Cuz you wannid to hep us. To hep *me*. I's always sposta be th'one savin evrabody. An th'on'y person other'n you who ever tried savin me . . . was that man we done laid to rest t'day.

"An even with all m'pow'rs, m'dad-blasted, planet-shakin, world-ifyin pow'rs," he said, the corners of his mouth curling down like he'd just sucked up rotten milk, "I caint bring Hawk King back anymore'n I can grab a coupla fistfuls a yesterday."

He sniffled, touched my arm gently with his massive hand, and then pushed open the door before walking out, out, and away.

WHEN HEAVEN SHRIVELS, WHITHER THE EARTH?

For Wally, the death of his icon was only at that moment becoming truly real. While non-powered citizens live daily with the reality of their powerlessness and have no choice but to make their peace with it, for you as a hyper-hominid, facing the fact of your own ultimate powerlessness can be devastating. I asked Wally to come see me to ensure that he, a saviour suddenly bereft of his own saviour figure, wouldn't plunge perpetually into the jack-booted tentacles of the slavering mouth of the black hole of despair.

Others, however, were legendary for their capacity to slough off the slivery yoke of mourning to don the newly dry-cleaned uniform of self-actualisation.

Mr. Piltdown was not one of them. Hampered by his own over-glorification of his mentor and pinned to the mat of political intrigue by his contempt for Kareem, Mr. Piltdown was haranguing anyone who would listen—in this case, Dow-Man, the Downsizer, and Smithing

Wesson—with his diatribe over the day's events. I took a seat within hearing distance, signalling S. Bruce Pippen for a piece of Original Leeby's Cosmic Cheesecake.

"—nerve of that knot-muscled blunder-boor to come here, just for the sake of appearances. Watchtower hasn't stepped foot inside this establishment in years. Yes, Soup 'n' Heroes might be cramped, run-down, with passé blue-collar kitsch for cuisine, and blue-haired biddies named 'Madge' and 'Eunice' serving low-end coffee, but for those of us who honour tradition—"

"I haven't seen you here once in the last year, Squirrel," dead-panned Original Fabulous Man, swivelling around on his counter-stool.

"Maybe if you didn't spend all your time here in a men's room stall," said Mr. Piltdown, his cohorts snickering viciously at his riposte, "you would have."

"I still have my membership card, Squirrel. I'm still fully paid up. And I'll remember what you said on ratification day."

"You do that," said Mr. Piltdown. "Assuming you can tell the difference between a voting box and what I believe you people refer to as a 'glory hole.'"

"Right now, Squirrel!" said Original Fabulous Man, standing to his full six-and-a-half feet and shoving his rainbow flag off of his immense biceps.

"Hey! Somebawdy here wanna get banned?"

It was S. Bruce Pippen speaking, his non-eye-patched eye trading glowers between both men. "Cuz I am itchin to ban somebawdy! Snappin and fightin in here, on the day a Hawk King's fun'ral, like a coupla dawgs out in the street. Samatta witchu guys?"

"Sorry, Bruce," said Original Fabulous Man. "I'll stop if he stops."

"I've already stopped," said Mr. Piltdown, turning back to his own group while Pippen monitored a moment for compliance before putting my cheesecake on my table. "Can't you do sumthin about these mugs, Doc?"

"I'll do my best, Bruce," I reassured him. He winked, then glowered at the would-be combatants before limping back to the kitchen.

"Anyway," said Mr. Piltdown, "Watchtower's a fraud *and* a liar. Always hinting about his pathetic secret identity as some unnamed metropolitan intrepid reporter—"

"You mean he aint?" asked Smithing Wesson.

"Hardly. He's actually the 'acclaimed' advice columnist of 'Ask Aunt Edna' in the Blandton *Gazette-Dispatch*."

"An ad*vice* columnist? You kiddin me? What a sham artist!"

"Indeed. It's one thing to lie to the public, but to us? So what does this 'resignation' mean, anyway? Nothing but a failed publicity stunt."

"From what I heard," said the Downsizer, leaning forward and checking each man's face in turn, "this is for real. I heard Wally's so depressed he's thinking about getting the ol' snip-snip."

"Naw, no way!" said Smithing Wesson.

"Yeah. Depoweration."

"Hah!" sneered Mr. Piltdown. "Well, regardless, he may as well've done so decades ago for all the good he's ever done. Certainly with his ... *mm* ... problem—"

"Oh, y'mean," said Smithing Wesson, "with the ... ?" He crushed his fist repeatedly in a mysterious gesture.

"Wait, you mean with the—?" added the Downsizer, flicking his fingers at the side of his eyes with equal mystery.

"I thought those was just rumours," said Smithing Wesson.

"Far from it, gentlemen," said the Squirrel. "And while I hate to give credit to any lunatic utterance of that refugee from the Laboratory of Apoplectic Baboons, we are now in a dire security situation. Much as I'm loathe to concede the point, brain-power aside, Wally was our ultimate line of defense. Combine that with Hawk King's intellect, and our planet was safe. But now ...."

"So whaddaya sayin, Fess?" said Wesson. "You sayin the King really was murdered?"

"If he was, my friend, then I suspect the mastermind behind it will attempt to bury several more hatchets in the livers of our individual brothers ... before he drives a combine over us all."

"You think it's Warmaster Set? Or," whispered the Downsizer, then gulping, "Menton?"

The name, uttered even in a hush, chilled the already quiet room, drawing icy glares.

"I think I'd rather not say," said Festus, "just yet."

"Now wait a second, Squirrel—back up to Wally," said Wesson. "What's with this Wally stuff you guys were hinting about? Are you talking about those rumours a him bein like Fabulous Man and them?"

"No, not specifically," said Mr. Piltdown, "though it wouldn't surprise me. Wally's never been married, never had a girlfriend to anyone's knowledge despite those shams of high-profile relationships with Ticker-Tape Girl in 1947 and then Princess Astra in the early 80s. The nickname Impotent Man didn't get whispered for nothing—"

"Festus!"

Mr. Piltdown looked up into the eyes of the ravenish woman standing in front of him, draped in black. All whispering around the deli died.

"Our King iss dett, Festus," said Iron Lass, glaring at him from behind her veil. "Iss zis respect? Unt Vally, however flawt he might be, vuss vun of us. Unt now ... now our two mightiest are gone ... unt neizer vun even set gootbye ... to me."

A metallic tinkle splintered the silence, a sound like dimes dropped on a tile floor. And for the first time since I'd seen him in Soup 'n' Heroes that day, Festus closed his mouth, his jaw muscles powered by an emotion almost certainly new to him: shame.

Iron Lass strode through the sclerosis of the crowd without pushing as a path opened before her. Once she was before the dimmed jukebox at the wall, S. Bruce Pippen limped quickly towards her, kneeling to plug in the music player before putting a quarter in it for her.

"Ich danke schön," she whispered, touching his shoulder like a queen bestowing a knighthood on a commoner. She pressed keys for her selection, then walked back through the crowd. No one met her gaze except me.

Perhaps that's why she sat with me, her face smeared between outrage and relief at what she no doubt regarded as hubris on my part for being there at all. It was the first time she'd volunteered to speak with me about anything.

But she didn't speak, not immediately; we sat silently listening to a jukeboxed Patsy Cline twangingly explain the single greatest mistake of her life.

"Ah ha!" whispered Mr. Piltdown over at his table, scanning his Squirrel Screen which blazed with graphs, numbers, and two images: a swelling face-shot of the Flying Squirrel, and a diminishing one of the X-Man.

Gloating over his requested poll, Mr. Piltdown watched while the PNN anchor explained that X-Man's racial allegations about Hawk King had driven support for the X-candidacy down to fifty percent. Support for the Squirrel had rocketed up to twenty-five percent, strongest among white male church-going Republican NRA members.

"Mr. Piltdown," I called to him softly, "clearly you're heartened by the PNN poll results."

"Nevertheless, surely you must be concerned how the F*L*A*C will respond to your bout of fisticuffs with Kareem at this morning's funeral."

He walked over to our table, stood in front of me like a barricade of squirrelly muscle.

"Are you *threatening* me, Miss Brain?"

"Mr. Piltdown, I'm asking you a legitimate question about your feelings—"

"—because I'll re*mind* you not to exceed your mandate, which is limited to what transpires *in*side that brain-beautician salon you call a clinic. You are here, just as you were at this morning's sacred commemoration, *solely* at the sufferance of the men and women of the F*O*O*J—"

"Mr. Piltdown, the F*L*A*C has given me broad authority to conduct my analysis wherever I choose, and base my report and recommendations on all observable behaviour. So I repeat my question: how do you think the F*L*A*C will respond to your actions this morning?"

He breathed in, leaned down, spoke to me inches from my face.

"Given the current instability caused by the death of our king and the resignation of our atomic-powered jester," he whispered, "regardless of this farce you call 'therapy,' the F*L*A*C wouldn't *dare* take action against me right now. Not when the alternative would be to hand over the election and Operations to that racialist rabble-rousing Reichstag-torching Rwandan."

He straightened up, turned around, returned to his seat.

> *I remember that night*
> *And the Tennessee Waltz*
> *Only you know how much*
> *I have lost . . . .*

Suddenly I heard more metallic tinkling. Shining on the glass table top in front of me were droplets of metal, hissing steam and cooling.

Iron ingots.

Hnossi Icegaard dabbed her fingers beneath her veil. If what Jack Zenith wrote in *Unsafe in Any Cape* were still true, no one in history had ever seen Iron Lass cry.

Until that day.

"You're—" I began, when suddenly something crystallised for me. "Those . . . aren't just for Hawk King, are they?"

She stared back at me from behind her veil, motionless, silent.

"It's a lot to take, isn't it, Hnossi? To lose both your mentor and someone else so important to you in the same day?"

She waved her hand with false dismissal. "Vy are you so surprised, *Doktor*? Becoss at a moment of dire crisis, when everyvun's spirits are at stake, a husbandt valks out unt—I mean, a *hero*, Vally valks out unt simply abandons us at our time of greatest neet?"

"That's an interesting slip, Hnossi."

She rolled her eyes. "Ymir's penis, *Fräu* Eva," she sneered. "Surely you can access better clichés zan Freudian slips."

I stared into her twin amethyst ices, waiting for her to own her admission.

And so we sat like that until she finally got up and walked out, leaving everyone else to their quiet elegy of cheesecake and beer.

What will it mean for your life, and your view of yourself, if the glory days never return?

Iron Lass: "The death of the father is the death of life."

TRAUMA: THE ENEMIES WITHIN

Of course, Iron Lass is not the only hyper-hominid grappling with the grieving process and ending up in a full-nelson, face down on the rank gym-mat of denial upon the dingy floor of despair.

Trauma always reactivates the entire unexamined repository of unprocessed misery in the psychemotional cache, much in the way that the flatulence of a diseased colon is particularly fetid, given the abundance of undigested organic material in its crevices.

When you engage the grieving process, you're not sobbing simply for the sadness at hand, but for every sadness you've ever suffered, from dropping your ice-cream cone when you were four to the humiliation of vomiting from anxiety at your senior prom, to soiling your tunic during a particularly frightening melee with a super-foe.

While I'd been able to observe some of my sanity-supplicants first-hand to assess their post-funeral psychemotional de-griefing, I also noticed that the grievers had split along the same lines as those in the funereal battle. Not a single active or former member of the L*A*B (or any other non-white crime-fighters with the exceptions of Sanford Cowl, HKA the Spook, and Gustav Gorditas, HKA La Cucaracha) had assembled at Soup 'n' Heroes.

After making a few inquiries I took the subway. Leaving behind me the mourning silence of downtown Bird Island, I crossed the Mantlo River over to mainland Los Ditkos and the borough of Langston-Douglas, cheekily dubbed by its residents as "Stun-Glas." From there, the only sign of the upscale Bird Island I'd left was the erect grandeur of the Tachyon Tower in the distance.

Negotiating the borough's crumbling streets, graffiti-scarred buildings, and urine-soaked bus benches, I navigated along a depressing procession of gun stores, pawn shops, nail shops, beauty shops, barbershops, rib-shacks, chicken shacks, martial arts schools, and Squirrel Burger franchises, until I eventually found the seedy red-black-and-green soul-food restaurant called The Dark Star.

SELF-DELUSION: GRIEF'S SUPER-POWERED SIDEKICK

Entering the dark and dust-choked interiors, I beheld a myriad of black men dressed in colourfully elaborate native costumes and fezes decorated with arcane symbols and icons.

All of them turned slowly to stare at me silently.

The only sound was the blare of a clanging, bass-bursting reggae instrumental with electronic bleeps echoing as if into the depths of space. A man behind the counter glared at me. I found myself momentarily hypnotised by his upside-down U-moustache and the sculpture of his pectorals and biceps beneath his tight white t-shirt, before noticing him nodding to his right, directing me to sit.

Around the corner sat the X-Man, drinking tea with a smooth-skinned Asian man in a suit—Tran Chi Hanh, FKA Chip Monk and, briefly, long ago, as my patient.

Their cups emitted ghostly trails of steam into the dark air. Kareem looked up at me narrowly before rolling his eyes and whispering something to Tran. Both men stood, and Tran excused himself to walk past me with only minuscule acknowledgement before he was out the door.

I asked Kareem if I might sit with him. He grimaced, finally pointing to a chair for me and motioning towards the counter man before sitting himself.

"What're you *doing* here, Doc?"

"Well, Kareem, in therapy yesterday, weren't *you* the one who told me I wasn't making accurate observations because I was only seeing all of you in the clinic? That I had to get out of my comfort zone and see you in your natural habitat?"

"I don't think I'd ever've used *those* words—"

"Regardless of the semantics, I'm here."

"Doesn't this violate confidentiality," he hissed, leaning forward, "you coming here like this? And how'd you know I was here in the first place?"

"A good therapist always knows where to find her patients. And as to confidentiality, these people don't know who I am—"

"Yeah, you're only the most famous tunic-shrink on the planet—"

The man with the upside-down U-moustache brought me a cup of coffee. After he departed, I told Kareem how much the man resembled African-American CNN anchor Bernard Shaw. Anger flashed across his face before Kareem stashed it behind the barrier of a cold smile.

"That's quite the set of facial reactions, Kareem. Tell me what they mean." He said nothing. "By any chance were you going to tell me that I think all African-American men look alike?"

He almost smirked, then ripped the expression into the shreds of a scowl.

"You *were*, weren't you?" I said. "Except I was right, and *you* think I'm right, too, don't you?"

"Most people say he looks like the lead singer from Cameo. That's a funk band." He paused, smiled against himself. "I'll give you this, Doc . . . you've got a real pair of meteors, coming here like this. Anyway, could we get to the point, here? What do you—"

"Kareem, I'm worried about you, how you're handling the passing of Hawk King. First your claims that someone conspired to do away with him, then your claims that he was an African, and then getting into a brawl at the funeral—"

"Number one, I haven't 'claimed' any conspiracy—I'm investigating the *likelihood*. Two, I didn't 'claim' Hawk King was a brother—I asserted what I *knew* from direct experience. Third, I didn't 'get into' a brawl. Festus attacked me! What, you think I should've just stood there and let him beat me like I was Rodney King?"

"Well, as I recall, Rodney King did fight back—"

"What the hell are you—"

"—but that's not the point, Kareem. Surely you have to know how all these things will affect your electoral ambitions with the public, not to mention your membership status in the F*O*O*J which the F*L*A*C could—"

"The public wants to know, Doc. They're sick and tired of being lied to, and sick and tired of *being* sick and tired. People want somebody who isn't afraid to speak the truth. And as far as the F*L*A*C, well, just *let* em try to throw me out now, after revealing the truth about Hawk King. People'll be in the kot-tam *streets* they try that foolishness now!"

Rather than engage Kareem's delusions of popular support, I gestured to the décor: wicker chairs, a zebra-skin rug, what looked like a Masai shield, and finally a wall of framed pictures of Afro-American men. The only face I recognised was that of dietician Dick Gregory.

"That's Marcus Garvey," said Kareem, picking up on my curiosity and pointing to each photo in turn. "The Mighty Sparrow, Bob Marley, Son Of Nat Turner, Paul Robotson, Rakim, Steve Biko, Redd Foxx, Fela, Sun Wosret, Richard Pryor, the Brother from the H.O.O.D., Maximus Security, James Brown . . . and *that's* Dr. Jackson Rogers—"

"The man you claim was Hawk King."

"I don't claim anything. I assert the truth."

"Interesting that there's not a single picture of a woman on the walls. And other than me, no women in here at all."

Kareem appeared startled, first perhaps because he'd never thought of that before, and next that that he'd let slip his startlement. Finally he shrugged. "There *should* be pictures of strong sisters on the wall. I'll mention that to Brother Larry. Make em myself if I have to."

"These other men—they're your old comrades from the League of Angry Blackmen, correct?"

He nodded, pointing them out where they stood or sat in front of murals of pyramids, primitive art, and African idols. "In the long black coat, almost see-through in the shadow, that's The Grand High Exalted, Never Faulted, Rock of Gibralted, Atomic Sucker-Breaker, the Dark Fantastic."

"That's his name? All of that?"

"Yeah. We all had long titles in the L*A*B. Part of our mystique."

"So what was yours?"

"'The Kinetic Kemetic Magnetic Mystic Majestic.'"

"Very colourful! And the rest of these gentlemen?"

He scowled, as if he mistook my delight in the L*A*B's poetical (if juvenile) fixation for condescension. But he continued anyway. "In the pyramid hat over there, that's the Pyramidic Gikuyu Mau-Mau Hip-Hop Master Blaster, Ahmed Q. Wearing the suit with the badge over his breast pocket, that's the Universal Stimulator and General Overseer, the Black Lieutenant. Loves to yell—he was always saying how we'd 'gone too far this time'—kind of our coordinator.

"In the cape, carrying the double-headed axe? That's the Cosmic Soul Controller and Planetary Roller, Shango. Guy with the glowing knife is the Hyper-Gravitic Invincible Convincer Eldritch Cleaver. Obviously the brother in the locks is the Political, Poetical, Polemical Dreadnaught the Dreadlocker."

"His hairdo is alive? Like Medusa's snakes?"

"Yeah, but they don't turn you into stone. They're like tentacles. Over there with the ãnkh-staff, ãnkh-fez, and the black ãnkh turtleneck is the Star-Breathing, Hyksos-Crushing, Sucker-MC-Smiting Mystical Militant, Professor Grim, HKA Grimhotep, the Living *Ka*. In the bowler hat and the Edwardian coat, that's the Righteous, Tonighteous, Fool-Smackin, Punk-Attackin, Preachifyin and Testifyin Upbraider, the Player Hater. And finally, the tiny dude next to him in the suit is the Litigious, Pernicious, Trouble-Making, Shit-Shaking Arnold Drummond, HKA Mofo Jones. Brother clerked with Johnnie Cochrane. He was the one who got us our HUD contract to protect Stun-Glas—"

"—before you lost it."

"Before somebody 'lost' it for us."

"And who 'lost' it for you?"

"IT'S A BLACK THING": RNPN
(RACIALISED NARCISSISTIC PROJECTION NEUROSIS)

The X-Man snorted. "That *is* the question, isn't it?"

"So you don't think it had anything to do with the L*A*B's anti-white rhetoric?"

"Being *accused*," he sneered, "is not the same thing as being guilty. But in your line of work, I suppose that's difficult to understand—what with Freud blaming mothers, sexual perversion, and everything else for causing the planet's problems—everything except the white power system and the people who own it—"

"And you don't regard that as anti-white rhetoric?"

"Hey, if the hood fits . . . ."

"It's exactly that kind of language, Kareem—"

He held up an index finger, yelled toward the counter-man. "Brother Larry, can you turn that up?"

I looked behind me at the television that'd caught Kareem's eye. According to the news report, now that word of Omnipotent Man's resignation had become widespread, tributes were piling up for him outside the fence of the F*O*O*J's Fortress of Freedom—thousands of bouquets, drawings, cards, action figures, and tied to the fence, red-white-and-blue ribbons and cape-like flags with the letters "O.M." on them.

The images were followed by a shot of dozens of tiny Egyptian statuettes in tiny cardboard boats set adrift by citizens across Eaton's Bay towards Sunhawk Island.

"Disgusting," growled Kareem. "Hawk King's death is *world* news, right? So why is it when that steroid-popping bozo up and quits for reasons I wouldn't buy on an expense account, suddenly everybody forgets the King and starts celebrating the kot-tam jester?"

"How does that make you feel, Kareem?"

"That the best you can do, Doc? 'How does that make you feel?' Maybe it's time to buy a new CD, y'know?"

"Why are you afraid to discuss your feelings?"

"Afraid's got nothing to do with it. But didja ever think that maybe what people think is more important than what they feel?"

"Don't over-think, Kareem—that's where you'll get blocked—"

"What I *think* is that the day I announce that Hawk King was a brother, public tears—*white* public tears for him dried up from the millions to the dozens. But when some brain-canned putt-nuts submits his decades-overdue resignation, he suddenly gets the honours due a *genuine* hero!"

"So all of this is about race for you? Omnipotent Man has been a celebrated hero for decades, co-founding the F*O*O*J back in the forties—"

"Man's a fraud—even the Fascist Squirrel said so. You ever read Zenith's *Unsafe in Any Cape*? If Wally'd been named Kwame, Ali, Juan, or Sanjit, you think the press would've overlooked his Peter Sellers routine all these years and crowned him 'world's greatest hero'?"

"What makes you think the public even accepts your claims about Hawk King's secret identity? Enough that they would actually reject him posthumously?"

"What've I just been saying about the tributes drying up?"

"The resignation of Omnipotent Man *matters* to the public, Kareem, whether *you* respected him or not. And if you think others believe your racial claims about Hawk King, I'd suggest that's more a matter of projection than observation."

Kareem snorts. "In all his papyri and public statements of the last ten years, Hawk King called the Ancient Egyptians 'Brothers on the Nile.' You think that was an accident? You think it was coincidence that after he went into exile in the Blue Pyramid, the only domestic Hawk King sightings were in black neighbourhoods? That he—"

"There are also sightings of Elvis, the Gold Glider, and Poe-Bot around the country every year. Surely *those* aren't evidence of anything other than wish-fulfillment self-delusion."

"What about breaking exile to destroy Hutu militias in Rwanda after the F*L*A*C refused to intervene? Think that's nothing?"

"If you're right, then why didn't he intervene more often? Overthrow apartheid or something like that?"

"Because Hawk King wasn't simply living out a self-imposed exile in the Blue Pyramid! He was living more and more of his life as Dr. Jackson Rogers, to try to understand the struggles of flesh-and-blood human beings and how we can fix our planet without the 'help' of a bunch of phonified freaks hyped up on their own zap-powers. Dr. Rogers, he was old and sick, even depressed. He spent the last twenty years in a wheelchair, the last three unable to speak without his Data-Vox. I don't think he even had the energy to transmute himself back into Hawk King very often anymore—"

"Then even if you're right, doesn't that suggest he *wasn't* murdered? That this 'Dr. Rogers' simply died of natural causes?"

He raised an eyebrow. "Look, I was in touch with Hawk King regularly, and while he wasn't well, he wasn't *dying*—"

Suddenly I became aware that Kareem's former gang had been staring at us throughout our discussion and was even then menacing toward us like a fleet of gaily-spotted leopards.

"World's smartest hero," the Black Lieutenant yelled at me, "dies of 'natural causes' but fails to predict his own death? Get the hell out my office!"

"And the planet's strongest 'hero,'" rumbled Grimhotep, his voice like the unmuffled motor of a dump truck, "up and resigns only a couple of days later, with no previous indicators?"

"And all of it happening," said the Dark Fantastic, a shadow in voice as well as form, "when the King's F*O*O*J is in a leadership *and* membership crisis?"

And then another voice rose up barkingly from behind their dark phalanx, amused and vicious at the same time, like that of a disgruntled carney vowing vengeance against every townie on the midway: "Which one-a you buncha ignant-ass negroes gots to get blown fore the Fly can get hisself some *ser*vice up in here?"

THE RUDOLF SYNDROME

The wall of men parted down the middle, revealing the Brotherfly standing behind them.

Despite the darkness of the interior, André was still wearing his tinted Fly-goggles. He'd retracted his wings, and instead of his usual tunic and its fly-with-afro emblem, he was sporting a tight black t-shirt glittering with a sparkly disco-font logo announcing him as "Baby Daddy."

"Fuck you want, fool?" asked Ahmed Q.

"Why, you gonna take my order?" laughed André. "In that case, give Mista Brotherfly a Cristál-an-cream-soda anna bacon double cheeseburger."

"Figures you'd be eating the devil's hound," growled Ahmed.

"We don't serve alcohol and we don't serve meat round here," said Larry the counter man. "Specially not no pig."

"Swine," said Ahmed. "One third rat, one third cat, and a third dog."

"Must be the new Biology," said André. "Never realised y'all could do genetics in thirds. Somebody gots to tell Mendel he screwed the mock pooch, knawm sayn? Kay, then, Mister Chef—gimme a plate of goat roti, with a extra shell."

"Like I said, this establishment," said Larry slowly, "is veg-e-*tar*-ian: tofu cutlets, bean pies, parsnip smoothies. Dig?"

"Brotherfly hafta dig *two* latrines if he ate that shit! *Bzzzt!*" howled André, shifting his hand side to side, palm up, as if expecting someone to put something pleasing into it. "Can Brotherfly get a *bzzzt*? People, people, can a Brotherfly get a *bzzzt*?"

Even from where I was sitting I could smell André, a reek like apricots and cleaning solvent: maki. He must have been chewing it ever since he left the funeral, if not during.

"So Brotherfly's flyin over here," said André, strutting and waving his arms as if they were his wings, "an he's thinking, on this most auspicious day when we is all sposta be layin to rest our greatest hero an teacher, when we sposta be payin homage, keepin it real, pouring out the first spurt of the forty an sendin props to the other side, knawm sayn?—an André's thinking, what would the hyper-righteous Zulucentric Q*R*I*B negroes be discussin inside the whitelessness of the soulified Dark Star?

"An what do he find here but all you intellectual ultramandigoes speculamatin on y'all's conspiracies! What a surprise! Feelin all important bout y'selves cuz y'all is crackin the case of the mil*len*nium, bigger than 'Who shot Crispus Attucks?' Bigger than 'Who killed Uncle Ben and Aunt Jemima?' Bigger than—"

"André, you come here shit-talking us," said Kareem, "when you are so fucked up on maki you smell like you've been lying in a bathtub of Lysol and apricot jam, and you think *you're* the one showing respect?"

"So who's behind this grand-ass plot to kill Hawk King, Kreem-pie?"

Before Kareem could speak, Eldritch Cleaver, fingering the edge of his luminescent soul-blade, cut him off. "Kyklos," said Cleaver, "the Imperial Grand Dragon. He killed SONT. If he found out bout the King being a brother—"

André's laughter stopped him. "Even if Kyklos *did* know, that double-amputee gots to be seventy years old, not to mention tough as Dream Whip by now. Brother from the H.O.O.D. ripped *both* his cross-burners off, remember?"

"He could be in a conspiracy with Warmaster Set," said the Player Hater. "Or Set could be acting alone."

"Damnation . . . it could've been Omnipotent Man himself."

The accusation hit like a bird into a bay window.

Everyone turned, waiting for the Dark Fantastic to explain himself.

"Think about it. He's one of the only beings on this planet powerful enough to be able to kill the King. And with his 'problem'—damnation, if Hawk King tried to intervene—imagine how O.M. might've reacted. And the resulting guilt . . . " he said to his crowd's knitted eyebrows and nodding heads, "that could explain the sudden resignation—"

André kissed his teeth. "Should I come back when y'all worked out your story together? Maybe *y'all* did it, cuz the man wouldn't eat y'all's *bean* pies!"

"It's Menton," said the X-Man.

The name ground the butt of the conversation into the floor.

Even a decade after the Destroyer's butchery was brought to an end by the combined might of the F*O*O*J and its unaffiliated allies, the name Menton could still pour liquid nitrogen down the slacks of anyone in the hyper-hominid community.

"Unless you aint heard," said André, "Menty done got his ass thrown in the clink way the hell up on Asteroid Zed five years ago. Kinda hard to kill anybody from up there."

"Really, André? Then why to this day are people still afraid even to say his name? Knowing that he used to be able to use just the *cognition* of somebody vocalising his name as his portal? You ready to bet your life he's no danger anymore?"

"Y'all is too hilarious, quivering like the babies of Dorothy and the Cowardly Lion. Can't even work up a *bzzzt!* for all y'all scararanoid niggity-knights—"

"Maybe that's cuz pork-suckin house negroes like y'self don't care," said Ahmed Q, "if the Destroyer's huntin down an killin off the brothers."

André snorted extravagantly.

"Snort all you like, Hyksos-muthafucka," said Ahmed. "Brother from the H.O.O.D., Maximus Security, Lou Mumba, SONT . . . now Hawk King. Two weeks ago in Cripton somebody almost took out Pimp Man. Got beat-down to half a fuck from death—"

"Uh, actually . . . " said the Player Hater, "the Pimp Man thing . . . that was me."

Everyone turned on him. Ahmed howled, "You *crazy?* The man personally paid to build the on'y decent playground in Cripton!"

"What, 'Players Paradise' over on Smalls Street?" cried Player Hater. "Place's a disgrace—kot-tam 'Merry-Ho-Round' an all that shit! An don't be lookin at me like that—fool was holdin back the race! And Fried Chicken Man better watch his ass, too!"

"Hell yeah!" said someone.

"All you self-righteous, sanctimonious negroes," sing-songed André, "accusing anybody you don'like, beatin em down, drawin up enemies-lists almost longer than my dick—y'all a buncha perfectest, holy-rollin, no-smokin, no-drinkin, no fun-havin, no-dancin, no-sexin, impotent limp-dickin Thirty-Six Chamber havin, monkey-ass—"

"This ain'no kot-tam *Wu Tang* album," snapped Ahmed, "'Baby-Daddy'-shirt wearin ho-ass tricketty-split nigga! This shit's fuh real, Forty-Two Chambers, word, not thirty-six! Somebody call 9-11 on the pre-emptive fuh this Dead Fool Walkin fore I sweep out the john with this fool's conk!"

"Y'notice, breddren," said the Dreadlocker, his hair-tentacles writhing like a gang of cobras at the sight of a squadron of mongeese, "how dis ere sell-out naa even join hour side durin di FRAcas at di fun'ral? How im slink out di BOCK widdout even trowin a single punch in hour MUtual diFENSE?"

"Like a *byatch*!" said somebody.

"Too busy 'swinging' to do any swinging," said X-Man. His line got the laugh he was looking for. Whatever his flaws, Kareem was a gifted verbal improviser, as he continued to demonstrate: "Telling everybody how he's 'the shit' and never realising just how right he is. So busy chilling, he's completely frost-bit. A slack, slick, loose-dicked, willingly-no-self-control, no-zipper tan-man who maks-out his mind to convince himself he *isn't* a senseless, thoughtless, shiftless, aimless, brainless, oversized pants-wearing, 40-ounce loving, penis-fixated, self-under-rated, supreme cham-*peen* of galactic niggativity!"

"And you, 'Philip,'" said André to Kareem, "the biggest hypocrite of them all! You think I don't know why you 'left' the L*A*B? When's the last time you were welcomed here at the Dark Star, huh? You're what, half a degree more welcome here than I am?"

I'm shocked, bearing witness to this transformation of André's vernacular (and even his accent) into something I've never seen from him before—clipped and pristine, like Bryant Gumbel's.

"But now that you're pimping Hawk King's corpse," André railed on, "the L*A*B's got no choice but to deal with you, am I right? So why don't you tell 'the brothers' here what you've told the good Doctor here about you, the L*A*B and your secret scandals? Or should I tell them myself?"

"I aint told her *shit*, you kot-tam liar, and these brothers don't doubt that for a second!" yelled Kareem, scanning the faces around him for the doubt I saw wriggling like maggots in the corners of their eyes.

"Don't say another word, Kareem," yipped Mofo Jones from down below, before turning to André. "And *you* say one more word, you blue-bottled wigaboo, and I'll sue your slandering ass back into the Stone Age!"

X-Man: "Better get the hell outta here while you still can, Super-Tom—"

"Motherfuck all y'all!" yelled André.

And just as the L*A*B moved against him to rip him wing from wing, André zipped out of the way with the proportionate speed and agility of a fly and was out the door, yelling *Bzzzt! Bzzzt! Bzzzt!* and howling a manic, deranged sobbing laugh as he flew away.

UNDERSTANDING RNPN AND RUDOLFISM

Whereas racial discrimination was once a daily fact of American life for many, legislation and social progress have ensured that what was only a dream on the steps of the Lincoln Memorial a few decades ago has become a reality for all.

Yet for many heroes of colour, the collective memory of that discrimination—and the habits secreted into our culture around commemorating it—have produced a rabid, slavering Cerberus whose heads are Self-Defeatism, Self-Fulfilling Prophecy, and Pervasive Expectation of Exclusion.

If you're an ethnic crime fighter who believes everyone is against you, you may find yourself caught in a manifestation-cycle of overt or passive-aggressive behaviours that drive away your colleagues and potential friends. Constantly super-charged by your own anti-social aggression, you are so aswim in your conviction that "discrimination" exists, you remain convinced everyone else is wallowing in that "awareness" with you.

The belief that everyone shares your world view, while imputing your own aggression to others' motives and self-servingly transferring back to yourself the victimhood you impose on them, is a toxic mindset known as Racialised Narcissistic Projection Neurosis. It is this delusory perspective, rather than supervillains, that is the leading cause of injury among heroes of colour, because the distraction and poor judgement the neurosis engenders leads to irrational choices, needless danger, and fruitless fighting.

Of course, people who believe they are victims of exclusion frequently become excessive excluders themselves. This is the Rudolf Syndrome. The atmosphere I observed inside the Dark Star was clearly one of hostile competition, one-up-manship, alpha-doggery and vicious pecking-orderism. Outsiders, even "outside insiders" such as the Brotherfly, must be attacked bloodily (in body or in spirit) to satisfy the need for a scapegoat. Without such a sacrifice, the self-defeating community would dissolve into civil war; to "riff" upon an Afro-American proverb, the crabs in the bucket would be forced collectively to jump into a boiling pot.

Examine your behaviour patterns closely. Are you constantly crying victim? Do you perceive the world as composed of antagonistic institutions whose "propagandised minions" are wittingly or unwittingly "oppressing" you? Do you ever find yourself using expressions such as "the system," "the Man," "our people" or "further evidence of the vast conspiracy against us/me"? If so, you may be suffering from RNPN. And if you are punishing others with the very exclusion you claim afflicts you, you are probably enforcing the ruthlessness of the Rudolf Syndrome.

To deal with your RNPN, begin by recognising that you are an individual, not a social abstraction. Your destiny belongs to you, not to history, and whatever successes or failures you experience are solely of your own making. Take responsibility for your own happiness, rather than claiming telepathy you don't have (unless you are telepathic) or ascribing to others ugly thoughts you can't verify, and aiming endless, nonspecific blame for your mediocrity on the Trilateral Commission, "the media," S.K.U.L.L., the RAND Corporation, the long-disbanded Treemasons, the M.A.N., the Black Helicopter Legion or the perennial favourite of paranoiacs, "They."

Finally, if you're the victim of a Rudolfian attack, remember that it's neurotic to desire the company of those who loathe you. And remember also the lesson of Rudolf, the legendary luminescent crimson-proboscused reindeer: if you continue developing your own abilities and doing what honours you without anxiety over other people's judgement, eventually even those who despise you shall be constrained to honour you. It's a paradox, but only by abolishing your craving for your critics' respect will you ever achieve it.

WHEN A Q*R*I*B IS ONLY A CRIB: VICTIM-IDENTITY AS SELF-INFANTILISATION

Eager to expel me from his former hang-out spot, Kareem "offered" to escort me to a gypsy cab or the subway. I was just as eager to probe his perspectives and self-delusions while he was still in his native environment, so I persuaded Kareem to take me on a walking tour of Langston-Douglas, including to the headquarters of the League of Angry Blackmen, the Q*R*I*B.

A couple of blocks away from the Dark Star loomed a renovated building that had once been a bank, but had taken on an entirely different appearance for an entirely different purpose. This near-legendary edifice was, according to Kareem, sometimes called "the Underground Shrine," despite the fact that the slightly trapezoidal fortress stood above ground and five stories tall: the Quarters for Revolutionary Intelligence, Blackified: the Q*R*I*B.

Its architecture vaguely suggesting the Grand Temple of Luxor, the Q*R*I*B boasted wrap-around murals crawling with hierograffiti and giant native black African figures dressed like Ramses gripping sundry white characters by the hair while smiting them (including caricatures of select US presidents and members of the F*O*O*J itself). The display was nothing if not a vast, three-dimensional incarnation of the Racialised Narcissistic Projection Neurosis which undoubtedly helped cost the L*A*B its HUD security contract to protect Langston-Douglas.

Kareem paused to look up at the images, and even with his eyes masked by his black "G-man" sunglasses, his face was darkened by the unmistakable soot of melancholy. I proceeded gently, asking him what André meant by saying that Kareem was hardly more welcome than he himself was at the Dark Star.

He cut me off, pretending he hadn't heard my question, listing instead a myriad of L*A*B miscellanea such as how some artist named Emory Douglas helped design the Q*R*I*B's murals; how the Q*R*I*B was built on the border with Cripton (the most dangerous part of Langston-Douglas) as a warning to the gangs which infest it; how independent crime-fighters were shattered by the death of Maximus Security in 1984 and finally formed the L*A*B in 1987 to continue his work; how those same L*A*Bsters only later realised that each of them had gained his powers from being exposed to the contents of mysterious, hieroglyphic-inscribed containers called Canopic jars, which, said Kareem, they "found in obscure corners of places such as libraries and the Special Collections Rooms of the Schombro Museum."

Eventually Kareem and his comrades came to believe that the jars were the divine gifts of Hawk King.

"He interceded into the affairs of Stun-Glas to raise up among us a generation of heroes," said Kareem, his sentence creaking beneath its own obese grandeur, "so that his people—our people—could save themselves. Now maybe we didn't have the deputised supra-legal exceptionalism of the F*O*O*J, but we gave a damn about Stun-Glas. Protected it. Against gangstas, racist cops, and supervillains alike."

As soon as we resumed walking, Kareem pedantically listed and explained the L*A*B's Forty-Two Point Platform (subdivided into "What We Want" and "What We Believe"). And once again I tried to steer Kareem towards examining what must have been for him an unbearable truth, that his awesome rage against white society, contained in his words and his racially-fixated delusion about a supposed secret identity for Hawk King as a black, are contributing to a build-up of his paranoia; that this paranoia could have only dreadful results for him if he refused to resolve it and integrate true reality into his awareness.

His grin grew colder every second I tried to persuade him; when I asked him why he was smiling, he said mysteriously, as if he hadn't understood a word I'd said, "'Integrate?' You people think integration's the solution to everything."

"Kareem, I'm talking about psychemotional integration—"

"I know what you meant," he sneered. "And I don't expect a damn shrink to understand a kot-tam thing about the *real* world. The only two 'ation's I'm interested in are *libe*ration and in*vest*igation. There are suspects we can't even find and might never be able to—Warmaster Set, Cosmicus, the Einstein Baboons. But up in orbit we've got three bad-actors I want some answers from, and I intend to talk to em as soon as I can arrange it."

"You mean Gil Gamoid, the N-Kid, and . . . ."

"Yeah," he said, "and Menton."

Kareem didn't even flinch when he said the name. Indeed, he seemed to enjoy uttering those fearsome phonemes.

We were only a block from a subway entrance when Kareem stopped with his arm out, holding me back. He pointed along both sides of the street towards the boarded-up faces of a half-dozen businesses, one after the other: Ruby's Ribs, Deacon's Gumbo, Junior's Jerk Palace-an-Ting, Down Home Chicken, 'Bama-Ass Chicken, and Git-Yo-Chicken. Finally he pointed to the far end of the street, and the bustling business enjoyed by the Squirrel Burger franchise enthroned there.

Because of my access to F*O*O*J files, I wasn't surprised that the X-Man would single out the burger business. Indeed, the battle between the young Philip Kareem Edgerton and the Squirrel Burger Corporation had nearly prevented Kareem's membership in the F*O*O*J, and had ensured a hatred between Kareem and the ultimate master of Squirrel Burger, a division of Piltdown Edible Products International—Festus Piltdown III.

THE BLACK QUIXOTES
TOWARDS WINDMILLS OF COLOUR

In 1986, when he was still operating under the hypernym of Mac Rude, Kareem and several other proto-L*A*Bsters went to war with every Squirrel Burger outlet in Langston-Douglas. While Arnold Drummond launched dozens of frivolous lawsuits against franchise owners, the Dark Fantastic used his shadow-powers to make every restaurant so dark that the kitchens were unusable, and Kareem deployed his rudimentary logogenic ability to manifest 3-D graffiti above Squirrel Burger restaurants declaring such phrases as "Squirrel Burger is Destroying Black Business."

When that campaign had minimal effect, Kareem changed his slogans to urge ghetto residents to "Stick it to the Squirrel—Buy Black." That campaign's failure prompted Kareem to develop his power further, creating mobile "word swarms" or "hyper-tags" which followed Squirrel customers after they left the restaurants. Diners found themselves returning to school, home, and work with 3-D phrases such as "I Licked the Squirrel's Nuts" and "I Drink Nut-Shakes" orbiting their heads. Squirrel Burger business plummeted, and local restaurateurs rejoiced.

But eventually Squirrel Burger Corporation regrouped with its franchise owners by offering free burgers, Squirrelly Fries™, and Chocolate Bushy Tails™. Exhausted and overstretched, Kareem and his comrades couldn't maintain their crusade with its homophobic slogans against the sheer numbers of new Squirrel diners; eventually they surrendered completely.

"Makes me sick," said Kareem, glaring at the giant scowling Squirrel mascot as if he were Dante in the Pit staring up at the Beast, and then at the people waddling in and out of the fast food outlet. "But it takes a nation of millions to keep us fat. And stupid. And that nation's *us.*"

"Don't you think people should have the free choice to eat where they want, Kareem? Do you think *you* should have the authority to tell everyone what to do, how to eat, or what to think? To say nothing of depriving local people of jobs?"

"Shit, Doc, are you kidding? Don't get me started on jobs—minimum wage, no benefits, swing shifts? How about down here in Stun-Glas we get some of that high-tech investment from the dimensional research contracts they do up there in the Tachyon Tower, and all the spin-off jobs that go with that? *That'd* be some jobs!

"Can you even see what's in front of your eyes? Look across the street! Fools weighing three hundred and fifty pounds ordering a mega-meal Kilo-Burger, a gross of Squirrelly Fries™ and a Half-and-Half Shake thickened with Crisco? See that man right there—that one? Can barely walk, but he's walrussing around like some NBA star in his Adidas sneakers and Nike track pants—I mean, they must be knock-offs cuz Nike doesn't make size infinity—but this mad-ass madness of tryin to look athletic when you're lethally stuffing yourself with the filthiest foods on the planet? Diabetes, heart attacks . . . used to be poor people *starved* to death. Now we *over-eat* to death! Killing us off with low quality, high-fat food, obesing us all into the grave. And 'Squirrel Burger' isn't just a name, Doc. That shit-shack serves *actual squirrels!*"

"Now, Kareem . . . we both know that's not true."

"Isn't it?"

"You're telling me the FDA has approved the sale of wild rodent meat to the general public?"

"You think the multi-billion dollar Piltdown Group doesn't get whatever it wants, whenever it wants it? The FDA's a three-dollar-an-forty-two-cent ho, Doc! Wake up! And the squirrels aren't wild . . . Piltdown's got huge factory farms down in Alabama, Kentucky, Arkansas, everywhere Piltdown pulled out his high tech manufacturing and moved it to Mexico or New Atlantis. Got all those downsized crackers, some of em just eighteen years old—*salteens*—working his squirrel ranches, which're really just factories with billions of squirrels in teeny-tiny cages getting force-fed ground-up rats that were fed ground-up roaches that were fed ground-up brains of all the mentally-retarded prisoners they execute down in Dixie-land! You heard of the China Syndrome? A nuclear reactor burning all the way down to China? This is *Piltdown Syndrome*—burning us all down to nothing. To *nothing.*"

He threw up his arms, aiming his tirade like a wrecking ball at all the empty buildings.

"But people are deaf, dumb, and blind. You can scream the truth in letters ten miles tall, and still the only thing they'll notice is nothing. Whole reason brother Larry opened the Dark Star was so people'd have suh'm tasty and healthy to eat after Squirrel Burger drove everybody else outta business. You know you can buy and get stoned from a whole bag of maki in this neighbourhood easier and cheaper than you can buy a kot-tam *salad?* But if it weren't for the L*A*B and a few others, Larry wouldn't even be able to keep his doors open."

SLICING THROUGH THE GORDIAN KNOT

Kareem's rant veered wildly, even into how the L*A*B operated its own "social programs to counter white influence," including "Free Breakfast for Shorties," "Africa Medallions for Homies," and "Free Fades, Flat-Tops and Afro-Picks for Soul Brothers," the last of which was undermined by something Kareem called "the Jheri-curl plague," which left what he claimed were "Jheri-bags and activator-empties lying in the gutters of the MLK boulevard of dreams deferred."

Suddenly Kareem turned on me with accusation burning in his eyes like lit cigarettes.

"I sure hope you aren't planning to turn this conversation or any of our sessions into one of your books, Doc!"

"Well, Kareem, I'm sure if you actually were to *read* any of my—"

"I checked out your stuff the second we got sentenced to your therapy. All of it. I pity the poor mopes you psycho-catalysed. I read what those suckers said—although I'd hafta read between the lines to deduce what you'd cut out since the way you'd edited everything was so self-serving—and then I'd read your diagnoses and speculations and bizarre psychosuperstitious slop—*damn*. The least insightful, most outrageous conclusions, like you couldn't see cute on a puppy!"

"Be that as it may, Kareem—"

"I mean, in the dictionary, next to the definition of 'unreliable narrator,' there's gotta be a picture of your degree. I hate to think how you'd be framing anything *I've* ever said. You take one little word of what people say, then psychopontificate the hell out of it until you've got readers thinking the afflicted are the afflictors, and the afflictors are the afflicted! No different than the F*O*O*J helping destroy New Atlantis while protecting the people bringing maki into our neighbourhoods—"

It was time to cut through the Gordian Knot of Kareem's white-persecution complex. "If everything you're saying is true, Kareem, why did you even *join* the F*O*O*J? Why not remain in Stun-Glas full time, fighting alongside the L*A*B?"

"What, remain ghettoised, cut off from the reach that only the F*O*O*J has, unable to effect change past my own neighbourhood, prevented from joining a wider cause? Then you'd accuse me of—"

"Did the L*A*B expel you?"

He stopped, his jaw half-open.

He closed it, then opened it again only long enough to say, "No." He shook his head. "No."

"André said you weren't welcome at the Dark Star. You didn't rebut him. What did he mean?"

"Look!" he yelled. "We are in serious danger, Doc—can you get that through your head? Omnipotent Man's resigned! Hawk King's dead by causes unknown! The F*O*O*J is a kot-tam *disaster!* This morning, at the funeral, the appearance of the Netjeru—that was a warning to us all, a harbinger that if we don't—"

"The what? Natcheroo?"

"*Netjeru,* Doc! Don't you know anything? The so-called 'gods' who took Hawk King's sarcophagus away! They haven't appeared on earth in maybe six thousand years. You think they don't want his killer caught? And what do you think they'll do if we don't avenge his death?"

"Are you saying that these gods are inferior detectives to you?"

"I'm saying that—look, even if they don't, I dunno—whatever—what do you think's gonna happen if we don't bring his killer to justice? Who's next? And how many after that? Because if you can kill someone of Hawk King's power, then nobody's safe! How can you not *see* that?"

"All right, Kareem."

"All right, what?"

"You believe that Gil Gamoid, the N-Kid, and/or the Destroyer could be behind this alleged crime, correct?"

"*Yes,* for the ninth time!"

"Then let's go ask them."

"What're you *talking* about? Thanks to you jailing me in therapy, my investigation's barely started! And a detective doesn't tip his hand to a suspect until he's—"

"I'm worried that you're manifesting a vast, disabling paranoid fantasy, Kareem, and *that's* what's *really* jailing you. I'll go to Asteroid Zed tomorrow to interview them myself, if you won't, so we can rule out Gil Gamoid and the N-Kid as suspects—"

"You do that and you're gonna destroy the element of surprise and blow the one chance I've got with them!"

"So I'm going to Asteroid Zed, Kareem, to speak with your triumvirate of terror myself. Unless you want to go with me to rule them out yourself."

He flailed his arms, yelled at me, explained his case a dozen times, haranguing me, threatening me, and finally pleading with me not to go. I wouldn't budge.

Finally, after hectoring me for a full ten minutes he fell silent, and his shoulders drooped while his gaze scoured the weeds creeping out of the cracks in the concrete.

He shook his head, chewed his lip. "When?"

"First space elevator up. Five A.M., if memory serves."

"Kot-tam. *Fine.* Five A.M. lift to the kingdom of the damned."

How will you face knowing that you will never exceed, or even equal, the accomplishments of your predecessors?

X-Man: "Catching this super-assassin is all the glory I need."

THE FACE OF THE FOE IS A CRYSTAL BALL

Whether combating the RNPN of the X-Man and his comrades or the end-of-epoch *ennui* of mainstream F*O*O*Jsters, an ascent to the orbital penitentiary where the worst super-criminals in history were entombed alive seemed at that moment to be our only path towards mental clarity. The death of Hawk King had so damaged the already fragile psyches of my group that unless they engaged in a mythopoetic descent to an Underworld, my sanity-supplicants would find themselves lost in the sewers of self-delusion until finally drowning in the waste treatment plants of depression.

Perhaps it would take the horror of staring into the face of the villain who had murdered so many heroes—or the faces of two founding F*O*O*Jsters who had gone mad and nearly murdered them all—for my team to pull back from the brink of self-destruction and be reborn from the psychotherapeutic womb of self-redemption.

CHAPTER SIX

Up is Down:
The Path Inside is Outside

MIRROR, MIRROR, ABOVE THEM ALL

TUESDAY, JULY 4, 5:27 A.M.

"To know one's enemy," wrote Iron Lass many years ago in *Towards a Practical Götterdämmerung*, "is to know oneself."

To test that theorem, I gathered my patients together to voyage into that inferno of foes, Asteroid Zed. And indeed since in space, as in psychotherapy, there is no true up or down (only centeredness and dissociation), it is just as legitimate to say that we *descended* that morning into orbit, because in a relative universe, any place on our planet can be the bottom of the Earth.

Rising (or falling) inside the StarCase™ Space Elevator at sunrise, we slipped the surly bonds of Earth to dance the skies on laughter-silvered carbon nanotube Herculon™-filaments. I was struck how at our altitude even the titanic Tachyon Tower was shrunken into little more than a pepper shaker, and how the gridwork of Los Ditkos's streets was reduced to an Eggo waffle. From there in that high, untrespassed sanctity of near-space, it seemed impossible that down inside the city's golden pockets, the cholesterol-laden butter of dysfunction and the sweetly seductive syrup of neurosis were citizens drowning in a chaos of psychemotional condiments.

But in leaving behind our breakfast of super-champions, we were venturing towards a far more dangerous zone wherein we all were to put out our hands to touch the face of madness.

Everyone in the group was upset about our trip and its timing. Two hours before dawn I illuminated the Psych Signal above my Mount Palomax Laboratory to draw forth my team. Each member complained bitterly upon arrival—Iron Lass argued that our mythopoetic journey was not to a psychic underworld but to a technological "over-world;" Power Grrrl repeated *ad nauseum* (and with many expletives) that she didn't appreciate being ripped away from a warm and triply-occupied bed; the Brotherfly, apparently under the influence of some substance(s), issued a slang-soaked diatribe against mornings in general ("André don't do AMs, knawm sayn?"); and the Flying Squirrel railed against using a vehicle from the rival StarCase™ Corporation to achieve orbit when either his Squirrel Shuttle or an Allosaurus-Class rocket from Piltdown-Dynamics would have been faster (if more ecocidal).

But the F*O*O*Jsters' verbal complaints failed to camouflage the true animal of their anxiety. Obviously nothing upset them so much as the prospect of facing the sociopathic sadists—including former friends—who had hunted, haunted, and attempted to slaughter them.

But sanity is a demanding master, and insists we seize our traumatic experiences so as to integrate them into our daily consciousness, where their psychic "charge" can be grounded and thus neutralised.

Of course, one didn't have to be a therapist to deduce from my patients' repetitive gestures, scowls, and agitated body language, that morale inside the Space Elevator had become a quicksand of terror swallowing them whole, especially at the thought of standing in a room to breathe the air exhaled by Menton the Destroyer.

Strapped in next to the only F*O*O*Jster who hadn't been complaining, I observed Kareem preparing for his imminent encounter with former F*O*O*J friends and foes. He was literally absorbing the text from hundreds of hardcopy pages, holding his right hand over an open book and "scanning." The letters flew off the page in a black stream, only to replant themselves in place. According to his personnel file, he called this process *medu gi-orema*, or "word-eating." He was absorbing one page approximately every ten seconds.

Interrupting his studies, I gently warned Kareem that if he were still intent on interviewing the Destroyer, he'd have to save that villain for last, and keep his interrogation as brief as possible to minimise Menton's ability to unleash his mental horror-hold.

"It doesn't take a rocket surgeon to figure that out, Doc," whispered Kareem. He flashed me a smile, but it was a warning. "Howzabout this: you don't tell me how to conduct an investigation, and I won't tell you how to head-shrink."

I reminded Kareem that he had, in fact, told me numerous times how to "head shrink."

He smiled brittlely, but I sensed it was less from anger than from anxiety. "I guess I hafta write you a cheque made out to 'touché.'"

He folded up his papers and flicked on a satellite monitor, flipping feeds until he found a Pacifica station running a program called *Democracy Now!* It was the tail end of an archived interview with a black, wheelchair-bound cosmologist and archaeologist named Dr. Jackson Rogers, discussing the relevance of ancient Egyptian astronomy to recent telescopic discoveries in the galaxy. He looked like an old, withered version of calypso singer Harry Belafonte or TV's Sherman Helmsley.

The archived segment ended, and the screen then switched to a female anchor and a bespectacled, gap-toothed Afro-American guest in a too-tight suit and a long, untamed, greying afro.

> **HOST:** So what do you think, Professor West? Could Dr. Rogers actually have been a secret identity for Hawk King?
>
> **GUEST:** I think, Amy . . . the possi-*BIL*-i-ty that he could have. Been. The incre-di-ble *Hawk*. King. And the-resulting-dichotomous-reactions-of-the-American-people-and-the-backlash-against-Brother-X-Man-raises-some-important *QUES*-tio-o-ons . . . Amy . . . . Questions. About the fundamental re-*FU*-sal of certain segments in our soc-*I*-e-ty . . . to ac-*KNOW*-ledge . . . the-inherent-capacity-of-African-American-people-living-under-White-supr—

The feed clicked to another channel on its own. When Kareem spied Mr. Piltdown clicking the controls on his glove, an argument erupted which only intensified when X-Man and the Squirrel overheard the panellists on the next news station. Those panellists were discussing how following the loss of two F*O*O*J icons, X-Man had become the vanguard of the new hero generation, deriving legitimacy from his Hawk King-connection and credibility from his forward vision; these same panellists dismissed Festus Piltdown III as "yesterday's man."

At that point Mr. Piltdown shut off the satellite feed completely and launched an invective against affirmative action in general and the L*A*B in particular (citing its lost HUD security contract), and finally referring to the L*A*B as the League of Apoplectic Baboons. Only seconds into Kareem's rebuttal, Iron Lass threatened to depressurise the compartment and kill everyone unless the bickering stopped. Mr. Piltdown dropped his voice, muttering about my alleged breach of professional ethics by "coercing" them into imminent reunion with their murderous ex-nemeses.

For me, Mr. Piltdown remained a fascinating figure, an omelette of a man, rife with the green onions of bitterness, yet held together by the tangy Velveeta of integrity. Despite the Squirrel's cantankerous persona, in the wake of Hawk King's death and Wally's resignation, much of the F*O*O*J had coalesced around Mr. Piltdown's inspirational words (less than, perhaps, his presence). In general Mr. Piltdown seemed fearless.

Yet he, perhaps more than any member of the group, seemed horrified at the prospect of setting foot on the prison planetoid.

Then we all saw it through the window, a few dozen miles away, little more than a black space blotting out stars. As it rotated slowly into view, we beheld its sunlit face, and it seemed to me that the silvery-steel facility planted upon the dark rock resembled a Zippo lighter stuck into a coconut.

Asteroid Zed.

Our elevator *thunked* into the "top floor" Space Elevator terminal, and we unstrapped ourselves, cycled through the airlock and floated through the station to board the Space Bee transport over to Asteroid Zed.

Gazing back, the StarCase™ glinted in the darkness like a child's tin can telephone, taught on its string. If anything were to go wrong, if the Destroyer were still the menace Kareem feared him to be, if he were indeed free of his mental restraints only to have assumed dictatorship over the asylum, then that tin can telephone would have transmitted our final conversation to our lost home and life itself.

THE LEGACY OF MENTAL DIS-EASE

Asteroid Zed had hardly changed since when I first visited it in the early 1980s: a cold, gleaming white-walled and steel-barred environment, sickly with the stench of boiled cabbage and baking soda. Walking its tiers, one would have the impression of being locked inside a giant refrigerator.

The prison's very existence was a layer-cake of irony, iced with the stale frosting of our society's failures. Once an emblem of the triumph of superheroism in the *Götterdämmerung*, the Asteroid was originally conceived, designed, and constructed in 1971 by none other than Gil Gamoid and the N-Kid themselves. Fourteen years later, those two champions would find themselves interred in their own creation after the F*O*O*J's foiling of their conspiracy to blow up the Fortress of Freedom and murder all the heroes inside it. Refitted in 1985 by Piltdown Dynamics to prevent an escape by its own designers, Asteroid Zed would soon house countless villains who'd once fought against Gamoid and the Kid.

Our guide through the tiers of the technological Tartarus was the warden, Doctor Rudy Wells. On our way through the various holding units, Warden Wells pointed out to us the many prisoners put there by my own patients. In the Fish & Reptile Villains Unit, Codzilla, Monitor Lizard, Black Mamba, and Nemesaur, all captured by Iron Lass; in the Techno-Villains Unit were Robot Stalin, and MicroCrip and his Nanogangstas, defeated by the Flying Squirrel, as were incarcerees of the Crime Lord Villains Unit such as Tong Triad & the Iron Eunuch, and Pauli the Living Mafia. Bio Villains such as the Dessicator, the Devolver, and Zee-Roks the Imitator required special containment, explained Wells, which is why they were kept in Unit X on the other side of the asteroid, so as to minimise contamination of the orbital biocosm.

The only unit no one ever saw, of course, was the one that was invisible to the eye, the Metaphysical Villains Unit. The MV was an upper-string-dimensional confinement zone at a -3483°angle to our reality and specially designed by Hawk King himself for nemeses such as the Infinity Farmer and his Time Tractor. Technically, we were walking through it at the very moment its existence was being explained to us—but then again, we were always walking through it, and we never were, as it was everywhere and nowhere simultaneously.

I had no idea if the F*O*O*Jsters were pondering that intersection of physics, philosophy, and psychopathology, but it was clear that walking the ultra-bright corridors between cell-rows of such monsters was exacting a psychic toll on my team. Iron Lass projected a gaze even colder than usual, surrounded as she was by the prisoners of the war she'd declared and led; Power Grrrl had resisted turning on the speakers of the most sombre bustier I'd ever seen her wear, glowering at every cell door we passed; flicking his gaze fly-like from cell to cell, the Brotherfly seemed to be scanning everywhere either for spiderwebs or Venus fly-traps (understandable, given that Spiderbyte and Venus the Fly-Trap were both incarcerated there), as if fearing he'd be dragged inside one of these cells and ripped apart, antenna from antenna; X-Man's jaw was clamped tightly enough that I could see his mandibular muscles bulging up along the height of his skull and disappearing into his short hair. His fists were clenched so tightly that his knuckles were rendered beige.

But no one looked more agitated than the Flying Squirrel himself, who was gunfighter-flexing his fingers beside his utility pouches, as if expecting to unleash any of his numerous high-tech weapons at a moment's notice. Combined with the sweat glistening on his upper lip, he resembled no one so much as Humphrey Bogart's immortal Captain Queeg, quivering with increasing paranoia at every second.

"Should've just put down the lot of them," snapped Mr. Piltdown, cutting off Warden Wells in mid-lecture. "Would've, too, if not for the goddamned shyster queers in the ACLU. At any rate, Wells, other than by using the psionic-impotence helmets, how're you keeping these mega-misanthropes from staging a coup on this hell-rock?"

"Well, Mr. Squirrel, sir," said Wells, anxiously huffing steam onto his spectacles and cleaning them with his tie, "the psionic-inhibition helmets do their job on all the most, well, disturbed cases, especially the psychics. But intensive use of psychoceuticals, mostly from Piltdown-Sorus-RX, keeps most of our patients from hurting others. Or themselves."

"Mighty nice racket for Pilty, Wells," said Kareem, just as we entered the Political Villains Units and glimpsed the Leninoids and the Eiffel Terrorists through the door monitors. "Piltdown-Sorus-RX *created* half this villain epidemic in the first place when it invented Nouitol—like we *needed* a cross between LSD and thalidomide—"

"Shut your crack-hole, Edgerton! You don't know the first thing that you're braying about—"

"Your company made the damn drug which got half these fruit-bats addicted, mutated, and mind-smacked in the first place, Fasces—"

"So blame the god-damned FDA, not my company! If that gaggle of pink-eyed Poindexters can't conduct a simple double-blind study—"

"—not when you've got a thousand lawyers and lobbyists hammering them and the kot-tam administration to fast-track all your junk into the veins of old folks and babies—"

"Mr. X-Man," attempted Doctor Wells, "while it's true that Nouitol can induce intense feelings of entitlement, superiority, megalomania, and homicidal rage, it can also push the very limits of mental acuity in otherwise limited intellects—"

"No wonder Festy had it invented. Must be injecting himself twelve times daily—"

"Why, you *fil*thy little—"

Doctor Wells: "To this day, carefully monitored doses of Nouitol are a regular part of our treatment here."

Kareem stopped dead. "You mean you're *still* injecting people with that poison? Are you insane?"

"I assure you, Mr. X-Man, that all safety protocols—"

A techno-music dance beat erupted down the corridor, bulging with raunchy samba-salsa-mambo-rumba "samples." I rushed back to find the music blaring from Syndi's bustier woofers and crotch tweeters. Through the door monitor, I could see the target of Power Grrrl's HEAT-ray—she'd turned every member of the aging Mongoose Men, the Anti-Castro Cubanitos Crew who destroyed much of Florida during the *Götterdämmerung*, into dancing versions of herself. Inside their cell they were gyrating in sync to her music, all twelve of them howling out her Top 20 hit from the previous year, "La Vida Cola."

"Now Syndi," I said, "we talked about this, and I said no."

"Oh, *ga*-awd," she whined. "Fine."

Released, the Mongoose Men resumed their ordinary appearances, blinking at each other in dawning comprehension before turning away to slump in their respective corners and avert their gaze from each other.

Before I could catch up with my group, a frantic Doctor Wells ran back to me, telling me that Mr. Piltdown and Kareem had broken off on their own after insisting that they interrogate their intended targets immediately.

Rushing me along to the Secure Room, Doctor Wells signalled the guards to let me through, and I dashed in past the security checkpoint to see the Squirrel and X-Man glaring through the letho-glass at two of the most beloved—and feared—figures of the twentieth century.

WHEN HEROES GO BAD

Even sans their glorious armour, clad in simple orange jumpsuits and with faces ravaged by their decade-long sedation, these two super-beings were unmistakable.

Francis Ford Coppola was often compared to the elder of the two with his wild beard and eyes, although to my knowledge, the talented director never reached a height of eight feet, achieved arms like a body builder's thighs, or had a mouthful of teeth like gleaming metal rail spikes. His younger companion, while shorter at a mere six feet, was every bit as remarkable, with his opalescent ram's hooves and horns, his golden body-fur like the mane of a California model, and his smell pungent enough that even through the letho-glass I felt as if I were bathing in coconut milk.

Heroes and villains in the same bodies.

Gil Gamoid and the N-Kid.

Of course, there were obvious changes. The N-Kid no longer carried with him his heralded Grail Pail, and both ex-champions were fitted with specially-designed psionic impotence helmets to accommodate horns or oversized head. Their psionic restraints looked like football helmets made of black glass, detailed with silicon circuits and frizzed out with flickering, brain-draining psiber-optic filaments.

With nothing on their side of the glass to sit on but the floor of the featureless white cube, they stood, their faces rigid but flickering with faltering self-control.

Mr. Piltdown stepped forward, opening his hands in anxious supplication

"If there's anything you need, Gil, Kid, just name it," he said quickly. "If it were up to me you'd be at the Squirrel Tree right now being tended to by my personal physicians, not up here in this ghastly—"

"Get out get out get out GET OUT GET OUT *GET OUT*—" screamed the N-Kid, leaping from his seat and hurling himself against the glass, kicking his hooves against the barrier, while at every contact the glass seared his fur with awful purple arc-light.

Doctor Wells yelled, "This isn't going to work, Mr. Piltdown, sir! I think we should leave—"

"*NO*, HUMAN," intoned Gil Gamoid, his voice like it was in his glory days, a love-child of tuba and gong.

Even the N-Kid stopped long enough for us to focus. Gil said, "DOCTOR WELLS. GO. FESTUS. GO. OTHERS, STAY."

Doctor Wells gestured towards the door as would a *maître-d'*, but Mr. Piltdown refused to look at him, glaring instead at his former team-mates. Finally, he said, "I just want you both to know . . . that I forgive you. Both of you. We're even."

The N-Kid emitted a horrible goat-like *b-a-a-a*, a *b-a-a-a* of rage, a *b-a-a-a* of vengeance. Mr. Piltdown backed out of the room so slowly as to be almost comic, but the mood was nothing short of tragic. Doctor Wells sealed the cubic chamber on his own way out.

I leaned towards Kareem, whispering that he should beware; while he might have gained personal satisfaction in seeing the Flying Squirrel ejected, he needed to remember that the two converts to sociopathy before him were master manipulators. Ejecting their greatest defender, the man who paid their multi-million dollar legal fees and refused to denounce them for conspiring to kill him and blow up the Fortress of Freedom, seemed calculated not only to wound Mr. Piltdown, but to create the illusion of alliance between them and Kareem.

To my surprise, Kareem actually whispered back, "Good call, Doc. Thanks."

"Why you here?" jabbered the N-Kid. "What you want?"

Kareem sat in one of the two chairs. "Information."

"About what, X-Man-man?"

An eyebrow from Kareem. "So you know my name?"

"Of course know your name. Who you think you dealing with? Celebrity nitwit? President of country? No. You X-Man-man, formerly of League of Angry Blackmen-men, currently seeking information."

"Okay. You're obviously as insightful and intelligent as your reputation suggests," said Kareem, sliding into the trick-bag of the interrogator. "So why don't *you* tell *me* .   .   .   .   w h y   *am* I here?"

The N-Kid *b-a-a-a*-ed a chuckle, horribly. "Gil, him try flatter me. Think that get him information."

Gil Gamoid narrowed his eyes at his smaller companion. "TELL HIM ANYWAY," rumbled the voice inside my skull like someone jackhammering girders. "WITHOUT WASTING TIME."

"You want know," said the N-Kid, wincing from the rebuke, "how Hawk King die."

Kareem leaned back, both eyebrows creeping up before he returned them to default position. "Well then?"

"DENIED RIGHT TO ATTEND FUNERAL," gonged Gil. "HUMILIATING. EMBITTERING."

"That wasn't my call," said Kareem. "But you, you *wanted* to be there? Despite your two-man conspiracy to murder Hawk King and the rest of the F*O*O*J in 1985? Why? So you could finish what you started?"

"EARTH YEAR 1985, UR-PRIME YEAR BILLION-AND-SEVENTEEN, WHAT ALL MEAN? CROSS ALL THAT SPACE-TIME TO CAUSE HURT? WHY? TOO CREDULOUS, X-MAN."

"So why'd you want to come to the funeral?"

"PAY RESPECTS," said Gil Gamoid. "AND FINISH WHAT STARTED, YES."

GRASPING AT STRAW-MEN

"So you're admitting—"

"Admitting nothing, X-Man-man! Separate issue! Never want hurt Hawk King. Never! Wouldn't!"

Kareem leaned forward. "So you're saying . . . you had a different target? You weren't trying to kill Hawk King either in 1985 or last week?"

Silence.

"Then who—"

"Enemy among you . . . not what seems."

"Who? How? A shape-shifter? Mind-control?"

Silence.

Kareem stared at the two prisoners, trying to out-wait them.

A minute clambered past, like an ant across a salt heap.

Then a second minute.

And a third.

The glitter in the eyes of the two aliens had disappeared; their faces were still enough to appear waxen.

Finally Kareem leaned towards me, whispering. "I thought they were refusing to talk, Doc, but . . . is it just me, or are they actually zoned out?"

"I think you could be right, Kareem."

"Their speech, their grammar, the difficulty with the pronouns— they haven't talked like that since they first arrived on Earth. Is it the drugs? The P-Imp hats? Both?"

"Both, I suspect. Their charts indicate substantial decline in language and social skills since incarceration here ten years ago . . . but that could be part of a long-term deception, Kareem. Be careful not to—"

GONG! GONG! PING!

The sound was like that of a calypsoan Triclops striking a Trinidadian steel pan a mile wide, but it was Gil. Having broken free of his momentary catatonia, he'd begun flicking his metallic fingernails against the iridescent horns of the N-Kid. One horn maintained its basso drone, while Gil flicked the other one into trilling treble.

> *WHERE'ER BLASPHEMING LIARS RAIL*
> *TO SMOTHER TRUTH BENEATH LIE'S VEIL . . .*

chanted Gil Gamoid, the crispness of his language once again what it was in his prime:

> *. . . LET INNOCENTS REFUSE THEIR TALE*
> *FOR JUSTICE MUST ALWAYS PREVAIL!*
>
> *UNFURL THE SAIL!*
> *SEEK OUT THE GRAIL*
> *SO GLORIOUS HOPE*
> *MIGHT NEVER FAIL!*

FOR EVERY BREATH THAT WE INHALE
LET EVERY VILLAIN E'ER BEWAIL
THE POWERS STRONG OF HEROES FRAIL
WHO DRINK THE MILK FROM N-KID'S PAIL!

The gong-and-chiming ended, but hung in the air, like a cruel sentiment.

Once upon a time, millions of cape-fans and capecard-collecting school children knew that oath by heart as much as Gil Gamoid did. Upon reciting that creed, the uncanny N-Kid would be transformed into a Q939 creature resembling an Earth goat, complete with teats protruding from the apertures of his goat armour. Continuing his incantation, Gil would kneel, and taking the N-Kid's Grail Pail, "milk" his companion, the rhythmic motion resounding like an underwater *didgeridoo*. Thus was produced the awesome ultraviolet Q-ichor that, when quaffed, would grant the two titans twenty-four hours' worth of their cosmic Q-powers, or if refined into Q-cheese, a week's worth.

But for ten years both the Grail Pail and the star-emblem armour of the duo had been locked far away from Asteroid Zed inside the armoury of the Fortress of Freedom, while prison authorities daily injected N-Kid with lacto-suppressants. And despite Gil Gamoid's invocation of his pledge, the N-Kid stood in front of us untransformed, a humanoid goat-man with a perpetual young child's/old man's face, gouged by the aching tragedy of a life consigned to nothing but the long, long wait for death.

"Milk-milk's gone," whimpered the N-Kid. "No more cheese for me."

"AND POOR GIL'S COLD," rumbled the elder. "ISHTAR CRIES FOR US ALL."

"N-Kid, you said," tried Kareem again, "that there's an enemy among us. Who is it?"

"So far from home, X-Man-man. Understand? Been gone so long, been gone so long, been gone so long—"

"SO LONG," echoed Gil.

"Fabled city of Uruqanthl, capitol of Ur-Prime. Old Gil and me . . . children there. Ancient here. Everything small here. Small planet, small distance to sun. Ur-Prime orbits quasar Qanthl from 100,000 light years away. Even at that distance, radiation would burn humans into slices of toast—"

"N-Kid, please, I'm asking you to focus. You said you'd never want to hurt Hawk King. So help me find out who did."

"How can us help inside here? You the detective, out there."

"Your Q-perception . . . they say it's strong enough for you to see into the future, or the past . . . ."

"Hat-hat hate perceiving," said the N-Kid, pointing towards his P-I helmet, holding his fingers at a cartoonishly far distance that suggested he were feeding piranha. "No Q-ceiving in, what, eight years, Gil?"

"TEN. TEN YEARS."

"Even so, maybe . . . look, have you observed anything else? Anything here out of the ordinary? Other inmates acting unusually?"

The N-Kid and Gil Gamoid laughed awfully, like grave robbers joking about bloated corpses lying in suggestive positions.

"Okay . . . I mean 'unusually' for *here*. Anyone been asking you about your visions, like if they relate to Hawk King? Anyone asking questions, asking you about Hawk King's defenses, or his weaknesses, or the defenses of the Blue Pyramid?"

"Asking questions, X-Man-man? Years and years and years and years of questions-questions-questions—"

"POOR GIL'S COLD . . . ."

"—and filling Gil and me with druggies, can't-thinkies, P-I-shitties . . . done something to old Gil, so he can hardly talky-thinky. But never forget truth, X-Man-man. Never."

"Which is what?"

"Bad moons rising—"

"TROUBLE ON THE WAY—"

"—serpent's egg a-hatching, dragon's unfurling, talons scraping, knives sharpening, bloody tide rising, leviathan rising from the deep-deeps, slithering and slouching forth, hungry-hungry-hungry—"

"Who, N-Kid? Who is it?"

"Secret! Mystery! Twilight of the century! Midnight of the millennium! Sky rains, stars darken! Butchering of the prophets! Burning of the scriptures—"

"KILL THE KING—"

"—and disappear, watchers with slaughtering knives and fingers cruel, into night, to butcher children with parents' own blades—"

"AND THE KING FALLS, NEVER AGAIN TO GLIMPSE THE MOON, AND DOES NOT FLY LIKE A BIRD, NOR ALIGHT LIKE A BEETLE—"

"Gil, N-Kid, help me out here! Who *did* or who's *gonna do* what you're saying? Who killed Hawk King?"

"Mystery! Mystery wrapped inside enigma, wrapped inside tortilla, wrapped inside light, fluffy nan bread, wrapped inside flaky phylo pastry!"

"*Was it Menton?*"

Instantly, Gil and the N-Kid ceased their ranting. Kareem had asked the ultimate question, played his highest face card. Whether or not Hawk King's death was by natural causes, this question revealed Kareem's yearning for a pat and simple answer. As an interrogator, he was now at his greatest moment of vulnerability to a mad prisoner's manipulation.

"Hard to say," leered the N-Kid, cocking his head. Then, slowly, he said, "Who's . . . Menton?"

Kareem's lips parted, then nearly closed.

"Kot-tam," he mumbled. "We're done here."

"No! No-no-no! Listen, X-Man-man!" said the N-Kid, kicking the letho-glass with his hooves, ignoring the arc-shocks. "Who's Menton? Who's Menton? Understand?"

"FOOLED, X-MAN? FOOLED TO DEATH? DEATH TO FOOLS? WHOSE?

A PLAN, A PROSPECT, A PROJECT—FOR A NEW HEROIC CENTURY OF DEATH DESCENDS, LIKE THE BULL OF HEAVEN UPON THE WORLD, TRAMPLING TOWERS LIKE GRASS, CRUSHING SKULLS BENEATH ITS HOOVES LIKE GRAPES—"

"Listen, X-Manny-man! Listen!" Kick, arc-shock, kick, arc-shock. *"'Whose?'* Understand? *'Whose?'"*

Kareem shook his head, pushed himself out of his chair while the electric shocks strobed the white room into blinding whiteness. "C'mon, Doc!"

"WHOSE, X-MAN!" Gil Gamoid plastered his massive palms against the glass, arc-shocking his body into a giant humanoid fireworks display, his rail-spike teeth turned into a pan-pipe of awful electrical music. *"WHOSE* MENTON? *WHOSE* X-MAN? *WHOSE* MENTON? *WHOSE* X-MAN? *WHOSE—"*

TO FACE THE DEVIL HIMSELF

Exiting, we found Iron Lass waiting by herself down the corridor, agitatedly stroking her cheek, ear, and neck with an index finger. An insignificant gesture from anyone else, the fidgeting was practically a panic attack from her.

I caught her eyes, but only for a moment before they flickered away. There was dread in the black of her pupils, but far more guilt in the white of her scleras. She'd always been close to the two heroes of Ur-Prime; by some accounts, she'd never forgiven herself for her rôle in their incarceration.

When I asked Hnossi where all the other F*O*O*Jsters had gone, she said that the Flying Squirrel had ventured into the bio-containment Unit X to interrogate the Devolver, who'd once failed at devolving Hawk King into a tuna fish. André and Syndi, on the other hand, had retired to the staff commissary.

With Doctor Wells' guidance, Kareem, Hnossi, and I proceeded with growing trepidation to Unit Zed, what was sometimes called "the M-Wing." Past numerous security checkpoints, EEG/EPG monitoring stations and ever more obvious and numerous psi-dampeners, we descended to the cell-within-a-cell-within-a-cell wherein dwelt the Destroyer.

Portalling through multiple metallic vault doors and rumbling scanners, and finally passing beyond anxious armed guards, we arrived at the penultimate chamber. Doctor Wells reviewed with the three of us the psychic safety protocols he'd outlined when I contacted him the previous day, techniques to use in an emergency to stop Menton from terror-shackling our minds. Wells made us sign our final waivers, indicate next of kin, and check off the DNR and TWEP boxes.

I reminded Kareem that if he wanted to turn back, there was nothing stopping him.

His glare, a costume of bravado and contempt, couldn't disguise its fear.

"We're ready," said Doctor Wells into the wall comm. "Release Unit X Door 1, code delta-epsilon-alpha-theta."

Instantly, brutal blue light screamed into our vestibule through the retracting iris door until blue enveloped us, until blue was thick on our tongues like the taste of blood, until blue clogged our nostrils like the stink of gasoline.

We stepped through the circular doorway.

The prisoner was shackled into a massive P-I chair, wires and cathodes and tentacles sucking every psion of phagopsychotic energy from of his body. His head was crowned with a specially designed P-I helmet, its diodes drilled directly into his brain. Despite the chair's imprisoning purpose, I couldn't help but notice how much its technological grandeur had turned it into a throne, how much the modified helmet resembled a crown of silvery spikes, the tip of each spike twinkling like an electric ruby. And so as I looked at him burning in the centre of the chamber, an ultraviolet star at the centre of an ultrablue nebula, I was forced to remember Milton's description of the Fallen One who disdained service in heaven for rule in hell.

I'd studied the manifold clinical and mental techniques of this "man" once known as Doctor Napoleon Orator, corresponded with him, even published articles and books about him. But this was the first time I'd ever stood in the presence of the villain who'd murdered ten thousand people in a single, awful day in Las Vegas, 1983: Menton the Destroyer.

My bones felt like eggshells. And I was cold.

"Welcome, Iron Lass," stage-whispered the Destroyer.

The Valkyrie said nothing in reply.

"It's been a long... long time," he continued. "Especially for me. But of course, I have you to thank for my stay here. And I've been ... longing ... to express my gratitude."

Beside me, Hnossi stiffened, swallowed.

"And at last we meet, Doctor Brain," he said. "I've enjoyed our epistolary conversation over the years, some of which informed my article on therapeutic addiction for *The Journal of Clinical Psychiatry.*"

"Yes, Doctor. Doctor Wells showed it to me. Quite impressive."

"And you," he said, his light bulb eyes flicking onto Kareem. "You must be the uncanny X-Man."

"That's right," said Kareem.

He clearly intended defiance in his voice, but the words stumbled and tripped their way out of his mouth, rendering them almost inaudible.

"So ... you've ascended to my realm. Supplicants seeking my counsel, obviously."

"Ve don't vant your 'counsel,' Destroyer," hissed Iron Lass. "*You* are not in charche here. *Ve* are."

The man formerly known as Doctor Orator emitted a sound that was probably supposed to be a chuckle.

It drilled into my skull like a mosquito piercing my ear drum.

Standing for lack of chairs, Hnossi and I watched while Kareem began his interrogation. Painstakingly he waded through Menton's ominous sarcasm and the events of his criminal career, both matters of public record and details sealed in F*O*O*J files.

But Kareem's self-proclaimed status as the world's *new* greatest detective soon revealed itself as self-delusion. Throughout his ping-pong evocation of Menton's life, he mixed up numerous facts, from the number of patients Doctor Orator "treated" at his clinic during the first known year of his criminality, to the number of days to which he subjected Princess Astra and the Supersonic Snail to the unspeakable horrors of his phagopsychosis.

Yet for reasons surely unfathomable to any human mind, the Destroyer humoured Kareem, allowing him to disgorge a steaming puddle of inaccuracies that caused even me a profound, sympathetic frustration. Whatever evils Menton had committed, surely the very diabolical brilliance of his villainy merited an investigator's astute attention, rather than the dithering dilettantism of Kareem's detection.

"Kareem," sighed Iron Lass at last, "vere are you goingk vis zis?"

He flashed angry eyes at her, his entire body tensing visibly, and immediately resumed his inquiry.

"So lemme get this straight, Destroyer—you're saying that the only thing that kept you from mind-chewing the entire F*O*O*J in 1983 was the Flying Squirrel's Hypothalamic Scrambler?"

"Yes, yes, yes," muttered Doctor Orator, audibly irritated at last. "Why are you wasting my time with such inane queries, you cretinous—"

And then the X-Man clutched his head, releasing a burbling cry and collapsing, as if he'd been struck in the teeth with an axe.

RUNNING AWAY FROM ANSWERS

"Menton!" yelled Iron Lass, her hands instantaneously clutching her eldritch black and white blades. *"In ze name of ze late Princess Astra, I commit you to ze grafe you deservedt fifteen years ago—"*

"NO!" screamed X-Man.

Struggling to get up, he barked into his wrist-comm, "All F*O*O*Jsters: emergency evacuate! Repeat: emergency evacuate!"

"Vunce I strike down zis Loki-bastart, Kareem, z'emerchency vill be over!"

"There's no time! Asteroid Zed's about to be—"

Suddenly I collided with the bulkhead. Everything was sideways, then upside-down, and sound exploded in my head like a locomotive engine, wheels, and whistle screeching all at once. Even Menton howled, his light bulb eyes blazing blue horror. Kareem reached up, yanked on the upside-down door-release without effect.

Iron Lass sliced through the foot-thick steel of the iris door as if it were made of aluminium foil.

"Kareem—get *Doktor* Brain to safety!"

Kareem grabbed me, helping me up and through the ravaged doorway. Iron Lass howled, *"Miscreant!"* and everything around me burned into agonising blue supremacy while Kareem pulled me along the up-ended corridor.

And then the angle of gravity shifted again and we plummeted.

"Pillow!" yelled Kareem, falling, and just before impact could grind our bones to pebbles, we slammed into the soft embrace of a ten-foot thick black cushion.

While sirens squealed and flashed, Kareem yanked me along behind him. Guards and technicians were yelling and dashing all around us along the ceilings-turned-floors while prisoners were screaming from their inverted cells. Kareem was pouring with smoke, but before I could ask him if he were on fire, I saw a dark cloud spilling from his mouth like a legion of blackflies in a summer breeze. Muttering over and over to himself, Kareem suddenly stopped and yelled into his wrist comm, "F*O*O*J squad! Come in! What's happening to the Asteroid?"

"Kareem!" crackled Syndi's voice. "Thank god it's you! Are you all right?"

"I'm all right, Syndi! You okay?"

"Yes, I think so—"

"What's happening?"

"They're telling me the Asteroid's been, like, hit or attacked or something! They're trying to evacuate, but—oh god, no!"

"What?"

"The Space Elevator's been destroyed!" she said. "Kareem, we're trapped!"

"All F*O*O*J units!" yelled the comm voice of the Flying Squirrel. "Converge on . . . on the Crystal Module, forthwith!"

"Squirrel, what's going—"

"I said 'forthwith,' you missionary-boiling grunter! *Forthwith!*"

Resuming his muttered whisperings while pulling me behind him, I finally heard what Kareem had been saying. *"Find! Find! Find!"* he chanted, and for the first time I saw what the smoke was composed of: tiny logoids, none taller than a snowflake.

The cloud dispersed itself into the walls, floor, and ceiling, while the explosions grew louder by the second.

X-Man scrambled up the tiers of a shelf bolted into the wall until he came eye-to-screen with an upside-down display. After punching keys, he jumped down and yelled, "Follow me!"

We raced towards the Crystal Module through the madness of evacuating personnel, sirens, flashing lights, and the overlapping, overhead voices announcing the double-doom of Asteroid Zed:

Facility breach on tiers ten / Lockdown breach!
The prisoners /nine, eight, seven / Rupture /Are escaping
Lockdown breach / and vacuum protocols
The prisoners are escaping!

Staff and prisoners trampled each other in the strobe-lit race for life-pods, while screaming and the stench of charcoaled meat meant that inmates had begun exacting vengeance from their guards.

My heart hammered kettle-drums in my ears, but Kareem didn't even slow down, yanking me into the stairwell and "down" to the sixth story—the last unbreached tier of the tower—where we scrambled into the spherical observatory called the Crystal Module. Iron Lass ran in behind us. André and Syndi had already donned void suits, and through her helmet Syndi beamed at my arrival while looking at Kareem.

And then Mr. Piltdown burst in, pointing what looked like a personal cannon right at us, and yelled "Close your eyes!"

We heard an explosion.

Kareem, Hnossi, and I were knocked over and bubbled inside a canvassy-aluminum sack hiss-filling with air and choking with the reek of gunpowder. Through the bubble's porthole I saw Mr. Piltdown press a button on his belt, and then the Crystal Module's outer wall disintegrated into flaming shards before belching out into space.

We were all sucked out into the void like Pinocchio into the belly of Monstro the whale.

Escape pods piloted by surviving staff fell into the darkness all around us, like jellyfish fleeing the moonlight at the roof of the ocean . . . .

And then I saw it above us: a Squirrel Shuttle descending upon us, its robotic bushy tail scooping us up into its underbelly.

As soon as the airlock pressurised, Iron Lass ripped open our emergency bubble. Through the window and across the chasm of the vacuum, we witnessed the prison asteroid convulsing, sprouting tumours of blue and purple fire, before finally cracking and spilling rubble and debris and wriggling bodies into space.

"So do you finally see what I was *talking* about?" yelled Kareem at his fellow F*O*O*Jsters. "You think I don't know what you were saying about me? And now somebody blew up the whole kot-tam asteroid! Why? To stop my investigation, or wipe us all out, or both!

"Any of you freaks wanna call me paranoid *now?*"

PARANOIA: WHEN THE UNDERWORLD IS SO DARK YOU CAN'T SEE YOURSELF IN THE MIRROR

Paranoia is, ironically, a defense mechanism. Learning to deal with pain, disasters, and the loss of loved ones means accepting that we can control neither life nor death. Because they control us.

The self-delusion that mysterious forces and persons unknown are conspiring against us is, ironically, a comforting belief, because it means we're significant enough in this anarchic world to warrant someone's enmity. That delusion saves us from the far more difficult-to-accept reality: that we're simply not that important to anyone. That the universe just isn't that "into" us.

Paranoia is the emotive-psychestructure's response to feeling ignored, unloved, or forgotten in an existence filled with random acts of destructive indifference emphasising the inherent futility of life and struggle. If you're ever to achieve serenity, ultimately you must accept that in such a vast cosmos, you simply don't matter very much.

The F*O*O*Jsters' journey to the archetypal underworld, and the chance to employ their enemies' faces as crystal ball to their own future, should have been enough to show all my patients how they could end up, unless they renounced their failed vision and bankrupt misconceptions about the meaning of their "heroism." At the moment of our return to Earth, it still was not clear whether any of them had learned their lesson—and in the case of Kareem, it was clear that his condition was only deteriorating.

So unless you want to devolve emotionally into the deranged, desperate, degraded depths of a Gil Gamoid, an N-Kid, or an X-Man during their final days, you need to make peace with your finitude.

Visualisation and trance-work can help. Try picturing yourself as a single grain of sand inside an hour-glass. You are not the first grain of sand through the spout, nor the last, but the middlest. But once the hour is up and all the sand has fallen, the hourglass is smashed to pieces and left on the floor, and no one will ever clean it up. When you can trance-contemplate that image for an hour without sobbing, you'll know you've successfully suffocated the influence of self-grandiosity, and that you're well on the journey towards psychemotionally integrative recovery.

Unfortunately, as I was about to discover, my F*O*O*Jsters, especially the X-Man, were going to eschew integration in favour of paranoia . . . which ultimately led to a terrifying tragedy for everyone.

CHAPTER SEVEN

Who Are You, Really?
Secret Origins and
Secret Shames

FALL-OUT

TUESDAY, JULY 4, 3:59 P.M.

"Goddamned coach-class StarCase™ Corporation!" growled Mr. Piltdown while piloting us back to Earth.

"If man were meant to conquer space inside a goddamned dumb waiter he'd've been born looking like laundry! If not for me, all you ninnies would be vacuum-roasted and gut-burst right now, you hear me?"

By that point, the tenth minute into our rescue, Mr. Piltdown had already explained to everyone several times the mortal debt owed to him for having a Squirrel Shuttle standing by on remote, and how no Space Elevator was or would ever be a dependable means of transit, whereas Piltdyne Scramjet-Rockets held the proprietary "future of mankind" in their Pulstar-class engines.

But our brush with asteroidal immolation wasn't my focus. I was worried about Kareem, who was sputtering in zero gravity through the labyrinthine warps of his conspiratorial delusion, raving that Menton had orchestrated everything from the "assassination" of Hawk King to the destruction of Asteroid Zed itself.

"What," said André, "and get his own ass smoked?"

"Menton," snapped Kareem, "wasn't even *on* Asteroid Zed!"

Syndi exploded with a manic laugh-cry of having narrowly escaped death. "Really, Kareem? Like, who exactly were you interviewing, then, huh? Dracula?"

Kareem snorted haughtily. I'd noticed his tendency to delight (perhaps especially) in moments like these—at hoarding what he considered critical facts, like a dragon leering from atop a mound of cubic zirconia. "Figure it out," he sneered. "That wasn't Menton."

"Really. Like, who was it, then?"

"I don't know—yet. I haven't gotten all my *medu-kem* back," he said, referring to the logoids he'd dispersed in his frantic mantra of *Find! Find! Find!* "Probably stuck on the outside of the shuttle. But when we're on the ground and I open the hatch, I'll know for sure."

"Strap yourselves in and cut the chatter, scatter-wits," said Mr. Piltdown. "We're entering the atmosphere."

Everyone complied with the strapping-in, but none with the command for quiet.

"Kareem, uff course ze man I dispatched vuss ze Destroyer!" said Hnossi. Her face was flushed and puffy, the flesh under her eyes like raw steak. For a woman who'd seen combat on a global scale, she was taking these events much harder than I'd've expected. "You yourself shriekt horribly in hiss cell unt collapsed ven he vuss usink his phagopsychosis on you!"

The lights shut off, and our only illumination came from the flames beyond the portholes as we hurtled planetward.

Kareem claimed he'd collapsed not due to any Mentonian attack, but because of a desperate, telepathic gambit by Gil Gamoid and the N-Kid to warn him—an effort, he said, which had to have cost them the ultimate price.

Their message: that Asteroid Zed was about to be destroyed.

"They combined their Qosmic Qonsciousness," he said, "and pushed right through their P-Imp hats. *And it killed them.* I smelled it inside my own skull, their brains burning into briquettes. Tasted like a tray of lasagna left in a kot-tam furnace."

The portholes were orange disks in the darkness while the heat shield ripped through the superheated air around the plummeting shuttle.

"Unt even if you're mistaken about *how* zey diedt, zey are *det*," said Hnossi, her eyes heavier than dumb bells. She touched her mouth with quivering fingers. Noticing the shaking, she grasped the digits with her other hand and tucked both hands between her thighs. It was an incongruously girlish, vulnerable image for a steely, immortal woman.

"At least, at last . . . zeir Q-souls are hettet beck to Qvasar Nine-Sree-Nine, beck to ze Ur-Prime vich produced zem."

"Yeah!" yelled Kareem, his voice nearly swallowed by the roaring engine deceleration. "Hope that's a comfort for all the families of Asteroid

Zed's guards and the technicians! Looks like half the life-pods didn't even eject! Last five minutes on the asteroid was the dance called 'prisoners' revenge,' and the band was on fire! So what we've got is an attempt to shut down my investigation and kill more heroes—us! Not to mention wiping out all the remaining villains!"

"Kareem, is you crazy?" shouted André through the descent. The portholes were orange heating elements atop a black stove. "You sayin Menton not only wanna kill Hawk King, he wanna destroy us an all other villains, too? Why? What's in it for him?"

"My god, doesn't anybody have a kot-tam brain up here? Look! Hawk King's dead! Omnipotent Man one day just up and resigns? We almost get slaughtered up there, and almost every remaining rival for anyone who wants to take over is wiped out in one shot!"

"Take over what, Kareem?" howled Syndi.

And Kareem shouted one last sentence before re-entry wiped out his voice: "What do you *think?*"

INSIDE THE FORTRESS OF FEAR

Conversation was dead until we'd landed safely inside the Fortress of Freedom, where scores of heroes crowded round their comrades to make sure they were all right. Outside the Fortress wall, dozens of camera crews awaited interviews, since by then satellite photography had beamed images of Asteroid Zed's destruction around the world.

Although I'd been inside the Fortress of Freedom several times, I was still then, even after having survived the orbital disaster, awestruck by the stained-glass windows depicting the tragedies and triumphs of the F*O*O*J's history, the vast 2.5D mural churning with the chaos of the *Götterdämmerung*, and the titanic, soaring, gold and platinum statues of the founding F*O*O*Jsters together with the Flying Squirrel holding up the celestial ceiling.

(While the Flying Squirrel didn't join the F*O*O*J until 1946, he was able to add his own colossus to the Fortress's Age of Heroes caryatids because the F*O*O*J, in fact, were his tenants. Mr. Piltdown not only paid for the construction of the Fortress, he remained the owner of the building and the land beneath it; to this day, the F*O*O*J pays rent from its federal operating grants to the Piltdomain Holdings Group.)

I was about to enter Heroes' Hall when the guards almost stopped me, but after Syndi vouched for me and I was let inside, I saw a storm swirling with Kareem as its eye. F*O*O*Jster novices and veterans alike seemed to have decided that the X-Man was the answer man. Mr. Piltdown looked none too pleased at the gravity wielded by his front-running rival for the post of Director of Operations.

I scanned the assembly, sensing these heroes' seething anxiety. At the back, Syndi was twirling and tugging at her hair hard enough to yank it rootless. On the far side, André affected detached cool while leaning against the wall, but he could not stop glancing upward constantly as if anticipating the collapse of the ceiling. I couldn't see Iron Lass anywhere.

Kareem eventually took to the stage, framed by a backdrop mural of F*O*O*J martyrs such as Captain Manifest Destiny, Doctor Patho, and Liberty Belle.

"Menton the Destroyer," said Kareem into the microphone, employing the profane name to shock everyone into shutting up, *was not on* Asteroid Zed. I believe he had been replaced by an imposter. Specifically, Zee-Roks the Imitator."

With everyone rapt upon him, Kareem reported what we saw in the space prison and laid out his "evidence," such as it was: that he fully expected Menton to be a terrifying figure, yet he felt no fear of the man whatsoever; that his interrogation plan was to state incorrect knowledge about Menton's career and crimes to lure the egomaniac into "correcting" him, yet his subject affirmed Kareem's inaccuracies without hesitation; that his last-minute logoscopic investigation of Asteroid Zed's computers revealed "micro-gaps" in the data—so small only his logoids could find them—indicating an attempt to erase all record of at least two unauthorised prisoner transfers: one to and one from Unit Zed, three years ago; that the "comatose body" occupying the cell assigned to Zee-Roks the Imitator in the Bio-Villains Containment Unit was actually synthesised from a combination of medical waste, rhinoplasty, and Swanson's Hungry Villain Dinners™; that contrary to early supposition, Asteroid Zed wasn't destroyed by any outside force, but instead annihilated by a malfunction in its gravity reactor, "unquestionably" due to sabotage; and that since Gil Gamoid and the N-Kid proved they could overcome their P-I helmets, the more psionically powerful Menton could have developed the same skill, but without burning out his own brain . . . and if he had, only he would have had the means, motive, and opportunity to overcome prison authorities, escape, kill Hawk King, terminate Omnipotent Man's career, and wipe out his enemies, his potential rivals, and his tracks all in one shot.

It was a thrilling, intoxicating, highly speculative, and totally circumstantial concoction Kareem had brewed, and the hundred or so terrified F*O*O*Jmates in attendance, still reeling from the loss of Hawk King and Omnipotent Man, were all too willing to snort it up by the mugfull. But unfortunately for sanity's sake, Asteroid Zed's destruction (which by Kareem's own admission was due to a structural defect) meant no one could verify X-Man's claims. And lack of verifiability was a paranoiac's playground paradise.

But what happened next stunned even me.

"I agree with the X-Man," announced Mr. Piltdown, taking a step onto the stage.

Every head swivelled towards the Flying Squirrel. Kareem was agog.

"Our organisation is under threat," called the Squirrel, moving towards the microphone. "Perhaps its gravest threat since the *Götterdämmerung* itself. And whether we're facing an escaped Destroyer, or person or persons unknown of similar threat-level—my own investigation, which for reasons I'm not yet at liberty to reveal—points to none other than Warmaster Set—we are clearly being hunted by a shadowy foe of enormous cunning, power, and danger."

With greater delicacy than I'd ever seen him employ, Festus Piltdown wedged himself between Kareem and the microphone, saying, "On the authority of F*O*O*J General Security Order Number One, we are now at Defense Condition Cyan."

With that, he clicked a button on his glove and the auditorium plunged into deep cyan.

Confused mumbling flooded the hall. Mr. Piltdown shook his head, finally shouting at the questions only he could hear: "No, no, no, you shankshaft, you put on scuba gear for Def-Con *Mauve*, not *Cyan*! Are you colour blind?"

"Yes!" cried an indignant Dober-Man.

"Why couldn't it be L-Raunzenu?" shouted somebody, slicing through the din.

Mr. Piltdown flushed darkly while the challenger railed on. "Everything Kareem said about the attack, the plot against us, all of it could've been carried out by L-Raunzenu. Which you know better than anybody, Squirrel, since Piltdown Psychotronics synthesised the damn thing outta ten million neurocorded nightmares—"

"—at the cost of a billion dollars in defense contracts of taxpayers' money," said Kareem, grabbing the microphone. "Look—Heli-Cop, isn't it? Listen, I hear where you're coming from, but L-Raunzenu has no need to free Menton, right? And I'm telling you, I was up there on Asteroid Zed, and Menton wasn't. If you wanna pursue that as a complementary investigation, we can continue this conversation in camera. But for now," he said, appealing to the crowd, "this is the angle I'm working."

"That *we're* working," said Mr. Piltdown, glaring at Heli-Cop. "Def-Con Cyan, everyone! Action stations! Action stations!"

And off they all shuffled beneath cyan lighting. By then there wasn't a hero in the Fortress who hadn't been swept up in Kareem's cyclone of neurotic panic. And when all those airborne heavyweights eventually smashed into the earth, inevitably the innocent would be crushed.

When the Hall was clear, I was alone in the cyan light except for one man. At six-five, he was hard to miss, but it was as if he'd been invisible until that point. Yet at that moment he was a lightning bolt of a presence in his dark blue suit and red tie, with his coal-and-silver hair greased into a single e-curl in front. His face looked as if it'd been dipped in tempura and yanked from the deep fryer five minutes too soon.

"Doctor Brain, sir, ma'am," he whispered, shuffling towards me as if his every bone ached. "I . . . I need y'hep."

WHAT TYPE OF SANDWICH ARE YOU?

One glance into Wally's eyes communicated an epic of disorientation and dysfunction. If you've ever looked yourself in the mirror at 3 A.M. and seen such distress, felt so out of control, and been so desperate for answers, maybe it's time to stop looking around you, and start looking *behind* you. Your pain and life-disorientation may *seem* to be the products of your present, but they're not; your present is merely the effect of your past.

Just as a ham sandwich is composed of ham, bread, and condiments such as mayonnaise, mustard, and relish, and occasionally a slice of lettuce, avocado, or a sweet pickle, every human being is formed of experiences, some of which are supplemental, and others of which are primary. The tastes and textures of a smear of emotional relish and a leaf of psychic lettuce change drastically in relation to the bread and ham of your primary development.

Ask yourself honestly: are you two slices of rich, multi-grain whole wheat sandwiching a fresh serving of organic country ham? Or are you two easily-torn white wafers of over-processed flour mass-cooked into a lifeless loaf, trapping the fatty, cold, red-dyed sinews of a factory reconstituted swine-product?

Only when you've answered that can you start asking the questions to unlock the mysteries containing your misery. And if Wally couldn't do that for himself, there was no telling how far he'd plummet, or if he'd even survive.

PAYING THE POWER BILL

"Listen, Miss Brain—are you listening to me? Because so far I don't think you've heard a god-damned word I've said about anything."

I assured Mr. Piltdown that I was indeed listening, knowing how oblivious he was to the irony of his insistence, since he rarely listened to anyone. Because I sensed that Wally needed the comfort of meeting with his age-mates, I'd sought out Iron Lass, who was unfortunately unavailable; the normally steely heroine had been so psychically fatigued by the events of the past few days that she'd been returning nobody's telephone calls. And so I invited Festus Piltdown to join Wally and me.

Having reconvened at my Mount Palomax offices, I quickly tucked away the **Elect X-MAN Director of Operations, F*O*O*J!** pamphlets Kareem had somehow managed to leave around—whether for electioneering purposes, or simply for antagonising Mr. Piltdown, I was not sure, although by then it was clear that antagonising the Flying Squirrel was difficult to avoid, even for someone with my training.

"You were expressing," I mirrored to Mr. Piltdown reassuringly, "your reservations about Wally's performance in the Id-Smasher™ simulation we ran last week."

"Expressing my—did you say *expressing my reservations?* I was detailing the eight hundred and twenty-three reasons why that man is an unapologible cock-up!"

He tugged at his neck straps, removed his squirrel mask and put it on the leather of the sofa seat beside him, then ran his fingers through the chalk streaks of his blackboard hair.

"He's a fraud, Miss Brain. Earth's greatest superhero, my *colon.* He's a panty-willed, 'aw-shucks, ma'am', fermented possum-swilling, unmitigated ultra-ninny. Times got tough, he resigned. And at Hawk King's funeral, no less, stealing the spotlight for himself. He's a serial spotlight-stealer, I hope you realise—has been for decades. And now that the destruction of Asteroid Zed is capturing the headlines he wanted for himself, he's back here whimpering to *un*resign himself—"

"I didn'*un*resign, I'm still *resign*-resigned, an you're just sore cuz y'almost got blowed up t'day an I couldn'be there t'save ya for the eightieth time on accounta m'health!"

"Save *me?*" yelled the Squirrel. *"Me? I'm* the one who saved the entire *mission!* But go out to any tin-kettled flap-jack shack and ask 'Charlie Spam Sandwich' and 'Edith Dishsoap' who's saved this republic more times than there are stars on the flag and *your* name'll be the first one on their slack-jawed, bespittled lips . . . . So if that assembly of brain-stemmed dinkle-wits that dares calls itself the F*L*A*C wants to address efficiency or diminished morale in this time of Cyan-level crisis, they might first try addressing the profound misallocation of credit foisted upon the galactically undeserving! That'd be *one* man's modest proposal."

Throughout Mr. Piltdown's venting, Wally sat surprisingly placidly, as if he were listening to delightful, faraway *oom-pah-pah* music only he could hear—of course, with his omni-hearing, he might very well have been doing that. I returned him to our world by asking him how he felt about what Mr. Piltdown had just said.

"Wellsir, I respect Festus's opinion, and I respect his right to *have* an opinion, ma'am. Which is what makes our country great."

"Yes, I see, Wally. However—"

Mr. Piltdown: "Do you even listen to the pap that dribbles out of your mouth, Wally? *You respect my opinion?* My *opinion* just burned you down to a primary-coloured cinder, and you *respect* it? Is there so much as the *smell* of a thought inside that high-density skull of yours?"

For the first time, Wally smiled, opening his hands in concession.

"Wellsir, Festus, you've got me there. I'm still an old-fashioned man. It's how I was raised. I b'lieve you should be able to disagree without being disagreeable, and, wellsir, I admit, I'm a might taken aback when you start, well—"

"No, Wally. You're not taken aback. You're weak. And stupid. You were a liability to this team since it formed, and in the years since then you've only deteriorated, and, QED, you've cast this country into jeopardy, including through your capricious crybaby resignation—"

Suddenly Mr. Piltdown shuffled himself in his chair, reaching inside a utility pouch at the armpit of his left flap as if he were itching from ants.

"Good god-damnit! How in the hell did that Congo coon—"

"Whatcha got there, Festy?"

"I take my cape off for two minutes at the Fortress to use the damned rest room and that sociopathic sleeping-car porter stuffs it with one of his Mau Mau-ing election pamphlets! If that switch-bladed Australopithecus gets on our F*L*A*C, I'm telling you, we'll all be speared in our sleep!"

"Mr. Piltdown," I say, "let's stay focused on—"

"He's got no respect for private property! This is my *cape*, for god's sake! You don't touch a hero's cape! My *life* depends on this thing operating properly—"

"Festy, calm down—it's just a lil ol brochure—"

"Wally, while illiterates such as yourself may not care about the power of the written word—"

"Mr. *Pilt*down, let's focus on what you were saying about Wally. The words you chose carried an intense . . . certainty, and by your own description, they defy common wisdom. Why do you feel that Wally hasn't earned his fame? He was, after all, a founding member of the F*O*O*J, whereas you joined only after the original six members had returned from Germany."

"Actually, ma'am, Festus tweren't a member til the next year—'forty-six."

"Thank you, Wally. Yes. So what is the nucleus of your concern?"

Mr. Piltdown laughed, coldly. "Ah, Miss Brain. Further proof that initials after one's name mean nothing insofar as intellectual credentials or even a child's capacity to peer through the viscous veneer of venerability. During the War, Earth's champion, there—"

"The War—you mean the *Götterdämmerung*?"

"World War II! Two seconds ago you were talking about Germany, so why would I be talking about the *Götterdämmerung*? I don't expect you to keep up with me, but at least muster the cognition to keep up with *yourself*, if you don't mind."

I paused, allowing him to continue.

"—*As I was saying*, this man is celebrated for having somehow put the kibosh on that moustachioed Austrian misanthrope in 'forty-five, when in reality as a result of his staggering incompetence, before Wally even got to Berlin he'd already destroyed a dozen Allied refuelling ships and actually protected a U-Boat by mistake!"

Omnipotent Man chuckled. "Well now, that there's kind of a funny story—"

"A funny story—helping the Nazis. Here's a funnier story, Miss Brain. Wally's entire origin is a sham. You've got yard-chimps from Bangor to Buckskin Falls collecting trading cards and memorising statistics about this atomic-powered flatworm, and every last one of them knows the messianic story of his origin: baby Karojun-Ya, rocketed to Earth from the exploding planet Argon by his philosopher-king father Jobuseen-Ya and gaining powers over mortal men—half Hercules, half Jesus.

"But has anyone ever actually *seen* this planet Argon?"

He let the question smoulder, his baleful eyes burning like heaps of garbage.

"No, you see," he resumed just before Wally could defend his origin story, "because it just happened to be destroyed before anyone on Earth could even take a picture of it, even though his rocket got here faster than the speed of light? Nothing but snake-milt.

"Wally has—what's the media buzzword?—he's 'sexed up' the truth. He's no extraterrestrial. He's nothing but white super-trash. Have you ever seen a picture of his real family, Miss Brain? They're trailer-trolls from Out House, Kentucky!"

"Wellsir, if I'm not from the planet Argon, Festus, then where'd I get my omni-powers?"

"People acquire powers for any number of reasons, Wally! Genetics, childhood trauma, cell-phones . . . maybe you got yours in one of those Mexican clinics—I really don't know. Some of us don't depend on 'powers' to do our damned jobs, which you don't manage to do anyway. We actually have to *work*, understand? Be productive? Actually possess our own working testicles?"

"I'm a—now, you see, Doctor Brain, sir, ma'am, this is where Festy has a tendency to take his horsing around a bit too far outta the barn—"

"You know what this keen little patriot did during the OPEC crisis?"

"—I'm a very hard worker, always have been, been workin hard since I was nothing but Omni-Lad—"

"—eating 'omni-grits,' no doubt. During the OPEC crisis—"

"—been savin folks in this here country since I was old enough to—"

"*During the god-damned OPEC crisis* Wally promised Carter he'd use his 'Omni-Power' to create a new energy source to free us from the tyranny of those tablecloth-headed hand-choppers. You know where Wally tested his brainchild? You recall a little gem of real estate called 'Three Mile Island'? To this day the entire country still believes that was a nuclear power plant, instead of the argonium processor it actually was. Now *that's* P.R., when the President himself covers up for you. Covers up for you being a filthy junkie!"

"Now Festus, you wait just a golly-shocking minute! I aint never had no problem with argonium—"

"What she ever saw in you, I'll never understand—"

"'What she'—? Who ya talkin bout, Festy? Princess Astra?"

Festus shut his mouth, his eyes flashing onto me and then away as if he were afraid he'd said too much. Then he regrouped and regained my gaze, thumbing his accusations toward his colleague.

"Those same hero-card-collecting urchins who believe his rat-excrement nonsense about being from the planet Argon are true believers in his idiocy about argonium. That meteor-fragments of his 'exploded homeworld' are the only substance that can kill 'Omnipotent' Man. Brilliant bit of logic, there, by the way, being allergic to his entire home planet. Just how does a species like that evolve, hm? Gloves? When the truth is, he's as addicted to argonium as a common coolie is to opium!"

"Festus, now dontchu be, be spreading any a your, your . . . exaggerations again," said Wally, as if the word were the foulest curse he'd said in years.

"Look at him, Miss Brain," continued the Squirrel. "We've been trapped in your therapeutic clutches for over a week now. Could even you be so dim as to've failed to notice how often he excused himself to go to the little cretin's room, and how when he came back, his nostrils were dusted with a fine, blue powder?"

I glanced at Wally nipping the nail of his right index finger. Given the omni-density of his nails, his chewing sounded like a boxcar locking into a train.

"This man," said the Squirrel, thumbing, "so successfully hoodwinked that peanut-harvesting huckleberry of a president that he managed to turn the entire Department of Energy into his dealer! Three plum-sized glowing blue crystals *per day* back then. I haven't a clue where he's getting his supply now. Perhaps from somewhere out in the asteroid belt, which would explain all those 'exploratory missions' he's been on of late, and probably explains his resignation itself! Instead of being up on Asteroid Zed today making himself useful, he was probably out getting his fix—"

"Doggonit, Squirrel, y'all better hush, now—"

"Did you know, Miss Brain, that this apple-gnawing rum-donkey doesn't even restrict himself to one secret identity? He has at least three that I know of, presumably so he can be an utter failure in as many places as possible. How about it, Wally? Did you know I knew? Junkies tend not to hide things very well, but neither do they tend to realise what nakedly strolling emperors they actually are."

Wally's eyes became twin sunny-side-up eggs on the plate of his face, his lips an O of two crispy-curled slices of bacon.

"Wally," I asked, "what does Mr. Piltdown mean when he said you have more than one secret identity?"

"Festy, you nuthin but a lyin, steamin heapa goat shit, dj'know that?"

"Oh ho! The monkey finally finds his mouth. But which of the three monkeys? Nothing but a disgrace to Hawk King's entire legacy—"

Suddenly the Flying Squirrel was flailing backwards across the room because of the whipping, screeching tentacle of blue-white brilliance extending from Omnipotent Man's mouth to the centre of the Squirrel's chest. Smashing into the opposite wall and crashing to the floor, Festus clutched the blackened, flaming hole in the tunic above his armour, gasping awfully.

I glimpsed myself reflected in the glass of a framed Munsch print—my hair, static-charged, upright and stiffened into the shape of an upside-down Daddy Long-Legs.

The entire room reeked of ozone.

"Festus," said Omnipotent Man, electric sparks spraying out between his clenched teeth like neon spittle, "you'd better tuck-tail on outta here 'fore I lose my temper . . . suh'm fierce."

ACHILLES' REAL HEEL WAS HIS WHOLE BODY

If you're like Omnipotent Man was, you may have spent much of your career, if not your life, hiding behind the fig leaf of your physical indestructibility. But having a diamond-hard body doesn't guarantee you freedom from a costume jewellery soul, or that the gold of your mental health won't oxidise into an unsightly green.

Achilles, the "invulnerable" hero of the Trojan War, was vulnerable supposedly because of his very mortal heel. But even a cursory reading of The Iliad shows that Achilles maintained very weak interpersonal relationships and was frozen at a child's stage of ego development, sulking in his tent even while war raged around him. Clearly, Achilles' true vulnerability was actually his invulnerability, or what I call the Achilles Three-Fold Folly of Superior Ability.

The Achilles Three-Fold Folly of Superior Ability

1. Achilles believed in the myth of his own invulnerability, so he never attempted to understand the meaning or ramifications of others' vulnerability.
2. Achilles' inexperience with physical pain meant that he never developed a common lexicon of misery, the key ingredient for human connection.
3. Achilles, believing in his supposed inability to feel pain, and because of his lack of compassion, never grew to understand his own or others' emotional pain, which imprisoned him inside an inescapable confinement of existential solitude. When the poisoned, flaming Trojan arrow struck him, Achilles died as likely from heartbreaking loneliness (the narcissistic fantasy that he alone could feel such pain) as from toxins, infection, third degree burns, and massive blood loss.

Unless Wally could rise to the challenge of confronting the reality of his own essential fragility, particularly during a time of such instability for the organisation that gave his life meaning, he would never be able to achieve true strength and would instead die a broken, embittered, delusional man.

SECRET ORIGINS AND SECRET SHAMES

Without exception, every family keeps a veritable mausoleum of skeletons in its closets. Innumerable patients of mine have discovered only in adulthood that they're in fact adopted, or abuse survivors, or human-alien hybrids, or even cerebro-boosted Globus monkeys.

So when Mr. Piltdown attacked Wally on his origins, I couldn't help but ask myself some questions: *Are* Wally's parents extraterrestrial quasi-gods possessing powers surpassing our "awe-capacity" and intellect impenetrable to mortal men? Or are they salt-of-the-earth country folk from America's deep-fried gristle belt? Did Wally invent a myth of grandiose origins to over-compensate for his personal mediocrity? Or is it something else entirely? Or not?

In order to help Wally feel truly comfortable exposing himself, I dismissed Mr. Piltdown to seek medical care and resume his "independent investigation" into Hawk King's death. To aid in getting towards Wally's inner truth, I brought out my DynaScan Reflective Spectroscope Junior®, and while giving Wally a few hours to compose himself, I pored over the "Omnipotent Mess" chapter from Jack Zenith's *Two Masks of a "Hero,"* and contacted Mr. Piltdown to have him courier me his own Squirrel Intelligence files on Wally. And, as a precaution, I arranged two lightning rods on either side of my desk.

If Mr. Piltdown's claim about multiple secret identities had any truth to it, Wallace W. Watchtower was in far greater pain than I could ever have guessed.

EXCAVATING THE ICE AGE OF JOBUSEEN-YA

"So, Wally," I asked, while sunset sweetened the room into a glowing ketchup smear, "how does it feel to be out of the F*O*O*J? Sitting on the sidelines, watching the accidental destruction of Asteroid Zed, and the impending election for the F*L*A*C?"

He gazed at me glumly, slumping in his chair like a mound of mashed potatoes.

"Wellsir, asteroids are always blowin up somewhere, y'know?" he mumbled. "An's far as th'lection, well . . . never really cared for thet administrative guff. I like *do*in thangs. Actin. Not fussin over forms an such."

I flipped through my file and the file Mr. Piltdown sent me. "Hm. But . . . yes, you *did* serve on the F*L*A*C a few in the late 40s and early 50s when the F*O*O*J was still new. There were some . . . problems . . . ?"

"Tweren't really my thang, like I said, ma'am. Gil Gamoid stepped in for me, an Hawk King, may God rest both their souls, suggested I retire from the F*L*A*C so he could hep me keep refinin m'powers. The King hepped me find m'real callin: rescuin, savin, inspirin. I'm a 'big pitcher' sorta feller, not a dottin-tees an crossin-eyes man, y'know. Hnossi, Festus, they're better with that sorta stuff."

"I see. Would you say then, Wally, you've taken seriously, or not seriously enough, your history of failure?"

"Wellsir, ma'am, I'd like to say that I always never don't fail to take serious things seriously. I mean . . . wait a minute. Uh . . . yes?"

"So you agree then, that—"

"Now hang on, ma'am . . . you kinda rattled me there a minute with that question. So no, I don'think that I haven't taken . . . I mean, I have taken—look, I never said I was a failure. That's just not true. You know it, I know it, th'entire 'Merican people know it. They call me a hero. Now, I don'call *m'seff* a hero, but that's what they call me. And two hunnerd and fifty million people can't be wrong, no sir, ma'am."

"Now Wally, it's interesting to me that you phrased your response the way you did. Because I didn't say you were a failure."

"What? I coulda sworn you just—"

"No, I asked you to characterise, or reify—*measure*, if you will—how seriously you've *taken* your failures."

Wally looked back at me with his eyebrows knitted into a muffler of confusion, until finally scratching beneath his right armpit. "Now maybe you didn'hear me right, ma'am, but I just said I'm *not* a failure, I'm a hero. Hero-fyin is what I do. It's what I'm good at. Always have been."

"Wally, how realistic, really, is it to think that you're perfect?"

"I never *said* I was perfect, ma'am-Doctor. *No*body's perfect. Even Hawk King, and I adored the man, so don'get me wrong, but even *he* wunt perfect, though you might think so, listenin to Festus. Okay, no one cept maybe my daddy's perfect. An he's passed on."

"So how did that make you feel, when Festus referred to your parents as, and I'm quoting from my notes, here, as 'nothing but white super-trash . . . trailer-trolls from Fried Possum, Kentucky?'"

"Actually, ma'am-sir, he said, '*Out House*, Kentucky.'"

"Right. Of course. So, how *did* it make you feel?"

"Wellsir, twasn't nice, course, but I'm a big boy. But I was talkin bout m'real daddy, not m'step-pa."

"You mean . . . 'Jobuseen-Ya,' from the planet Argon."

"Yessir, ma'am."

"Because we had a bit of an incident here when Mr. Piltdown started questioning whether 'Jobuseen-Ya' and Argon actually existed."

Wally wrinkled his nose, turned to his side, sucked in a deep breath, then let it out over the course of a full half-minute. Frost formed a huge white circle on the window in the path of his exhalation, and even the spectroscope next to me scummed over milkily. I couldn't stop myself from shivering.

"Sorry bout that," he said.

"That's fine, Wally." I crossed my arms for warmth, noticing how my skin had pimpled like a plucked chicken's. The air had to have dropped twenty degrees.

Omnipotent Man leaned forward, pushed himself up and out of his chair and ambled over to the window he'd just made opaque. He put a fingernail into the frost which I could then see was at least half an inch thick.

"Don'much care for people suggestin, Doc," rumbled Omnipotent Man, "that I aint tellin th'truth."

COLD REALITY

"You listen to Festus long enough," he whispered, maybe more to himself than to me, "y'start not even knowin' what's true about *y'seff*. He c'n tear a strip off ya long enough to make a runway. On'y three or four people in th'world he don'never talk like that about. One's Hawk King, who he thought was doggone infalpable . . . infabbubull . . . inflabbubble—"

"—infallible?"

"Zackly. Then there's Ir'n Lass. An', I spose . . . yeah, Chip Monk, his ol sidekick, even though they had a powerful fallin out, but he still don'never say s'much as a bad burp about him.

"But *me*, he's always ridin' me like a fat jockey on a poor man's pony. Sayin' Argon didn'ever exist, that I done wrong by 'Merica, that I'm, ha ha, that I'm addicted t'Argonium. I mean, don't that just take jake-all?"

He glanced up at me for affirmation, while his fingernail continued cutting shapes into the frost-field on the window, whether randomly or by design, I wasn't sure.

"So . . . all these accusations are false, Wally?"

"Yes'm."

"Let's take it that they're false, then. On a scale of one to three, with one being 'quite a bit,' and three being 'one hundred percent,' how much truth would you say Mr. Piltdown's claims contain?"

His fingernail stopped on a downward diagonal line. "Well, I . . . I mean . . . I guess then I'd hafta say . . . one? Wait, wait a second—is there a zero?"

"No. How relieved do you feel that you've been able to release yourself even a little bit from the burden of these self-deceptions, Wally? With one being 'very relieved,' and three being 'extremely relieved?'"

"Now, I didn'*say* that I was relieved, ma'am—"

"So how much do you wish that you had not let me know how relieved you are, with one being—"

"Now, Doctor Brain, sir, ma'am, what I'd, I'd, I'd really like to talk with you about is how gosh-durn unfair it is for Festus t'be stompin' on m'good name like that. An not just, like, a hour ago but for the last dad-blasted fifty years!"

I tapped the device next to me. "Wally, do you know what this is?"

He resumed drawing his frost-image, his finger cutting and dancing faster than I could see and raising a cloud of snow. Without even looking back at me, he said, "A DynaScan Spectroscope Junior®."

"Very good. Do you know why I have it with me?"

He stopped, silent, his finger suddenly stuck in mid-draw.

"I've set it to scan for a rare substance," I said quietly. "Do you know which one?"

"Listen, ma'am, in my line-a-work I fly through solar prominences, planetary cores, Cirque du Soleil shows—I could have any number a things stuck to my suit an cape—"

"According to the scanner, this substance isn't on your suit, Wally, and you're not wearing your cape. It's on your fingers, teeth, lips, and nostrils."

He turned to face me, stepping away from the window. Only then could I see he'd drawn three startlingly detailed portraits, each one slightly different, but clearly all versions of the same face.

His own.

And then he turned back to the window and expectorated a gob of electrons onto the glass, and the images *pfft!* into steam.

"I aint no junkie!"

Grateful I'd taken the precaution of wearing a rubber undersuit and wooden shoes, I adjusted the lightning rods on either side of me. "Wally, I never referred to you as a—"

"I aint!" he said, pointing at me, and without any warning his fingers fell off his pointing-hand and hit the floor.

"Ah, H-E-double oil derricks, not again," he said, stooping to pick up his scattered digits with his other hand.

"'Not *again,*' Wally? Are you saying this has happened before?"

He nodded, holding his fingers up against their stumps, spitting electrical fire upon them to weld them back into place.

I got up to pat the chair across from me to get him to sit down when he'd finished with his hand. He didn't budge. "Wally, tell me about your father. Your real father: Jobuseen-Ya."

"Y'mean, you don'believe Festus's foolin? You think I'm tellin the truth?"

"Wally, I *know* you're telling the truth. At least, part of it. Now let's see if together, we can get the rest."

THE ORIGINAL GOLDEN AGE, OR THE AGE OF FOOL'S GOLD?

"My daddy, m'real daddy, was the greatest official on th'entire planet of Argon," said Omnipotent Man after a long, long silence in which the Los Ditkos night began to flow through my bay window like a cola beverage into a crystal decanter.

Wally hardly looked at me, staring instead into the twinkling Bird Island skyline and the neon-metallic phallus of the Tachyon Tower throbbing above it.

"Daddy was a genius," he said eventually. "Knew our whole planet was in danger."

"What type of danger?"

"Oh, all kinds. Aliens, especially. And traitors. Plus, Argon was gonna splode if we didn'keep relieving the planetary pressure of all its excessive energy, which Daddy was a pioneer in removing."

"I see."

"So anyway, he realises one day thet the whole planet's gon implode—"

"Explode?"

"—right, splode, like that very week, an he wants t'warn the public, but the damn gubment says he's jess causin panic is all, an they orders him to shut up or else they gon throw him in jail. So they won't let im say nuthin, he caint do nuthin, except one thing: save me. So he up and puts me in a rocket ship f'Earth."

"You were how old? In Earth years, I mean?"

"I reckon round eight."

"Now, Wally, what about the rest of the family? Your mother, siblings—you had two brothers and a sister—and everyone else in the extended -Ya family—didn't he try to save any of them?"

"Naw, see, he could only spare the one rocket, so he couldn'send any a them. Else he mighta got noticed and got in trouble."

"But if he were going to die with the planet anyway, then wouldn't jail-time be a rather empty threat?"

His forehead furrowed into a farmer's field.

"So why," I probed, "do suppose your father saved you alone, out of your entire family?"

His bright blue eyes blinked onto mine, glittering in the lamplight like two big drops of Windex. "Well, I . . . you know, I never actually . . . I mean, nobody's ever asked me that before."

"Wally, I want to show you something, if I may."

Drawing him over to my desk, I selected some images on my computer while he stood behind me.

"When you resigned, I was very worried about you and your processing of these recent experiences. Because I hoped we'd continue our sessions, I asked Gagarina Girl to search through some of Hawk King's galactic records for me, do some astronomical detective work, if you will. And she's come up with some very interesting results.

"It appears that you've been a bit off regarding the location of Argon, which you'd always said had been *here*," I said, pointing to the screen. "But if we look *here*, we get an entirely different story."

A high-resolution image of an alien world appeared, a Christmas tree of a planet with millions of tiny lights, like fireflies orbiting a foolishly wrapped and rotting Yuletide ham.

"You ... you're sayin ... that's Argon? It's still there? No, that dun't ... now wait, ma'am," he said, breaking into a relieved grin, "the light to take this photograph caint travel faster than the speed of ... of light! Which means this image is from *before* Argon exploded."

"But Wally, Hawk King invented the Khu-Kheperi imaging technology that makes these photographs possible. This is a picture of Argon as it looks today. And this," I said, clicking further, "is a picture of the capital city, what you've always called Nietchion."

I clicked open an image of a giant tower shaped like a man hefting two massive weapons of indeterminate use.

"And this, assuming Gagarina Girl's translation is correct, is the Citadel of Galactic Security. And if we take a closer look," I said clicking again, "on the top floor, in the office on the side facing us, is a man who looks like an older version of you, drinking what looks like a mug of something hot, what with the steam coming off the top, and he's dropping in something and stirring—perhaps an Argonian low-calorie sweetener of some sort, since he's in such good shape. And there, on the desk behind him ... let me bring up the magnification, yes, a name plate, which the translation says means *Jobuseen-Ya, Director of Argonian Security,* and right there on the side of the desk, that's a holograph of what looks like him, a wife, two grown boys, and a girl."

I looked back up over my shoulder.

Before I could see his face, Wally W. Watchtower had turned around; he was trying to muffle the snuffling sounds he was making.

Pulling his expando-cape out of his jacket and tying it around his neck, he began flying slowly around the room at less than walking speed. His cape was drooping sadly at his sides like the jowls of an aged hound dog, tears dropping from his face like that hound dog's melancholic slaver.

The icon trap had imprisoned Wally with even greater power than I had realised, but with a twist: the icon splintering Omnipotent Man's psyche into fragments was made of two persons fused into a single dominating demon of disapproval: Jobuseen-Ya, and Festus Piltdown III.

THE INNER ABANDONED CHILD

"Wally, please—it's better to talk this out."

"Why bother?" he said, flying snail-speed laps around the room. "Argon never was under no threat! You done just proved that! M'daddy jess wanted to get ridda me! Like tyin up a big ol sack fulla kittens an droppin em in a dirty ol creek!"

"Now, Wally," I said, rotating in my chair so I could keep him in sight, "Earth isn't exactly a 'dirty old creek', and your father didn't kill you, now did he? Maybe originally he thought there really *was* a threat."

He turned to look at me. "So why didn'he try an get me back, then? You know what he *did* do, though?"

Distracted, Wally made a low-speed collision with my fig tree, knocking it over. "Aw, pig-snickers," he said, surveying the dirt. "Sorry bout that."

Before I could coax him into sitting with me, Wally was in flight again, but he hadn't made it five yards before he hit the floor like a flying pelican mistaking a black tarmac for a lagoon.

I rushed to help him into a chair. It was like trying to lift a sack of bowling balls. I asked him to tell me about his father.

"That ol' bossy such-an-such!" he choked. "You know what he left me? Th'on'y thing? This here cube," he said, producing a glinting black box no bigger than a sugar cube. "Had it since I was hip-high to a mule, when I was a kid growin up in Mannsfall, Kentucky, and confused as all jolly on accounta I couldn'member anything bout who I was before age eight. But I had this here necklace, see, which Ma and Pa said I was wearin when they found me in th'swamp. An when I got older an walked to An'ar'tica—"

"You *walked* to Antarctica?"

"—yeah, an this here box started tellin me how our planet'd been destroyed an how the box was the sum a m'daddy's intelligence an it was gon guide me throughout m'life in his stead."

He shook the device in his closed hand, next to his ear, as if he were about to shoot craps. "Even has daddy's voice," he said.

He opened his hand, gazed. "But all this durn thing ever did was insult me. 'Karojun-Ya, how can you be so stupid?' an 'Karojun-Ya, you failed again, liver-brains,' an all that kinda guff."

"Do you think . . . that's maybe why you put up with Mr. Piltdown's insults?"

He fixed his eyes on me again.

"Because the whole world calls you a hero, yet you let Festus talk to you like that constantly, as if you're worthless."

"I don'know."

"How did all your father's comments make you feel?"

"I don'*know*."

"Did they make you happy?"

"*I. Don'. Know.*"

"When you swore at Mr. Piltdown and then electro-spat him across the room, do you think in some part of your mind, maybe you were spitting at your father? Was that the saliva of 'You can't hurt me anymore'? Or was it the albumin of a frightened little boy who was angry that his 'daddy' had rejected him?"

He looked down, mumbled, "I'ont know *what* kinda hork it was, ma'am."

"Because saliva—the water of life in your body—"

"Actually it was a beam of electrons, ma'am—"

"But the deeper truth of the saliva *behind* the electricity is what matters, Wally. Look at the rage you released in that single thousand-volt expectoration. You're the most mild-mannered man I've seen in this practice in decades. But then, one remark too many—"

"Yeah," he chuckled grimly. "Fried squirrel. Courtesy of m'omni-gob."

"Exactly. Being rejected by your father like that, believing that you're never good enough . . . do you think that might have something to do with your stunning achievements in anti-success?"

"Well, I mean, I spose that . . . wait, what?"

"Tell me about walking to Antarctica."

THE BLACK BOX OF THE SOUL

"Yeah . . . when I was sixteen. Ma an Pa, well, they's Jehovah's Witnesses, but I didn'know what I b'lieved. I was gettin inna trouble, drankin an messin around an tryin to vote an such. I still didn'know bout m'powers, y'unnerstan. An Ma an Pa, they was always talkin about doomsday—seemed evra time a doomsday come up an didn'happen, they always had another one waitin.

"So I stopped wannin t'listen to em, specially when they wannid me t'go out witnessin, farm-to-farm an door-to-door an such. So they was fightin with me suh'm fierce t'go, an I up and decided to spite em by gettin as far away from em as I could.

"So I started walkin, an I member being s'prised by how far an how fast I could walk without ever gettin hungry. An before I knew it—like, on'y a coupla months'd gone by, an I was at the south end a Chile. And the cold didn'bother me neither, which I never knew before on accounta Kentucky always bein s'hot. An I was jess so fulla spite I had to go th'whole distance, so I decided I'd swim over to An'ar'tica, which wun't the smartest thing to do, I admit, considerin I didn'know bout my powers yet, but I was always a good swimmer an figured why not? So I did. I made it.

"But I musta lost m'necklace with the black cube on it or suh'm, cuz when I came out the water, it was gone. But I looked behind me an all th'penguins an walruses were swimmin away cuz a big black iceberg or suh'm was comin up out th'water like a mountain bein born.

"On'y it wun't no mountain. It had a huge blue doorway glowin like one a them neon signs, an it was willin me to go through it! So I walked on inside an there was all sortsa blinkin machines, like chairs an beds an treadmills—like, like a big ol health-spa from the future or suh'm. An I felt this powerful urge to sit inside one a them chairs, an when I did, suddenly I could feel all kindsa powers surging in me.

"An then I looked up and seen right on top a this pedestal—it's m'black box! Beamin out a ghostly image of m'daddy—that's what it said to me, that it was m'daddy—talkin to me bout how he sent me to Earth to save m'life an so at least I could be a success *some*where."

He sat across from me chewing his lip. "Guess I never really paid attention to how he worded that before."

"Go on."

"Well, I got up outta m'trainin machine to pick up m'box, but I'd become so strong, I accidentally ripped the machine outta th'floor an knocked th'pedestal down an then, well . . . pretty much after that was a blur on accounta th'whole black iceberg commenced t'comin down. An so I flew back home—I could fly now, see?—an all th'while my box-daddy was tellin me I was a complete nimrod, though that wun't th'word he used.

"I got back to Mannsfall, an I went to see m'step-pa an -ma t'tell em all what'd happened an that I fin'ly knew I was adopted, but I still hadn't quite got th'hang a m'powers, so I accidentally burned down half th'town and then when I was trying to use m'frost breath to put out the fire I accidentally shrank th'whole place with some other power I didn'even know I had. Still don'know how I did it, actually . . . so I been workin ever since then to figure out how to unshrank em."

"The whole town just disappeared? And no one noticed?"

"Well, it was a small town to begin with. An the war'd just started. So anyway, I went over into Cloverport, bought me a aquarium, an put the tinier town of Mannsfall inside it."

"And you just left it there?"

"No, I took it with me. It's in my condo, now, right on top the toilet tank, so at least once a month I member to bring in fresh food and water, which I shrank down to their size."

"Are your step-parents still alive inside the aquarium?"

"Yessir. Time seems to've slowed down on accounta the shrankin. Or suh'm . . . don'rightly know, akchully." He chirped up, "I can bring in the tank, if you like, to show ya."

"If you'd like to, Wally. For now, tell me more about what you did after you returned home."

"For a while I did some hero-fying as I was learnin m'powers. That's when I was Omni-Lad. Then the war got worse, an the call went out from Hawk King. I mean, actually from his hawk legion, which was searchin th'whole country lookin for superheroes to help fight the comm'nists—"

"The Nazis."

"—right, an that's when I hooked up with him, Iron Lass, Captain Manifest Destiny, Liberty Belle, Gil Gamoid an th'N-Kid—"

"—actually, Wally," I said, leafing through the heavily redacted contents of the OMNIPOTENT FRAUD folder Mr. Piltdown had couriered to me, "I meant, what did you do when you *weren't* performing superheroics? Tell me about the jobs you held, the friends you had, the kind of life you led in your secret identity."

"Course, y'already know m'secret name, ma'am. An I expect y'already read Jack Zenith's book, since darn near everybody in creation did. So y'know I led a quiet life as a grade school teacher."

"But what about writing, Wally?"

"What about it?"

"You also—as I've learned," I said, flipping through the files, "worked at a small newspaper in Blandton—"

"Now where in tarnation dja'ever hear suh'm so silly?"

"—where you were apparently known as a shy and awkward proof reader named Willis Nesbin. But 'Nesbin' was secretly the writer behind the popular syndicated advice column 'Ask Aunt Edna'. Which means this additional secret identity of yours was actually a two-for-one."

"Who toldj'all that?"

"You even rented an apartment under this Nesbin persona. Your neighbours there describe Nesbin as—I've got it here, quote, *Quiet and polite, but not in that creepy serial-killer way,* end-quote."

"What, doc, you been spyin on me?"

"So you admit it's true."

"No, consarn it! I mean, you been spyin on somebody else but thankin it were me, when in reality—"

"In fact, Wally," I said, taking out a set of photographs from Mr. Piltdown's folder, "you seem to have a great number of secret identities." I held up photos one at a time, each one paper-clipped with relevant news print-outs on its back, and then set them on the coffee table between us.

"Billionaire playboy Ricky R. Bustow . . . pious conservative televangelist Jebedai 'Crawdad' Crocket, ruthless fight promoter Francis 'The Musk Ox' Miller.

"Since your resignation, Wally, no one's heard a peep from any of them."

He stared back at me emptily.

"And earlier today," I continued, "you carved portraits into the frost you made on my window. Portraits of these men, who, despite slight differences in hairstyles, glasses, and so forth, all look remarkably like you."

"Doc, you'd hafta have a sweater th'size a Kentucky t'pull that much wool over th'eyes of th'Merican people. How could I be all those men an still be me?"

"Only someone with powers beyond those of mortal men could do such a thing."

"Well why would I even wanna?"

"How terrified are you of rejection, Wally? Mercilessly esteem-hammered by Festus, rejected by your own father who cast you out of his entire world, a misfit in your adopted hometown, a fraud in the field of superheroics, and no known romantic relationships to speak of? So if you can hide who you really are, and become something which is appealing to enough people—"

"Doc, I'm loved over this whole tadpoled planet! Why should I need any more adulation than I already got?"

"You tell me, Wally. Tell me why it's never enough."

"I never said it wun't! Now you jess quit all this crazy talkin! So *what* if I look like summa them fellas? Jess a coincidence! I'm Wally W. Watchtower, Karojun-Ya, last son of Argon . . . well, okay, maybe not th'last, but—I'm th'invincible Omnipotent Man. That's it, that's all, no more!"

"Wally . . . are you saying . . . are you saying that you actually don't *know* about these other identities?"

"Doc, I jess said—"

"Maybe . . . originally you had yourself in check, this craving of yours for validation, but the more the public fed you, the hungrier you got—as if you had a tapeworm burrowed in your psychemotional gut—and the emptier you felt. So you found something you thought could fill you up. But what you didn't know is how much that very something would fracture you further."

At that moment, I reached beneath the coffee table to produce a leaden grey lockbox no larger than a lunch kit. I opened it and placed it on the coffee table between us.

Wally blinked, his nostrils flaring, his lips crimping inside his mouth.

The stench of ozone wafted from the interior of the grey box, which glowed electric blue.

"Obtained courtesy of the F*O*O*J laboratories," I said. "Fifty-five grams of powdered argonium."

"I'd reckon it," he said after a taut twenty seconds, his eyes nailed onto the box, "more like fifty-four."

SUPERVILLAINS ARE NEVER AN EXCUSE, ONLY A REASON

I reached to close the box. Wally jerked nearly all the way out of his chair before he looked at me and stopped himself; his eyes locked onto the box, and then back to me. Settling himself down, Wally flitted his face as if the iconic masks of Comedy and Tragedy were battling upon it for supremacy.

I waited with the powdered argonium open and available in front of him, counting out the seconds and then the minutes on the clock beyond his shoulder.

All the while, Wally's face and body clicked and contorted through a chaos of ticks and spasms.

Finally, his lower lip trembling, he almost begged me. "Doc . . . y'know—*please*—"

"I will help you," I whispered. "Wally, did you know that one of the effects of argonium is personality fragmentation?"

His eyes flickered over me, over the photos arranged before him, over to the window where his frost portraits no longer were.

He sniffed, nodded, defeated.

"And I can't help but wonder whether it might also induce delimbification in Argonians. How long has argonium use been affecting your work?"

"I'ont thank it affected m'work, ma'am," he growled. "I always showed up, I always—"

"Was that why the attack on the Allied ships, and saving the U-Boat?"

"Naw, naw, naw—back before the war I aint even ever heard about no argonium. That was jess a mistake is all."

"So when did you first begin using—"

"Rex Mirthless," he said.

"The Vocabularian?"

"One an th'same," he said, drawing in a long, ragged breath. "M'first real super-opponent . . . a true arch-villain. We'd been havin these off-an-on melees for about a decade already, him always managing to slip away, like a coon dipped in bacon grease. Now Rex, he were this snootified, citified, sissified N'Englander. Wore a, whaddayacall them thangs—a *cravatte*, c'n you b'lieve it? Wellsir, this was back in fifty-eight, an he were threatnin to take control a th'energy market, introduce some sorta sun-powered thang. It woulda destroyed th'whole economy. So I stormed his fortress—he had this base inside a volcano, an he was wearin one a them Beatles-type jackets, on'y it were white—"

"A Nehru?"

"—right, a Nero. He was th'first guy to do that, by th'way, th'whole volcana an white jacket dealy. Evr'body after that was jess copyin im. So he tricked me, knocked me out with some kinda cosmic beam, an then when I woke up he started goin inna all his plans, splainin em to me like he's braggin. I figured, heck, let em talk, right? Every second he gave me was time to plan an escape.

"But what I didn'know was that his cosmic ray-beam couldn'kill me physically, but he *could* kill me brain-wise, jess by *talkin*. I mean, he was planning to bore me to death, *literally*. He had some sorta thing funnellin his gol-dang voice straight inside m'brain, wipin out m'memories, makin me all crazified . . . an th'whole time, like, days, he was standin in fronta me takin little sniffs offa his flouncy sleeve collars, from some kinda blue powder he kept puttin on there from his snuff box."

Wally's eyes were far away, slipping from the window to me to the box.

"So he forced you to snort argonium?"

"Naw. Rex'd always been real jealous of me, see? Fraid I was more manly'n him, which is why he tried to neutralise m'powers." He chewed his lip, pausing. "So I told him, now thet your machines done wiped out m'omni-powers, whyonchu an me duke it out, mano-a-mano? And zap, for the first time in three days he'd shut his yap, and jess like that he had me outta his Zero-Chair or whatever it was."

"So what was it like, for the first time in your career, to have to fight a villain without being able to use your powers?"

"Well actually, I still had em, see? Rex thought his cosmic beam's effects were permn'nent, but no sir, once he got me outta the chair, I jess ripped his arms and legs off."

"I see. So how did you save him? Cauterise his wounds with your omni-breath?"

"Naw. He bled to death pretty fast after being de-legged. But he'd dropped his snuff box. Now, you gotta unnerstan—I hadn't slept or eaten or had anything to drink in three days, an thet blue powder, wellsir, it smelled powerful nice . . . like wakin up and goin t'sleep at the same time."

His eyes were super-glued onto the strongbox, blinking so rapidly I almost didn't notice, while his nostrils repeatedly flared and his fingers clenched and strummed like white tarantulas undergoing seizures.

"I asked you before how self-medicating with argonium has been affecting your work."

He glared at me. "I'ont *know!*"

"Has anyone ever said anything to you about it?"

"Maybe . . . maybe Hawk King, once or twice . . . an, well, Ir'n Lass . . . an Gil Gamoid fore him an th'N-Kid up an went ker-nuttified an hadda be locked up on Asteroid Zed . . . ."

"So your colleagues, your oldest friends . . . how does it feel, knowing that they knew and some still know about this weakness of yours?"

Omnipotent Man leaned forward, gripping his skull like it was a fortune cookie he was about to rip open.

"Wally . . . do you want to be able to wake up and go to sleep on your own, without any blue crystal to help you do it? Do you want to be yourself, and not billionaire Bustow, Reverend Crocket, 'Musk Ox' Miller, Willis Nesbin, or Aunt Edna? But just plain old Wally? I mean, omnipotent *new* Wally?"

As if trying to drown out my voice, he was muttering to himself, rocking and rocking and rocking in his chair.

"Wally! Listen to me! Do you want your life back?"

On and on he rocked and muttered.

Finally I shouted, "Answer me, Wally! Do you want to be one sane man instead of a half-dozen fractured ones?"

And then I put a hand on his shoulder, and both his arms slipped out of their sleeves and rolled across the floor. He keeled forward face-first, his left leg ejecting from his pants like a slippery wiener squeezed out of a bun. What remained of contiguous Wally was sprawled out before me like a giant flesh tennis racket.

"Wally, goodness, let me help you!" I said while struggling to turn him face up. I scrambled for his limbs; he moaned awfully. Opening his jacket,

I ripped open his dress shirt and attempted to reconnect his detached right arm to its shoulder stump.

What I saw shocked me: the wound was no bloodier or bonier than a sliced-open tube of liverwurst, as if Argonian flesh were all undifferentiated tissue. The arm wouldn't take. "Wally, can you try welding your arm back on, like you did with your fingers?"

Keening, he tried spitting out an electron burst, but all he could manage was the sparks that a spent lighter produces. He wailed, "I'm all out, Doc!"

Helping him to be as comfortable as I could manage, I had my secretary Ms. Olsen retrieve the containment suit I'd employed during my treatment of the Detached Man, whose body began crumbling into pyramids, cubes, and dodecahedrons without his conscious command. After opening the armour, Ms. Olsen and I hefted Wally and his parts inside it and sealed it shut, tightening the connections with everything in place but the boots and neck collar.

Just as I was calibrating the penultimate settings, I heard the telephone ringing in the other room. After running to answer it, Ms. Olsen informed me that the call was urgent. Since Wally and I'd already been interrupted, I pressed the Erect button on the containment suit so Wally could at least stand while I took the call. There was no point leaving the room for privacy given Wally's omni-hearing—assuming he still possessed it.

"Miss Brain," said a voice as raw as freshly killed deer, "it's Festus Piltdown."

Ordinarily I would have avoided using Mr. Piltdown's given name, but taking into account the direness of his tone and the fact that he was calling past eleven o'clock at night, I asked, "Festus, what is it?"

"It's Hnossi," he finally begrudged. "She, she wants you. To talk to you."

"Why? What's wrong?"

"Apparently . . . the, the immortal Iron Lass," he said, clearing his throat, "is dying."

I heard and felt the clap of thunder. I spun, finding Wally back on the floor like a tipped mannequin, his feet detached and upright a yard away from him as if his legs had simply stepped out of them.

What will it mean for your life, and for your view of yourself, if the glory days never return?

> **Omnipotent Man:** "For the first time I can remember . . . I'm totally afraid."

IT'S ALWAYS DARKEST BEFORE THE DAWN (OR WHEN YOU'RE BLIND OR DEAD)

One of life's greatest paradoxes is that only when we see ourselves at our most naked, weak, foolish, ugly, disappointing, cowardly, broken, repulsive, selfish, and stupid, can we really appreciate just how special we are. For Wally to fill up the tank of personal re-integration, he was going to have to pull into the filling station of exhaustive self-assessment. And so will you.

Get writing tools and a quiet space, and block off enough time to write out all the occasions in your life in which you've been weak, foolish, ugly, disappointing, cowardly, broken, repulsive, selfish, and/or stupid. A day should be enough. Don't hold back. Total honesty is absolutely necessary.

When you're done, ask yourself the following questions:

1. *Who else other than I am to blame for what I've done?*
2. *How did I personally choose to be a victim of myself?*
3. *How did I enable myself to become a perpetrator against myself and everything I hold dear?*
4. *How many of the psychemotional barnacles attached to the ship of my consciousness am I willing to burn off in order to sail freely across the ocean of well-adjustedness? And why am I too cowardly to burn them all off at once and be done with it? Is it because I'm confusing the barnacles for the ship?*

As you're about to see, the challenge to Iron Lass's immortality would threaten not only her own survival, but Wally's recovery . . . and Festus Piltdown's soul.

CHAPTER EIGHT

Unrequited Hate

THE ROOTS BENEATH THE TREE

WEDNESDAY, JULY 5, 9:16 A.M.

I sat upon the immaculate silver sofa in the immaculate bronze room across from immaculate ivory suit and golden cravatte inhabited by the slightly maculate Festus Piltdown III. His hair was greyer than usual, and somewhat unkempt; the bags beneath his eyes were heavy enough to be considered luggage.

Sitting there in front of me, roiling with his usual stew of emotions, plus a few choice new ones, he had no inkling of the reconnection—or confrontation—I'd already set in motion, to bring him the peace he so desperately needed from a man he considered an enemy.

Yet the desperation and fragility Festus felt at that moment in his life demanded that I act, in secrecy, to bring to him a one-man intervention.

While Festus and I watched highlights from the 8:30 A.M. Fortress of Freedom press conference on the wall screen, his aged manservant placed a cappuccino on the marble coffee table beside me before disappearing.

> **NBC Reporter:** "—believe the destruction of Asteroid Zed to be in any way connected with the death of Hawk King?"
> **X-Man:** "I can't confirm that, no. Not yet, anyway."
> **CBS Reporter:** "There are reports that Iron Lass is dying from unnamed causes, possibly connected with the orbital prison disaster. Can you comment?"

X-Man: "That's true—there *are* reports."

CBS Reporter: "Yes, but, but what about them? Are they true? Is her condition connected with the bombing of Zed or the death of Hawk King?"

X-Man: "I can neither confirm nor deny that at this time."

ABC Reporter: "Are you investigating Iron Lass's condition to see if there is a connection?"

X-Man: " . . . All I can say is, and I'm not saying she even has a 'condition,' but I will follow to the ends of this solar system any lead which points to a threat to the F*O*O*J, to this country, or to our planet—"

PNN Reporter: "Following the destruction of Asteroid Zed, a Knight-Ridder poll put you fifty-five percentage points ahead of the Flying Squirrel for Director of Operations. How do you respond to those who say you're exploiting the death of Hawk King, the resignation of Omnipotent Man, and allegations about Iron Lass's health to advance your own personal political aspirations?"

X-Man: "My—! Look here! My only aspi*rations* . . . are truth and justice! And let truth and justice prevail though the heavens fall!"

"Can you believe that hyperactive hypocrite?" snapped the Flying Squirrel, and then, as the image switched, he moaned, "Oh, not this again!"

Onscreen rolled the by-then infamous funereal footage of Festus punching Kareem and Kareem hitting him back, with the anchor's voice-over about X-Man's "meteoric rise."

"Meteors *never* rise, you sub-cretinous discombobulators! They only fall, crash, and burn out!"

At that moment, Festus's butler, Mr. Savant, so ancient and withered he might conceivably have been an unbandaged mummy, returned to say, "Madame is ready to receive visitors now, Lord Piltdown."

Noticing my reaction to his title, Festus shrugged and said, "I acquired a lordship a few years back. Thatcher owed me for all the good press. Come on."

While Mr. Savant led us on the motorised pedway, we winded our way through the labyrinthine corridors of Festus's legendary crime-fighting headquarters, the Squirrel Tree. Every hallway was actually the interior of one of the Tree's "branches," and each chamber the interior of a giant "leaf." Vast, hydrogen-powered magnetic counter-gravity kept the entire assembly, minus the trunk, suspended above ground. With the facility's "smart garage," Trashbots®, Lawnbots®, air traffic dominance and D.E.T.H.Scan security system coordinated by the SquirrelBrain 9000X, the Squirrel Tree made Bill Gates' "smart house" seem like a Fisher-Price playset.

Passing through the cavernous Vehicle Hollow containing the Squirrel Copter, Squirrel Sub, and Squirrel N-ICBMs, and a fabulous five-story-tall replica of a one-million dollar bill, we finally entered the Medical Hollow. Mr. Savant led us to the room, pulled back the curtain, and stood aside.

From her bed, Hnossi Icegaard stared up at us.

The whites of her eyes were like filthy old pennies. Her face and neck were splotched ashen red and brown. In the worst sections, her skin was flaking off like the scales of a dead rattlesnake dropped in a campfire.

"Rust poisoning," muttered Festus. "Advanced."

"*Ja*," rasped Hnossi, chuckling out of a bravura smirk. "But you shudt get a look at ze *uzzer* guy."

"When the cells opened on Asteroid Zed," explained Festus, "the Dessicator attacked her, that god-damned bastard."

"He dit not suffer long—" she said, only to pitch forward in a hacking fit, grating out a sound like someone repeatedly hitting the ignition on a running car. Finally she slowed, cleared her throat, and finished her sentence: " . . . vizzout his torso."

I approached her, gingerly touched her wrist. It felt like phylo pastry. I told her Festus had passed on her wish to see me.

Mr. Savant left the room. Festus sat in a corner chair.

"*Ja, Doktor*. I am a varrior deity. Ein Aesir gott. My people . . . haff no Apollo, no Sos," she said, I believe referring to Thoth and by extension all deities of science and medicine. "Unt Festus's human doktors, for all zeir learnink, cannot heal vun uff us. So I am now facink my own personal *Götterdämmerung*. My own private tvilight uff ze gotts.

"Unt I haff been sinkink...about our sessions. About your qvestioning uff my, my relationships . . . vis my children. Unt now zat apparently . . . zere is no more time . . . I vant you to broker—"

Hnossi snapped forward and back, exploding her coughs like a Brinks van backfiring repeatedly. Festus leapt from his chair, yelled into his wrist for the doctor, then grabbed Hnossi's hand and roughly rubbed her neck and back to loosen her potentially lethal congestion. A doctor and nurse appeared, swept us out, and drew back the curtain.

Festus and I stood in the hallway not looking at each other.

Silence sandpapered a minute off the clock.

With his gaze nailed to his toes, the battle-hardened billionaire stooped before me, his six-foot-four frame fragile, faltering.

"She beat every villain on the planet," he whispered, then captured and released a long, hissing breath. "She'll beat this, too."

I stifled my professional duty to ask him *And what if she doesn't?* long enough for Festus to say, "And then, then, then that bastard . . . Warmaster Set . . . he'll pay for this."

"You're sure he's the one responsible?"

He glared at me. "*Everyone* responsible will pay."

The withered Mr. Savant appeared once more. "Your . . . other guest . . . has arrived, Lord Piltdown."

"My what? I wasn't scheduled for any—"

"Master Festus," said the old man, his watery eyes trembling with sympathy, "it's Master Tran."

Festus straightened up. His spine crackled audibly. He swivelled his face to level his blast furnace gaze upon me.

"Now why in God's good hell, Eva," he growled, "would I be visited this morning . . . for the first time in fifteen years, by my ungrateful . . . insubordinate . . . back-stabbing . . . renegade of an ex-protégé, Chip Monk?"

SIDE-KICKED: PRODIGAL PUNISHMENT

Beneath the grandiose high ceiling of the Allen Dulles Room, Tran stood by the mantle examining a framed, sepia photograph of a little boy wearing a suit-and-tie and fire helmet and wiping away his tears. He turned his forty-five-calibre eyes on Festus as we entered.

"Hard to believe you were ever this young," said Tran to his former alpha-hero, putting the photo back on the mantle. "Or that you ever cried. For anyone."

"So," said Festus, his colossal frame regaining its lethal rigidity. His arms crossed his chest like battering rams. "You've returned after all these years just to abuse me, then? My, how your imagination has failed during your supplicant service to that Marxist menace."

Tran, although elegant in his cream-coloured suit, was more obviously his fifty years in the full light of the drawing room than he'd appeared in the shadows of the Stun-Glas restaurant Dark Star. Wince-lines crinkled the amber skin around his eyes; while he still had a swimmer's build, his movements were deliberate, as if he were consciously confronting arthritic agony. Given Festus's unusually youthful appearance, Tran appeared even older than his former mentor.

"I'm not here to abuse anyone," said Tran at last. "I'll leave the abuse to experts like you."

"This is pointless, Miss Brain! What possible good did you think would be produced by this pathetic pup's point-blank petulance?"

"I'd hoped, Festus, to see you finally able to aim the extinguisher of healing upon the kitchen grease fire of your relationship with Tran. And you can only do that when the sous-chef of your most important recipes—"

"I get it, all right?"

"All right, then. Let's begin."

I took a seat, gestured for both men to sit facing each other. Neither did.

"Both of you men are clearly suffering," I said anyway. "You were once the most celebrated superhero partnership on the planet. For the entire 1960s, no duo got more magazine covers than you two. You were the model. You took down Pauli the Living Mafia, Black Mamba, the Iron Eunuch, the Monitor Lizard, Standing Buffalo . . . the list goes on.

"And then the 1970s came, and slowly news dimmed of your brave biumvirate, and before long all your 'busts' were solo efforts. And then 1980 came and you were finished. Kaput. No more. The media—"

"The *media!*" snapped Festus. "Lying, distemperous pack dogs! Rabid, mangy curs with more hours spent tongue-bathing their own scrota than investigating the truth!"

"Spoken like the true media mogul of PNN *et al* that you are."

"You haven't lost a nanogram of your snide superciliousness, boy."

"And you haven't gained an iota of introspection, *milord.*"

"Gentlemen, please. As I was saying, the media implied that you two—"

"I don't need to hear from you what those filthy—"

"—were lovers."

Silence. And glaring.

"And," I continued, "after your four-year disappearance and resurfacing to work at Human Citizen, Tran, that your falling out was the result of Festus's having discovered that you were having an affair with Jack Zenith."

More silence. And more glaring.

"Well?" I finally prodded my way into their staring match. "To what degree were those claims true?"

Further silence.

I leaned towards the younger of the two men. "Tran?"

"Jack Zenith is a brilliant, dedicated man," said Tran, sculpting the air with his balletic hands, hands so deceptively delicate-looking one expected to see a cigarillo dangling smoulderingly between their slender fingers. "And he is beyond question the finest American of this century—"

"*Bah!*" said Festus, making him the first human being I'd ever heard use that interjection. But Tran batted not so much as an eyelid at the usage.

"—but Jack isn't gay, Doctor. Not that he's straight, either. He's just . . . he's *just.* In a decade of working with him, I haven't seen him so much as smirk a randy thought towards man, woman, animal, or alien. All he does is write, organise, eat tabouli, and sue."

"You haven't answered my question, Tran. Why did you two split up?"

"I was ten years old when . . . when Lord Piltdown 'adopted' me from a South Vietnamese orphanage. Took me into his home. And trained me in his cult—"

"'Cult!'"

"—his cult of hero-worship. Him worshipping Hawk King, and me expected to worship him. And, god help me . . .

"I *did,* Doctor. If that isn't the most sickening truth I could ever divulge. *Everything about him.* I identified with my master more than my master identified with himself. Even used his Squirrel Erasing Spray to try to whiten my skin, if you can believe it. It just rotted off all my body hair and left me with first degree burns from brows to balls. I was fourteen when I did that. And all to become like this man. Did he ever tell you his secret origin?"

"No. But I'm familiar with the story."

"The *offi*cial story, I'm sure. I only heard it, what, a thousand times … a month? How about the *real* story?"

Tran produced the very cigarillo I'd imagined he would smoke, made a show of lighting it, and blew decorative smoke-trails and twirls in between holding his cigarillo upwards as if balancing an invisible plate upon its tip. He seemed to be waiting for Festus to fight back.

"Yes, the *real* story," he finally said, lacking any verbalisation from Festus. He began pacing and smoking. "How in 1942 when he was only eighteen, his blue-blood bee-baron father, Fountroy Prescott Piltdown V, sicced Hinkleton leg-breakers on the Okie, Mexican, and black migrant labourers trying to organise on his bee fields? How a young public interest lawyer led a class-action lawsuit against Fountroy to get redress for these men, some of whom were stung into hospitalisation after the Hinkletons fed poppies and coca blossoms to the bees? How this same public interest attorney investigated Fountroy and discovered he was selling honey by the megaton to the Nazis?"

"This attorney was Jack Zenith?"

"*Yes*, Jack Zenith! By the time Fountroy's collaboration made the cover story of *The Wall Street Journal* he was so mortified he played a round of 'PGA roulette.'"

"What's that?"

"Golf in a mine field. Grenades instead of balls. Daddy Piltdown didn't make it to the first green."

I looked over to Festus, half expecting to see steam shooting from his ears, but he was as silent as his heroic namesake, perched and waiting for the precise moment to strike with deadly, nut-gnawing accuracy.

"So orphan, heir, and faux-Libertarian Festus, suckled in the pouch of luxury, swears unholy goddamned vengeance against Zenith and the wretched of the earth he represents. I must've heard him ten million times on the poor: Parasites, leeches, tapeworms, foreskin-fleas … as if the *poor* had killed his father, rather than his own greed and Nazi-trading treason!"

Once again, I looked towards Festus expecting an explosion. Yet he offered nothing but his cold blue eyes glinting like sapphire ice picks.

"So what does he do with his daddy gone and the war on, you ask?" asked Tran, pacing, smoking and gesticulating. "He retreats to his family's Floridian properties in the swamps, a southern manor on a not-so-former plantation. All by himself in the spooky bayou, except for an army of butlers, maids and indentured lick-spittles.

"So during a moonless midnight of the autumn equinox, while he was reading Nietzsche or Blumenbach or de Molay, a *Glaucomys sabrinus*—a northern hemispheric flying squirrel—plowed right through the twenty-foot high bay window and showered him with glass, bloody fur, and squirrel musk. Making the young Master Festus soil his silks, I'm sure."

"Your mawkish, mocking attempts to provoke me, Tran," whispered Festus, "will be fruitless. But after you're finished ripping into me with your Zenith-certified rib-spreader, I'd suggest you re-read *Lear*, Act One, Scene Four, for some self-description."

"And I'd suggest you remember, Lord Piltdown," said Tran, "that even while ranting about serpent's teeth, Lear was not only a foolish, bad, and stupid king—he was loopier than a snake in a garden hose."

Neither man talked until I asked Tran about the squirrel collision with the window.

"Yes," said Tran, "that, apparently, is when the light goes on over young F.P.'s noggin regarding the power of the flying squirrel to instill terror in the reptilian brain, the 'dominant portion,' he said, of 'your typical urban phrenological reprobate.'

"And he also told me, as I recall, that he identified with squirrels because they're 'so productive . . . they collects nuts and store them while lazy animals freeze to death, as befits their miserable existences.'

"Somehow he never bothered to notice the obvious: that the trees are the ones making the nuts, and all the squirrel does is take them. Parasitic, not productive. Like his family."

THE TRUTH ABOUT
SQUIRRELS AND CHIP MONKS

Tran's tirade, unsolicited, uninterrupted, and unanswered, proceeded for several minutes. And whereas I'd assumed Festus had been lying in wait for the perfect opportunity to destroy his former apprentice, I soon lost that certainty. The elder man, who'd finally sat down, looked less like the poised hunter than the felled hunted, like an agèd hound dog on its side breathing shallowly and awaiting the ripping teeth of rats.

Then Tran shifted to a new topic: hypocrisy. Tran said that Festus had spent years of their time together exhaustively denouncing Wally W. Watchtower's argonium addiction. But the seventy-year-old Festus had the body and looks of an athletic forty-five-year-old for a reason no one was ever intended to know.

"He's," said Tran, shaking his cigarillo at his ex-mentor, "been riding on his argonium high-horse like English royalty on a fox hunt, when he's a god-damned junkie *himse-e-e-elf!*" He elongated the word as if he were kissing it. "Addicted to 'G.I. juice,' Doctor. Ever heard of it?"

"That's . . . Hyper-regenerative Growth Hormone?"

"HGH, the one and only. The steroid of the long-underwear world. And ten thousand times more expensive." Tran blew an *O*, then shredded it with a spear of smoke. "The army stopped using HGH after Lance Lanternman was the only G.I. to survive the trials—"

"That was Captain Manifest Destiny?"

"Yes, yes, Cap. Another addict, thanks to the army. Took HGH until his death in '56, when, according to the newspapers of the time and the history books of today, the Iron Kross killed him. But you can thank Piltdown Propaganda News for that. Why don't you tell her, Lord Piltdown? Tell her!"

After ten seconds burnt away, Tran answered for him.

"The Iron Kross," he said, tracing the air with his figure-skating hands and jerking agitated strides across what must have been the largest Persian rug anywhere in the world, "was already dead a year when he supposedly assassinated Captain Manifest Destiny! He'd died in Argentina, on the F*O*O*J's own secret-ops payroll!

"Yes, he hadn't even lived long enough to finish crushing the Arbenz Avengers in Guatemala, the very project the F*O*O*J had commissioned him to do! But thank heaven the Iron Kross's body could be journalistically exhumed and resuscitated long enough to frame him for an assassination . . . so that nobody would ever know the Captain had died a needle-plunger. Nobody except for the 'world's greatest detective,' of course, who found the corpse.

"Don't believe me, Doctor? I read the sealed medical report in the Squirrel files myself—oh, trust me, he's got secret files on everyone, including you, I'm sure, better than the FBI, SWORD, and the Church of Spyontology all rolled together. But the pathologist, yes, the pathologist at Fort Detrick who autopsied Cap said he was so deformed by tumours he looked more like a potato patch than a man. His wife'd had nothing but miscarriages—something else you'd never've read in any newspaper.

"Now, the *human* reaction to this is to want to expose the government for what they did to the man and get compensation for his wife. That's what a *real* man, a man like Jack Zenith, would do. And it's also what a self-proclaimed 'enemy of Big Government' should want to do.

"But not the delightful 'Lord' Piltdown, no! He took one look at the scene, found the drugs, figured out what they were for, arranged the cover-up, and began injecting every day for the rest of his life since that night! Go ahead, Doctor—swab his mouth. Get a blood sample. Hell, take his cappuccino cup to a lab! That was his little joke, you know—he called it 'G.I. joe' when he put it in his coffee! This man—"

"Tran, I'd like to ask Festus—"

"Look at him sitting there! He doesn't even de*ny* it!"

"Tran, just a moment, please!" I said. The ex-apprentice stopped rigidly in mid-step and half-gesture, like a live shrimp flash-fried.

"Festus, I have to ask you—I've seen you emit devastating verbal attacks against anyone who even so much as raised an eyebrow in a manner you considered challenging. But you've just allowed Tran to upbraid you almost without interruption for ten minutes. Please . . . share with me what you're processing right now—verbally integrate it. Own your feelings!"

Festus let out a long, low sigh, like a zeppelin deflating from a penknife's puncture wound.

"He," said Festus, "was an orphan."

I wait. Finally I said, "Go on."

"Like me."

"Yes."

"I took him in. Gave him a home. Treated him like a son—"

"'Like a son?'" spat Tran before shutting up again, I initially assumed because of my cautioning glance.

But then I saw the look in Festus's face.

"I never . . . never—." He swallowed heavily. "Do you know what it feels like to have people write appalling, sickening lies about you, Eva? I've endured such filth being sprayed on my family's name ever since I was a child. I knew what it was like to be alone, vulnerable, despised. My own mother died when I was a boy, and my father never remarried. I found this child, afraid and alone, a refugee from a travelling Vietnamese circus. I took care of him. Trained him. Taught him everything I knew.

"Loved him."

Tran's eyes opened so wide they looked as if they'd fall out.

"Tran," I asked, "you look . . . as if you've never heard Festus say those words."

The former sidekick was frozen. He'd trapped his flapping, fluttering hands inside their opposite armpits. His cigarillo dangled limply from his lips. Not a word slithered between them.

Festus continued, "And so when those scandal-mongering filth-rags accused me of, of 'touching him' because of some anti-academic 'repressed memory' idiocy in that 'abuse-recovery' necronomicon called *The Courage to Fly*—mythology packaged as science!—I sued every one of those libelling lycanthropes into an early grave.

"But it was too late, Eva. To this day, go ahead—look in any book, any article, any 'web page' on my career or on the F*O*O*J. All of them cite that toxic spew, even though there's not a syllable of supporting evidence. Because the controversy itself became news. Save a country, save a world, save a child—it doesn't matter. You don't need proof or even evidence to burn down a man's soul. All you need is accusation.

"So to answer your question at last, Eva, to answer the world's question at last, my . . . association with this young man didn't end because *I* made homosexual advances upon *him*."

Tran was turned to face out the window. His eyes were closed. He sniffed continually as if trying to read the flowers on the Piltdown estates with his nose.

"So, Festus . . . you're saying—"

"I'm *saying*, Eva, that as much as I tried to help this boy . . . there were things he wanted that I couldn't give him. And maybe if I'd . . . if I'd done a better job . . . he wouldn't've *wanted* them—"

"*Stop* it, Festus," choked Tran.

"I'm just trying to tell you that it's not your—"

"Stop it! Just don't—"

"Lord Piltdown," wheezed Mr. Savant, shuffling his way inside the vast room. With obvious agitation he said, "Ever so sorry for the interruption, sir, but a third guest has arrived—"

"Another one? Eva! What baffle-gambit are you trying to pull?"

"Festus, I didn't—"

"No, sir, it's a Mister Zenith, sir—"

A lanky, soil-and-ash haired septuagenarian marched in behind Festus's centenarian butler. Opening his jacket, he revealed a chest strapped full with explosives, like a smokehouse wall of dynamite. And it wasn't bad dentures distending his mouth, but a detonator clamped between his teeth. I noted with a certain detachment two things: my second brush with explosives in forty-eight hours, and the complete relaxation of my sphincter muscles.

"Jack!" yelled Tran. "My god, what are you *doing?*"

"Zenith!" yelled Festus. "Have you completely fallen off your bean?"

"Gmph-KWUH!" shout-mumbled Zenith. *"Wruh-NNMMR!"*

With deadly acrobatic fluidity, seventy-year old Festus vaulted from his chair, reached inside his jacket, and hurled something at Jack Zenith before he landed and rolled towards the wall to smack a hidden panel. Whatever he'd thrown at Zenith erupted into a cumulus cloud of something like shaving foam which apparently hardened on contact, immobilising Zenith.

"Out, *now!*" yelled Festus, grabbing Tran, Mr. Savant, and me and launching all of us through the opening of the retracting window. The four of us spun plummeting towards death on the Zen garden boulders five stories below, when at the last moment nets shot out from tree-mounted launchers to break our fall—

—and above us, the Squirrel Tree drawing room from which we'd just escaped erupted into orange, flaming death and raining, burning rubble.

COLLATERAL DAMNATION

"Security!" yelled Festus into his wrist, jumping up. "Get to the Medical Hollow now. Status on the patient!"

Within seconds, a battalion of gliding, cybernetic Squirrelbots descended to secure the area and protect us while flame-defense mechanisms choked the inferno above. Less than a minute later, Festus's human security guards had scrambled to our location, providing first aid for Mr. Savant and taking me inside for a change of clothes from the extensively stocked manor.

I emerged within minutes to find Tran sitting at the stone enclosure base of the smoking remains of a massive topiary squirrel. He was an agony to behold, his body shaking in utter silent sobs.

I put my hand on his shoulder. He went rigid. And then, in the random association grief begets, said, "We just . . . we just lost the only man alive . . . who's fit to be President of the United States." He wetly sniffed back mucous. "Not that he'd ever've been even . . . allowed to debate . . . ."

Across the grounds, Festus was loudly excreting abuse into his wrist comm.

" . . . I don't care, Doctor! You god-damned get her whatever she wants or I'll have you shipped to the Congo to spend the rest of your career harvesting pygmy organs, you understand?"

Absorbed as he was, Festus hadn't even noticed the arrival of an unlikely partnership: the X-Man and the Brotherfly, there to investigate the near-assassination. Kareem was heading towards Tran, so I intercepted him and explained that he needed to allow the former Chip Monk time to process his psychemotional state.

"Of course, Doc," whispered Kareem. "Poor freaking guy. To finally have replaced *that*," he chin-wagged towards the invective-lobbing Festus, "as your 'father' with someone as great as Zenith, and then only to lose him, too."

He shook his head after another outburst from the lord of the manor. "Look at that—I mean, I've seen him flip out on people for bringing the wrong shade of orange juice," he said, "but thousands of people've been trying to assassinate him for decades. Why's this attempt got him so spooked now? Does he think this was the work of Menton or Warmaster Set?"

I explained to him Festus's concern over how Hnossi Icegaard might be reacting to the sounds of the explosion.

The X-Man surveyed the elder hero. "Who woulda thought?"

"What do you mean?"

"That he actually could give a demi-damn about anyone other than himself. Hm. If I didn't know better—"

"Good god," groaned Festus, no longer speaking into his wrist and having finally fixated on Kareem and André. "Dinosaurs, buffalo, the dodo . . . and merit-based hiring. All truly extinct." Then he shuffled off to examine the burnt remains of a narcissus flowerbed.

"I'm a bit surprised," I told Kareem, forestalling the inevitable fight, "to see you and André working together."

"Call came in. We were both at the top of the duty roster. Anyway, Doc, what hap—"

"Oh, *bzzzt*, Squirrel-dawg! Yo house is da *bomb!*" André howled laughter at his own repartee. He sang, *"The roof! The roof! The roof-is-on FI-YAH!"* Then, shifting into a Joe Friday voice, he said, "What happened here, ma'am? Just the facts."

"I'm the Primary, here!" snapped Kareem. "Why don't you buckdance on over there and try not to contaminate the crime scene?"

"'I'm the Primary!'" mocked André, flying up to examine the smouldering drawing-room charcoaling out the midday sun. "Looks like the HNIC got a big ol stick up his Primary ass."

I asked Kareem to explain yet another F*O*O*J acronym. "HNIC," he said dryly, "means Head Nigger In Charge."

Kareem said into his wrist comm, "André, locate the butler and find out whatever you can about when Zenith pulled out the detonator, his state of mind, whatever." He clicked off just as Tran walked up, without waiting for André to respond. After the former Chip Monk had composed himself enough for the two of us to brief Kareem, Festus strode up and said, "They actually put you on this, Edgerton? Investigating a bombing at my house? Isn't that a conflict of interest?"

Kareem chuckled, apparently enjoying the sight of Festus's distress. "Look, Fasces. You gonna obstruct the investigation, or are you gonna be helpful for a change?"

"Just don't fuck this up. Do you think you can handle that? This is my home, for god's sake. My headquarters!"

Kareem closed his eyes, breathed in deeply, and enunciated the word *kheperi*. Around us, a hundred or more glistening black beetles—from the size of my fingernail to the size of my palm—shadowed into existence. For a few seconds they all crawled about and tested their wings with a sound like an orchestral string section warming up. Then up and off they flew, half of them zipping across the Zen garden and grounds, the others flitting into the interiors of the Squirrel Tree.

"The forensics are covered, Pilty. Now I've got some questions for you."

Looking aghast at the insectoid investigators, Festus said, "Questions about that ACLU anarchist who tried to assassinate me, I hope!"

"No, but about Jack Zenith," said Kareem, completely straight. "About why a distinguished lawyer and civil libertarian would suddenly transmute into a suicide bomber."

For several minutes Kareem drilled into Festus, demanding to know precisely what happened and what if any recent interventions Human Citizen had taken against the Piltdown Group, or vice-versa. Throughout Festus's response, the X-Man dug into him repeatedly with one of Zenith's most persistently devastating charges: that the Flying Squirrel had pushed the F*O*O*J into starting the *Götterdämmerung*, and then into prolonging it, because Piltdyne Defensive was its sole supplier of arms, exoskeletons, vehicles, and materiel throughout the war, leaving the American taxpayer footing the bill for the F*O*O*J's multibillion dollar appropriations budget. Even the mid-1980s retrofit of Asteroid Zed was a Piltdyne project, "when according to Zenith," said Kareem, "two dozen other contractors could have done this stuff for a tenth of the price. Or less. C'mon, fifty-thousand dollar shower curtains? A half-million dollar bidet? Who's gonna use a bidet on Asteroid Zed?"

"I made regular trips up there to supervise reconstruction, Edgerton, and those of us on the *winning* side of evolution care about hygiene matters. I wouldn't expect you to understand."

Before Kareem could counter him, Festus's security agents ushered in a contingent of the LDPD. Before the tycoon could say a word, the X-Man stepped into the path of the lead detective.

"This is F*O*O*J jurisdiction, officer. So why don't you take your little men back to your brother-shooting clubhouse while we solve this case? Bye," said Kareem, turning his back.

The lead detective flushed borsht-red. "Now you listen up, 'X-Man'—"

"No, *you* listen, Detective McDevil," said Kareem, facing him, "I've got full jurisdiction here, and you're standing on my crime scene. So unless you want *me* to arrest *you*, get out of here now. André!" he yelled into his wrist. "Get down here!"

The detective, outraged at being trumped in front of his men, looked toward Mr. Piltdown for support. Festus shook his head in sympathetic disgust and shared impotence.

"Don't look at him. Look at me." Kareem smiled. "The one ordering you to get your ass out of here."

"You better watch yourself, Edgerton," said the detective. "The bigger you get, the harder—"

"—the harder I'll kick a fool in the ass. See ya!" said Kareem, walking away and waving bye-bye over his shoulder at the retreating LDPD.

"Edgerton!" snapped Festus, sticking a finger in Kareem's face. "Leaving aside how you treated those peace officers, you've wasted ten minutes berating me about a man who tried to murder me in my own home as if *I* were the bomber and not the man who blew himself to bloody bits! Maybe you should be leaving this investigation to someone who isn't conflicted by pursuing a personal agenda—or a political one!"

"Irony—cute. Might want to reflect on that irony yourself, Festes. So you'd have me believe that out of nowhere, one of the most brilliant investigative litigators in the country—"

"Maybe never being able to finish his vendetta against my family finally got to him, and he snapped! Maybe he had terminal cancer and this was his last chance to get me! Maybe—"

"Maybe Menton got to him."

Festus stopped, placing a thumb and crooked finger to his chin.

"May*be*. But . . . Menton wouldn't've been able to mind-master the Tree's bomb-sniffing technology. It'd take someone like the supreme *khemist* of ancient Egypt, Warmaster Set, to do that. He'd be eminently capable of devising an explosive my sniffers wouldn't be calibrated to detect."

"But why would Jack Zenith work with Set? I mean, Menton could've mind-chained Zenith, but Set doesn't have—"

"The Sceptre of Typhon. Obviously you're not the Hawk King authority you think you are."

The blackboard of X-Man's face chalked with exasperation before he wiped it clean.

"The Sceptre of Typhon," said Festus slowly, as if to an immigrant, or a deaf person, "discussed in the papyrus The Book of Lesser Portals as a staff of mental domination. It was lost around 1400 BC—but perhaps now found and used again." He snorted. "Not that I disagree with Set's choice of targets in this case."

"You son of a bitch!" said Tran, suddenly at our side. "Jack Zenith wasn't like all us, us *clowns* in the F*O*O*J prancing around in our three-colour lingerie. He changed America more for the better than all of us combined. Combined a thousand times!"

"Well, evidently," quipped Festus, "the author of *Unsafe in Any Cape* was unsafe in his final suit."

And with that, Tran spat on Festus's cravatte and stormed off.

TOWARDS A TOTAL X-SANGUINATION

"What're you smirking at, Edgerton?"

"Admiring your spit-shine. Focus, Fes-face! There's another angle to the Menton lead—I've finally finished analysing all the data my *medukem* brought me from Asteroid Zed's computers.

"Turns out Menton wasn't the *only* prisoner missing from Asteroid Zed. Sarah Bellum should've been in lock-down since 1972. But she never made it! With her powers, she could've mind-scribed everyone concerned into believing she was up there. For all we know, she could've been the one who initiated Menton's powers—"

The Brotherfly swooped down, brushing his feet on Kareem's shoulders and head.

"Get the hell off me, you moron!" yelled Kareem. "What took you so long? I called you down here five minutes ago!"

André landed, ignoring the question. "Yo, Kreem, you gots a *army* out there, son. Army of reporters. Looking to talk to y'all."

Kareem turned his back on Festus without so much as a word. I followed him towards the entrance with André flapping directly overhead.

"Got some fine-ass news-ladies out there, K-dawg," said Andre. "But what with your 'investigation' making you the Zulu-flavour of the week, André gon hafta work his *bzzzt!*-mojo extra hard to get any attention, specially since you light-skinned negroes always get all the play—"

"What kinda bullshit have you been drinking, André? You and I are the exact same colour! And *you're* the one who was on the cover of *The Source*, on *Essence*, you were *People*'s 'Sexiest Superhero Alive,' so don't be giving me your—"

"Whoah-whoah-*whoah!* You red-bone dodecaroons are so touchy! André gots to be calling you Detective Defensive! Don't worry, bruh—soon you can be releasin all the tension you got to with them repor-teurs. They's a fox from FOX out there with ta-dow who's bizanging!"

"I'm in the Forty-Two Chambers, André! Vow of chastity, remember?"

"All that means is more for André, dawg!" he said, rubbing his hands together and grinning. "All-you-can-eat hoes!"

At the gates of the estate, cameras and reporters swarmed X-Man, demanding answers about the status of his investigation and his reaction to polls showing him with a sixty percent lead over Flying Squirrel. And then a reporter in a pinstriped pant-suit and push-up bra shouldered her way to the front of the throng, holding up a book with the face of an angry, hyper-muscular woman on its cover.

"Jaylene Dander from FOX, Kareem. This's an advance copy of Billi Biceps tell-all autobiography, *Butch Like Me*—"

"I don't know anything about Billi Biceps, Jaylene—she was never in the F*O*O*J, she doesn't—"

"Billi said she was the victim of a cruel lie—that her year-long relationship with Power Grrrl was nothing but a heartless sham—"

"—I'm here to investigate an attempt to assassinate one of this country's most esteemed superheroes, part of an *on-going* investigation into the assassination of *the most* esteemed superhero—"

"—a heartless sham designed to cover up the fact that Power Grrrl was never a lesbian, that in fact she was having a secret affair with *you*."

Suddenly every camera and microphone was shoved in Kareem's face, and for the first time since I'd met him, he was speechless.

"How do you explain this, Kareem?" said Jaylene. "You, the radical, militant, anti-white, black power crime-fighter, sleeping with someone that *Hero Threat* calls 'a skanky, white, kryptosexual, pop-tart heroine-poseur?'"

André howled from above, buzzing his wings in hilarity. "And he aint even supposta be sleepin with no ladies at all, *no* how!"

Cameras swung up towards the Brotherfly. "Him an all his Forty-Two Chamber-havin blackocentric homies, they all supposta be 'chaste,' an now it turn out he been doin the chasin? He been lying down on the job to be eating off th'blonde rug?"

"Shut up, you mak-head! Look, Jaylene, your allegations are a complete, utter colostomy bag! I—listen, I never, ever—"

"How do you respond to newly-surfaced documents, Kareem," said the newswoman, "showing that you actually hated Hawk King?"

"*WHAT? Are you NUTS?*" he shouted. "What kind of insanity is *that*? Hawk King was my hero! My teacher, leader, and mentor—"

The statuesque reporter took out a thin newspaper. "This is a 1984 copy of *Mama Said Punch Whitey in tha Throat*, the Langston-Douglas underground newspaper you used to write for under the pen-name 'Anavidge Blackman.' You wrote, quote, *Hawk King . . . is a stooge for F*O*O*J-led white domination of the planet*, end-quote. And in another article," she said, producing that issue, "you wrote, quote, *I've been proudly hating all my life, hating the nation of millions holding us back. We opposing jive turkeys.*"

Cameras were clicking, whirring, and whining faster than ever. Kareem's face had drained to beige.

"Because your allegations about Hawk King's secret identity," said FOX's Ms. Dander, "and the alleged 'secret connection' you supposedly shared with him has been the key to your electoral legitimacy—"

"Tomorrow, look, tomorrow, everyone—listen! I'm scheduled, I told you all at Hawk King's funeral, that I would be revealing the contents of Hawk King's final papyrus, contents which will—"

"—a papyrus whose authenticity, given your molecular word-powers, will be impossible to prove, I'm sure," said Jaylene Dander, who then shook the newspaper articles in the X-Man's face. "But how do you rate your chances of being elected Director of Operations, Kareem, now that these extreme documents showing your extremist views have seen the light of day? How can you expect voters to trust a white-hating extremist?"

"How do I—I don't hate white people! You just used the word 'extreme' or 'extremist' three times, you freaking Hyksos—"

Kareem spluttered to a stop while cameras clicked all over him like a plague of crickets.

"No kot-tam *comment!*" he yelled.

He shoved himself into the choke of reporters , trying to wedge his way back inside the grounds and through the gate. Blocked by photographers, he finally started shoving and cursing and got shoved back and cursed at, which made him counter-counter-shove and -curse. Every moment of it was immortalised in photographs and news video that soon would be beamed around the nation.

"You'd better back up off me, punks!" Kareem yelled, swinging blindly and punching a coiffed white reporter in the throat, knocking him to the ground gasping.

In the ensuing chaos, Kareem scrambled up the wrought-iron fence, but while clearing the top spikes, he snagged and ripped his pant legs with a cartoonishly extended tearing sound while he fell. He bounded back to the Squirrel Tree with his torn black trousers flapping like pirate flags while the cameras recorded every second of his ragged retreat.

WHEN DISTRACTION BECOMES DESTRUCTION

Left unchecked, the Quixotic and paranoid paradigm so typical of superheroes can become self-destructive at even the cellular level. In fact, the awesome psychic weight of believing that others depend on you for their very lives can be lethal. For instance, new mothers suffer from post-partum depression not only because of tectonic hormonal shifts, but because of the juggernaut realisation that motherhood will be a lifelong, relentless burden of worry, moral (and mortal) responsibility, and embittering power-struggles.

Iron Lass had laboured as protectress for two thousand years, but the protector-burden had finally crushed her immortal-immune response, giving rise to a lethally opportunistic infection from an otherwise minor attack. X-Man's Herculean yoke was his racialised narcissistic projection neurosis—his irrational urge to view all phenomena as the effects of a vast, encompassing, imaginary "white power structure," rather than recognising the inherently orderless nature of human societies, the fundamental indifference (or seen another way, impartiality or justice) of the world, and the inescapable ennui that ultimately euthanises all joy, satisfaction, and human connection.

When dysfunctional self-distraction devolves into delusional self-destruction, neurosis turns into psychosis. If Iron Lass and the X-Man could not discharge their neurotic need to be needed and yearning for vengeance against nonexistent enemies (whether Menton or "the Man"), their psychotic mortiquaerotic (death-seeking) urges would seal their doom . . . and the F*O*O*J's with it.

PART THREE

APPEALING TO A HIGHER POWER

CHAPTER NINE

Paranoia:
It *Can* Destroy Ya

X-COMMUNICATION

MONDAY, JULY 10, 3:57 P.M.

It was the morning of the press conference, Kareem's first statement to the press since the previous Friday's shocking revelations. At the back of the Fortress of Freedom's Hall of Proclamations, I was standing beside the Brotherfly looking upon a veritable herd of journalists awaiting their chance to graze upon a fallen hero's next—and perhaps final—words of his career.

While some of Kareem's comrades had turned out to show their support, including attorney Tran Chi Minh, Original Fabulous Man, and the L*A*B's Shango and the Player Hater, the absence of the majority of F*O*O*Jsters was a death-knell indictment of his credibility, and of his bid for the Directorship of the F*O*O*J's Operations.

Polls shunted him down from 75 percent to bottom out at 15 percent of decided voters. The Flying Squirrel had glided up to 50. Even Spoiler Man at 18 percent had pulled ahead of Kareem.

In the three days since the story had plopped into the fan, media had subjected Kareem's life and career—his every article, utterance, deed, failure and foible—to a public colonoscopy. The only division in the electorate seemed to be over which of Kareem's "betrayals" was worse— violating his own vow of chastity to prosecute a "racially hypocritical" relationship with a white woman, or his racially-paranoid denunciation of Hawk King.

(Shockingly, the media-ravenous Syndi Tycho had completely vanished from journalistic sonar screens; not even X-ray paparazzi had been able to snap a shot of her emerging from a trendy bath house or a four-star Kabbalah temple. Her publicist had issued only a single statement in the face of the Billi Biceps autobiography and Kareem scandal: "Ms. Tycho wishes to express her profound sadness at the lack of happiness being experienced by her colleagues at this time.")

In the previous day's edition of *The Langston-Douglas Crisis*, two former comrades from the League of Angry Blackmen had accused Kareem of being a "super-sell out;" on the AANT program *Oh No She Didn't*, Ms. Thang of the Supa Soul Sistas had demanded "the return of X-Man's race card." And civil rights-era icon the Spook had called Kareem "a militant negro threat to democracy as great as that of Kyklos the Grand Dragon."

Amid editorials describing Kareem as a "black supremacist" and "race-fixated head-case," *Sentinel-Spectator* accusations that he belonged to "a black hate group called the L*A*B, an 'Ebonics' acronym translating out to 'Lots of Anti-white Blacks,'" and even an editorial cartoon depicting Kareem as a bell-bottomed pimp wearing a KKK hood while soliciting Power Grrrl on the streets of Langston-Douglas, came the calls for Kareem to drop out of the election, recuse himself from investigating Hawk King's death, and even resign from the F*O*O*J itself. The turkeys of racialised narcissistic projection neurosis had come home to roost, and were laying their eggs all over Kareem's face.

Flashbulbs erupted like mortar fire when Kareem stepped awkwardly onto the stage at precisely 4 P.M.. X-Man took his place at the table arranged with microphones from two dozen news outlets, and was shortly joined by other members of the so-called X-Slate in the then-impending election: candidate for Director of Personnel, Gagarina Girl; candidate for Director of Finances, Dynamiss; candidate for Director of External Affairs, Shockra; and candidate for Director of Investigation, the Spectacle.

Flashes illuminated the emptiness of the final seat behind the nameplate for X-Slate candidate for Director of Research + Development, the Periodic Man.

Kareem's neck rocked side-to-side in the then-loose collar of his ubiquitous white shirt, while his by-then skullish eyes stared straight ahead, a poker face for facing the Grim Reaper. He looked as if he'd hardly slept or eaten in days.

Having escaped the labyrinth of Langston-Douglas to fly within tanning distance of the sun inside the F*O*O*J's leadership nucleus, the wax of racial rage had melted and scattered the crowfeathers of X-Man's afro-paranoia, leaving Kareem to plummet into the seat—and fate—he'd taken at that very moment.

"Time to watch this muthafucka *squirm*," giggled André, grinning while literally rubbing his hands together.

I tried to catch André's gaze, hoping to glimpse some of whatever could motivate such an intense psychemotional response towards the X-Man. But he was as fixed on the proceedings as a Roman senator in the Coliseum about to watch a Christian become cat food.

Kareem's sole opportunity to salvage his career and psychemotional wellness from the Minotaur of his own delusions, and to flee the maze of his own misjudgement, was to accept full responsibility for his grievous errors and beg the public for forgiveness. Only by throwing himself on his sword, battle-axe, dagger, and pocket-knife could he excise the cancer that was consuming his very soul.

MEET THE PRESS, BEAT THE REPRESSION

Complaining that he'd been "quoted out of context" and citing his need as a young hero "to shock a deaf, dumb, and blind public into consciousness," Kareem's opening statement fell desperately short of the apology for which the press had clearly come looking.

His defensiveness intensifying during the "media analysis" section of his rant, he threw back into the reporters' faces his by-then infamous quotation "I've been proudly hating all my life, hating the nation of millions holding us back. We opposing jive turkeys."

"What I *actually* wrote," he said, reading, "was, quote, *In the 1960s at least we knew were fighting the Man. We should've called him the Punk. But then in the 1970s, we lost sight and got obsessed with opposing 'jive turkeys.' By the 1980s, we'd whittled down our objective to battling sucker MCs. And by the nineties, the best we could do was oppose 'playa-haters.' Well, I have been proudly 'hating' all my life, hating the fools, suckers, and liars with expensive amplifiers who are blinding, deafening. and dumbing-us down, and opposing the nation of millions holding us back, which sometimes—guess what?—is us. We spent too much damn time getting down. Now it's time to get up.* End-quote.

"So listen, press. If you people're gonna to attack me for what I wrote, at least have the intellectual integrity and the professionalism to quote me in full and attack me for what I *actually* said—"

Reporter #1: "Kareem, if you're saying you don't really hate and want to destroy all white people, why did you say you did? If you didn't mean it, why did you say it?"

Reporter #2: "Is it true you own a spear inscribed with the words 'I'm Gon Git You, Whitey'?"

Reporter #3: "Why, after Professor Hnossi Icegaard's declaration of the *Götterdämmerung*, did you say that, quote, *The world might be a whole lot safer if Iron Lass had a husband*, end-quote?"

Reporter #4: "Kareem, do you lust after all white women, or just Power Grrrl?"

Reporter #5: "X-Man, will you offer a complete and unqualified retraction and apology?"

"Listen, *listen!*" he said, and when he lifted his hands in a gesture of quiet, flashbulbs erupted like a prairie lightning storm, photographing his every gesticulation into an image which would later be given meaning through captions.

"Let's get this in perspective, all right? *The F*O*O*J is under attack,* do you understand that? Hawk King is dead, quite possibly murdered, Omnipotent Man has resigned under mysterious circumstances, somebody destroyed Asteroid Zed, someone tried to assassinate both the Flying Squirrel and the hero formerly known as Chip Monk, Iron Lass is dying—"

Kareem froze, wincing with the knowledge that he had not been authorised to release that information.

Every reporter screamed for verification and elucidation of his slip.

"—and, and, and *mean*while you people have derailed my investigation *for three days* because of something you ripped out of context that you don't even understand that I wrote *years* ago, when meanwhile a murderer, possibly one of the worst supervillains in history, is systematically wiping out the most powerful champions on the planet! And by focusing your attack on *me*, you people are playing right into his hands, while the *real* enemy—"

Questions inevitably and correctly called for Kareem to address his own delusional paranoia. Angrily battering the inquiries, he tried shifting focus onto his Five Point Platform and his proposed "*Götterdämmerung* against Corporate Crime and Ecological Evil," and his slate's whimsical schemes to use the F*O*O*J to promote their "Mission for Quality of Life."

But throughout Kareem's weak dodges, reporters tossed stage-ward the literary bones they'd exhumed from Kareem's corpus of writings, seeking his reactions if not retractions: his rage against white people who wore "dreadlocks" or who used the phrase "ghetto blaster," his charges that "the Beatles had less talent in four voices than James Brown has in a single scream" and that "Elvis was a talentless chicken-fried-steak-gnawing junkie thief who should've been charged with grand larceny for stealing black music and executed for the treason of expropriating the title 'King of Rock and Roll,'" that Civil Rights-era pioneering hero the Spook was "a Driving Miss Daisied, ham-hock-swallowing, 'yassuh bossing,' friendly-firing, stealth-flying, five-star general house negro," and that Kareem had once said that "the only position for a woman in the F*O*O*J is 69."

"—kot-*tam* it, how many times do I have to apologise for that '69' remark? I said that *eleven years ago*—when I was *drunk*—at a Stun-Glas wake for Maximus Security when the F*O*O*J was on the wrong side of the Atlantis war that killed him, and some pretty-boy reporter from the *Sentinel-Spectator* was there—"

A reporter: "Isn't drinking against your black power religion?"

"I wasn't even *in* the L*A*B or the Forty-Two Chambers at that time—and it isn't a 'black power religion'—and I told the reporter right away I didn't mean it, but he still up and printed it anyway—"

And on and on went the media melee, with André cackling beside me at every drop of Kareem's blood.

Reporter #113: "—hate *all* white people, or just *most* white people?"

Reporter #98: "—and so how soon will you resign from the F*O*O*J?"

Reporter #141: "—initiated the relationship, you, or Power Grrrl?"

Reporter #72: "—still in love with Syndi Tycho or just using her for sex?"

Reporter #122: "—did Hawk King know what you said about him and did that break his heart and if so do you think that may have killed him, Kareem?"

Reporter #37: "—true you repeatedly had sex inside the F*O*O*J Fortress's Mission Simulator, which led some F*O*O*Jsters to nicknaming it the 'Emission Stimulator'?"

Kareem rocketed to his feet and flipped the table, scattering the microphones. His slate-mates backed up, stunned. A hundred lash-bulb flashbulbs bleached him white. "All y'all can KISS MY MUTHAFUCKIN *BLACK ASS!*"

THE DESPERATE NEED FOR A CHUM
WHEN THE SHARKS ARE FINISHED DINING

By the time André and I squeezed through the crush of reporters to enter the green room, the emaciated Kareem was still as haggard and harried as he'd been onstage. He didn't even raise his head from cradling it in front of the vanity mirror.

His wrist buzzed, petitioning him hollowly: "X-Man, some reporters from *Jet*, AANT and *The Crisis* are insisting you speak with them—"

He smacked his wrist, crushing the voice.

I pulled up a chair beside him, sat down, and asked him how he felt.

"That," he muttered, not even looking up, "was a galactic fucking disaster."

The sigh he let out was so heavy, deep, and cold, it merited its own frost warning.

"Whole kot-tam world's falling apart, asteroids exploding, Squirrel's a corrupt corporate-welfare bum, people-of-capes dead and dying, and the conspiracy to bring down the F*O*O*J is working on hero number four. You got Wally the junkie jonesing for glowing blue crystals—"

"Kareem," I asked, "what makes you think that Wally—"

"—give it a *rest*, Doc! Half those kot-tam reporters out there've known the story for years, but do y'think they'd ever report it? You're never gonna see *Wally* on the cover of the *Urinal-Expectorator* with his nostrils and fingertips dusted blue an looking like a kid fiending on powdered blueberry Tang! Wally coulda single-handedly stopped

Asteroid Zed from being destroyed if he hadn't quit his job while fucked up on argonium, and then Iron Lass wouldn't be dying—"

Flashing into existence during his diatribe were various logogenic apparitions from his speech, including disembodied nostrils and fingertips. The black bodyparts rotated around his head, disintegrating randomly into black silt-shadows.

"—and damn in a can," he railed on, "the man was caught flying under the influence how many times? And the argonium exacerbating his MPD? *That's* a bigger kot-tam scandal than anything *I* supposedly wrote, said, or did! That's a matter of kot-tam planetary security! Where's the kot-tam press on *that* shit?"

In the corner of the green room, a large, steaming, malodorous pile of logogenic feces manifested itself, at which point André said, "Whatever you do now, Kareem, don't say the word 'muthafucka.' *Bzzzt!*"

Kareem looked up in exasperation, his black irises like two Rolos dotting twin scoops of vanilla ice cream.

"Can you be serious for one stinking minute, André? What if . . . look . . . Wally, right? He's cracked, MPDed, strung out on argonium . . . what if—I mean, Menton's powers were always strongest on people hiding secrets—maybe he puppet-mastered *Wally* into killing Hawk King! Wally's one of the only beings with enough power to do it, and then, even if Menton suppressed his memories, guilt from that could be seeping into his conscious mind, which motivated his resignation—"

"Tha fuck you talkin bout, Kreem? That got to be the stankiest heap a Tyrannosaurus shit André ever took a whiff of!" The Brotherfly affected his trademarked hiss-laughter despite his obvious rage. "Evrabody, evrabody in the whole world guilty a suh'm but *you*. Reporters didn'quote you right, Festus is a corrupt rich man, Wally killed Hawk King, an Hawk King worked f'the white man! But what about Ka-*REEM?*" said André, grabbing X-Man by the face and shoving it back like a tether ball.

Kareem snapped back and leapt up out of his chair, staggering to stay upright, swinging back at André who danced out of the way, causing Kareem to pitch forward and nearly hit the floor.

"Don't you get it?" spat Kareem. "You've gotta put all that you-me shit aside, Andrew, long enough to see this attack's *bigger* than me! This's about my investigation! I should be pursuing this Sarah Bellum angle, tracking her connections to Menton! Maybe they've been working together all along . . . or maybe she *is* Menton! Brother, the timing of that smear-job on me was no kot-tam co*inc*idence!"

"Don't 'brother' me, punk-ass nigga! You *deserve* this shit. Biggest accuser who ever shit on somebody he don'like now gettin the shit he dumped, dumped back on him. Where I come from, that's called justice, dawg. *Natural* justice."

He stepped forward to lean down his six-three frame and shove his face in front of Kareem's, close enough for each man to smell the other's breath, to see the sleep (or lack of it) in the other's eyes.

"I hope they rip your ass in two, Kareem," he said, "which's maybe the only way t'finally clear all the shit outta you!"

"André!" I said, shocked for a moment from my professional detachment. "Why do you hate Kareem so much?"

He didn't shake his gaze from Kareem for a moment. "I don't hate *anybody*, Doctor," he said crisply. "Unlike *this* person."

How will you face knowing that you will never exceed, or even equal, the accomplishments of your predecessors?

> **The Brotherfly:** "Glory's a hole. Gimme that mo-nay! *Bzzzt!*"
> **X-Man:** "I don't give a fuck about glory. Give me truth."

DENIAL AND DELUSION: ALWAYS UNHELPFUL?

Kareem demanded I leave him to his green room solitude. I spent the next two days at the Hyper-Potentiality Clinic anxiously awaiting his call. Beyond the fright-show skullishness of his looks, it was the crumbling desperation in his voice, so striking in a man ordinarily so strident, that worried me. Polls showed him crashing through the basement of his previous disapproval ratings. I hoped that wherever he was, there were neither pills nor rope.

And there was no word from Syndi, either, the target of her own backlash after having been "inned" by Billi Biceps. There'd been a public-tearing-up of her membership papers in GLAAD, and the weekly *SuperherOUT* had denounced her for "pimping queerness to advance her shallow career through poseuristic lesbian chic."

Iron Lass had been too sick to see me, and neither Festus nor André had anything to say outside of anti-Kareem gloating. And so the only person left attending therapy was Wally.

As Argon's only son on Earth continued to integrate the experiences of his many personalities (or *alters*) into his central persona, his powers continued to malfunction and fade. It was as if his hyper-capacities depended on his own lack of self-awareness to function. And the picture that was emerging of Wally's alters wasn't pretty.

As playboy Ricky R. Bustow, "Wally" had left a trail of businesses he'd plundered, insider-traded, or plunged into the ground; as fight promoter Francis "Musk Ox" Miller, he'd built his Vegas sports book and his fortunes entirely on Omnipotent Man's battles—not whether he'd win, but how long it'd take to defeat his foes, which powers would be used, and which buildings would be destroyed; as Reverend "Crawdad" Crocket, he'd built a televangelist empire exploiting his congregation's fears that the *Götterdämmerung* was Armageddon, but behind the scenes he'd left collection basketsful of broken hearts and at least one very reluctant abortion.

Fascinatingly, the alters possessed qualities of shrewdness, discernment, and intellect that Wally had not yet manifested in his own life. Perhaps a rural upbringing had wilted such capacities in the young Wally, and an overbearing influence such as Festus Piltdown III had stifled them afterward. But argonium had stimulated them and set them free. If Wally, free from his destabilising argonium addiction, were able to harness the alters' mental faculties and awaken them inside a unified Wally-prime personality, he might be able to save his sanity and himself.

But we were not even close to such a dynamic integration.

Even the existence of Wally's retreat, his Stronghold of Standing-On-My-Own-Two-Feetitude, had come into question, when satellite telemetry in Flying Squirrel's Omnipotent Man file challenged the Stronghold's "Antarctic" location by showing no such location had ever existed. In fact, the real Stronghold was in the Andes. Faced with such photographic proof, Wally confessed, "I never was no good at d'rections."

Every session, Wally's powers failed further, his panic escalating the closer he got to realising that his extra-terrestrial hyper-abilities might have been at their end. I encouraged the desperate Wally to use visualisation and the serenity affirmation to picture himself without his powers, yet completely at peace. But my request merely drove Wally into such deep despair that he'd begun regularly articulating suicidal ideation.

Desperate for a solution, I asked Wally if he were willing to go along with a last-ditch gambit for his survival.

"Yes!" wailed Wally, rocking and sobbing in front of me, cradling his head between his knees, pounding his fists into the back of his head heavily enough to elicit gongs. "But how, Doc? I feel like I'm dead already!"

Locking Wally into the Id-Smasher®'s psyche-simulated environment for a continuous session stretching over a week, I induced in Wally the mental experience of having all his powers back. To restore his confidence in own his character, I created a simulated Hawk King who walked with him, talked with him, and flew with him, who constantly reminded him to assert ownership of and become a stakeholder in the Hawkish qualities he so admired, to own the target of his own admiration.

It was a grave risk. Such an auto-belief in his career and his powers required Wally to activate vast mental energies into a delusion of his own competence and that the future would see the return of his powers to their original magnitude. My dangerous strategy was predicated on the psychestructure's enormous capacity for denial, an evolutionary defense mechanism intended to preserve the sapient organism against overwhelming odds.

Given sufficient time and safety, Wally might eventually have come safely to integrate full awareness of his failures and accept his im-omnipotence. But that time had not yet arrived.

SELF X-AMINATION

THURSDAY, JULY 13, 9:59 P.M.

At last, on the third night following the press conference, while Wally was still contained inside the Id-Smasher® for his ongoing personality reintegration, Philip Kareem Edgerton showed up at the door of my Hyper-Potentiality clinic.

He was unshaven, appeared to've lost even more weight, and looked and smelled as if he hadn't changed his clothes since Monday.

"How'm I supposed to do my job when I've become the story?" he said by way of greeting. "That's not a rhetorical question, Doc. I'm asking you."

"Kareem," I said, showing him into the encounter room and frothing him a whippaccino, "what these people are all expecting from you is a statement of accountability. All you have to do is accept responsibility. Then they'll let you do your job."

He sat, looking out the window towards the hundred and fifty stories of neon in the distance called the Tachyon Tower. Based on his sneer, I doubted he was pondering the cosmological-dimensional research being undertaken there.

"Re-spon-si-*bil*-ity . . . " he drawled. "You know, that's the one word Hawk King used in his Instructions papyrus more than any other. For all the good the papyrus'll do anybody now. Might's well seal it back inside a canopic jar, let some other brother try again with it in a thousand years . . . when the world's ready to listen. To believe. No—scratch that. To think."

Disconnecting, Kareem asked me if I'd seen the latest press on him. The stories had mutated into a public version of the childhood game of telephone, with various sources alternately claiming that Kareem's brief article on Hawk King from years before was in fact an essay, a thesis, a dissertation, or even a two-volume set called *Ofays Aint Shit*. *Esquire*'s apparently last-minute cover story, featuring a file photo of Kareem crossing his forearms into an X, was entitled "X-Man Hates Your Cracker Ass."

"You see what that *chai*-sucking, sub-intellectual yuppy pinhead wrote?" asked Kareem in reference to Shauna Slyming's column on him in the *Sentinel-Spectator*. "She ignored everything I explained, and then wrote that I 'used words like bullets'—never mind who's using *actual* bullets against black folks, which apparently doesn't concern her—and then she denounced, quote, *all black radicals,* and accused me of being sexist!"

"Kareem, can you blame her for being upset with you? You must've hit her in the head with a microphone when you flipped the table. Did you see her photo? Her face looks horrible!"

"Naw, she always looks like that. You know she actually phoned me later that day before she wrote her 'opinion piece'? Told me that when I'd written this one article a couple of years ago saying, quote, *There should be more female superheroes,* that—get this—*that* was somehow sexist! Slyming's a krypto-conservative supra-moron, Doc! And you know what else she said? She tells me . . . ."

The hour wore on, with Kareem frantically spewing out his elaborate theory of self-justification which, because of his severe RNPN, he could not recognise as proof of his subconscious acknowledgement of his own guilt, and the fundamental irrationality of his black-panic paradigm.

"Kareem," I finally interrupted, "what about when we were at the Squirrel Tree, and you called that policeman 'Detective McDevil'? That's a racial slur. That's the kind of thing the public and the press expect you to take responsibility for. You claim you're against racism, and yet you're guilty of exactly what you accuse others of doing."

"First of all, that isn't racism. I can't deny McDevil or his people their jobs, their homes, or their lives. Second, that punk deserves the name. Wanna know why I call him that? Back before I had my powers, he was a patrolman at a Stun-Glas demonstration after Maximus Security got killed in New Atlantis. Punk's practically a Klansman. He beat my *legs*, Doc, beat my legs like he was tenderising rhino meat!"

"For someone whose very powers are based in words, Kareem, you're employing a double-standard on hurtful language. The children's rhyme about 'sticks and stones' isn't true—hurtful words hurt, Kareem, no matter who's using them."

"The cops *have* sticks! What do you think McDevil was beating my legs with?"

"Kareem, when life gives you lemons, make Lemon Pledge! And then take that Pledge and clean up your act! You're losing an opportunity to see yourself for who you really are and therefore to self-actualise—"

"'Losing an opportunity'? Have you opened your eyes once in the last week? Have you seen what's happening? A conspiracy to murder one hero and neutralise three others, destroy an asteroid, get two supervillains disappeared without a trace—"

"Look inside yourself, Kareem! What opportunity for *yourself* are you missing?"

"*This is not about me!* Why can't you shrinks ever get that, that the world is bigger than the kot-tam individual? The F*O*O*J is nothing but Lost Opportunities, Inc.—doesn't do a damn thing to solve actual problems. Best it ever does is put out fires, but it's spent way more time *settin* em.

"You know what Colonel Strom Flintlock spent his whole career as Director of Operations doing? Trying to keep black, women, and gay heroes out of the F*O*O*J, stick the Ten Commandments inside every hero's oath, and overthrow the government of New Atlantis. That paleo-conservative's a hundred-and-seventy-three years old, did you know that? The only soldier the G.I. juice experiments successfully revived from—as he loved to call it—'the War between the States.' He wasn't fit enough to fight in WWII, and he didn't join the F*O*O*J until 1946, but he's occupied the D.O.O. chair ever since. A kot-tam joke! That swasti-fossil's so right-wing even a super-sell-out like the Spook was too black for him!"

"Kareem!" I snapped, standing up. "Listen to yourself ranting about and casting blame on everybody but you! Here's a question to which you have still not given a straight answer to anyone yet which is at the heart of your current calamity! *Did you or did you not have an affair with Syndi Tycho?*"

He shoved himself out of his chair and raged out of the room like a zephyr in a rumpled black suit-and-tie.

THE X-FILES

According to the F*O*O*J's psychological profile, Philip "Kareem" Edgerton was a complicated young man. At thirty-four years old, highly intelligent, and with a corrosive personality, the X-Man had gained (and has just lost) enormous public standing, an ironic indicator of his interpersonal isolation. In a survey, not a single member of the F*O*O*J had described him as either "a very close friend" or even "a good friend." And despite Kareem's "good old days" affirmations about the L*A*B, I had seen little indication of those halcyon times when I'd visited the Dark Star restaurant and he'd appeared only marginally more welcome than André.

Facing black racist accusations of "lily-diddling," Kareem found himself denounced by almost every member of the L*A*B and the Supa Soul Sistas. A would-be leader without followers, a lonely man alone inside a mob of his own making, the secretive Kareem was a fascinating contradiction: for one who'd railed so long against white society, he'd immersed himself in the nearly all-white F*O*O*J, and apparently conducted a secret affair with a scandal-magnet white heroine. Although he screamed that he was drowning in it, Kareem apparently loved the tub.

Unlike his fellow L*A*Bsters, Kareem had never been a street tough, but a quiet, bookish Political Science student at Langston-Douglas's Robeson College. Finding a voice through his writing, Kareem had grown in confidence enough that his development of super-powers had led him almost instantly into crime-fighting and a subsequent recruitment into the L*A*B, providing him what he'd never had before: comrades, a base, training, and technology.

But despite the awesome destructive capacity his logogenesis afforded him, the X-Man rarely got into melees; he'd preferred to devote himself to becoming, in his words, "a thinking-man's hero, and the world's greatest detective, but for real."

Yet his own awesome anger had continued to plague him, causing fractures between him and his editors, his first super-team and later within the F*O*O*J itself. If Kareem failed to destroy his own anger, that anger would finish destroying him.

In the days that followed, despite uninterrupted therapy being a condition of maintaining active member status, most of my F*O*O*Jster patients stayed away. I did receive updates on two of my sanity-supplicants: Hnossi had declined further, while Festus kept vigil at her side, leaving only to pursue "leads" in his investigation of Warmaster Set.

Only two F*O*O*Jsters continued their sessions: Wally maintained his feelings work, sealed inside my Id-Smasher® for continuous, uninterrupted reprogramming. And André continued seeing me, splitting his session time between bragging about his sexual conquests and condemning Kareem. Once, for variety, he informed me that he'd visited Syndi in her undisclosed location, and that "she be doin all right."

The only subject which slowed down André's leering litany of lust or his cantankerous anti-Kareem catechism was the death of Hawk King. At any mention of the fallen mentor's name, André's smile turned inward; he chewed his lips, nodding and staring at the floor, saying only, "Ain't no justice in this world, Doc. No justice for nobody."

THE PARABLE OF THE TWO WOLVES

SATURDAY, JULY 15, 8:30 P.M.

When Kareem finally returned to the Hyper-Potentiality Clinic on a Saturday evening, he was calm but sullen. He opened our session complaining that his investigation had been all but destroyed since he couldn't gain access to the "crime scene" of the Blue Pyramid (sealed by the *Ka*-Sentinels ever since the funeral), and because wherever he went he was mobbed by reporters, yelled at by angry citizens, and stonewalled by uncommunicative witnesses.

But that tirade soon gave way to his obsessive attempts to convince me that his recent reversal of fortunes was the result of a "white power structure" bent on destroying him.

"Is that really true, Kareem? I mean, take that editorial cartoon in the *Sentinel-Spectator* that made you so upset. That was by Melvin Moal, and he's black, I believe."

I pulled the cartoon from my file, but he refused even to look at it. I glanced at the image of the Klan-hooded Kareem in a "pimp suit" prostituting Power Grrrl on the streets of Stun-Glas, with its embittering caption "X-Contender."

"Melvin Moal," sneered Kareem. "The kot-tam Moal-man. Never even stepped *foot* in Stun-Glas. That Toby-tron belongs to the Cartoonist Council of White-Gloved, 'Yowza'-howling, Tom-osexual House Negroes.

It isn't just me he sold out—you should see the racist shit this guy drew about the Crimson Kafeeyah, the Palestinian crime-fighter. Drew him like a mad dog, actually used the words *Arab, animal, savage*, and *killer* in the background—I mean, no wonder he's fucking with me like this! This sell-out punk Moal, I swear, he got named 'Tom of the Year' by *Tom Magazine* three years running—"

"Now, Kareem, we both know there's no such thing as *Tom Magazine*—"

"Well there should be!"

"You can't heal yourself of your toxic, boundless rage if you don't admit some culpability, Kareem. Are you really saying that *everyone* is to blame but you? That this is all the result of some vast, white conspiracy to, how did you put it, 'keep the black man down'?"

"I never said that!"

"I think you did, Kareem."

"Wouldn't I know what I said?"

"So *I'm* wrong, the media is wrong, the *F*O*O*J* is wrong, *Hawk King* was wrong, the *L*A*B* and the *Supa Soul Sistas* who denounced you are wrong, *everyone* is in on this vast, white conspiracy and they're *all* wrong except you, the very person who wrote the words that are now coming back to destroy you?"

"*This is bullshit!* You're setting up a freaking battalion of straw men! And whatever book you plan on writing about all this, I hope you announce yourself in the foreword as being the most unreliable narrator since Jonah went deep throat!"

Feeling the frustration of the impenetrable wall of Kareem's X-rhetoric, I decided it was time to allow Kareem a break.

How will you face knowing that you will never exceed, or even equal, the accomplishments of your predecessors?

X-Man: "I don't give a fuck about glory. Give me revenge."

After Kareem had discharged some of his anger through a journaling session, I shared with him a Native American parable. It was my hope he'd be able to use the story in visualisation to help him contain his raging self-destructive tendencies.

"There once was a tribal elder who found an anxious young brave," I told him, "who was perched atop a butte beneath a moonless night sky. It was the night before the young brave was to begin the trials of his manhood initiation, his 'vision quest'. The brave told the elder, 'Medicine Man, every night I dream that there are two wolves fighting inside me. In the morning when I wake up, I feel as if I've been ripped apart during the night. What does it mean?'

"The shaman told the young brave, 'Inside everyone there are the same two wolves. One is white, and one is black. The white one is Joy, Hope, Courage, Loyalty, Justice, Honour, and Love. The black one is Rage, Despair, Fear, Selfishness, Revenge, Cowardice, and Hate.' The brave asked him, 'Really? That's what these wolves are inside me? Then which one will win?' You know what the medicine man answered, Kareem?"

He shook his head.

"'Whichever one you feed.'"

Kareem argued with me at length over the colours for the wolves, but I refused to budge on the deeper truth of my story, and throughout his dinner break he ate his bean pies quietly, his every munch a munch of intense, self-actualising introspection.

CHAOS X MACHINA

After supper, a mellowed Kareem still refused to discuss Syndi, but neither did he launch himself out of the room when I asked him about that relationship. Instead, the ever highly-strung ex-L*A*Bster suddenly uncoiled like a black mamba on muscle relaxants, waxing nostalgically on the first hero he'd ever wanted to emulate—not Hawk King, but the Langston-Douglas legend Maximus Security.

Rising to prominence as a crusader against neighbourhood drug dealers and the "corrupt police" supposedly in collusion with them, Maximus Security left America in 1975 to fight alongside the "MPLA" in Angola. The young Kareem, then known only as Philip Edgerton, had idolised the maverick crime fighter throughout those overseas adventures and even more so upon his return to the neighbourhood in 1977, following his every move and filling scrapbooks with everything he could find on the man.

"Old people used to look at Brother Max and shake their heads," laughed Kareem, imitating their scowls. "They thought he was gay. See, he used to wear this shiny yellow disco shirt open down to his navel, these tight blue pants and this huge, oversized chain around his hips—"

"Would that bother you? If he were gay?"

"What're you talking about? I don't give a frosty freak about any gay-straight yah-yah. Coulda been gayer than Oscar Wilde and Felix Unger for all I cared. He was my hero, understand? That cat had his own style. Always using weird expressions like 'Holy ship!' and 'Jesse H. Chimpmas!' and saying to the cops stuff like 'You jive turn-key'—I mean, corny as all hell, but he'd wink and all us kids'd laugh, and he'd toss us some goat jerky. Man was so popular, they actually based the movie *Shaft* on him, and *School House Rock* even did a cartoon that everybody in Stun-Glas just *knew* was really supposed to be him: 'Verb! That's What's Happening!' I mean, you know you hit it big time when they start making cartoons of you!"

"There was a cartoon of you, Kareem. Do you feel fulfilled to have 'hit the big time'?"

"Editorial cartoons depicting me as a Klan pimp and drawn by step-and-fetching, massa-sucking, porch-monkeying, professionally-hamboned ultra-Toms don't count, Doc. And you already knew that, so quit talking shit," he sniffed bitterly. "Like I was saying, Brother Max, he was every ghetto kid's hero. So when he up and joined the New Atlantis International Brigades against Reagan's terrorists, we all wanted to go off with him, be his Stun-Glas junior troopers. He was so tough that if we could be like him we'd never die, cuz he could never die. And then it was 1984, and he did."

"Did what?"

"*Did die,*" he said darkly. "So yeah, you've been blasting me, blasting me, *blasting* me about being angry, that I have to 'take responsibility' for what I wrote about Hawk King. Yeah, I was angry. And I had a right to be angry. I wrote it and I was right: from Guatemala to Congo to Iran, the F*O*O*J were, quote, agents of global honkification and leucogemony. And yeah, that *included* Hawk King, going along with all this shit about truth, justice, and the American way. I wrote that you could have truth and justice, or you could have the American way, but you couldn't have em all together. And you know what happened? After I wrote that?

"Hawk King, who'd supposedly exiled himself inside the Blue Pyramid almost every day and night for the previous nine years, came to visit me."

"You? Personally?"

He nodded slowly and heavily, as if the power of his claim were in the mass of his chin. My wristband buzzed three quick vibro-bursts into my skin; I subtly tabbed the **Acknowledge** key to let Ms. Olsen know I'd received her message.

"I was sitting up on the roof of my apartment building drinking coffee," said Kareem, unaware of what I had waiting in store for him, "pounding out my column on my manual typewriter like I did every Sunday night. Every once in a while I'd look around . . . maybe at all the network transmission towers, at the lights of the Hermes Theatre, or over at the Tachyon Tower, wondering what kind of astonishing discoveries they were finding in their dimensional research labs, scanning out past the edge of the galaxy, spelunking black holes, gazing at quasars . . . .

"And while my head was all whirling inside those mysteries, suddenly the moonlight went out.

"I looked up, and I was staring into the moon-frosted silhouette of a man-hawk.

"He swooped down, landed in front of me—six-four, golden beak, and gold-rimmed eyes glittering, flapping his huge black-and-gold wings with enough strength in em to crush me like a ripe tomato.

"I thought . . . I thought he was there to *kill* me, Doc."

He shook his head again, got out of his chair to gaze through the window across the Bird Island skyline.

"But he'd come to tell me he'd read what I'd written," said Kareem, " . . . *and that he thought I was right.*

"I couldn't believe it. I was completely in awe, humbled that he'd even read something I'd written, that he'd been moved by something I said, so moved he actually came to see me? And so somehow I managed to cough up the guts to ask him why.

"And then he invoked a spell . . . and transformed himself. Into a man, an old man in his sixties. Withered, short, maybe five-seven, in a crummy, crumpled suit looking like something my grampa would've worn in 1945. He was sitting there in front of me, an African. Just like me. Just like all the people in the neighbourhood, just like Max, just like the Angolans Max fought with. But in a wheelchair. Told me his name was Dr. Jacob George James 'Jackson' Rogers. That he wasn't a god, but a man from the dawn of civilisation who'd gained his 'celestial powers' by leading a war to avenge his slain father, the ancient Sudanese mystic named Lord Usir.

"I mean, it's a Sunday midnight and I'm sitting at the feet of the man Hawk King's turned into, who's revealing to me his life story underneath the city lights and the moon and the stars. He told me that after ruling over the lands of the Nile for a century as its Hawk King, he felt empty. Except for his great grandchildren, he'd outlived everyone he'd cared about: wives, mother, friends, cousins . . . and in all that time he'd never gotten over the loss of his father, which happened even before he'd been born. So he left. Went up into the stars to try to find his father's souls. Found himself still in battle against his evil uncle, Warmaster Set, and holding back the chaos of the cosmic serpent Ããpep.

"Sometimes he'd come back for a while, help rescue Egypt when she was in trouble . . . and after Egypt fell, he helped out in other places where people still knew his secret names, in Meroë, in Namoratunga, in Timbuktu . . . but he'd always go back out into the rolling deeps of space, searching for his father.

"And then one time after searching for he didn't even know how long and still not finding him, he came back. But everything'd changed. He realised it'd been seven thousand years since he'd been born, and he hardly even recognised the world anymore. But he saw a war going on— World War II—took a side, raised his own army. The F*O*O*J.

"But when the war was over he wanted a life, not as a hawk king but as a man. So he transmuted himself back into his human body. It'd aged—not seven thousand years, of course, but still. And when he went looking for a place to live, he made a discovery: most places in the city where his own F*O*O*J was based wouldn't rent to a black man.

"He knew what it was like to be a persecuted refugee—that's how he'd started his life, since his uncle'd murdered his father and he was raised by his single mother, a warrior-woman on the run. So he decided to blend in. Got an apartment in Ellison Heights in Stun-Glas. Practiced medicine for people who couldn't afford it. Got his doctorates in archaeology and cosmology and taught university and tried to just live as a man by day while guiding the F*O*O*J as a mystic-philosopher-king by night.

"But Doctor Rogers... he was devastated by what he saw in the world. And he just . . . he couldn't figure out what to do with his powers that wouldn't involve conquering the planet, without killing and destroying to impose his will, and he didn't wanna solve things that way. Said it wasn't right, and that it wouldn't work in the long run anyway. So he'd decided to bide his time, do his research, figure everything out.

"He told me, when he came to see me that night, that he'd finally figured it all out. Partly because of the death of Brother Maximus Security. And partly because of what I wrote.

"He told me he was reaching out to what he called 'the virtuous young' to become his *Shemsu-Hru*. That he would entrust us with certain powers, his to enhance and his to take away depending on what we did with them. And then he gave me a papyrus roll, what he called The Book of Doing Knowledge. Told me to search out the canopic jars he'd left around the city, across the Americas, across Africa . . . and write down whatever words I found in them.

"Within a few months I'd found a dozen jars, mostly in Stun-Glas libraries and in the Schombro Centre—they were like glowing turquoise, and after you opened em, they spoke their words to you and then— *whoof!*—they just disappeared. And because I was searching for them,— I met a bunch of other young brothers and sisters looking for them too. That's how I met the people who'd end up forming the L*A*B and the Supa Soul Sistas. It was like a, a, a Hawk King affirmative action program. Not like the one that's mostly just helped white women get ahead, by the way—but one that actually worked for *us*.

"At last, deserving people weren't gonna be held back by where they were born, or what they sounded like on the phone, or looked like when they showed up for the interview. Brother Grimhotep, he found so many jars and gained so much wisdom, he was the one who created the Brotherhood of the Forty-Two Chambers and initiated the rest of us.

"We connected, selected, directed, and defended Stun-Glas. And waited for the day Hawk King promised when we'd be trained enough and ready for him to reveal to us all his celestial, revolutionary vision."

"So," I asked, "with all that success and what you saw as an inspiring vision, Kareem, what happened? Why did the L*A*B to which you were so devoted decide to excommunicate you?"

He looked back towards me, his lips parted, not even trying to hide his shock.

"I *am* a psychiatrist, Kareem. We don't get our degrees for being completely dim, you know."

I got up, joined him at the window, noticing how the street lights turned into stars in the blackness of his eyes. "Did the L*A*B kick you out... because they found out?"

He looked down. His jaw muscles bulged visibly around the base of his scalp as he ground his teeth against each other.

"So this is it, huh?" he chuckled grimly to himself. "This is how my career ends. Not because some dickwad's laser beam cuts me in half, not because the Ammit Monster chews me to bits, not because the Turner Diarists blow me up in the Los Ditkos Federal Building . . . but because of the kot-tam *lie* that I hated Hawk King . . . and the truth that I . . . that I—"

"—that you *did* have an affair with Power Grrrl."

He stood, still as a statue.

"Yeah," he said finally.

I touched my wrist. "Ms. Olsen, would you please show in Ms. Tycho now?"

Kareem looked up at me, eyes bulging as if he were choking.

Syndi walked in. Gone was all her glamourous glitteralia, the *look-at-me!* paraphernalia and the outrageous temporary tattoos, all replaced by a simple black **PG!**-logo t-shirt and jeans. Even her trademarked blond mane had changed—faded to black.

"Hello, Eva," said Syndi, her mascara drenched into raccoon smears. "Hello, Kareem."

THE LONG KISS GOOD MORNING

The two black-garmented heroes sat as far as possible from each other on opposite corners of my wide, white leather chaise lounge.

"This is *bull*shit!" rumbled Kareem. "I should be investigating a murder case, here! Hawk King's dead, Jack Zenith's dead, Asteroid Zed's destroyed, Iron Lass is dying, Menton and Sarah Bellum are missing—"

I cut him off. "Syndi, how do you feel about what Kareem's just said?"

She shook her head. "It's just, like, sad, Eva? Because Kareem was always, like, afraid to look inside himself. Which is why he was always looking 'out there.' But *snap:* like, let the world save itself? You've gotta save yourself, you know?"

"So you don't believe Kareem's claims about the Destroyer being responsible for this current crisis?"

"Gawd, no. Even when we were together, Kareem spent half the time talking about these, like, elaborate conspiracies. This Menton-thingy's just the latest one."

"So, Syndi," I asked, "why did you lie about being a lesbian?"

She twirled her hair, rolled her eyes at the ceiling and then back towards me, indignant at being questioned. "I didn't, like, lie, Eva."

I produced the advance copy of *Butch Like Me* that Festus had acquired for me, flipping through the ghost-written Billi Biceps auto-herography until finding the first of many passages I'd marked. "'In eight months together, Syndi never even let me get past first base. Or maybe second—I never really got that whole baseball thing. That's a man's game, anyway, what with all the phallic crap. So let's just say volleyball.

Well, I never spiked her or anything like that. Just over-hand serves. But regardless, the point is, she's no dyke, you understand? I don't think she's even bi. She's just the world's biggest poser. Everything is all about appearances with her, and it's always all about her.'"

I closed the book and kept my hand on the cover image of Billi as a steroidal Rosie-the-Riveter. "Well, Syndi? Is Billi lying? Or are you?"

"I never, never said, Eva, that I was a lesbian. Never! I just created provocative imagery and let people think, like, whatever they wanted to!"

"You joined GLAAD."

"You don't have to be lesbian to join GLAAD. They got something *they* wanted out of it, and I got something *I* wanted out of it. Everyone profits. What's your hyper-damage?"

"So your profit was more albums sold, a possible film deal, more make-up endorsements, and more sales of your books, perfumes, breast enhancers, Power Grrrl Dental Dams®—"

"—and they got to use me for their own PR. Everyone wants to use me. Even these men who think I'm lesbian and buy my posters and videos and go to my movies . . . I mean, how insane is that? I'm more popular with men because they think they *can't* attain me?"

"You lied to Billi."

She glared back at me, her eyes blue radiant rage inside the black halos of smeared make-up.

"According to this book," I said, tapping the cover, "you broke Billi's heart. Did *she* profit?"

Deformed into its trademarked pout, her mouth suggested indignation far more than photogenic lust.

"How does it make you feel . . . to know what you did to her?"

"I feel *ashamed*, okay? Are you happy? Is that what you want to hear?" she yelled. "I never meant to break her heart. No one was supposed to get hurt. It just . . . things got out of control. Like they are now. Kareem won't even *talk* to me, for months he's refused to even *look* at me, he won't even say my fucking name, people are dying left and right around me and I'm gonna be left alone . . . ."

"Tell me," I said, "about your relationship with Kareem."

At that, the two former lovers finally looked at each other, their faces crawling with the crabs of conflicting emotions.

When neither broke from their eye-war, I finally asked, "Which one of you initiated the relationship?"

Kareem raised a black eyebrow with all the menace of a Jolly Roger, but Syndi didn't flinch.

"I did, Eva," she whispered, her voice puckering with melancholy. "I first saw Kareem in the press, like, five years ago. I thought he was hot. And dangerous. And hearing him speak . . . it was like watching a panther run after a gazelle. I'd catch stories on PBS's *Langston-Douglas Black Journal* about him and his L*A*B patrolling Stun-Glas—"

"You watch PBS?" I asked. *"You* watch *Langston-Douglas Black Journal?"*

"Yeah," she said, flitting her head in an unspoken *no duh.* "So then they got their HUD contract, and Kareem was this up-and-comer, sexy, angry, successful, going places. So, like, this was four years ago and I was still an up-and-coming singer/heroine myself, and I was the opening act for Salt-N-Pepa's *Let's Talk About Sex* tour at the Hermes Theatre in Stun-Glas, and the L*A*B was doing security that night—"

"Four years ago . . . so Kareem, you would've been thirty, and Syndi, you would've . . . been only seventeen?"

Kareem's and Syndi's eyes faxed multipage documents to each other in text too small for me to read.

"Uh . . . yeah," she said. "Anyway, I arranged to meet him backstage after the concert. And I thought we, like, had this chemistry, but he was all, like, 'Aren't you a lesbian?' and I was like, 'Don't try to put me in your little box, baby. So are you down or what?' and he was like, 'No, I'm a black nationalist, I'm chaste, and even if I weren't I don't do white girls, and plus you're just a kid,' and I was like, 'Whatever! You're a man! You really think you can resist me?' And so I started tracking him down, and he was like, 'Stop following me,' and I was like, 'Nuh uh! *You* stop following *me*—'"

"Damn, Syndi," groaned Kareem. "Would you please give it up with all this 'like, like, like' shit? We're *here*, all right? Doctor-patient privilege? And after everything I've been through . . . ."

She looked at him, suddenly even softer.

"That's the first time you've called me by name since . . . ." She sighed. "All right, Kareem."

I said, "You're not twenty-one, are you, Syndi?"

She shook her head.

"And not a lesbian, either. So what else isn't real? The bubble-head act, obviously. So you really did write all those books, then."

"She's a marketing genius, Doc," said Kareem. "And one of the smartest women I ever met. That's why . . . why I started liking her."

Syndi glowed like an aromatherapeutic candle.

"So who was driving the bus?"

Kareem scrunched his face disgustedly. "What?"

"She's asking who 'wore the pants' in our relationship, Kareem. I'd say . . . it was pretty even, Eva," she said, nodding to encourage him to agree with her.

He laughed bitterly at her non-verbal request. "I'da been happy just if it'd just slowed down long enough for me to get *on* the bus! I spent the whole time running after it with my coat caught in the kot-tam *door!"*

Syndi wince-smiled abashedly. "She came on so strong, Doc. Wouldn't leave me alone, kept following me, until I couldn't get her out of my head. I knew I shouldn't've, but . . . kot-tam it, I was lonely. I've always been lonely. Wasn't like I'd ever had women chasing me. I'm not made of stone. She wore me down. So finally I agreed to meet her—incognito."

He sighed, deeply.

"I told her to drive out and meet me in San Sebastino at the only Ethiopian restaurant in town, a little place called Emerald Lion. She wasn't all tarted up that night. She was elegant. Wore a long black skirt. Her hair . . . it smelled like salt water and hot sand. And we just . . . talked. For hours. About music, food, books, comedy, art . . . .

"I'd been angry so long, *serious* so long . . . and suddenly there I was laughing, reminiscing about cartoons, toys, games, things I hadn't thought about since I was a kid. And feeling . . . totally free. In my life, I always had to set a conscious example, come correct, what we used to call in the L*A*B, be blackified.

"But with . . . *Syndi*," he said, visibly forcing himself to say her name again, "I didn't have to do that. Or need to do it. It was like, suddenly, all I had to do was just one thing: be happy. When I was with her, suddenly it was like there was no world, no politics, no mission, no duty. It was just us."

"And you so fell in love with her."

His mouth opened angrily, as if he were about to spit denial. But then he softened, looking at Syndi, then at me, and finally granted a single nod in defiance of himself.

A sigh almost broke into a sob in Syndi's throat. But she was smiling enough to crinkle her eyes.

"But then the L*A*B found out," I pushed. "What'd they do?"

Kareem glared out the window.

Syndi leapt in: "They told him to stop seeing me! What the hell business is it of theirs?"

"Why's this gotta be the big bad fetish—black man, white woman—like it's the end of the kot-tam world?" said Kareem. "You see these newspapers? These punks'd happily be printing headlines like 'Nigger B&E's Whitey's harem' even if the planet were plunging into the sun!"

"But didn't you used to feel the exact same way, Kareem? Isn't that what you said in your article?" He said nothing. "And you were denounced by whites for your *hypocrisy*, not your transracial eroticism. Those denunciations were almost all by blacks." He wouldn't answer. "So the L*A*B kicked you out. How did that make you feel?"

"I talked with Doctor Rogers," he said, "asked him what to do. The L*A*B was already under fire—we were about to lose our HUD contract, and now I was in the middle of a relationship I shouldn't've been having at all, for several reasons . . . . He said that everything was unfolding as it was meant to, that my destiny was ultimately to lead the F*O*O*J.

"I laughed! I mean, I figured he was yanking my spear, trying to cheer me up. But he wasn't kidding. So before the L*A*B could force me out I quit. Syndi'd already been in the F*O*O*J a year by then, done her probation, was already a made member, so she sponsored me. No one made the connection. But I'd already shocked the hell out of everyone just by asking to join."

"So what happened? Clearly you were both passionately in love. What went so wrong between you two that you even stopped saying Syndi's name?"

This time, instead of their eyes sending faxes to each other, the two turned towards opposite walls, my question rebuffed by their receivers being taken off their hooks.

LITTLE WHITE LIES AND BIG BLACK SECRETS

Unravelling the bandages covering Kareem's and Syndi's psychemotional wounds was exhaustive work, since their bloodied psychic linens were so crusted into each other they'd made a congealed experiential gore. As the night deepened, we baby-stepped our way through the basic facts towards what I'd sensed was a devastatingly destructive betrayal.

We established the basics: that the relationship was passionate but rocky, its secrecy deemed necessary by both but frustrating to each; that over time, Kareem saw Syndi as selfish, shallow, vain, and narcissistic, whereas Syndi came to see Kareem as obsessive, deluded, impersonal, and emotionally retarded.

And as was generally the case, the sexual problems that erupted during such a contrapersonal disconnect were misdiagnosed by the couple as cause rather than as effect.

From Kareem's perspective, Syndi had grown sexually unresponsive in the second year of their secret tryst, "after the kink wore off," he sneered, and also, according to him, because she was terrified that he was finally seeing through her multiple layers of deception and self-deception to gaze upon the "real" Syndi. The more she shut down verbally, psychemotionally, and sexually, the more frantically Kareem inverted their preset rôles of hunter and prey, driving her further from him and him deeper and deeper into chasing the connection with her and drowning himself in self-loathing.

And then, one night, in a desperate attempt to restart their physical passion and emotional intimacy, Syndi made a snap decision that shattered something in Kareem which apparently had not healed a bit in the two years that had followed. And the closer we moved towards gazing into that smouldering crater, the more Kareem's body stiffened and his face splintered.

"It'd been two months, Eva," said Syndi. "Since we'd. You know. Made love. I mean, we'd sleep in the same bed, but we wouldn't even hold each other.

"I was desperate, just . . . terrified it was over. I mean, I loved him . . . but all we did anymore was go through all the cloak and dagger bullshit just to see each other and spend the night together without any witnesses connecting us, and then we'd just argue! All night! Or sit in silence! Or sleep together without even touching each other. I just . . . I wanted to feel close to him, for the sex to be good again, for everything to be like it was in the beginning."

"So what did you do?"

Kareem's eyes flared. "So, great, not enough I'm humiliated in front of the kot-tam world, now I get humiliated here, too?"

"Kareem—" she said, reaching out for his knee or arm or shoulder or cheek, but he shoved himself off the chaise lounge and walked to the furthest point in the room from her, pretending to read a book he'd pulled from my shelf.

I forced her to look at me. "What did you do, Syndi?"

"I . . . " she said, trying to decide whether to confess, and finally: "I used my HEAT-ray on him."

"Your . . . your hyper-emulation beam? You . . . turned him into a copy of you? Which you controlled?"

She nodded. Kareem looked angry enough to bite through the wall.

"And it was amazing," she said. "I'd never felt anything like that in my life. Ever. It was so good . . . the best—"

"Kot-*TAM!*" snapped Kareem. "Can you *hear* yourself?"

"Kareem, please. Let Syndi process this. Continue, Syndi."

"That's it. I mean . . . what else can I say? It was really that good— mind-blowingly, Richter-scale fantastic. But after I relea— . . . when we were done . . . Kareem, he was shaking. And he . . . he cried. For an hour. And he wouldn't let me touch him. I'd never seen anyone react to the HEAT-ray like that before, but—"

"Had you ever used it in sex before?"

"No, but . . . no."

"Syndi, don't you think it's odd that although you've told me you're not a lesbian, you've presented yourself to the public as one for years, and that after finding yourself sexually unsatisfied with a man," (even without looking at Kareem I could hear him react) "turning him into a woman re-ignited your erotic energy?"

"No, Eva, you, you don't get it—that wasn't it at all. It's not that I turned . . . I mean, that Kareem became a . . . look, it's not that I was making love to a woman—"

"It's that you were making love to *you.*"

She swallowed, looked away from me, then down at the floor. "Yes," she whispered. "Yes."

"Kareem . . . you obviously had a strong psychemotional response to this sexual engagement—"

"'En*gage*ment!'" he hollered at the roof.

"You're verbalising a great deal of anti-happiness. Could it be that you're actually manifesting this anti-happiness towards yourself?"

He turned to me. "What in the hell are you talking about?"

"Are you 'angry' at yourself because you liked the experience so much? Of becoming a woman?"

His arms and legs slackened, and Kareem slumped against the wall, his jaw seemingly unhinged. He was literally panting with speechless rage.

"Gender confusion is a common experience, Kareem, and nothing to be ashamed of."

"I don't have 'gender confusion'!"

"Not to mention the psychic clash with your pronounced homophobia of being suddenly transformed into a lesbian—"

"I am *not* homophobic and I didn't 'become' a lesbian—"

"—well, a clash of your becoming a woman despite your deeply-held sexism—"

"For fucking out loud, *I AM NOT SEXIST!*"

"—well, whatever label you choose to affix, you were frightened by this experimentation—"

"It wasn't 'experimentation,' Eva! It was exploi*ta*tion! Complete kot-tam humiliation! So I got angry—to use a word you fear so much—angry because someone who said she loved me could make me her puppet, her toy, her kot-tam slave, and then have the gall to expect me to like it! To expect me to willingly throw up my wrists for her to lock the cuffs on again! And because she couldn't muster up a gram of shame or face a milligram of my righteous rage at her betrayal, she, can you get this, *she* dumped *me!*"

"But look at your every word and gesticulation, Kareem," I said, gesturing gently to reassure him of the liberating truth of my diagnosis. "It's not her you're angry at. It's yourself."

He howled at the ceiling. "Do you ever listen to anyone but yourself, Eva? Ever think an original thought that hasn't dripped like toxic sewage out of one of your head-shrinking, misanthropic, pseudo-science textbooks? Man, *Stalin* could've paid you to write narration!"

"So you're telling me you're not angry at yourself? Not even a little?"

"If I'm angry at myself, it's not because I 'liked' what she did to me, but because I put up with her as long as I did. I'm angry because she had the means and motive and I still gave her the opportunity to fuck me over like she did, literally! And because I didn't dump her ass before she could dump me!"

"Kareem, anger isn't the opposite of joy any more than hate is the opposite of love. Both are manifestations of intense attention, focus, pre-occupation: your anger and hatred toward Syndi are proof of your joy in her and your love of her."

"So you're telling me that if a woman is raped, her obsessive anger and hatred prove she loves her rapist?"

"Kareem, the effort you devote to dodging obvious realisations proves my point. The very intensity of how much you deny having enjoyed your experiences as a woman—"

"I didn't! How many times do I have to say that?"

"—case in point—are simply denial. Obviously you loved being dominated by Syndi, and your enjoyment in becoming a woman is directly proportional to the effort you expend bearing the awesome psychic yoke of rigid African-American machodeterministic phallarchical gender rôles. It's been amply documented in studies of heterosexual Afro-American drag-queen subculture that many black men harbour psychefragmentary 'lesbians' inside themselves—alternate sexual personalities or 'sex alters,' if you will—a condition referred to on the street as being 'on the down-low, sideways.' Do you deny that?"

"Deny what?" guffawed Kareem. "That you're psychotic?"

I waited. When he refused to say anything else, I shifted angles.

"Kareem, Syndi . . . do you hate each other . . . or do you still love each other?"

Again, each one turned to the other, glaring in agonised aggravation, anticipation. Desperation.

"Well?"

Suddenly Syndi was sobbing.

I offered her the box of tissues.

Kareem, against himself, staggered towards her, finally sitting on the end of the chaise opposite her.

I asked about her tears.

"Because, because," she wailed, "because everything's falling apart, because he hates me, because everyone's leaving me . . . ."

"That's the second time you've said that, Syndi," I said, gesturing for her to take another tissue. Her cheeks were channelled with black lines, a white porcelain sink dirtied by a child's playground mud. "What do you mean, 'everyone's leaving me?'"

She shook her head again and again while blowing her nose. "My mother," she said at last.

"Yes? What about her, Syndi?

"My mother . . . my whole life, she always, always put me last. I was like a dog, you know? Waiting on the couch by the window the whole day for its master to come home, but the master never does, and so the dog practically breaks its fucking tail off wagging and whimpering and whining alone . . . . That's why . . . when Kareem was always so obsessed with his job instead of bothering to spend time with me, focus on me, take care of me, I just couldn't take it. I got scared, and I pushed him away. Because he was already pushing me away, don't you get it?" She hiccupped her sobs. And while the exhaustion on Kareem's face suggested he' heard her story before, the pain on his face was as real as hers.

"I'm surprised, Syndi," I said, "because from everything you've ever told me, you and Bianca have an excellent, close bond, not to mention the most famously successful—and lucrative—mother-manager/daughter-talent relationship in either showbiz or in superheroics—"

"No!" she choked, looking up and moaning. "No! Bianca's . . . she's not . . . she's not my mother, Eva, she's just my agent. That was just a cover-story. I'm crying . . . because my real mother's dying.

"What?" said Kareem. "Syndi, then who's . . . Kot-tam, Syndi, are you saying—"

"Yes," she said, choking back a sob and visibly making a decision. "My real name is Inga Icegaard. My mother is Iron Lass."

And suddenly, there it was.

With her hair now ravenfeather-black and her eyes bright sapphires on the black felt of smeared mascara, the axe-blade of her cheekbones and the taper of her chin, it had been hidden right in front of us all along.

Looking into his pinballing eyes, I could see Kareem was as stunned as I was. His face was a sorting machine, visibly re-evaluating his every experience and conversation and fight and sorrow with Syndi, not to mention his workplace-relationship with Iron Lass and her witness of the last two years of his behaviour towards her daughter.

And then something else suddenly stormed into his eyes, like a vision of thundering horses and a chaos of lightning.

The X-Man bolted out of the room without so much as a glance goodbye.

"Kareem!" shrieked Syndi, crying again. *"Kareem . . . ."*

How will you face knowing that you will never exceed, or even equal, the accomplishments of your predecessors?

　　Syndi: "I never asked for glory. Just unconditional love."

DOES YOUR HEART COME WRAPPED IN YOUR CAPE?

Now that the age of heroism is drawing to a close, or even when it was at its peak, if you've found yourself spinning from one frantic come-here/go-away relationship to another, then it's time to start owning your rôle in creating your own misery, loneliness, and feelings of worthlessness.

As a superhero, you may have told yourself that your central purpose was saving lives and protecting the public peace. But now that your apartment is empty, your bed is cold, and your freezer contains nothing but Lean Cuisine Depression-Buster Parfaits®, then it's time you took ruthlessly courageous action.

Ask yourself: while donning the cape and tights may have seemed to be about helping others, was it actually always about helping you? Were you actually connecting in your heart and mind the applause of the crowd with Daddy throwing you in the air and saying "Attaboy!" and Mommy nuzzling you to her chest and telling you that you'll always be her "bestest widdle girl?"

Now that the world has gone quiet around you, you have the time to face the ultrafoe who's been stalking you all along: your fear of being forgotten, unloved, and alone.

Don't back off from the challenge. Don't surrender. In the jungle of your unfolding developmental path, don't let yourself sink beneath the psychemotional quicksand of alcohol, drugs, cybendorphins, serial sexual conquests (or surrenders), or krypto-suicidal reckless adventurism. Because you need to capture the destructive nemesis known as Doctor Despair, since he's been holding in his cold, cobalt claws the two powers you've always truly needed but never known how to attain: self-awareness, and through it, self-actualisation.

CHAPTER TEN

The Battle of All Mothers, the Mother of All Battles

YEARNING FOR DÉTENTE ON THE EVE OF WAR

SUNDAY, JULY 16, 10 A.M.

It was a Sunday morning. And quiet. A family reunion in the hospital.

Festus, Syndi/Inga, and I were sitting in the silence of the Squirrel Tree Medical Hollow suite of Hnossi Icegaard.

The dying goddess was writhing in tortured sleep.

Once raven-haired, she now had a mane of oxidised hospital green; once cream-complexioned, her skin was a minefield of festering red-grey craters. She was covered in sensor pads feeding biometrics to the machines counting out her final days on the planet, like a female Gulliver roped down by med-tech Lilliputians.

Festus, who'd never hidden his contempt for Syndi, had maintained an undeclared truce since we'd arrived at 9 A.M. and she'd explained her genealogy. His face betrayed no surprise; perhaps the self-proclaimed "world's greatest detective" had already known, or perhaps his affect had been steam-rollered into a parking lot by recent events. Either way, he'd accepted Power Grrrl's "new" civilian name, dark hair, and altered clothes and speech without comment.

Syndi/Inga looked especially tragic that morning. She was clad in a tight black leotard shirt and skirt, and her white pancake make-up and black lipstick and eye shadow were framed by her black hair, the so-called "Neo-Orc" look she'd popularised on the cover of her first multi-platinum album, *Jagged Little Pudenda.*

The quiescence splintered when Festus suddenly whispered into his wrist while cupping his ear. "How long was he there? . . . Well, if he comes back . . . . Yes—like a hawk. The second that recidivist reprobate—yes, exactly."

"What's going on?" asked Power Grrrl.

"It's your boyfriend," growled Festus.

"He's not—what about him?"

"After he fled Miss Brain's clinic last night he went to the Fortress. Spent all night on the computers."

"So what, Festus? He's a F*O*O*Jster. He's got a right to be there. But now you've got someone spying on him?"

"Apparently your ex-lover was hacking into private F*O*O*J personnel files, 'Inga,' and focusing his search on the known weaknesses of his colleagues."

He leaned forward, narrowing his eyes and scanning her frame as if deciding on which of her limbs he should barbecue first. "Any idea why?"

Indignantly, she said, "How would *I* know?"

"I expect you *might* know, you little—"

Wet hacking—a sound like the plungering of a soup kitchen sink—drowned the proto-fight. Festus rubbed Hnossi's back with rough gentleness, holding an emesis bowl beneath her bowed face. Wiping the bright copper sputum from her lips, he asked her what she wanted him to do for her.

"Nussink, Festus," she whispered. "You'ff been grandt." Turning to Power Grrrl, she said, "Miss Tycho. How nice uff you. Sank you for comink—"

"I told them, Mother," she said. "They know."

Hnossi fell silent, her face a Mona Lisa of melancholy, a Klimt of verklempt.

"Come on, Miss Brain," said Festus, standing. "These two need to be alone."

"No, Festus," snapped Hnossi, raising her hand in *stop* and dragging tubes, wires, and sensors with it. "I tried asking *Fräu Doktor* ze uzzer day . . . to help me . . . to help Inga unt me . . . put behint us all our discort. Before ze ent. Vich now . . . is almost here."

SHUTTING OFF THE CURRENT OF THE PAST

If your family contains intergenerational hyper-hominidism, then whatever dysfunctional tendencies exist inside your relationships are magnified by the proportional strength and agility of the powers you collectively manifest. In order to discharge the psychic voltage between mother and daughter, as in the case I had that morning, we first had to shut down the breakers whose power had been convulsing Hnossi's consciousness into an id confrontation-loop for decades.

"To help both of you sort out this mother-daughter contradynamic, especially given the . . . shall we say, 'time constraints' involved," I told them, "since we don't have the option of years of therapy, we need to delve immediately into your relationship, Hnossi, with your own mother."

Staring at me with her icy amethyst eyes, Hnossi reached weakly for her emesis basin, loosened her lower lip, and let drip a long, viscous, purple-green cord which plopped into the pail, which she rested back on her side table.

That was her only response.

"Hnossi," I tried again, "without examining your mother's template that you inherited and which formed you—the same one you used unconsciously to draw the contours of your own relationship with Inga— we can't reformat it so you can redraw your relationship with her now."

"Surely, *Doktor*," she rasped, "you haff more to help us in our hour uff neet zan zese barkain-basement Freudian clichés about muzzer-blamink!"

"Eva," said Inga, holding up a warning finger, "don't listen to her. She's trying to bat your arm away because your aiming your arrow right at the bull's eye."

Hnossi glowered at her daughter, a look cold enough to freeze sunshine and shatter it on the pavement.

"Ze real proplem for me, *Doktor*, is ze pain of realising zat my daughter hass vasted her talents unt her career gallivanting arount in front of ze cameras for nussing uzzer zan fame, fortune, unt scandal, like a golt-luffing little slut—"

Jutting her head forward, Inga scalded out the words: "You mean. Just. Like. *Gramma?*"

I waited for Hnossi to deny the charge, but she maintained the killer frost of her glare.

"My mother, Hnossi Icegaard," said Inga at last, "is the accidental feminist icon who secretly spent her career trying to keep women out of the F*O*O*J or from climbing the ranks, and is maybe the most sexually repressed woman I've ever known."

"Inka! You shut your mouse! You don't know vut you're talking about!"

"And all of it," said Inga, "because she's disgusted by her own mother! Did you know her own father left them? She's spent her whole life looking for a powerful man to pull her wagon. Why do you think she was so devastated when Hawk King died? But then, when whatever man she'd finally tricked into falling in love with her eventually, inevitably turned out not to be strong enough to reach her stratospheric standards— because, I mean, who could ever be as strong as the strongest woman in the world?—she'd crush him like a monk stomping grapes and then go on a bender with the wine. And that's," said Inga, "what she did to my dad!"

And so with Hnossi's eyes aiming liquid nitrogen all over her daughter, Inga-Ilsabetta Icegaard revealed the neurotically distorted prunings of her family tree, and hinted at how her mother's problems with love resulted in a failed marriage, damaged children, and a terrible fate for her daughter that Hnossi did nothing to prevent.

CURDLING THE MILK OF HUMAN KINDNESS

From the contents of Hnossi's F*O*O*J personnel file, and from my own observations of her and her daughter's interaction, a three dimensional image had begun to emerge. It's the Hnossi who stood beyond—or lay behind—the iconic warrior goddess and the type-A professor of Military History, Political Economy, and German and Scandinavian Literature.

Clearly, Hnossi Icegaard was a woman who'd been upset about many things for many centuries, and was, no doubt, sexually repressed, quite likely in reaction to the extensive coitalambulation of her own mother, for as Inga/Syndi put it, "Gramma Freyja was a major ho."

Content for millennia to be mistaken as the daughter of the Aesir goddess Frigg, wife of Odin and Queen of Aesgard, Hnossi hid the shame of her true genealogy as the daughter to the Vanir goddess Freyja, who was commonly mistaken either for the regal Frigg, or for Idun, keeper of the Apple of Youth. History recorded Hnossi as having only one sister, Gersimi. But according to Inga, "gramma" Freyja actually had nine hundred and ninety-nine daughters, all of whom she raised on Mount Snafulnir near the "party halls" of Folkvangar and Sessrumnir.

By all accounts, Hnossi's mother Freyja was exceedingly beautiful; but her marriage to the god Odur ended when he "disappeared." Distraught to the core, Freyja wandered Midgard in despair for him while crying tears of purest gold. Intensely vulnerable, Freyja engaged in tens of thousands of dalliances with gods, humans, elves, dwarves, giants, and sundry other magickal beings, all the while sinking into the disreputable practice of *seidr* magic.

Eternal scallywag and Ragnarokian rogue Loki went so far as to accuse Freyja of sleeping with every god in Aesgard, every elf in Alfheim, and even her own brother Freyr; while the trickster deity and storm giant was forced into a retraction and a sealed settlement in Aesgard's Hall of Judgement, the victory was purely Pyrrhic for Freyja ("her *only* purity," quipped Loki famously) since her own actions had already ruined her reputation.

But Freyja was also a goddess of combat and death whose lust for men was equalled only by her lust for war and gold. Possessing a birdfeather cloak which she used to transform herself into a falcon, and a chariot drawn by two iron cats, Freyja sometimes wandered the earth at night disguised as a goat, and when not transporting the souls of the slain to Valhalla, she was adding to her jewellery collection, as when she famously acquired the necklace Brisingamen as payment for sleeping with the four Brising dwarves.

Witnessing this sad, pathetic, carnal crusade for love, and embittered by the booty of shame and humiliation she'd amassed as a result, young Hnossi sought recruitment into the sorority of battle-maiden Valkyries, clutching at the hope that by joining an organisation she'd equated with purity, she could escape one side of her family history while embracing the other.

Historical accounts listed Hnossi as an unflinchingly brave warrioress who personally dispatched untold thousands of elves, dwarves, giants and monsters back to the Niflheim damnation of the nethergoddess Hel; in the modern era, Iron Lass had masterminded the *Götterdämmerung*, conceived its strategy, issued its battle cry, and even written its manifesto.

Having broken from what she saw as her own mother's lack of control, Hnossi Icegaard became the quintessential controller, a strategist supreme of global affairs. But lacking a model for wife-and-motherhood, the control she so desperately wielded could not but cause chaos inside the family she was about to create.

As Inga/Syndi said, Hnossi—perhaps to replace the father whom she never knew and to repair the psychemotional damage caused by the mother she did—pursued extremely strong men. In the 20th Century she fell in love with and married the human mortal Hector "Quetzalcoatl" El Santo, HKA Strong Man. Five months later, Inga-Ilsabetta El Santo y Icegaard was born, who was followed two years later in 1964 by younger brother "Lil Boulder" Baldur.

Strong Man was indeed a strong man. Having risen to prominence in the Mexican wrestling circuit, Strong Man claimed to have derived his powers by ingesting the miraculous "Maize of Chac Mol;" his strength increased with every year of his life until he could pick up entire oil tankers with his gloved hands.

But Strong Man's powers weren't limited to physical deeds; he invested his profits from wrestling and crime-fighting back into Mexico's wrestling and film industries. Capitalising upon his own reputation and the putative source of his powers, he invented Corna Cola (which despite its Anglo name became Latin America's third most popular soft drink), created the Yucataxi Cab Company, bought out the entire Volkswagen manufacturing base in Mexico, and founded the popular fast food "Milk Chac" chain in the USA.

The union of two such attractive, dashingly heroic figures led to a decade of magazine covers and idolisation; the story-book couple of the hyper-hominid world was considered the marriage to emulate.

But it was all a sham. Despite the passion of the relationship, by 1974 the milk of loving-kindness had curdled under the heat of acrimony whose causes neither spouse ever revealed. Separating from his wife,

Hector El Santo returned to Mexico to raise both his children in a remote Mayan fortress in the Yucatan. From that familial stronghold, he rebuffed her ever-increasing attempts at reconciliation, rejecting her ever-greater declarations of devotion, devotion which burned far more hotly during separation than it ever had during their togetherness.

Finally, in 1981, after seven years of separation, El Santo filed for divorce.

One month later to the day, Iron Lass declared the *Götterdämmerung*.

"I always wanted more for myself," said Syndi, concluding her matriography, "than the barren, angry, cruel life my mother'd hacked out for herself. All she knows, Eva, is how to keep people away, keep people on the wrong end of her swords, how to keep herself cold and hard. Like iron."

I turned to Hnossi, expecting rage. Instead I saw exhaustion: the rust craters dimmed her appearance as if she were fading into a red dusk, the medical webs strewn across her seemingly weighing her down like steel cables.

"Inka . . . " said Iron Lass, releasing a sigh over thirty full seconds, as if the effort to form the words is a mountain-sized yoke, *"grow up."*

Inga glared at the ceiling.

"Alvays it is ze same vis you. Vut do you sink zis vurlt is made uff, hmm? Nussing but canties unt sugar-cakes unt parties unt dencing unt booze-soaked sex?"

"Oh, right! Because there certainly were never any parties or drinking or sex in Aesgard!"

"Joy unt luff . . . zese are *illusions*, my daughter. If you luff a men he vill alvays hurt you—if you trust a friend she vill stab you in ze guts. Life is hard vurk, drutchery, boredom, exhaustion. At its finest it's honour unt devotion to higher ideals zan oneself, unt *ja*, higher even zan one's family, which you could never see! You're a demi-goddess, Inka . . . you must rise to assume your true status. Beingk in an organisation such as ze FOOCH means protecting mortal civilians, but not beingk *like* zem, not vallovink in zeir veakness unt self-pity unt ridiculous neet for 'luff'—"

"Like you did?" said Inga. "So why bother devoting your life to protecting people you despise, mother? Why not just abandon them, like you abandoned daddy and us?"

"I dit not abandon any of you! You all abandoned me, remember?"

"Even when you were with us," said Inga, "you weren't!"

THE BATTLE OF ALL MOTHERS, or;
NOT F*O*O*J BUT F*O*O*I: FAMILY OF ORIGIN ISSUES

Throughout their argument, both goddess and demi-goddess walked the brink of discussing what I suspected was the trauma that had caused the greatest tragedy between them. For a daughter to side with a father following a parental separation, and then to develop two nested secret identities to sever her connection with mother, indicated a profoundly violent amputation in the body of mother-daughter connection.

Despite Iron Lass's paradigmatic divergence from her daughter, Hnossi raised no objections to the biographical facts recounted by Inga. Nor did she say anything to rebut the charge that she both admired and despised the powerful males she pursued, squeezing from them whatever professionally nutritive juices she could before shoving them into the relationship composter, as her own mother Freyja had done before her and as Syndi would do after.

The sole counterpoint in Hnossi's behavioural script was her adulation of Hawk King. Because Hnossi's contempt for men had always become directly proportional to their desire for her, the Egyptian strong man's unavailability to any woman only magnified Hnossi's adulation of him, guaranteeing that the elder god's death would crack valleys into the lowlands of Hnossi's flattened affect. Arguably, the disruption of her immortal immune system which had led to her terminal condition should have been assigned in part to the psychemotional devastation caused by her true icon's death.

But Hawk King's allure for Hnossi went beyond his by-then-permanent unattainability. Hnossi had inherited her mother's magical feather cloak; while she could not transform herself into a falcon, in her possession the cloak transmuted into giant hawk wings. Hawk King had been famous for his impartiality, wisdom, and strict but compassionate leadership and guidance. His epithet among the super-community as simply "the King" spoke to the esteem in which he was held by all.

Unfortunately for Hnossi and her family, even while she'd admired Hawk King's character, Hnossi had failed to manifest his kindly demeanour. She didn't deny Inga's charges that on rare family "adventure" camping trips to Jotunheim and Pacari, Hnossi would become so enraged at her family's refusal to follow her strict camping protocols (for instance, prohibitions against sleeping late or intra-meal snacking) that she would go so far as to throw things at her husband—things such as boulders. Once when Hector failed to have the morning coffee ready at the instant of sunrise, she ripped down a butte and struck him over the head with it, terrifying the children, destroying their chariot, and badly denting their iron cats with the resulting rubble.

Mothering had come no easier to Hnossi than had wifing; despite nicknaming her son Baldur "Lil Boulder," the boy possessed neither super-strength nor invulnerability. Instead, much to his father's delight, he was a brilliant painter and muralist who emitted scented paints from his fingertips as a spider would secrete webbing.

Considered by many to be a prodigy of Diego Riveran proportions, the eight-year old took it upon himself to paint the entirety of Spectre Valley with a mural depicting the Mayan story of creation and doomsday. Art critics from around the planet flew at once to California to examine "the Work," as it was called, some hailing it as the greatest single giant artwork in human history, not to mention the best-smelling. Hnossi disagreed, ordering the boy to scrub off the entire work by hand since he'd painted it without state permission and was facing charges of vandalism, mischief, and destruction of a state park. Hector and Hnossi clashed bitterly over the incident, Hnossi going so far as to denounce "ze undik-nified life of an artist" to her former-actor husband before freezing and burning off the mural with her twin swords. The wedge between them crept deeper.

Hnossi's opinion of her elder child had been even less encouraging. While Inga's early powers didn't include hyper-emulation, her singing was hypnotic—literally. But since Hnossi disliked rival F*O*O*Jster the Siren (the heroine whose 1968 lawsuit forced the Fraternal Order Of Justice to change its name to the non-gender-specific "Fantastic"), Hnossi was entirely unsupportive of her daughter having any similar power. Desperately lacking her mother's positive reinforcement, young Inga soon began taking advantage of her hypnovocalism, singing to children and adults—especially males—to bend them to her bidding. The only people immune to Inga's powers were her kin. But her father and brother adored her because of their familial bond, not requiring any sonic manipulation for their experience of love.

"But there's something much deeper than this," I told Syndi. "Something your mother won't go near and something you're only hinting at. Something truly awful between you two which made you distance yourself from your mother so greatly that you created two secret identities with which to obscure your connection to her. What is it?"

Hnossi's ancient, deathly eyes fixed on her daughter like leeches, whether to shut her daughter down, or finally open her up, I was not sure.

Inga/Syndi got up and excused herself to go to the bathroom.

The moment she returned, I said, "Tell me about Cassiopeia Rand."

"What?" said Inga, floored. She clutched her hands to her chest as if my question has denuded her. "How the hell did you know about her?"

"Festus," I said, showing her a folder from my briefcase. "He's been very helpful with supplying additional background material from his extensive files."

"My god!" said Inga, shaking her head and looking with disgust towards the ceiling. "How long has that old fascist been spying on me? On all of us?"

"Ach, Inga," rasped her mother. "Stop beingk so dramatic. Ze man is ze vurlt's greatest detectiff. Vut dit you expect him to do vis his information-gazzering apparatus? Answer cross-vurt puzzles?"

"Duh, I dunno, how about, catch criminals? And not invade the privacy of law-abiding citizens?"

"Answer ze qvestion. Who is zis Cassiopeia Rand?"

"Inga," I pressed, "tell me about Space Girl."

THE DEBUT, DISAPPEARANCE, AND DOWNFALL OF SPACE GIRL

"I had problems igniting my career, okay?" said Inga, glaring at me with all the toxic, self-indulgent angst of her Syndi Tycho persona, but without the incessant use of *like* and *gawd*.

"It was 1981. I was nineteen. So I tried making my debut as Cassiopeia Rand, PKA Space Girl. I was singing Latin pop-lite tunes—this was years before Gloria Estefan blew up—and fighting a little crime on the side with my hypnovoice, just to get some press.

"I was starting to move up, get noticed. I even had a cable special with special appearances by Cher, Cheech Marin, and Tim Conway. But the *day* my special aired," she said, jutting her lower lip towards the hospital bed, "mother up and declared her global war. Every channel was glued on her and her crusade for the next month! Debuts are delicate, Eva! And mine, thanks to her, was a complete dud! And unlike in heroics, in showbiz, you don't get second chances."

Having believed her career was over, Inga-Ilsabetta exiled herself out east, eventually studying marketing, music production, and singing at the Alison Blair Institute for Advanced Disco Studies. Excelling in every course, she finally created a brand new persona through which to reinvent herself by 1987 and forge her own second chance.

Dyeing her hair, and with the almost-perpetually youthful looks of a demigoddess, she emerged as Syndi Tycho, HKA Power Grrrl, who in 1991 capitalised upon the need of the post-*Götterdämmerung* F*O*O*J to reinvent itself, too, in the wake of the promised "peace dividend." An angry, exhausted, and broke public needed happy, lively, pretty new faces if the F*O*O*J were to survive into its new post-villain era. Fast-tracked, the "seventeen-year old" became a made member in 1991 after a mere six month candidacy, and immediately launched extensive marketing tie-ins with her new "legitimacy."

"The government loved me, the F*O*O*J's corporate sponsors loved me," said Syndi, "the public loved me, everyone loved me. Everyone was happy. It was great."

"How about your mother?" I asked without malice, regretting the crumpling of her features as soon as I saw it. "How about you? Did you love yourself? Have you ever been truly happy?"

"Of course I loved myself! Of course I'm happy! What kind of question is that?"

"I think you didn't feel loved, Syndi . . .. or should I call you Inga? That you never felt you were getting enough love. That you had a hole in your soul. That you believed your mother'd never given you enough of what you needed. That you had to comfort your heart-shattered father and raise your little brother by yourself, depriving you of time just to be a girl. You feared Kareem would never put you first—"

"Is that a crime, Eva? To be more in touch with my need for love than other people are?"

"It's not a question of crime, but dysfunction, and of causing damage to others. You seduced Kareem emotionally, not just sexually. And the ramifications for him have been gigantic. Scandal might help you sell more albums, but this could quite likely be the end of Kareem's career."

"Unt you hat no right to treat Fraulein Biceps like zat," said Hnossi. "She vuss a gut varrior. She deservt better. Regardless of her uzzer . . . you know. Her . . . *liebenschtyle.*"

"After you felt your mother'd rejected you," I said to Inga, "you determined you'd never be rejected again. By anyone. Every relationship you've ever had—familial, platonic, romantic—you ended before the other person could, or controlled it financially, as with Bianca."

"God!" she said, pacing the tiny room like a black rat in a white box. "This is completely wrong, Eva! We're supposed to be talking about what my *mother* did wrong! *She's* the reason I'm so messed up!"

"'Messed up'? Earlier you claimed you were happy and felt loved. Inga . . . anyone as desperate as you were, as you still are, to avoid rejection—I mean, your entire career has been about attracting the attention you equate with love so as to guarantee yourself a never-ending 'fix.' Anyone that terrified of rejection has unquestionably harmed or debased herself in ways she isn't proud of. Ways she may never have told another living soul . . . ."

Inga froze, focusing on me tapping the cover of my **POWER GRRRL** folder. Her blue eyes paled into water.

"Vut is it? Vut's she talking about, Inka?" said Hnossi. "I don't understandt . . . vut are you getting at, *Doktor?*"

"You really should tell your mother, Inga."

"This is so unethical of you, Eva!"

"Inka," said Hnossi heavily, "tell me."

Inga scrambled up into a chair as if afraid of floor mice, hugged her knees against her chest, her eyes looking like huge balls of wet ice.

"I did the capes," she mumbled.

"*Vut?* Inka, you're not—you're not *serious*—"

Her daughter said nothing, except for what her glare said to me.

"Odin's eye," whispered the dying goddess.

The niche pornography industry called the capes, worth an estimated $2.5 billion annually in the US alone, served those men and women who sexually fetishised superhero tunics and the people who wore them. In rare occasions, though, a genuine superheroine or hero (but always a fallen one) gained "employment" in the field, appearing in films, videos, and holograms. Best known of these was the sole "success" story: Magna, the 1980s heroine and daughter of the Lodestone. At the height of the *Götterdämmerung* she'd left crime-fighting to begin her own highly profitable pornographic production company in whose features she'd frequently "starred."

Festus's file demonstrated with explicit photographic proof how Inga, then-HKA Cassiopeia Rand, took on the capes pseudonym Space Girl to appear in "supporting" rôles of "adventure" films such as *Magna: Pirate of Men's Pants*, "science documentaries" such as *The Theory of Magnajism*, and the "intellectual eroticism" of *Magna Cums Laudly*.

"But there's more, Inga," I said, "isn't there?"

"Mein todt, how can it get any vurse zan *zis, Doktor?"* moaned Hnossi, clutching at whatever frosted-green crabgrass remained attached to her skull. "Mein own dottir! A whore for ze cameras! Zis is all her fazzer's fault, ze filse of all his show-biz dreams—"

"Hnossi, please! Inga—all these years desperately craving attention, pursuing show business and reinventing yourself and even manufacturing scandals to guarantee the attention your mother denied you and that you equated with love. Always being the one to end relationships first. All of it to ensure you would never be rejected and that instead you would be the one doing the rejecting. What's the ultimate way to ensure that?"

I looked at both women. Neither would look at me.

"Ladies, please," I said. "The signs are all there, as giant and unavoidable as sky-writing. Will one of you please verbalise what happened to you and your family after you, Inga, at the tender age of twelve, attempted suicide?"

DISCOVERING—AND HEALING—
THE SCARED LITTLE GODDESS INSIDE YOU

Despite the younger Icegaard's propensity for blaming her problems on her mother, the suicide attempt was the sole damage zone even she had feared to re-tread, perhaps because once she began, there was no going back. If the "answers" her terminal mother gave her were insufficient, she would forever be denied her one chance to heal, even the opportunity to wonder "what if?"

Recounting her years in and out of therapy, Inga/Syndi parabolically approached the issue of her pre-teen attempt at self-murder.

"For years, I thought I'd done it because maybe I'd been abused," she said. "I had all these recovered memories from my other therapists . . . memories of mother . . . beating me. Cutting me with her swords, cutting my limbs off and magically reattaching them so the police wouldn't suspect anything.

"But then I had this one therapist, and he said I should talk with Daddy and Baldur about it, and, and . . . well, now I know it was just the other therapists screwing with my head, planting these ideas in my mind. But I've always had this problem with, you know, depression? And I used to cut myself, throw myself off of buildings and cliffs and things, burning myself, trying to hurt myself . . . . My therapist said it was Munchausen Syndrome. Said I was trying to get mother to rescue me."

She smiled coldly, then reduced her expression to a corpse's repose. "It didn't work," she concluded.

Of all memories, "recovered" ones are the most unreliable. According to Dr. Steve N. Strainge, the psychiatrist whose testimony interred Dr. Napoleon Orator on Asteroid Zed, Menton's career of manipulation began before even he realised he had such powers. For years during the therapy sessions he conducted, he had been implanting false memories of trauma in his patients, after which he was paid to supply expert testimony at trial for clients suing their former babysitters, coaches, pastors, teachers, siblings, parents, delivery men, meter men, and aldermen.

But since Inga had successfully detached from her therapist-implanted pseudo-memories, there was hope for her eventual recovery, even if we then had to descend deeper into the swamps of her dysfunctionally agonised adolescence.

I asked her to tell me what had precipitated her attempt.

"Mother," said Inga, "was out. Again. Always on some mission. She and *Papito* had been fighting for what must've been two days straight, and this was after two years of a downhill shit-slide with them. I mean, it was both of them, yeah, but it was *her* fault.

"So *Papito*, he couldn't take it anymore, said he was going out and she was screaming at him and telling him *Iff you go out now don't even* sink *about coming back* and he just said *Fine, maybe I won't,* and he rushed back in and packed a suitcase and I was trying to hold onto him and drag him back but he was almost as strong as Wally, and I was crying and begging him *Don't leave, Daddy, please don't leave!* and I was terrified, terrified that she'd finally driven him away and that I wouldn't ever see him again—"

"Zis is out*rageous!*" said Hnossi, her red-grey pockmarks glowing like campfire coals. "Zat's not how it happent at all! She vuss a childt! She doesn't remember how it happendt—"

"Hnossi, please," I said, forming my hands into a time-out **T**. "We all have our own truth—"

"Ach, vut *sheisen* you peddle! Zere is no *my truse* unt *your truse!* There is only *ze* truse, uzzerwise zere *iss* no truse at all!"

"Please don't interrupt. You'll have your turn. Inga, go on."

"—and so Daddy's gone and I'm on the floor sobbing, and like two seconds go by and then her *comm* goes off, for Ymir's sake, and then she's all *I've gotta go fight ze Gorgon Legion or some ice giants or vutever and you're in charch of your liddle brudder until I get back* and boom—she's gone, just like that!

"So she's gone and Daddy's gone and Baldur and I are alone all night and all the next day *and for the next two fucking days and nights after that!*" said Inga, plucking at her tight, black, long-sleeved shirt as if she were rehearsing ripping the skin and flesh from her skeleton. "I was twelve, mother! *Twelve!*"

"You vere a bik girl, you vere olt enough—people were goingk to be killt unless—"

"Unless you personally went and did your heroine-thing because it's not like you ever said no even though there were a hundred other F*O*O*Jsters who could've—"

"None vis my powers, experience, knowletch—"

"Sure, right, because it's all about proving how *you're* the toughest bitch who ever lived, that you don't need *anyone*, that *no one's* better than you, and that you have *no* weaknesses, not even a husband who couldn't take your shit anymore so he left you, or two scared little kids you abandoned at home that you could never wait to escape at the very first buzz on your wrist—"

"People *neetet* me! How can you not unterstant zat?"

"*We* needed you, Mother!" screamed Inga, sobbing. "*I* needed you!"

I cut in: "So what did you do, Inga?"

"I was so tired . . . of being scared. And lonely. And then all of a sudden I just felt this, this surge of power, of bravery, like nothing I'd ever felt before. Totally, one hundred percent determined—the 'will to power,' Mother always called it—like I was drunk or stoned or on fire. I knew where mother kept all her magickal implements, the stuff we were never supposed to go near, and I knew the spell to open the lock. I took *Jörmungandrstooth*, this *seidr* blade she had at the bottom of this one trunk . . . and I invoked the name of Ymir . . . and then I, I just—"

Her lips shut. Her eyes shut. She mimed a fast motion over her wrist, eight times in total.

Her eyes opened, ablaze from reliving her truth. "And then my soul was ripped out of me," she said, "and sucked right down into the depths of Niflheim and into the hands of Hel."

And Hnossi, despite her reputation for never crying, who only two weeks before had sat across from me at Soup 'n' Heroes crying iron ingot tears, sat upright in her hospital bed, seeping not liquid metal, but tears of pale, ordinary water.

"I came home," said Hnossi in a weakened voice that began shattering, "as soon as Odin's ravens fount me, tolt me vut you't done to yourself. I fought my vay srough ze ice-hordes of Niflheim unt zen against Hel herself to get you beck! Do you not remember zis? I risked my life, my soul to safe you, becoss you are my only dottir, my first born, my little—"

"And what did you do the very next morning after you brought me back, Mother?" said Inga with sufficient acid to melt both her mother's swords.

Silenced, Hnossi simply stared at her daughter with perfect vulnerability, that of the accused who'd just accidentally surrendered checkmate evidence to the tribunal, and who'd glimpsed the approach of the executioner.

"You went back to work," said Inga, her smile awful and vicious with irony. "You spent nine days in the netherworlds slicing the icicles off of frost giants, but for your weak, stupid daughter who tried to kill herself out of loneliness, you could not sit still for one lousy fucking day.

"After almost losing me forever, *you went back to work.*"

Inga waited for her mother to speak.

When Hnossi said nothing, Inga finally barked, "Nothing to say, woman?"

Everything was charged with emotion—even Inga's darkened mane and Hnossi's pale green tufts were puffed up, hairs splitting at their ends and vibrating in the tingling air.

"Inka," rasped Hnossi, "I'm . . . I—"

"Don't say it!" yelled Inga. "Whatever you're gonna say, it'll be all fucking wrong anyway, so just don't!" She stepped across to Hnossi's bedside, leaned down and yelled some more, and the highly-vincible goddess shrivelled like a weed sprayed with herbicide.

"And don't call me 'Inga' anymore! Inga died that day in 1974 because your neglect killed her! So you can stop wondering—assuming you ever did—why my official bio and F*O*O*J file say I was born that day, the day I left you and Daddy left you and Baldur left you! All you have to know, Hnossi, is that on that day I gave birth to myself!"

WHAP!—it was a sound like a whip cracking, and Syndi reared back and slammed against the wall, clutching her cheek. White smoke leaked from beneath her fingers. I reached for her, but stopped at the sight of electrical firecrackers exploding all over Hnossi's face and arms and above the white blanket covering her torso.

"Stand back, Syndi!" I shouted, just as all the medical equipment shorted-out in sparking mechanical death cries. My nostrils clogged with a burning stench. The air tasted like metal. "Doctor! Nurse!" I yelled out into the hall. "Code blue!"

The goddess who'd almost never cried, cried out her agony.

"Mummy!" said Syndi, releasing the burn wound and rushing forward to clutch her agonised mother. I tackled her before she could electrocute herself, knocking her against the wall beside the headboard and bouncing the two of us to the floor.

Her mother continued keening like an animal in a leg-hold trap. The only word we could make out, screamed over and over before the nurses dragged us out, was "Vally!"

IRON FATIGUE, OR RUST IN PIECES?

The finest specialists money could buy scrambled past us in their rubber scrubs, ready for the final stage of the disease. But while the metals of Hnossi's body were breaking down, deteriorating even faster was the hope for psychemotional reconnection between goddess mother and demigoddess daughter.

"Did you hear that? Did you god-damned *hear* that?" spat Syndi, again clutching the arc-gash on her face. "For Ymir's sake! Even now, even when she's dying . . . I mean, who's here with her? Not gramma, not Daddy, not even Baldur—me. *I* am."

Crying without trying to hide it, she dragged her sleeve across her face except for her burn, smearing her already smeared black make-up across her white features until she became a blurred mime. Festus raced up to us short of breath and stopped, glancing towards Hnossi's room and back to us, his eyes demanding an explanation.

Syndi offered him no comfort. "Even when she's goddamn *dying*, Eva . . . the only person she calls out for is some super-powerful unavailable loser who won't love her . . . and who walked away." She sing-songed bitterly, "Sur-fucking-*pri*-ise!"

For many second- or multi-generational hyper-hominids, the ability to achieve self-actualisation is hampered by the incapacity of their supposedly heroic and self-sacrificing parents to verbalise self-shame.

All too frequently in my practice, I've seen that the reason superheroes neurotically deny their own needs to the point of risking their lives originates in family of origin: the parents who modeled monkish asceticism, while forever failing to indulge their children's basic need to be the recipient of intimacy-behaviours and the centre of Mommy's or Daddy's affection- and caretaking-ideation. A parent who fails to recognise that a child's needs are distinct from and supersede her or his own is demonstrating a classic psychesituational signature of narcissism.

Resulting from the relationship Syndi had had with her mother, Syndi's relationship with Kareem was a paradox doomed to destruction. Far more than civilians, superheroes desire to change the past, some going so far as neurotically orbiting the planet at hyperspeeds under the delusion that they could reverse the Earth's direction and thus the flow of time, giving them a "second chance"—the most hoped-for boon in history.

So when Syndi selected a man whose workaholism, religion, and racial paranoia guaranteed he would be emotionally unavailable, she was assembling in the present a re-creation/rejection-cipher of her unavailable mother, thus giving her the opportunity to win his (and thus Hnossi's) love and attention. If she failed, she could "pre-emptively" reject him, therefore exerting the present-day capacity to deny the love that was denied to her in the past. Even her hedonistic hypersexuality/anguished frigidity demonstrated her paradoxical need to defy and reconnect with her mother, an anti/sexualism whose ironies she could rationalise/integrate only through her HEAT-ray experiment in "self-love."

While Syndi probably did love Kareem as much as she was capable, her own narcissism amplified her need and destroyed her capacity for genuine self-love (the pre-requisite for truly loving others), much as a burst of oxygen will engorge and accelerate the end of a fire.

TOWARDS RESOLVING PARADOXES,
AND PARADOXICAL SOLUTIONS

For the first time since I'd met the man, Festus Piltdown III was beginning to look his seventy years.

Slumped against the wall, his cravatte uncinched and asymmetrical, the wrinkles in his face suddenly as obvious as those of a suit that had been slept in, it was clear that no dosage of "G.I. juice" could forestall his aging process permanently, especially when deeply personal agony was hastening the inevitable approach of his own death.

Inside the sealed suite, specialists tracked their bootprints of vocal mud all over the plush white rug of our silence, while Syndi and Festus waited in medical impotence with wan faces and tears.

The wall-comm chimed.

"What is it, Mr. Savant?" said old Festus, tabbing the wall.

"Lord Piltdown, I'm terribly sorry for the interruption, but a Mister Fly is here to see you—terribly important news of some sort, he insists—"

"It's okay. Send him up."

Shortly we heard the familiar whine of André's approach, and then he was flapping down beside Festus, the bright yellow visitor E-tag hanging from his neck having prevented his incineration by the Squirrel Tree's D.E.T.H.Scan security system.

"What is it, Parker?" said Festus. "What's so important you couldn't simply use the comms?"

"Kareem's been acting crazy, Festus," said André; doing a double-take at a Syndi Tycho he'd never seen before. And then, bizarrely enough for him, he employed standard American English and the first-person pronoun *I*. "First I caught him hacking into F*O*O*J personnel files. But then he started cross-referencing everything on Menton with everything on Sarah Bellum, and making the computer correlate all of that with the F*O*O*J's records on Doctor Brain—"

"On *me?*" I blurted, stunned by a development I had not foreseen.

"—and he's been accessing all available Hubble imagery, cosmological records, everything on the Nistan dark matter nebula, downloading everything he could on the molecular physics and pharmacology of argonium," he said in articulate, almost broadcastable English. "He's up to something, Festus. Something I don't like one bit!"

Syndi's raccoon-eyes snapped up onto André. Festus put his massive hand on the younger man's shoulder. "Slow down. What're you talking about?"

"I think he's planning some type of *terrorist* attack," said André, his eyes wild, his posture bowed as if to confide a state secret. "And he didn't have time to completely wipe the computer of his work files before he figured out I was onto him. I un-erased his notes—*he thinks Doctor Brain is actually Menton.*"

The words hummed in the air. The three F*O*O*Jsters locked gazes among each other.

Then all their eyes turned on me.

"Well, come on, everyone," I reminded them, "*obviously* he's paranoid. You know that. Right? Remember the whole scandal? Let's stay focused, here—"

At that exact moment Doctor Singh, the specialist team leader, exited Hnossi's room. "What is it?" demanded Festus.

Remarkably, this middle-aged woman working for one of the most powerful magnates in the world ignored her tyrannical employer, and spoke directly to Syndi.

"Miss Tycho?" said the specialist.

"Yuh-yes, Doctor?" choked Syndi. "How's she doing?"

"Not well, I'm afraid. Your mother has perhaps two days to live."

THE MOTHER OF ALL BATTLES

Lacking external foes, one F*O*O*Jster was psychosomatically destroying herself, and collectively the remaining F*O*O*Jsters were turning on themselves in a psychotic downspiral of workplace-superpowered civil war. Most disturbingly, in the midst of the collective breakdown, F*O*O*J paranoia had plummeted even to the point of questioning the identity and integrity of their therapist.

Unless I were able to help my sanity-suppliants integrate the disparate lessons they'd gained from therapy into a new paradigm of post-heroic psychemotional equilibrium, they would soon destroy themselves . . . and countless innocent people along with them.

CHAPTER ELEVEN

Self-Distraction
is Self-Destruction

COUNTDOWN TO ARMAGEDDON

SUNDAY, JULY 16, 4:33 P.M.

"Perhaps I should leave," I suggested, "and let you all work during this obvious crisis."

"You're not going anywhere, Miss Brain!" said Festus.

"Surely you don't believe Kareem's delusion about me being . . . I mean, that I could be—"

"It's not whether *I* believe it. It's that *he does.* Which means you're his target. So you're not only in danger and needing our protection," he said, stepping towards me and clamping his gigantic hands on my shoulders in a gesture I imagined was intended to be reassuring, "you're our bait."

After forcing me to offer multiple reassurances that I was not Menton the Destroyer, the three F*O*O*Jsters focussed on the aforementioned frightening fracas soon to unfold. Not since the breakdown of Gil Gamoid and the N-Kid had there been the threat of terrorism by any member of the hallowed hall of heroes.

In a moment of silence, Festus said, "How do we know *Edgerton* didn't kill Hawk King?"

Syndi's lips parted, curled into disgust accentuated by the electrical burn on her cheek. "Oh, *shut* up, Festus! Why not just accuse him of killing Kennedy while you're at it? Oh, no, I forgot—Kareem hadn't been born yet, but *you* were in Dallas that day—"

"Naw, look here, girly," said André, regaining his trademarked urban drawl and swagger. "What if Squirrel-dawg be right? Check it: Major Ursa and the Spectacle said there were no signs of forced entry or teleportation at the Blue Pyramid. Whoever, y'know . . . *did* it, like, Hawk King had to've known im, right? So what if Kreem's tellin the truth about a special relationship with Hawk King? The King coulda let him in—"

"How, André? How would Kareem have enough power to kill Hawk King?" she said. "And more importantly, why would he *want* to kill his idol?"

"Look, girl, who knows how powerful Kreem really is? Think about what he could do with all his logo-magicalisms. He could send words down somebody's throat and clog their lungs or stop their heart, or inside their veins and explode their brains! F'all we know he could make poison gas or a nuclear bomb—"

"Why, André? You haven't said anything about why!"

"Why? Shit, P-girl, man's a Afro-paranoid! He prawly blieves Hawk King really *was* black, so maybe he went to im, said, 'Help me knock off whitey,' an when the King said Hell, no! and got ready to lock im up, *BAM!*, Kreem up an *words* im to death—"

"—and then leads an investigation not only to boost his electoral delusions," nodded Festus, "but as a diversionary tactic away from himself and onto an absurd conspiracy theory about Menton."

"Absurd?" spits Syndi. "You yourself said that—"

"And worse," said Festus, "his god-damned plan worked! That diabolical deviant is smarter than he smells. He wanted power on the F*L*A*C, power now denied to him—oh, you wouldn't believe how many transcripts I've read of his speeches to anti-white agitators and melanin-maddened malcontents over the years—"

"Damn, Peej, Kreem be usin his word-things to do his spyin inside computers, then he could be trackin anybody—maybe *ev*rabody! Think about it! Combine that with what he could do inside people's cells, they brains . . . *bzzzt*, he be on his way to becoming *the most powerful man in the world,* knawm sayn?

"The man hates the F*O*O*J," said Festus. "And he never hid it. Hates the F*L*A*C, hates the membership, hates our history, our traditions, our values, our mission . . . . The only thing he *didn't* hate—"

He stopped a second to rake Syndi's pelvis with his gaze.

"Fuck you, Festus!"

André: "People, *people*, eyes on the prize, here!"

"Obviously, Edgerton's aim," said Festus, "was to seize control of the F*O*O*J, by election if possible—remember, Hitler came to power by election—or by nefarious means if necessary . . . and eventually make the F*L*A*C all-black, contract all out-sourcing services to black companies—"

Syndi: "Do you have an atom of proof for any of this, Festus?"

"When you've been the world's greatest detective for fifty years, little girl, your instincts lead you far more than the evidence ever does. And you . . . weren't *you* the one who sponsored him to join the F*O*O*J in the first place?"

She rocked back. "Suh-so what?"

"How do we know you aren't spying for him right now, and that your perfectly-timed public 'outing' wasn't intended to distract attention from your continued collusion with him?"

"*Now* who's paranoid, detective?" she yelled at the exact moment something smacked her in the face and hovered above her head.

It was a black rectangle no larger than an ordinary envelope.

"It's from Edgerton!" said Festus, reaching for it, but Syndi got to it first.

"It's got *my* name on it," she scolded, turning it over to show us. Opening what was not an envelope but merely a folded sheet, she flashed its contents at us: letter-shaped holes in the black substance formed text. Placing the logo-gram against the wall for easier reading, she shielded it with her body for privacy.

"How'd that get in here?" said André.

"Perhaps it followed you," I suggested.

"But if it's for her," said Festus, "how would he've known André'd be meeting up with her?"

"Brotherfly's more concerned," said André, "that Kreem can be trackin anybody, anywhere. An next time he might not be sendin no *letter*, knawm sayn?"

"What's it say?" demanded Festus.

Syndi paused. "He . . . he wants me to meet him."

Festus glared an *A-ha!* at her.

"*I'm not working with him!*" she said. "He said he just wants to see me to tell me what he's figured out. He said," she choked, "that he's . . . he's worried about me. That he wants to protect me."

"Go to him," said Festus. "And we'll be right behind you with a hammer the size of his skull!"

"You think I'm gonna help you kill him, Festus?"

"For someone who said she's not working with him—"

"I'm not, but I'm still not gonna lead you to him like a Judas-goat—"

They shouted at each other for minutes, Syndi refusing even to take a holographic imager, tracking device, or microphone along. "And I'm not going anyway! Unless you forgot, my mother's sick and dying in there!"

"Oh, and you've always been such an attentive, devoted daughter!"

She drenched Festus in a steaming spew of profanity, but he ignored it.

"Your mother would want you to save lives, Syndi," he stage-whispered. "If you're going to live with yourself . . . *after*," he said, even touching her forearm with a gentleness of which I hadn't thought him capable (and even more shockingly, she didn't flinch at his touch), "then you know that carrying out what would've been her final wishes will be what you'll need to not spend the rest of your life with regret crushing you like a fallen building."

André and I were as stunned by Festus's reasoned delicacy as Syndi seemed entranced by it.

Quietly denying a final request to bring Festus along to the rendezvous location, Syndi said she would reveal any plans Kareem had only if they posed any sort of threat. After Festus made one last effort to divine the location of the meeting, Syndi conceded a single piece of information: that Kareem had asked her to meet at a place only the two of them would know.

"Where I first kissed him," she said, choking up, covering her face and dropping the letter.

Just before she could leave I grabbed her arm.

"Be careful, Syndi. The Kareem you fell in love with . . . he's suffering. And when people are suffering, they usually hurt the people closest to them, because those are the only people left around."

She showed me her white-and-black smear of a face, her eyes cold and deathly. "Kareem . . . my mother dying," she said. "This is all a wake-up call for me."

THE INTOXICATING AMBROSIA OF OLD HATRED (AND OLDER LOVE)

The moment Syndi exited the Medical Hollow, Festus stooped to retrieve the letter, but reared back when it broke up at his touch and its pieces scrambled away like cockroaches. "Disgusting!" he said.

"That's Kreem fuh ya," said André. "Just like cockroach: a low-down, dirty scavenger, who runs when the light's on im."

I hung back a few steps with the Brotherfly while Festus led us to his crime lab. "André," I said softly, "I asked you once before, but your answer was clearly hiding more than it was revealing. So tell me at last, why do you hate Kareem so much?"

"Damn, Doc, fool be threatenin mad havoc an you aksin me why I *hate* him?"

"Yes, but André, you felt this way about him long before today, which is partly why you ended up being ordered into therapy in the first place."

"André's whole life," he said, fussing, fidgeting, even fluttering his fly wings, "fools like him be all up in André's face, hatin, hatin, tryinna put they cleats all up in my ass—"

"Are you sure you have an accurate picture of your relationship with Kareem? At one point you even suggested you were jealous of him for, as you claimed, having fairer skin, when you're both obviously black. Truly, André, you seem far more antagonistic to him than the reverse."

"Only cuz he be reservin his best behaviour f'when he know he bein watched by you. Him an all his L*A*B-holes—nuthin but muhfuckin haters, fuh real!"

I tried probing further, but André was as agitated then as he was the day in therapy he'd thundered at Kareem to cease investigating Hawk King's death for evidence of a conspiracy. "Naw, Doc! Don't be defendin him! Punk aint nuthin but a bigot, knawm sayn? He a hatin muthafuck who gone crack-head on his own pipe fulla hate, an he deserve whatever he gon get when we put a super-stomp on his ass tonight!"

"But Syndi said she wouldn't—"

"Trust me, Doc. You cross Festus, you gots to pay, an he *always* got a way. Thass how it is. André get hisself some side-action for free, he aint complainin, knawm sayn?"

In the centre of the surveillance Hollow, Festus sat like a king bee in his hive, surrounded by an encompassing honeycomb of hundreds of hexagonal monitors beaming images of city streets, board rooms, industrial facilities, public parks, elevators, libraries, union halls, mosques, bedrooms, and more. He was tracking Syndi's path using a far more extensive network of cameras than I think anyone realised the Flying Squirrel possessed or could access, even greater than the F*O*O*J's own intelligence-gathering techweb.

"Damn it!" said Festus, pounding his console. "That cunning little tramp's smarter than she lets on."

On several hexagonal screens focused on the nearest DitkoTrain station, a knot of people suddenly melted into a contingent of shapely, black-skirted, black haired, white-pancaked young women, each of whom headed off in separate directions for various trains heading in every direction.

"That guileful little bitch," growled Festus. "Doesn't have a trusting bone in her body."

I pulled up the only other chair in the lab (a dusty one, its back monogrammed "C.M."), and sat beside Festus. He glared at me as if I'd used a piece of the True Cross for kindling.

I was struck again by how weary and worn he looked, slumped in his chair, his thinning hair whiter than ever and matted to his forehead. Perhaps he'd been skipping his "G.I. juice" injections, or the psychemotional stress had been diminishing their effectiveness. Even down inside the centre of his superheroic sanctum, his legendary yet no longer "undisclosed location," Festus Piltdown III looked like an aged farmer gazing impotently at the hail storm thrashing towards his fields.

"This is a very hard time for you, isn't it, Festus?"

"I can see why you need the Ph.D. after your name, Eva," said Festus, his eyes scanning his scanners without so much as blinking towards me. "Otherwise drumming up business while seeping anaemic banalities like that might be rather difficult." He snapped, "Of *course* it's hard on me! It's hard on all of us!"

"But on *you* personally. Only Syndi is taking Hnossi's condition as hard as you are."

"That's because I've known Iron Lass for five decades, twenty years longer than even her no-account daughter has. And now I've got to worry that these leads I was pursuing on Warmaster Set were all black herrings. Which means that even the destruction of Asteroid Zed—my god!—even *that* was the work of that Beelzebubian bastard Kareem—"

"Let's focus on your feelings, Festus—your worry for Hnossi. To see her in this state—"

"'This state'? *Dying,* you mean? In bed, the way no warrioress would ever want to go?"

"And before she can resolve her family troubles, her distance from her children, not to mention any other . . . unresolved interpersonal issues—"

He cut me off. "I was never married, so I can't relate to that. But missing your children—that I understand. I have compassion for *that* pain. And as her comrade."

"I'm not seeing comradely loyalty alone, here, Festus," I said, touching his hand. I expected him to yank his away, even order me not to touch him. Instead, he was frozen, his eyes unfocussed amid the flashing images from his surveillance honeycomb.

"I've been reading up on your non-caped careers," I said, anxious to maintain the opening. "You two not only worked together inside the F*O*O*J, but elsewhere. For decades, Professor Icegaard was a paid consultant of your defense contracting corporation. Piltdyne built the B9 bomber, which you christened the *Iron Lass* class; because of you, Piltdyne's nuclear submarine was named the *Icegaard*-class." I squeezed; his hand trembled. "For a hard-boiled industrial magnate like you, Festus, those were practically love poems."

He looked over to me, his eyes wet and glossy and twinkling from the banks of lights. Sitting there in his chair with his whitened hair, he was no longer the frightening, furry, one-man war on crime, and no longer was he even the towering tycoon of technology.

He was just an old, lonely man facing the truth of his own powerlessness.

"And yet," I said, probing this rare vulnerability to examine the psychemotional damage that was crushing the life out of him, "for all your devotion to this woman, now that she truly needs you and there's no one else in your way, you still couldn't and can't do anything to protect her . . . or save her."

"What?" he whispered, too horrified to be furious.

"Festus, you were up on Asteroid Zed with her, but when she was attacked by the Dessicator, where were you? And even now, with all your wealth, influence, and the awesome power of the surveillance you have at your fingertips right here, the woman you've been in love with for fifty years is dying, and there's nothing you can do to stop it."

His lower lip quivering, the spindly old teeth of his lower jaw exposed like a skeleton's, Festus leaned back in his chair, clutching his chest as if to keep his heart from exploding.

"Festus," I whispered, leaning towards him, "How does all that make you *feel?*"

His eyes were huge, his pupils swollen blackly, his face drained of all its colour.

Suddenly the high-pitched buzz-whine in the background noise climaxed to buzz-saw anxiety that ripped through Festus's misery. I glanced up, spied an agitated Brotherfly crawling the Hollow's ceiling in endless circles while fluttering his wings at just below take-off speed. Festus shook his head as if to wake from sleeping at the wheel, then shoved his chair back away from me and stood.

"Get the fuck out of my crime lab!" he yelled, flipping back the sides of his dressing gown, his hands hovering at the holster-level of his exposed utility belt. "And take that wall-crawling parasite with you!"

At Festus's behest, Mr. Savant, employing a crutch and with one arm in a cast, showed André and me to a drawing room. I offered André a tranquiliser, but he still wouldn't sit down, leaving his hand- and footprints all over the walls, windows, and ceiling.

Finally, following my special instructions, Mr. Savant left and hobbled back pushing a cart with a bowl of luxurious, exotic fruits, placing it on the grand marble coffee table at the centre of the room.

Lured down by the sweet scents and tropical colours, André perched on the coffee table to ingest the fruit, doing so by expectorating rancid yellow digestive juices all over the oranges, bananas, mangoes, papayas, and grapes which dissolved the produce—peels, stalks, seeds, stones, and all—into a steaming, stinking pool which spilled all over the table top. Opening his mouth, André unfurled his well-endowed proboscis and began sucking up the bubbling soda-pap he'd created.

Suppressing my gorge with an act of supreme will, I sat, removing my **ANDRÉ PARKER, HKA The BROTHERFLY** F*O*O*J file and the **MORRIS ANDREW PARK, Alias BROTHERFLY** file that Mr. Savant had brought me.

"You're twenty-six, André, correct?" He slurped and nodded, still sucking up the revolting stench and slime on the table. "And you've been in the F*O*O*J how long?" He held up three fingers.

André was a fascinating set of contradictions. As the hip, laid-back, fun-loving Brotherfly, he could not be a more profound counterpoint to the militant anal-retention of the thirty-four-year old X-Man. In one session, Kareem described André as a "hyper-womanising, anti-intellectual, willing slave . . . enough of a collaborator with every racist stereotype about young black males that he should be a PR man for the Klan," denouncing André to his face at the Dark Star soul food restaurant as "a slack, slick, loose-dicked, willingly-no-self-control . . . senseless, thoughtless, shiftless, aimless, brainless, oversized pants-wearing, 40-ounce loving, penis-fixated, self-under-rated, supreme champion of galactic niggativity."

But as the real man beneath the André Parker construct, Morris Andrew Park shared so much in common with Philip "Kareem" Edgerton that the toxic enmity they shared became all the more shocking.

Glancing through the file's photos, I was struck by how severely *André* deviated from *Andrew*: tiny four-year old Andrew in glasses on the back of a huge, shaggy dog; petite eight-year old Andrew as chess wizard; puny sixteen-year old Andrew in thick eyeglasses singing the rôle of Fortunato in his school's musical production *The Cask of Amontillado;* contrasting these were several photos of muscular, tall, sexually turbo-charged twenty-two year-old André "boogying" in Bird Island nightclubs The Meet Market, Bone Dancers, and Peacocks.

Undoubtedly Kareem would have approved of Andrew having attended the so-called "historically black college" Nat Turner U. It was there that the frail, awkward, genetics student became the victim of a fraternity "prank," and found himself forcibly gene-spliced with the dynamically altered DNA of a blue-bottle fly.

After an astounding array of mutations which saw Park autonomically spin a cocoon and retreat into it for the entirety of a spring break, Andrew emerged with an enhanced genetic matrix which imbued the brainy recluse voted "most likely to Urkel" (whatever that meant) with the proportionate speed, strength, agility, and "flyness" of a fly.

After first gaining his powers, the shy young undergrad who'd never shone anywhere but onstage or on the Dean's list looked for some way to employ his neo-talents to help pay the bills of the elderly aunt and uncle who'd raised him. But as his acne dried up, his vision improved, his chest rippled, and his coordination soared, Andrew found himself winning stage rôles as a leading man and attracting romantic attention of which he had never dreamed. After a fateful, confidence-supercharging, career-advising meeting with Dennis Rodman, "André" began earning more money than he'd ever seen—as an exotic dancer. Although crime-fighting as such had never been André's intention, the post-*Götterdämmerung* F*O*O*J was recruiting fresh faces for its own face-lift, and as André said in his job interview, "The benefits are to *die* for—*bzzzt!*"

Perhaps underlying the André-bravado and the anti-Kareem rage was the awkwardness of young Andrew, the tiny boy lacking in confidence everywhere but in the theatre. This frightened inner-child Andrew likely confused the hyper-verbal, hyper-confident, hyper-aggressive Kareem on a psychemotional level with all those who had ever bullied him—from the children who shoved his face in the urinal until he ate the cake, to the "frat boys" who so brutally got into his genes.

Yet there was more driving the Brotherfly's over-compensating humour, erotic aggression, and anger—another deeper node of sadness, pain, and, I suspected, guilt. Ordinarily André'd have been far too attention-deficit for me to probe into his deeper psychemotional workings, but as Mr. Savant had followed my instructions to inject the liquid tranquilisers I'd given him into the fruit, André was opening up like a can of soup.

"My uncle," he said when I inquired about the pain I knew he held in reservoir. "Poor ol Uncle Benteen."

"What *about* your uncle, André?"

"'s dead," he slurred sleepily. "My fault."

"Why would you say that?"

"I'd ... y'know ... *changed* ... a lot. When I. Went offta school. 'Slot ferimmta handle. Went away a liddle boy. Came backaman. Never toldimmabout my, my, my mu*ta*tion. Tion. That I wuzza supereero, that I joindaF*O*O*J. N one day, I, I, I didn'know hewuzzome. An I's getting into it ... an he—"

"Getting into what, Andrew?"

His eyes telescoped onto me as if I were a million miles away. But as he picked up speed, his hands and wings fluttered with ever-greater agitation, his face and voice rending themselves with greater tragedy.

" ... gettin inta my uniform," he said. "An Uncle Benteen, he juss walks right into my damn bejjroom an sees me there with my armzanlegs half innannouttuvvit ... an he grabs his heart, an he, he, he juss up an drops! An therewuzzn't fuckall I couldoabouddit! Dead's dead. *Dead*," he said, cupping his face in his hands, snorting and shuddering and wailing.

There was more, I sensed—something even more painful that André had yet to disclose. But before I could probe further, Mr. Savant appeared next to me.

"Madame," said the ancient manservant, "Ms. Icegaard is awake and is requesting your presence."

Stroking André's hair and straightening out his antennae, I assured him I'd be back as soon as I could. I hurried off for what in all likelihood would be Hnossi's final session.

WHEN "GOODBYE" IS THE ONLY TIME TO SAY "I LOVE YOU"

"Does Hnossi know, Festus, how you've felt about her all these years?"

He fixed his furious eyes back on me, already enraged that Hnossi had insisted on my presence during his last remaining hours with her. After he refused to acknowledge my question with anything other than rage, she spoke for him.

"*Ja, Fräu Doktor*," she whispered.

By then her skin was almost entirely racked with seeping red craters and brittle, white plates. Even her scalp was a tortured moonscape, with what had remained of her hair burnt off during her electrical discharges.

Yet when Festus turned to look at her while she struggled to talk, there wasn't a hint of horror or disgust in his eyes.

Only love and pain.

"Uff course . . . I knew," she said.

"Was there ever anything between you? Sexually?"

Festus's back stiffened, but neither of the two heroes answered.

Finally Hnossi said, "It vuss 1961. Five munse before I vuss to marry Hector. Unt Festus unt I vere vurkingk longk hours, heading up ze anti-Treemason task force . . . unt vell, zere hat alvays been zis . . . zis *potency* betveen us, betveen me unt Festus. Unt vun night after a battle, ve came back to ze Fortress, unt ve'd bose been drinkingk . . . ."

She sighed so heavily I feared the oncoming of another hacking fit—possibly her final one. But then she resumed.

"I felt so guilty . . . I couldn't even look at Festus, unt our friendship . . . vell, it never vent back to vut it hat been. Never. Unt me . . . my self-respect . . . after all zose centuries uff svearing I vud never be like my own muzzer. But it vuss like a curse. I vuss no better zan zat whore."

She gnarled her fingers together, gazed towards the ceiling with eyes almost entirely scummed white. "All my talk. About honour! Nussing but vurmvoodt."

"And so," I asked as delicately as I could, "you said this was five months before you married Hector. And four months *after* your wedding . . . ."

"*Ja.* Inka vuss born."

"And is she—?"

"She's Hector's," said Hnossi. "Sank Odin for zat. I put ze man srough enough pain. But Festus . . . venever ve hat FOOCH family picnics, I'd catch him staring at Inka ven he sought I vuzn't lookink . . . ."

Festus's eyes went wide. He'd apparently never known that the watchman had been watched.

"Staring how, Hnossi?" I asked. "At what?"

"Like . . . he vuss tryingk to see if somehow ze test hat been wrong . . . or if I'd lied to him about ze test, maybe? I don't know. And zen after she got to a certain age, he stopped lookink at her altogezzer, I sink, because . . . she remindtet him."

"Of what?"

She looked at me, twin tears glistening in the shock of her frosted eyes, stunned, apparently, that I could not figure it out for myself. "Of vut couldt never be!"

She beckoned in Festus's direction. He was at her side instantly, holding her crumbling hand with the delicacy of cradling a newborn.

"Festus . . . I vant to tell you sum sings . . . ."

"What, Hnossi?" he croaked, his throat a tuba of mud.

"I'm sorry . . . zat I made you suffer srough all of my, my—"

"This isn't the time for sorrys, Hnossi—"

"Let me finish!" she snapped, then softening instantly. "I'm sorry for hurtink you, rejectink you . . . for all my . . . vut does *Fräu Doktor* call it? Ze 'crazy-makink' behaviour, *ja.*"

"It doesn't matter, Hnossi," he said, clearing his throat and swallowing heavily, twice. "It doesn't matter."

"*Nein*," she whispered. "Uff course it mattered. It still matters. But at least now, at ze ent, I can say to you vut I shudt haff said back zen, back in 1962 . . . ."

He waited, stooping, clutching her hand to his cheek. When she said nothing, he begged, "Yes, Hnossi?"

He looked down into her eyes.

They were pale grey, motionless.

Her chest fell as softly as snow.

Red, rust-scented smoke was drifting from her mouth.

The medical monitors screamed as one.

"Hnossi!" shouted Festus. "Doctor Singh! Nurse! *DOCTOR SINGH—*"

The door swung open, and a suited and caped Omnipotent Man strode in.

"Wally, you idiot! What the hell are you doing here? Get Doctor Singh!"

"Step aside, Festus," he said. He clutched Festus's shoulder and plucked him out of the way like a mother dog retrieving a puppy by the neck.

Wally reached into the bed, sifted out Hnossi and clutched the red-ravaged body in his arms.

And then he kissed her.

Electricity crackled from Wally's mouth into Hnossi's, streamers of it whipping frenetically around the room and overloading the machines and exploding the light bulbs, plunging the room into flare-strobing darkness. Festus screamed at Wally to stop while Hnossi's limbs trembled and jerked and her chest sucked closed and inflated outward violently again and again, and still Wally welded his kiss onto her, and when the scorching blue luminescence brightened to the point of blindingness, Festus and I scrambled from the room in fear for our lives.

"*HNOSSI!*" screamed Festus from the hall, while light seared our eyes even from around the rim of the door for what seemed like forever.

And then there was silence.

The door swung open.

Standing beside the steely, confident Omnipotent Man was Hnossi Icegaard.

Reborn.

Her skin was gleaming copper, her hair was returned miraculously to its full thick blackness and lustre, and her eyes were shining like halogen amethysts. Wrapped only in a white bed sheet, she looked more Greek goddess than Norse, glowing before us and smiling with secret, joyful knowledge, as if listening to celestial music only she and the Divine could hear.

"Wally," gasped Festus, relief and horror fighting for control of his face, "what, what, what did you—"

"All th'little gal needed, Festy, was a little *gal*vanisin. Course," smirked Wally, "not every man knows how t'perform that."

Back in therapy after the excursion to Asteroid Zed, after Hnossi had already developed rust poisoning, Wally had fallen to pieces and electro-welded his own fingers and limbs back on. But none of us—not I, not Festus (whom Wally'd once electro-blasted across the room), and not Wally himself—had realised how that power might be applied towards transforming others.

I complimented Wally on his apparently successful transformation of Hnossi and, of course, of himself. He turned a sunrise smile on me, saying, "I couldna done it without ya, ma'am-Doctor."

"And your alters? Ricky R. Bustow, Reverend Crockett, Musk-Ox Miller? Are they—"

He tapped the side of his skull, eliciting a soft bell-tone. "Wellsir, they's still all up here—but now, they together. Uni-mah-fied." Even Wally's voice had been transmuted, expanded, as if the multiple "voices" inside him had harmonized sonically into a melodious choir, powerful and hypnotic.

"I did like you told me, ma'am," said Omnipotent Man. "I cogitated suh'm fierce upon who I wannid t'be, steada all the thangs I weren't an that I was a failure at. I put all m'shortcomins in th'closet an put on m'best Sunday-go-t'meetin-suit, an fixed m'self to bein like m'own mentor. An th'more I did, the more I realised the truth." His eyes shifted towards the ceiling, as if gazing past drywall and plaster and up into the majesty of the revolving, evolving galaxy.

"And what truth is that, Wally?"

"That I have a personal relationship with the *Ka* of Hawk King," he said, his voice riding a rhythm. "That I have accepted the *Ka* of Hawk King as my own personal superhero. That the *Ka* of Hawk King has saved me—"

"*Ka*-ka," mumbled Festus.

Wally's eyes flashed tiny electrical arcs, twin bolts of lightning, but he did not stop.

"—and that in his celestial crusade for justice, he has made me his own appointed deputy and knight. His Hawk Knight."

Draping herself from his shoulder, Hnossi stared up at Wally, her eyes sparkling as if his dynamic current were still surging inside her. Her flesh renewed, her muscles taut and defined, she'd never looked more powerfully beautiful or beautifully powerful.

I had never imagined I would see the dark-matter of disdain so disintegrated from her demeanour that she would shimmer like a nebula from the light of a hypermasculine supernova. Wally's omni-belief in himself, and the resulting growth in his own super-strength, had proved an old maxim: for many women, even goddesses, power was the supreme aphrodisiac.

And then Mr. Savant returned with Syndi, who was agog at the sight of her radiant mother. Mother and daughter embraced in a death-averted hug with more warmth than they'd likely ever shared before.

Festus Piltdown, on the other hand, slumped against the wall, looking as if he'd just been punched in his soul.

GRAFFITI FROM THE GHETTO OF THE MAD

Gathered with us back inside the crime lab, Syndi, flush with relief from her mother's recovery, divulged all the information she'd received from her rendezvous with Kareem, even revealing the location, since it no longer mattered: the now-abandoned Hermes Theatre in Stun-Glas.

"He told me to save myself," she said. "Because he said that you, Eva . . . that you're either Sarah Bellum, or Menton, or both."

Grimacing as if swallowing a pill the size and shape of a horseshoe, Syndi was clearly pained to be revealing her intelligence—whether from protectiveness of me or Kareem, I wasn't sure. The luminous Hnossi and Wally stood flanking her, each with a comforting hand on either of her shoulders.

Festus stared anywhere in the room but at that trinity.

There was a sudden whining buzz about my ears. I batted away the distraction.

André asked, "Why do that nut-job think she Menton or Bellum?"

Syndi shook her head. "Oh . . . it's . . . it's so sad. It's crazy. Paranoid. He was all over the place—because Eva'd written all those books on Menton, like she was the Earl of Oxford to Menton's Shakespeare."

I found myself startled by Syndi's reference, still integrating my comprehension that nineteen-year old celebrity puffhead Syndi was actually thirty-two year old intellectual Inga. "Why else, Syndi?"

She carefully laid bare the layers of Kareem's paranoia, as if opening a set of nested Ukrainian dolls. In addition to accusing me of being Sarah Bellum, Kareem claimed that I was originally the minor heroine "Right Brain Girl" rejected for F*O*O*J membership in the early 1970s; that he'd seen photographs of the "real" me standing in front of bookshelves full of Ayn Rand texts; that in the late 1970s I'd "assumed" the identity of Doctor Brain, and as therapist for Tran Chi Hanh had driven a wedge between the Flying Squirrel and Chip Monk, destroying their partnership; that I either had caused Dr. Napoleon Orator to become Menton so I could have the perfect mate, or that I had "doubled" my mind, placing half of it inside Dr. Orator as the first fiefdom of my geopsychic empire; that imprisoned on Asteroid Zed, I had evolved my phagopsychosis to absorb psinergy from the planetary unconscious itself, eventually enough to wreak murderous revenge on Hawk King; that I had used deceptive, destructive therapeutic techniques to initiate Omnipotent Man's breakdown; that I had manipulated my F*O*O*J patients into going up to Asteroid Zed where they could be mass-murdered, and barring that, where a Plan B could initiate the death of at least Iron Lass, which in turn would weaken Syndi and Festus; that I had accessed secret, comprehensive files on X-Man and Syndi, leaking the information to the press to destroy him in a scandal; that by establishing myself as the F*O*O*J's chief confidante, I had placed myself in the perfect position to gather supreme intelligence on them, exploit their weaknesses, and destroy them one by one, if not manipulate them to my further end of taking over the planet for a never-ending phagopsychotic feeding frenzy on the collective minds of the human race.

When Syndi was done, a cold silence clutched the crime lab like the metallic fingers of Count Speculum.

"It's tragic," I said, "that a young man so bright, with so much promise.... Ah, well. Now. Given the threat to public safety that Kareem's psychosis clearly poses, we need to focus now on what all of you are going to do."

"Oh, and there's one more thing, Eva," said Syndi, taking out and handing me an ordinary paper note addressed to me. I swatted at the Hollow's insect whining in my ears before taking the note.

"What's it say?" demanded Festus and André in unison, rushing me.

I scanned it, and then read aloud:

> First, "Doctor Brain," or whoever you truly are, my final ten-word answer to your recurring question about what I'd do if I could never equal the glory of my predecessors is as follows: "Pursuing glory is what created this mess. I'll take justice."
>
> Second, contrary to your psychobabbling parable intended to "heal" me, I want you to understand that I don't have two wolves inside me and never did. Just a single black dog with four paws: one of fear, one of hope, one of rage, and one of love.
>
> And he's a good dog.

Festus snapped, "What kind of Congo-jumbo is that Sambo sociopath dithering on about?" André shushed him violently, and remarkably Festus obeyed.

> And finally, before the end of this day, I intend to expose the real assassin of Hawk King, and explode an even more diabolical conspiracy which would otherwise leave thousands of American citizens dead, thus subjecting the country, if not the planet, to a never-ending war on freedom. And I swear by the Ujat, I will do so by any means necessary.
>
> Dã-fxu, us em maãxeru!
>
> The X-Man

"Y'hear that?" slurred André, still sobering up. "How he gonna . . . 'explode' a 'conspiracy . . . by any means necessary'? We can't wait any longer! If we don'put the smack-down on that psycho now, who knows what he gon do? An how many people he gon hurt?"

"Where do y'all think he's gon strike?" asked Wally. His voice echoed in the Hollow beyond its solitary sonic power. In the shadowy chamber, he, Hnossi, and Syndi seemed to be glowing.

Festus addressed his computer array, rather than looking towards the golden triangle. He swatted flies away from his ears. His voice was ice.

"Since Edgerton's attempting to blame the good doctor here for everything wrong in his misbegotten life, clearly he's going to attack her wherever he thinks she could be—which means her home, the Squirrel Tree, or her Hyper-Potentiality clinic. Don't worry, Doct—"

"Now dontchu worry, lil lady," said Wally. "We'll protect ya."

Festus bit his lower lip, hard, then keyboarded his console like a Bach playing his organ. The honeycomb monitors flared, fluttered, and flashed with millions of random images, and while we watched, the data-flood began channelling into select motifs.

"Good god damn," said Festus. Then, distracted by the buzz whining in the air, he turned around to glare at André.

"Hey, that ain'me!" said the Brotherfly.

"Vut is it, Festus?"

He shook his head disgustedly. "I should've caught this, but with everything going on, the conspiracy, me taking care of you—I can't keep absolutely *everything* under control, I never claimed to be a *god*, just a hard-working—"

"Festus!" snapped the Iron Lass, the syllables evoking the slash of a whip. "Vut. Is it?"

Still without looking towards her, he pointed at various monitors while electronically highlighting them.

"Here," he said, clicking on a hexagon of a black man and an Asian man in an office. "Footage recorded several days ago. Our X-Hero's retained legal counsel. With Tran." He snorted heavily enough to dislodge his pancreas. "Quite a turn-around for an ambulance-chasing back-stabbing barrister employed by an anti-superhero watchdog agency!"

Click. A desert canyon in searing daylight. The image scoped down to a network of drill holes. One after the other, four all-black baboons emerged from the holes, carrying tiny sacks and running. "Yuca Flats. The abandoned mine sites."

"So?" said Syndi, swatting at and missing the insects buzzing in the Hollow.

"That's where th'gubment was drillin f'argonium," said Wally, his tabernacle voice Pavarotting my brain. "I always told em there hadda still be some left down there."

I asked Festus why Kareem would send his shadow creatures to retrieve argonium.

"Who knows? A dirty-bomb? Insurance against . . . someone who might finally bother to return to active duty? Combine that with the argonium data he downloaded . . . . We've seen close-up how addictive it is. What if Edgerton could shadow-extract it or shadow-synthesise it, combine it with something else and mass-produce it? That racist reprobate has sworn revenge for the F*O*O*J 'denying' him his 'rightful place'. What if he's planning to drown white America in a tidal wave of argonium-crack?"

"That's complete *bull*shit, Festus," said Syndi, "and you *know* it!"

"*Ja*, Festus . . . Kareem may be a schwarzextremist, but still, I caun't believe—"

"Oh no?" he said, trying and failing to swat the insect buzzing near his ear. "Then what do you make of these?"

Festus clicked several hexagons: multiple angles of Sunhawk Island and the Blue Pyramid, time-jumping imagery of a black falcon entering and later exiting the Pyramid from the aperture of the mysterious shaft on the 42nd tier.

"The *Ka*-Sentinels sealed the Blue Pyramid," growled Festus, "three days after Hawk King's death. The drones wouldn't even let Major Ursa or the Spectacle back into the crime scene. And after the divine apparition at the funeral, no one wanted to risk trying to break in. And yet here," he said, pointing, "we see that Edgerton's been sending his shadows inside! For what purpose? What's he been doing?"

Suddenly Festus hammered his fist into his console. Syndi, André, and I jumped in reaction. Festus looked down at what he'd crushed: glistening, black fragments. Which then poof into nothingness.

"That *bas*tard! He's been *mon*itoring us this entire time! I should crush him with my bare hands!" he yelled, his voice resounding in the Hollow: *BARE HANDS BARE HAnds barehands .   .   .   .*

Panting with rage, he muttered almost inaudibly, "But that would be messy. *Gas* is neater for bugs."

A comm call came in from the Fortress of Freedom. Festus stabbed the "HOLD" key on his console.

I confessed to Festus that I could not see why the situation was as dire as he seemed to think it was.

"How can you fail to comprehend this, Miss Brain? That fanatic's been sending his word-things inside the Blue Pyramid! *He* killed Hawk King! And if he could do that to a god, how long do you think a defenseless human being could last against one of his nightmarish creations? And why murder Hawk King at all, unless he'd gone to the King under this delusional negroid-Hawk King theory, shared his plans with the King because he expected support, and when the King refused him any further access to the Blue Pyramid and its technology and threatened to turn him in, or attempted to capture him right there—"

"Technology? Inside the Blue Pyramid?"

"The ancient technology inside Hawk King's fortress, Miss Brain, could incinerate half the United States. If the X-Man were to use the Pyramid as his command-and-control centre, he could prosecute a one-man global race war . . . and possibly even win it."

PSYCHESITUATIONAL PRESENTATION
OF X-TREMISM

Determined to go into battle immediately, Festus sketched out his strategy, accepting brief-as-possible interventions from Hnossi, and fitting Wally with a device he called an "OM-meter" with which to monitor Wally's health in case the X-Man had acquired sufficient supplies of argonium to pose a threat. When I quietly pressed him on the "OM-meter", Festus conceded that he was more concerned that this "brave new Wally" was unstable, and he "refused to risk the success of the mission on the cultic conversion of any Kentucky-fried fanatic."

The monitors beeped impatiently with the call Festus had forgotten was on hold. He tabbed his keyboard, and the central hexagons of the honeycomb united into a single image: the black-furred Major Ursa, surrounded by a hundred F*O*O*Jsters, gathered inside the majestically muralled auditorium of Heroes' Hall.

"What is it, Major?"

"Uh, well—we've, we've all been waiting for you, sir."

"Waiting for me? What are you on about?"

"Your speech, sir—you were supposed to begin your speech ten minutes ago."

"Speech? I'm not giving any speech, Major!"

"But you used the Alpha-One channel, you asked us to—"

"I certainly did not use the—" He stopped. His eyes grew tiny. "Major Ursa, evacuate the fortress forthwith! Condition red! REPEAT, *EVACUATE ALL PERSONNEL FORTHWITH—*"

The honeycomb flared with sound and fury, and then went null, into default blue.

Festus stammered, "Good god—even *I* didn't think that madman would—"

Everyone gazed at the empty blue, dumb with horror.

Festus dialled into his hexagon-screen comm system, patching into both the Alpha and Zeta Channels.

"Ah . . . attention . . . cuh-calling all F*O*O*Jsters," he said. "Calling all retired F*O*O*Jsters and all independents. This is an Alpha-One and Zeta-One priority message, invoked under the authority of FEMA Protocol S.H. Two. The Fortress of Freedom has been bombed. Everyone inside has been . . . everyone is presumed dead."

"NO!" cried Syndi. "Kareem would never do that! It must just be, like, knock-out gas-bombs or something—"

Festus muted the comm to face Syndi. "You still believe that fanatic isn't dangerous? You heard him in therapy, in his note to Miss Brain! That he'd 'explode' a conspiracy! Well he's done it! With bombs!"

He unmuted his comm. "Stand by for scrambled mission strategy. Converge as outlined. Flying Squirrel out."

Festus turned, facing his troops. "Professor Icegaard. Contact the Spook directly—try him in Langley; I think he's speaking to the graduating class. He'll want a piece of this bastard boiled and dipped in butter. Wally. Try using your omni-hearing to locate Edgerton. We have to assume he's heading to the Blue Pyramid immediately—assuming he hasn't taken it already.

"Everyone: the only people we can count on now is us. We in this room may be the only surviving active members of the F*O*O*J. We have one mission, perhaps our most important ever: to neutralise the X-Man and his L*A*B fanatics tonight before they neutralise us all."

FAILING TO FIGHT THE SUPERVILLAIN WITHIN

Still unsure of the extant conditions and locked inside a psychemotional *grand mal* seizure of their own combative, antagonistic paradigm, the F*O*O*Jsters were determined to defeat their former colleague—not with reason, visualisation, feelings-work, journaling, or an intervention—but with naked, brute violence.

Even if the F*O*O*Jsters could somehow manage not to destroy each other, their capacity for psychic healing would be all the more diminished by their refusal to engage the most important hyperbattle of all: against the supervillain within.

CHAPTER TWELVE

Superheroes
Need Super-Egos

PROCESSING UNRESOLVED ISSUES

SUNDAY, JULY 16, 7:12 P.M.

In the bowels of Langston-Douglas, terror was growing like radioactive polyps. With news helicopters ratcheting overhead in the choking hundred-and-ten degree smog and the streets bloodied by sunset, the Q*R*I*B headquarters of the League of Angry Blackmen stood in dark defiance of the noose tightening every second around it.

Having divided all responding heroes into attack squads for three separate targets, the Flying Squirrel waited at ready with his own strike force from an undisclosed location, monitoring the shrinking cordon around the *faux*-Egyptian temple of the Q*R*I*B.

Including Power Grrrl, Red Squad was composed of eight trained and armed fighters, warriors who were straining at the ropes to begin combat while valiantly ignoring the shouted curses and tossed garbage of neighbourhood residents: fifty-three year old Kid Kombat, Sr. with his wrecking ball arms, buzz-saw "wings," and missile-launcher backpack; forty-three year old Sabre-Tooth Beaver, scourge of Treemasons and environmentalists, and champion of the nation's forestry industry; fifty-five year old Smithing Wesson, lord of firearms; fifty-one year old King's English, the super Bobby; the sixty-four year old Rock Breaker, armed with his mystic hammer John Henry; thirty-eight year old Super Bastard, half lawyer, half trailer park; and commanded by legend among legends (despite lingering court cases surrounding a few dozen friendly-fire deaths), the sixty-three year old military master, the Spook.

Safely ensconced inside the Squirrel Tree's crime lab, I was able to observe the approaching melee two ways: visually through the honeycomb of monitors, and empathically through the "OM-meters" the Flying Squirrel had ordered everyone to wear so he could coordinate the battle. Perhaps due to a malfunction, I couldn't pick up Festus's own cognistream, but I could experience the unfolding crisis from as many other psi-POVs as I could handle.

"I can't believe, like, what a bunch of pathetic, fossilised old geezers I'm stuck with," complained public-persona Syndi, perhaps having forgotten that her comm was active (or perhaps not forgetting).

"Cut the chatter, Red Two," snapped the Spook.

"Quit *calling* me that, Sanford! My name is Power Grrrl!"

The Spook: "Red Squad, prime powers and lock weapons in attack position."

Kid Kombat, Sr.: "Red Three, standing by."

Sabre-Tooth Beaver: "Red Four, standing by."

Smithing Wesson: "Red Five, standing by."

King's English: "I say, old chap, Red Six, standing by."

The Rock Breaker: "Yessuh, Red Seven hyah, stannin by-an-by."

Super Bastard: "Red Eight, frickin ready to rawk an ro-o-oll, good buddy!" (Pause) "Stanning by."

(pause)

The Spook: "Red Two, confirm readiness!"

Power Grrrl: (sighing) "*What*ever."

Still monitoring visuals only, I watched as the Spook, suddenly lit by red and blue stroking lights like the buildings around him, stood to address those bunkered inside the Q*R*I*B.

"ATTENTION, PHILIP K. EDGERTON AND OTHER L*A*B MILITANTS!" boomed the amplified voice of Red Squad Leader. "SURRENDER IMMEDIATELY. WE HAVE YOU SURROUNDED! COME OUT WITH YOUR HANDS UP AND YOUR POWERS OFF AND YOU WILL NOT BE HARMED."

Silent moments gouged into everyone's nerves. There was no response.

After forty-six seconds, Sabre-Tooth Beaver asked, "Are we even sure they're home?"

"Yes of course we're sure!" said the Spook. "Hold your positions, and your tongues!"

On the honeycomb hexagons haloing the combat theatre, video unfurled from the helicopters of the local and national news stations. Reporters explained that they were "live at the Stun-Glas stand-off" (and seconded by on-screen titles proclaiming the location as "KRIB Headquarters" [sic]) where "black L*A*B cult militants are under the command of disgraced F*O*O*Jster the X-Man;" PNN's story proclaimed

Kareem an "anti-white fanatic turned terrorist and super-predator" against whom the "dusk raid has been launched following a terrorist attack on the Fortress of Freedom where assembled F*O*O*Jsters are presumed dead . . . ."

Once sixty seconds at full alert had expired, the Spook ordered Syndi to deploy her HEAT-ray against the L*A*B to "dance them out." Syndi reminded the field commander that her beam worked only on line-of-sight, useless against the L*A*Bsters trapped inside.

The Spook: "Then hit the music, Red Two!"

Instantly:BUHM-BUHM-*BUHM*-BUHM . . . BUHM-BUHM-*BUHMti*-BUHM . . . .

Ripping her bustier speakers up to full volume, Syndi opened her mouth to unleash a sonic tsunami upon the neighbourhood, a herd of auditory woolly mammoths trampling over teepees:

> *I wanna SHOCK you, BABY*
> *ROCK you, BABY*
> *TALK you MAYBE*
> *Into GOING*
> *DOWN, DOWN, DOWN, DOWN*
> *DOWN on ME-e-E-E . . . .*

Rushing to their windows, ghetto dwellers leaned out screaming inaudibly against the aural assault; soon they disappeared only to return to their sills throwing bottles, forks, and burning trash—

The Spook: "Take em out, Red Two!"

Syndi's HEAT-ray bathed the tenements in intense swirls of disco light, and instantly the dozen window terrorists were transmuted into twelve individual Power Grrrls, all of them harmonising with her choral invitation to cunnilingual fury. When other residents emerged to pelt the Syndis in their own building with garbage, they too were flash-HEATed into singing submission.

When five minutes had passed and still no one had emerged from the Q*R*I*B, the Spook patched into Syndi's sound system to declare his ultimatum:

"ATTENTION MILITANTS! IF YOU DO NOT SURRENDER WITHIN THE NEXT SIXTY SECONDS WE WILL OPEN FIRE! YOU WILL MOVE OUT OF THAT HOUSE OR YOU WILL FACE THE CONSEQUENCES!"

Q*R*I*B DEATHS

When sixty seconds ended, the Spook ordered in the Rock Breaker.

With remarkable speed for such a massive, sixty-four year old man, the Rock Breaker leapt over the barrier and sprinted across the street, his mystic hammer John Henry in front of him like a sword.

At the final second before his strike could rip out the corner of the Q*R*I*B temple, dark tentacles tore out of the soil and tripped up the elderly black man, knocking him to the ground and seizing the fallen

John Henry. Rising from the soil with his tentacles like a giant black Daddy Long Legs spider, the Dreadlocker closed on the Rock Breaker to rip him to stumps.

And then a twenty-foot battering-ram of an arm smashed the Dreadlocker into a smear on the sidewalk.

Super-Bastard, piloting his giant "Transformer" suit of linked, robotic trailers, stood to his full six-story height, scraping the gore and dreadlocks from his arm before displaying evidence of his kill for the Spook.

"HOW'S SHE LOOKIN, PARTNERS?" he boomed, before the Q*R*I*B's roof exploded from the emergence of a six-story tall Arnold Drummond, Esq.

For terrifying seconds it was giant lawyer against giant lawyer, prosecutor against defense, locked in lethal litigative combat, until Arnold Drummond got the upper hand and knocked Super Bastard down with one swing of his massive subpoena. The trailer-transformer fell, crushing the Rock Breaker into the potholed street. Drummond jeered, "Whatchu *talkin* about, Bast'd?"

The Spook: "Red Five, take him out!"

Kid Kombat, Sr., knelt, bowing his head for clearance, and smoke streamed six hundred feet up from his back to touch Arnold Drummond's face, turning the left side of his giant skull into a cratered ruin of ravaged, sagging, burning flesh. An abattoir's worth of meat and bone pelted the ground like human hail.

Roaring in his death throes, Drummond charged the line before another tendril of smoke exploded through his midsection, dumping him dead overtop the struggling megaskeleton of Super Bastard.

Seconds before Kid Kombat could fire into the Q*R*I*B temple itself, his backpack exploded. Aflame, he fell to the ground screaming and flailing, dying like a crab dropped into a pot of boiling fat.

The Spook: "What the hell—"

I switched angles on the monitors. Charging across the street was Aunt Ester, who must've aimed her chemotrophic powers into the unarmed missiles on Kid Kombat's back. Still advancing, she transmuted five of Smithing Wesson's bullets into blossoms of steam before the sixth one punched a hole through her sternum big enough to reach through.

The scene devolved into chaos: Onyx Fox, another Supa Soul Sista, executed a hundred-foot arcing wire-work side-kick into Smithing Wesson's back—the King's English hurled his bobby-hat which transmuted in mid-tumble into a vicious, scrabbling badger which chomped onto Onyx Fox's leg—the Diva emerged, shooting her Look, and everyone in range dropped to their knees in worship until she and Syndi locked eyes and powers in diva-to-Diva combat—the Sabre-Tooth Beaver dashed across the smoking, flaming attack zone to start gnawing a new entrance into the Q*R*I*B—Anita Hill waded through strafing fire, her shield-law protecting her while she inched ever closer into range to unleash her power of discovery—

And then three giant silver-black wedges flew screaming overhead and dropped incendiary "eggs" on the Q*R*I*B.

The temple roared flame into the sky like Vesuvius.

Arcing out of their first bombing run, the Spook's terrordactyls circled wide, aligning for their second attack vector.

Having leapt all over the surrounding tenements, the fire transformed the entire block into a massive, multi-story bonfire. The Q*R*I*B's walls fissured and burst, and what remained of the roof crumbled and shattered through the four lower stories until all that remained was a rubble inferno.

For just a moment I activated Syndi's OM-meter, seeking an empathic survey of the situation. Beyond her horror, what I felt from her was a hammering heart, a throat raw from singing and screaming, and a nose scorching with the stench of smoke and burning meat.

The Spook: "Attention all units. This is Red Squad Leader. The target has been pacified. Repeat: the target has been pacified."

Regardless of what the adrenalin-addiction of superheroism may afford you, if you're serious about "pacifying" yourself, you'll need to look past such easy solutions as immolating those who spin you into a shame spiral or body-check you into belligerence. Remember: no one can "make" you "feel" anything.

The power is yours—and yours alone—to actualise yourself, to create your own reality, to free yourself of the illusions that imprison you more completely than could any malevolent mastermind. Had either X-Man or the Spook remembered such basic truths for achieving psychemotional equilibrium, they could have saved themselves not only lethal, destructive combat, but substantial consternation.

FINAL LESSONS AT THE ALMA MATER

By the time I scan-switched over to Sunhawk Island, Blue Squad had engaged its enemies. In the inky indigo dusk over the Blue Pyramid, orange flares and sparks lit up the combatants. But otherwise beyond those light sources I was blind, so I patched my OM-meter into Wally's cognistream:

~~What is all this crazy junk in m'face? M'team's gettin clobbered an I caint hardly see nuthin—better comm Festus. He'll know what t'do . . . .

"Mission C'mmand, this here's Wally—"

"Copy, Blue Squad Leader. Over."

"M.C., I'm getting blindeded out here—some kinda black cloud fulla lil ol squares is followin me—"

"Look carefully, Blue Leader—are the squares tiny words? Over."

"Uh, well now that y'mention it, *yes*, yes they is—"

"All right, then—they're logoids! Have you seen Edgerton anywhere? Over."

"No, not yet—"

"Blue Leader, White Squad's engaged Edgerton's word-creatures at the Hyper-Potentiality Clinic! He's over-extended—there's no way he can keep manifesting so many apparitions at once for long without completely draining himself. Hang in, Blue Leader! Over and out!"

"Over and out!"

~~Caint keep this up f'ever. Better spit on em. Now that's a sight! Fry, you stupid lil words! Golly, I always loved that smell—like burnin hair. That's better—now I c'n get me a clearer look-see. Goll dangit! Lookit the size a them boys, them whatchacallem—Ka-Sentinels? Like a football team of tar-black Goliaths with hawk faces. And who's that fightin alongside em? Whoever it is, they's beatin the stuffin outta Ivory Giant!

~~My gosh, it sure is a lovely night; stars all a-twanklin. Sunhawk Island'd be a nice place t'go campin some time. Think maybe when we're done t'night I should grab me some dinner at th'Olive Garden. They give ya extra breadsticks gratis if y'ask for em kindly. Maybe I should get me that collie-dog I been thankin about for a spell. They shed suh'm fierce, though . . . . Hm . . . is they re-runs of Rockford Files *on tonight? Always like that there Jim Rockford . . . .*

"Blue Leader! Blue Leader! This is Cathode Girl, do you copy?"

"Cathode Girl, this is Omnipotent Man, the Blue Leader. Over."

"Blue Leader, we need your assis—"

"Say, Cathode Girl, who's that fella leadin alla them *Ka*-Sentinels—the one wearing the golden skirt and whippin around that sceptre? Over."

"Blue Leader, that's the L*A*Bster, Grimhotep, the Living *Ka*! Blue Leader, please engage! We are currently having the sweet shit kicked out of us! Over!"

"Cathode Girl, this is Blue Leader—please keep th'profanity off this here channel! Over!"

"Blue Leader, Eldritch Cleaver has cut off Atomic Giraffe's legs, Ivory Giant's being kicked to death on the ground, and it's all Zed and I can do to shatter these Sentinels! We need your help, Blue Leader!"

"Don't get y'drawers in a knot, lil lady, I'm a-comin!"

~~Gotta plow through another cloud a these word-dealies. Worse'n Mexican skeeters. Lookit alla them animals runnin around down there—so dark out, it's tough to . . . what're them, crocodiles? An hippos! An a elk or suh'm? Hawk King shore had hisself a fine preserve, here. Okay, let's deal with these Sentinels.

~~Hm—skin feels like marble, cool and smooth. Still—uhn—they aint so tough. Just like crumblin crackers in yer soup. Ten-foot-tall black crackers with golden beaks, anyhow. How many left—okay, got those two. Get them over there—done and done. Spit down these six. Where's

Grimhotep? Fightin Cathode and Zed-the-Living-Phoneme. They'll be fine. Okay, smash this one. Crack them two. Spit these five down to—

~~*DMMMF!* M'dad-blamed skull feels like it jess been bocce-balled through a mine-field! Where am I? Up to m'neck in th'water—Sunhawk Island's way in the heck over there an I'm a-bobbin in th'Bay—

"Who sucker-punched me? C'mon, show y'self, unless yer yella! Don'make me smoke ya out!"

~~*NFFF!* Like takin a missile in m'sweetbread-section—an whoever's plowin into me is shootin us up outta th'water now—

~~kick him away—watch that crumb-bum spinning end-over-coffeepot. "Who are ya, y'no-good sucker-puncher?"

"You don't *know* me, Argonian?"

~~*Somebody's hovering out there with his back to th'moon, all shadowed an I caint see im fer squat—cept he's got a cape an he's holdin some kinda oversized double-sided axe or suh'm.*

"Sorry, buddy? Could y'all turn on a light or suh'm? I'm guessin y'all don'get many offers t'play basketball at night."

"Taunt all you like, *Impotent Man!* For I, *Shango*, will be the orisha of your doom!"

~~*OW! Betty Crocker, that smarts! Put his lil ol axe right in my turn-stiled kneecap! Let's see how he likes a little spit-shine! That's better, son—now I can see ya, lit up like a electric Santy-Claus on Bustle Avenue at Christmas!*

"How ya like that, Shangy-Man? You talk tough for somebody wearin such a funny little tiara!"

~~*uhff! Tough sumbitch, all right! Better shock him some more—still keeps on coming—burnt off most of his hair an clothes, an he's still swangin, grabbin me, wrastlin me like a Florida king-gator hopped up on funny-beans—hokay, gots to choke im—gon be tough—his neck's tougher'n m'thigh—practically huggin im he's so close—*

~~*now, there she goes, throat's finally crackin—*

~~*DAMN, he up an smoked me in th'eye with a head-butt—*

~~*what's all this sand or dust or whatever—hey, smells like—*

~~*everything's foggy an spinnin . . . world's gone blue an black an blue an black an blue—like I'm swimmin in Windex and crude oil, all hot an cold at the same time, I'm all tinglin an singin an laughin an m'heart's a-throbbin . . . . Why's the water rushin t'wards me like that? Okey-dokey, I'll take a little soaky . . . . Nice a Shangy to go fer a dip with me, even if he's lyin face down an all. Looks powerful peaceful. Think I'll try it—*

I de-selected my OM-meter link into Wally's mind and checked the honeycomb for visual scan of what was happening, but I could see nothing except darkness interrupted by flashes. And if there were some night-vision setting, I didn't know how to activate it.

I dialled up an audio link. "Anyone, anyone, can you hear me?"

"Miss Brain! This is the Flying Squirrel! Get the hell off this mission channel!"

"I'm sorry to interrupt, Festus, and I'm sure you're busy, but Wally's been incapacitated somehow—he may be drowning—"

"I was OM-metering the whole affair! He's been hit by an A-bomb!"

"An atomic bomb? Are you sure?"

"*Argonium,* you microbe! Probably laced with Edgerton's shadow-synthetic version. And I seriously doubt Wally'll drown . . . his brain can survive without oxygen for decades—hadn't you noticed? Now get the hell off this line and stay off!"

I hung up and spoke to the computer directly. "Where is Philip Kareem Edgerton, HKA the X-Man?"

The honeycomb flitted through thousands of camera-sights on Los Ditkos—the mainland, the Bird Island borough, and Sunhawk Island—sorting and filtering until dozens of urban angles on the same image lit up of a black car streaking at what must have been over a hundred and forty miles an hour—racing from Ellison Heights over the Rubicon Bridge and the Mantlo River, bypassing the clogged traffic of Bustle Avenue and ripping along Riverdrive beside the elite Bechtburton district, burning straight towards the northern plateau of the island—

But why was X-Man headed there? And why had the rest of his confederates thrown away their lives elsewhere? What had they been protecting? Or had it all been nothing but a diversion?

Flying Squirrel: "White Squad and all remaining units, this is Mission Command. Converge on Tachyon Tower! Repeat: converge on Tachyon Tower!"

WHEN WE LOSE OUR DELUSIONS, WE MUST NOT LOSE THE LESSON

Zooming every available city security camera I could, I tracked the shadow car as it rocketed up the hills to the plateau and then—astonishingly—straight up the side of Tachyon Tower.

The black blot further silhouetted itself against the scoreboard-style full-colour advertisements coursing the tapering heights of Tachyon Tower. Decelerating rapidly and then to a crawl just before it reached the tower's apex, the car braved an upside-down ascent from the bottom of the giant *faux*-plasma-globe, then inched up along the curvature until finally at the globe's equator . . . .

Switching angles to an interior camera, I gazed upon a vast window, on the other side of which the X-racer stuck to the glass like the world's largest refrigerator magnet.

Something extended itself from the underbelly of the vehicle, and then a neat circle etched itself in the glass, popping out a hole through which slid the cloaked L*A*Bster the Dark Fantastic, Chip Monk (in an altered version of his original costume—black tights instead of scaly green briefs), and the ever-white-shirted, black-tied and black-suited X-Man.

Kareem glanced back to the window. The X-racer disappeared. Through the crisp circle in the window, wind instantly whipped their costumes and scattered brochures across the Sunday evening desertion of the observation deck. The Dark Fantastic raised his arm—

—and every hexagon scanning that gallery of the Tachyon Tower deck blinked not to null blue but total black.

I flicked at the controls to bring up another image, but the invading trio was completely blacked-out.

Instantly another hexagon seized my attention: one floor upward, a wall shattered inwards, and then a woman in shining armour landed on the debris of steel and reinforced concrete—Iron Lass, her black wings transmuting back into her cloak, her twin swords bared for battle. Scanning her surroundings, she dashed towards the vault door overtop of which declared a sign:

CONTAINMENT UNIT X
FULLY AUTOMATED FACILITY
EXTREME DANGER

ACCESS RESTRICTED TO
SECURITY LEVEL INFRA-RED
AND ABOVE

Shoving her swords into the massive metal mechanism, she was showered by sparks and instantly lit up by flashing bullet fire from a dozen angles and splashed by sprayjets which coated her and everything around her in icicles. Throbbing lights plunged the room into red and purple.

While her armour protected her from whatever she didn't deflect with the nearly invisible speed of her swords, Iron Lass levelled both blades at the firing zones, emitting blasts of her own frost and fire until the entire room was a chaos of steaming and flaming destruction.

Vanishing her swords, she pried her way through what was left of the vault door, and I lost visual contact with her—apparently certain sections of the Tachyon Tower had no cameras in them, or required some further passcode or override for me to access them.

By the time I patched into Iron Lass's cognistream—

~~What is this contraption? Like planetarium projectors—seven of them? They almost look like psionic inhibition siphons ... but they'd be the largest ones ever built, all clustered and pointed at ... is that a person inside that cube? Like a man sitting inside a washing machine! Is he asleep?

~~Ymir's blood—can it really be?

"Destroyer?"

~~*withered, depleted, a human apple core left in the sun—eyes shuttering open, twin blue suns—*

"Menton! But . . . but I *kilt* you!"

~~*his mouth slowly working, chewing and swallowing, dryly forcing itself to work, as if the man's emerging from a coma—*

"Ah . . . Professor . . . *Ice*gaard? *Killed* me, you say? Your delusions . . . of grandeur . . . are as cloying as ever . . . ."

~~*Grendelsmuter, Darkalfheimsdottir, to me!*

"Surely . . . Professor . . . you have no need . . . of your weapons . . . against a desiccated corpse of a man . . . strapped into this . . . Torquemadan technology?"

~~*caution, Valkyrie—don't gaze into his eyes for too long at a time— he murdered ten thousand mortals in a single night, feeding upon their minds—*

~~*Grendelsmuter's silver light upon the butcher's face makes him look even paler—*

"How in *Niflheim* dit you get here, villain?"

"I be*lieve*, Professor Icegaard . . . I heard someone call it . . . Project . . . Paperclip? Transferred me on the CSV *Odessa*, if memory serves, from the Asteroid . . . I don't know how long ago . . . You'll forgive me . . . my mind's not quite what it used to be—"

"Haff you been behindt all zis? Destroying ze Asteroit? Murtering Hawk Kink?"

"*Me?* Hnnnh . . . hnnnh . . . excuse my, my wheezing, Professor . . . it's the only laugh I have left. I'm flattered, truly, but no . . . my glory days are long expired . . . time to lift me on the pyre. These days . . . I'm nothing but a humble document . . . in the archives of power. To be filed, refiled, *de*filed at the whim of a higher power—"

"Zen be filedt in ze grafe by my power, monster, for now at last you vill die!"

~~*Ach, sheisen! My sword—I've smashed one of the psionic inhibitors— his eyes—*

"YOU WILL LET ME OUT OF THIS ABOMINATION, HNOSSI."

~~*must . . . fight him . . . but I can't . . . stop . . . myself . . . .*

"EXCELLENT WORK, WIELDING THOSE BLADES OF YOURS LIKE SCALPELS. THANK YOU FOR FREEING ME. AH . . . FORGIVE ME IF I DON'T STAND UP . . . AFTER SUCH A LENGTHY CONVALESCENCE, MY LEGS . . . YOU UNDERSTAND? AH, I CONFESS, THIS INTIMATE TIME WE'VE SPENT TOGETHER HERE HAS GIVEN ME NOTIONS. WOULD YOU BE A DEAR AND SHARE WITH ME YOUR HEART?"

~~*no . . . my Grendelsmuter—away! Why won't you away? Ah—no, not through my armour—NOT INTO MY—*

Hnossi's agony momentarily blinded me, and I was shocked right out of her cognistream. I dialled through every camera I could, then through every OM-meter feed I could locate, until I clicked on to Syndi's.

"—how ya like me *now?"*

~~*that's it . . . sing it with me, asshole!*

"How's it feel being the one *controlled*, Menton? Oh, what's wrong, legs weak? That's okay, you dirty old bastard—dance! Dance anyway! You know this one? *'Hey!* MEN-*ton!* LEAVE *my* MOM *a*LONE!'"

~~*That's it, that's it—right on her goddamn sword, you old fuck! . . . Look at that . . . hardly even bleeding. Like a mummified mental Hitler . . . .*

"*Mütterchen!* Can you hear me? *Mom!"*

~~she's so heavy, all this armour . . . Odin, please don't let her be dead—

"Can you *hear* me?"

"Ah . . . my daughter . . . you'f . . . safedt me..?"

"Yes, Mutter!"

"Such . . . a gut . . . girl—"

"Mutter? *MUTTER?"*

"She'll be all right, Syndi!"

~~*who the hell? Chip Monk? Dark Fantastic? And—*

"Kareem! Oh, Kareem—why? Why'd you do all this? Why, Kareem? WHY?"

"What're you *talking* about?"

"All those, those, those people, Kareem, all those F*O*O*Jsters at the fuh-Fortress—we *worked* with them! How could you just, just, just *kill* them all like that?"

"I didn'kill *any*body, Syndi. Just hit em with the F*O*O*J's own knock-out gas, that's all—they'll be fine!"

"Thank god, Kareem! I told them, I told them, I said you'd never—but why—"

"I had to put em outta commission until I could get here—the stakes are too high to risk them trying to stop us—"

"But what were you trying to do? Take out Menton? Because I just did that!"

"That's who that is? For real? Shit, couldn't tell when you got him all *you*ed up like that. Kot-*tam*, I knew it! I *knew* it! Yo, 'Tastic, didn'I say?"

"Word."

"Syndi! Is Menton gonna die?"

"No, I don't think so—not if we get him to a doctor . . . ."

"How do you *know* he's not dying?"

"I'd know—if I want to, I can feel what they feel when they're HEATed—but he's out cold . . . I should *let* him die—"

"No, keep him alive! *We need him to testify!* We need the whole truth out on this!"

"Kareem, does that mean it's all over? I mean, I captured him, right? So now he can stand trial for Hawk King's murder, Asteroid Zed—"

"No, Syndi—Menton wasn't behind any of this—well, maybe behind killing Jack Zenith, but—"

"What the fuck are you talking about, Kareem? You're still fixated on Eva? Eva's not Menton! *This* is Menton! And she's not Sarah Bellum, either! Kareem, listen to me: you've been under a lot of stress! You're not seeing things as they really are. You need help! You need therapy!"

"Shut up, Syndi! I know Doctor Brain's clean!"

"Whu-what? But what about everything you told me at the theatre?"

"Yeah, I had my suspicions at one point, but—"

~~*Chip Monk's grabbing Kareem by the arm—*

"X-Man, we've got to move—"

~~*Can't let Kareem leave!*

"But Kareem, you told me yourself, this elaborate conspiracy theory about how Eva had—"

"I just told you all that cuz I knew you'd sell me out to those freaks the second you got back to the Squirrel Tree!"

"What? You . . . you *used* me? Why? For revenge?"

"For a diversion!"

"So you *did* use me!"

"Don't talk to me about *using* people or manipu*la*tion, Syndi—"

"So when exactly did you figure out this massive conspiracy, hm? And when were you planning to let me in on it?"

"It all clicked when you said who your mother was—everything fell together: Festus, Asteroid Zed, Menton—"

"That doesn't make any sense—"

"Who's the detective here? And besides, the proof is in the kot-tam pudding-pops!"

"How could you just, just use me like that, Kareem? As a diversion?"

"This aint fuckin *about* you, Syndi! I'm tryin to save the planet, here!"

"Always gotta be the one saving the planet, Kareem! How could you— just, just exploit me for your own personal goals?"

"Even-Steven!"

"Oh, *that's* mature!"

~~*Dark Fantastic is stomping his boot—*

"Dam*na*tion, Brother X!"

"Look, I'm not gonna argue with you, Syndi! How long can you keep Menton *you*ed-up like that?"

"I don'know—hours?"

"Good! Get him and your mom outta here, and evacuate the building—"

"Why? What're you gonna do?"

"We're gonna blow this entire dome if we have to! Chip, 'Tastic—split up—stay off the comms except for emergency! Find a way to get up to that dimensional research lab!"

~~*and now they're all gone, and I'm alone . . . .*

~~*Mütterchen . . . .*

SIBLING RIVALRY AND OEDIPAL COMBAT

I switched cameras, clicking through until I could find one of the three invaders.

I spotted Kareem, covered in an X-oskeleton, smashing through a window and crawling out onto the exterior of the building.

I clicked again, finding a dozen camera angles on the outside of the dome from which to choose. And on Dome Camera Ext. 11, I spotted Kareem.

Backlit by the twinkling skyline, he was climbing up the dome with his clawed shadow-gloves, his shadow-cables keeping him from plummeting a hundred and fifty stories to his death.

And above the whipping wind, I could hear the whine growing until it was like a bandsaw chewing into fresh pine. Kareem looked up—

"Okay, asshole!" shouted the Brotherfly. "Now you an me are gonna finish it for real!"

André opened his mouth wider than any human mouth should be able to and disgorged a steaming jet-spew onto Kareem that must have been some type of corrosive, digestive juice. Kareem screamed, wiping at his exposed flesh, then reformatted his X-oskeleton to seal itself completely—even over his eyes. With Kareem stuck blind on the curve of the dome, André flew closer, kicking and kicking and kicking into Kareem's shadow-armour until Kareem was swinging on his tow-cables from the impacts, his body and legs whipping side to side, and one of his feet went right into a camera, and the hexagon went null blue.

Flipping and clicking wildly to find another POV, I hit something that brought onscreen the phrase TACHYON TOWER - UPPER DECK CAMERAS - SECURITY OVERRIDE - ACTIVATED, and then I found myself witnessing an interior shot of Chip Monk and the Flying Squirrel smashing each other into the walls and across the chamber in a hurricane of weaponry and martial arts. In the brief moments when the two men stopped to circle each other, they hurled fragments of cruelty at each other, horrible claims about disloyalty and hatred and paranoia.

The Flying Squirrel: "So, you're mixed up with that communist coon, now, hm? He's doing for you what I wouldn't? Wouldn't Zenith be jealous?"

Chip Monk: "Zenith? The real hero that *you* murdered, Festus? Not that you'd do it yourself—that'd require you getting your hands dirty! You had your marionette Menton murder him *for* you!"

The Flying Squirrel: "How dare you question me! *Me!*"

The two men leapt, clashed, and the Squirrel fell onto his protégé. There was a loud crunch, and then Festus stumbled up backwards, gasping, holding his hands in front of him as if to push away the sight of the costumed body on the ground, so still that not even its chest moved.

Exactly at that moment, the exterior camera finally started working again.

André was still pummelling Kareem, but the X-Man wasn't even trying to fight back. Instead his X-oskeleton was growing something like a fiddler crab's oversized arm, a massive drill-like tool that chewed a hole through the dome wall until Kareem retracted his device and slipped himself through the gap.

Using the security over-ride, I dialled up an interior camera-view just as André followed Kareem inside the chamber, only to be smashed across the room by what looked like a massive, black fly-swatter. André careened off equipment, hit the wall, and landed on his side.

Given the angle of his impact, his body's contortion, and his screaming, I guessed his hip was crushed and at least one of his legs was broken.

Sirens were howling, and speakers were automatically chanting *All personnel, this is a Level One emergency! Hull breach in the dimensional interface chamber! Initiating full system shut-down!*

Behind André in the cavernous technochamber was a huge, radiant iris, a three-story gold-silver blossom whose centre shimmered with nebula and stars, vibrating with a disturbing violet luminescence.

Kareem staggered over to Andre, his X-oskeleton fading to grey and then to nothingness. Panting and groaning, he was clutching his side as if his ribs were broken.

"Now listen . . . you super-duper . . . killer house-nigger! I *know* . . . *you* killed . . . Hawk King!" His chest was heaving. He tried and failed to catch his breath. "Tell me why . . . kot-tammit! *Why?*"

"You *crazy*, nigga!"

"My *medu-kem* . . . found dust . . . from the Blue Pyramid walls . . . on your costume, André. But you said . . . you hadn't been there . . . since you were a kid—"

"So your logoids are wrong!"

"No way in hell. I also had them . . . go through Festus's computers . . . . Squirrel Big Brother . . . has got the whole city . . . under observation. Grimhotep . . . finally decrypted the file I retrieved. Shows you . . . flying away from the Pyramid the night the King was murdered. With a sceptre in your hands. The Sceptre of Typhon."

As his accusations grew in strength, Kareem regained his own.

"So how'd you do it, André? Mind-control him with the sceptre into revealing his transmutation-phrase . . . turn him into defenseless, old Doctor Rogers in his wheelchair, and then kill him? And then . . . use the transmutation phrase to turn his body back into Hawk King's so no one'd know? *Why*, muthafucka? How much did that son-of-a-bitch *pay* you?"

André yelled, "Fuck you, man! Ain'nobody pay me! I loved Hawk King! I loved him! He was my hero!"

Kareem put his foot onto André's pelvis and leaned.

The act—and André's scream—were so repugnant that even as a trained psychotherapist, it was all I could do to keep myself from turning away.

"*I aint fuckin around with you, André!*" yelled Kareem. "Now you tell me why you did it, or next time I'm standing up on that muthafucka like you a Stair Master!"

When André's eyes drifted back into focus, he said, "They were blackmailing me, man!"

"Who? Festus?"

"I don't know who! Guy came to me, told me he'd tell my aunt Maybelle that I was responsible for my uncle Benteen's death! It'd kill her if she found out!"

"His death?"

"Because, because my uncle, he . . . I was in my room one mornin, an I didn'know he was home, an he didn'think anybody else was home, so when he heard somethin in my room he just came up an barged in an caught me changin into my costume, an then he just had a massive heart attack—"

"He caught you fuckin a guy, didn'he, André?"

"*What?* No—no, that's not true, Kareem!" said André, or perhaps I should say Andrew, given his speech shift. "Who told you that? It's not true, whatever you heard!"

"No one told me—I figured it out days ago, after I bugged Doctor Brain's glasses. Your whole origin story—it didn't wash. All your 'womanising'—I *saw* the file photos of you at those nightclubs. Just cuz Eva doesn't know what kind of clubs the Meet Market, Bone Dancers, and Peacocks are doesn't mean I don't!"

"No, Kareem, please, just . . . look, don't tell my aunt, all right? Whatever you think of me, don't tell my aunt—"

"You're a kot-tam *murderer*, André! You think I'm just gonna give you a pass cuz you don't wanna get in trouble with your aunty?"

"It'd kill her, Kareem! Don't you understand? Just like my uncle—I was trying to pro*tect* her, that's all! She raised me!"

"I don't let murderers walk for any reason! Let alone the Judas who assassinated the greatest leader we ever had!"

"Oh . . . sure," sobbed André, catching himself before he continued. "Fine. High and mighty Kareem. So perfectly just. Judging me! The homophobic, white girl-screwing hypocrite, judging me!"

"This aint *about* homophobia!"

"Isn't it? When I went to join the L*A*B when you muthafuckas were recruiting? Remember that? I went down to the Q*R*I*B. All I wanted was to protect Stun-Glas. And all your friends, laughing about these applicants you'd rejected, 'fag' this and 'fag' that, and the Dreadlocker saying how he'd put some 'battiman' in the hospital just for *looking* at him and how he'd '*put fyah on di nex one*' he found!"

"*I* never talked like that, André—"

"No, but you didn't fucking stop it, either, did you? Did you have Dreadlocker arrested for confessing to a horrible, aggravated assault? Did you kick him out of the L*A*B? Even just fucking *talk* to him about it?"

X-Man looked down, opening his hands as if he'd left something important in them. "You're right. André. You're right," he said, clearing his throat. "But that doesn't excuse—"

Kareem was smashed against the wall.

I zoomed back: the Flying Squirrel was reaching into his utility pouches—

And then the monitors inked into blackness.

A FEAR-FILLED FINAL INVENTORY

I couldn't see anything. Even the eerie light of the dimensional portal had been snuffed out. The Dark Fantastic must've entered right behind the Squirrel. I clicked into the Brotherfly's OM-meter cognistream, but he'd passed out. Festus's link was still off-line. My only means of monitoring was auditory.

"What's a matter, Festus?" called Kareem. "Night vision goggles don't work? Even infra-red is light, you know!"

"So we're *all* blind, then! I'll find you, Edgerton. And when I do, I'll snap you into kindling!"

"I don't think so, Festus. You're tired. Exhausted! I can hear it in your voice! And there's just one of you, but two of us!"

Sounds of tripping and falling—perhaps one man, maybe more.

The Squirrel: "Ah . . . but *you're* injured and exhausted. As soon as I take out your hooded, hoodlum friend and his darkness dissipates, you'll be nothing but a lame, black cockroach that can't even dash for the shadows. And injured as you are, I'm guessing you won't have power enough for many word-monstrosities now, will you?"

There were more sounds of crashing.

Kareem: " . . . Hey, that's a great gamble, Piltdown. Sure . . . I don't have any Words left at all. I'm defenseless!"

The Squirrel: "You're bluffing."

Kareem: "Try me."

Silence.

Kareem: "I'll give you this, Festus—you had me fooled for the longest time. Didn't even cross my mind that you were the one who'd arranged Hawk King's murder."

Festus: "You Liberian lunatic, so now you've shifted your roving delusions from Miss Brain-as-murderess onto me? What's next? Accusing Iron Lass of assassinating Lincoln? Or Caesar? Or Abel?"

"It took me a while to put it all together, Festy . . . but when I saw how totally broken up you were about Iron Lass—you haven't just been mourning Iron Lass, you've been racked with guilt because you never thought your plot would get *her* poisoned!"

"That's why you went on this terrorist crusade of yours, you crackpot? Because I was mourning the impending death of a lifelong comrade?"

"No—because you, the world's self-proclaimed greatest detective, were dragging your feet on *two* investigations! I thought, why isn't he out rousting everyone he can think of? He loves this woman, and revenge is this bastard's middle name! So why wouldn't you be attacking somebody, *any*body, tossing whole neighbourhoods for suspects . . . unless you *knew* there was nobody to hunt down, because you *were* the one who'd arranged Asteroid Zed to be destroyed! Nobody wanted to go up there when Brain insisted, but *you*, you practically exploded a lung in protest! And then you wanted to take your own shuttle, but even when you finally relented and took the space elevator with us, you still had one of your ships standing by on remote?"

"You equate preparedness with homicide? Your lapses in logic have always been astonishing, Edgerton, but even for you, this is grand!"

More stumbling and crashing.

Kareem: "If I've got lapses in my logic, Pilty, it's funny how much your own computer records and surveillance footage helped form a picture of what you did, and what you're planning to do."

Silence.

"Nothing to say to that, huh? Yeah, I thought so. Even *I* didn't know I could do that until escaping Asteroid Zed gave me no choice but to send my Words inside the computers. But because of that 'crash course' I realised I could search your mainframe, and that's how I found out the people you'd had scouring the Middle East for years had just located the Sceptre of Typhon, one of the only things that could make Hawk King vulnerable. But you never turned it over to him, your supposed idol.

"Why wouldn't you? Unless you needed an ace up your sleeve? Or a dagger? You had to destroy Asteroid Zed because my investigation would take me to Gil Gamoid and the N-Kid, and you had no way of knowing whether their Qosmic Qonsciousness might've picked up on what you'd done, or the attack that L-Raunzenu was planning, that no one but you and Hawk King knew about!"

"*L-Raunzenu?* What in god's—you're truly deranged, do you know that, Edgerton?"

"—and you also couldn't risk me finding out that Menton and Sarah Bellum'd been moved. You were using them for your dimensional research, right? I mean, one of your holding companies owns Tachyon Tower! And after Sarah Bellum probably burned out or died, you went back to the store for something with a little bit more kick. And who better to arrange the destruction of Asteroid Zed than the head of the company that retrofitted it after Gil, the Kid, and Menton were transferred there in the first place, and the head of the corporation that ran the Asteroid after the kot-tam thing was privatised? You'd think—"

A crash. Huffing. Cracking.

The lights seeped back on, emergency lights in red and the dimensional portal in purple.

The Flying Squirrel was standing over the cloaked body of the Dark Fantastic, all of whose limbs were pointing in directions they shouldn't have. And right beside them stood the X-Man.

Kareem shouted something in an alien tongue, and four black baboons smoked into life and leapt on Festus, ripping at him, biting him, shredding his utility pouches and smashing whatever components they could find. The Squirrel whirled to fight off his attackers until he crashed into Kareem, knocking him down and sitting on top of him and reaching through the arms of his simian attackers to remove from his own neck the last item of Squirreltech he still had in his possession—a collar—which he locked around Kareem's neck.

The baboons *popped* away like bubblegum.

Kareem punched Festus in the throat, then heaved and shoved the old man off of him, struggling to get the shackle off his neck. He couldn't. "What'd you *do* to me?"

Barely able to push himself off the floor, the tattered, bleeding, and weaponless Festus, while panting, actually chuckled.

"Something . . . I whipped up . . . when you . . . affirmative-actioned your way into the F*O*O*J. Just in case. Scrambles your brain just enough . . . to stop you . . . from making your Words . . . come true."

Kareem backed away from the older man as far as he could.

"I don'care what it is," said Kareem. "Thing's got a battery—an since this is your first test, you don't know how long it'll last against me—"

"Oh . . . I don't need long . . . to kill you."

Both men were so injured it was remarkable that they could walk at all, yet still they stalked each other, pit bulls in a dog pit, waiting for the chance to rip out each other's throat.

"I found the footage in your mainframe, Festus. You're like Nixon—you're so paranoid, you even bugged yourself!"

"Keep talking, shine. Keep on using up your breath—"

"Hawk King came out to the Squirrel Tree to talk to you personally, to get you to shut down Tachyon's dimensional research labs. I read his astronomical notes—my X-falcon found them. He'd been scanning the Nistan nebula, and he found out that L-Raunzenu was planning to attack Los Ditkos . . . using the Tachyon Tower's dimensional portal to do it. But you wouldn't shut the portal down, would you? Because you had your own plans for keeping that attack secret . . . *and for letting it happen.*

"How many people d'you think an L-Raunzenu sneak attack from there could kill? Tallest building in the city, with nothing to block its nightmare-stream? I guess you'd know better than anyone, since Piltdown Psychotronics spent a billion tax dollars to *create* fuckin L-Raunzenu in the 'eighties. Your 'master weapon' in the War on Supervillains . . . but then L-Raunzenu didn't work so well in the *Götterdämmerung*, did it?

Unless turning on us, killing us, and escaping into another dimension rank as high quality control in your estimation . . . ."

The two men were now so close that they were stumbling and tripping to stay just out of the other's grasping range, each one trying to fake out the other—or attack.

"So what did Hawk King order you to do?" said Kareem. "Shut down the portal in forty-eight hours or he'd shut it down myself? But hey! The F*O*O*J was collapsing, right? Letting in darkies, letting in gays, just before its most important election ever . . . plus, you can't just stand by and let a little thing like global peace threaten the multi-billion dollar Piltdyne defense contracts supplying the F*O*O*J, could you?

"So you needed something, something big, an interdimensional Pearl Harbour, to justify a new *Götterdämmerung*, didn't you? A permanent one! With sweeping new powers for the F*O*O*J and for yourself, with you as Director of Operations! That's what Gil Gamoid and the N-Kid were trying to warn me about, only they were so fuckin cracked they could hardly string a coherent sentence together! And so what if a few thousand people'd die? I mean, they'd die anyway someday, right? And it's a small price to pay for Piltdown!

"But *I'm* gonna shut down this portal, Festus, if I have to use your skull like a fucking hammer to do it!"

Finally finding the right combination of buttons, I patched through on the speaker phone of the Brotherfly's belt.

"Kareem—please! You need help! Let me help you!"

"Doc? What the hell are you—"

The Squirrel leapt upon him, and the two men smashed each other against the walls, the machinery, the floor. The large man rolled on top of Kareem, punching him and ramming his head into the ground. And then the collar snapped open and fell off the younger man's neck.

Kareem yelled: *"GIANT FIST!"*

A black fist the size of a tank arced down from the ceiling, smashing through the edge of the portal and shearing through the floor and ripping open a huge gash in the wall extending to the level below and revealing the dark emptiness beyond. Ruptured by the impact, the metal floor buckled into an impromptu slide, and the two men, locked in each other's arms, shot outside into a one hundred and fifty-story plunge.

Exterior cameras caught strobing images of their descent:

145th floor: two bodies—

130th floor: tumbling feet-over-head in darkness—

105th floor: X-Man punching Festus—

70th floor: Festus doing nothing but gripping Kareem's mouth shut—

25th floor: *And a streak of light and one body still falling—*

And a sonic boom which erased the sound of impact.

REINTEGRATION

An hour later I was at the base of the Tachyon Tower inside the hot
darkness and the glare of emergency vehicle flashers and television
cameras, watching three injured but still-standing members of the
F*O*O*J issue their statement to soothe a concerned country and a
worried world.

" . . . and thanks to the superior strategic and defensive capacity of
this organisation," said Festus Piltdown III, scratched and scarred but no
longer bleeding, "once again, the F*O*O*J has saved America from the
threat of supervillainy: a sleeper-agent who was among us for years, part
of a diabolical plot to infiltrate the highest levels of F*O*O*J authority. A
sleeper working for a previously unknown network of new supervillains,
stretching across the planet . . . and right here in the homes of America—"

Festus broke off in mid-inspiration, visibly angry at the sight of a
swaying Omnipotent Man (his face still tinted blue) who was alternating
between flashing "thumbs up" and "double guns" towards the cameras.
Covering the microphones, Mr. Piltdown leaned away from the podium
and growled something to Hnossi, who steadied Wally.

Leaning back to the microphone, Festus said, "Understandably,
we're all exhausted. But our exhaustion, our injuries, even the sacrifice
of our fellow F*O*O*Jsters and other brothers-in-capes who perished
tonight . . . are a small price to pay for preserving the liberty of our great
nation, the greatest nation on this planet. Thank you.

"No questions."

EPILOGUE

Be a Phoenix,
Not a Dodo

THE PRIZE OF VICTORY

As you have seen throughout *Unmasked: When Being a Superhero Can't Save You from Yourself,* the struggle to achieve psychemotional wellness is far from hopeless. If you can muster all the members of your internal super-team and rally under the strategic command of the methods outlined in these pages, victory can indeed be yours.

You have learned that the vulnerability you experience to the greatest threats in your life originates in your own self-defeating behaviours. You have seen how your worst suffering originates inside your refusal to accept inevitable defeats. But when you choose to embrace such defeats, you will have achieved prizes that no villain, external or internal, can ever wrench from your gloved and mighty hands: the shield of clarity, and the sword of acceptance.

AVOIDING EXTINCTION
WHEN THE FOOD SUPPLY ENDS

As a superhero, not unlike a psychoanalyst, you dared to devote your life to saving others. As a reader of this book who has borne witness to the case studies within it, you have come to see that the reward for superheroic public service is usually nothing more than public adulation.

So when, as all things must, that adulation disappears, you come to see that the far greater daring is in the effort to save yourself. However, if the world has changed around you, you may find yourself without an environment that can support you. If so, and if you fail to examine your psychemotional circumstances, you may go the way of the dodo.

But mythology teaches that even if you face total burn-out, you can still be a phoenix.

Since the end of the *Götterdämmerung*, the heroes who have been entrusted into my care have come to me in two types, as distinguished by their attitudes: dodos and phoenixes. The dodos could not adapt to the new, exterior demands of a dynamically changing world and the intrinsic reorientation required to exist in that world, and therefore their own refusal to change led them to their ends.

But even those who were terrified by change, who nonetheless found the courage to seek psychic safety within, discovered their capacity to survive and even thrive in a world being recreated daily.

THE TRAGEDY OF A FALLEN F*O*O*JSTER

Whether because of the fantastical, delusional ideation of Racialised Narcissistic Projection Neurosis, or because he was acting on the orders of his masters in the recently-revealed Neo-Villain Network, Philip Kareem Edgerton posed a grave threat to the United States. His near-ascendancy to executive authority on the F*L*A*C of the F*O*O*J remains a cautionary tale, a "dodged bullet" whose *ka-blam!* still rings fear in the ears of the nation.

The F*O*O*J's special investigative task force concluded that Edgerton himself had murdered Hawk King, then exploited that murder to boost his electoral hopes. When his ascent to power failed, he exploded his "Plan B" in the July 16 Attacks.

For such a diabolical operative, Edgerton was ultimately incompetent at terror, surprisingly typical of one trapped in an id-reflexive conflict-loop. The task force discovered that the bombs Edgerton had planted at the Fortress of Freedom were so shabbily constructed that the chemicals they contained had been improperly mixed, which resulted in them emitting only gas instead of exploding, except for the "X-bombs" which destroyed the Fortress's comm system.

More worrisome was the task force's discovery of Edgerton's previously unknown capacity for mind control. Edgerton used this neuro-invasive variant of his logoid power to bludgeon a false confession from the Brotherfly. Another victim of that power was the late Tran Chi Hanh, as disabled by dodo tendencies as his confederate was, who died hating the man who had given him a home and who had treated him like a son.

Ultimately, the task force was unable to find a shred of evidence linking Hawk King to one professor Jackson Rogers of Ellison Heights, Los Ditkos, who coincidentally disappeared the same day that Hawk King did. While the task forced declared it had insufficient evidence to link Edgerton to Roger's disappearance, suspicions remain.

Fortunately for everyone, the containment of the Q*R*I*B was accomplished with only minimal casualties; aside from the members of the L*A*B, only a few dozen families died from fire or smoke, a statistic all the more remarkable when compared to the far greater number of homes destroyed. More lives might have been lost had firefighters not been ordered by the Spook to stay clear of their equipment for fear that they, too, could become targets of the L*A*Bsters.

HEALING THE NATION, HEALING THE SOUL

Fortunately for the plight of both freedom and mental health, most of my F*O*O*Jsters did learn the lessons I attempted to impart to them in the Hyper-Potentiality Clinic. Some, in fact, were learning those lessons before our sessions began, recognising the ways in which they would need to look past old ways of thinking, to make embassies of peace to those who previously had been adversaries, and to recreate themselves anew in a new world.

Explaining to the F*O*O*J special task force that Menton had been clandestinely transferred to the Tachyon Tower to serve in the highest level of Global Anti-Supervillain Intelligence, the Flying Squirrel demonstrated how the top-secret new Menton Protocols of GASI had helped the F*O*O*J keep tabs on all new developing hyper-threats everywhere, from scanning the minds of seemingly innocent Americans to checking what books they were reading and with whom they were socialising, all to pre-empt the development of the next generation of supervillains.

By Menton's analysis, the situation is disturbing.

There are somewhere in the neighbourhood of six million Americans with proto-villain tendencies, and hundreds of millions of foreigners around the world with such tendencies, not to mention those who are already acting upon such malevolent ideation. A grateful public has embraced this new "Mentology" surveillance service which ensures safety by stopping villainy before it can kill, so that, in the words of the Flying Squirrel, "the smoking gun is not a laser cannon burning down Los Ditkos."

THE NEW HORIZONS
OF PSYCHEMOTIONAL STABILITY

So how are my sanity-supplicants doing, now that they've completed the first phase of their therapeutic adventure?

Power Grrrl continues to process her narcissistic ideation and behaviours but has entirely overcome her Munchausen tendencies. Having left the F*O*O*J and superheroics altogether, she has moved her entertainment career completely out of the pop/dance/techno field, and is currently delving into an edgier, angrier "rap/hip hop" sound with a forthcoming album, *Straight Outta Virgins*. Since the events of July 16, she has refused to speak to the media about Edgerton.

The Brotherfly, after several months of physiotherapy and a hip replacement, has returned to me for an expanded rôle of talk therapy in his life to address his Secret Identity Diffusion and to finish exorcising the ghosts of Rudolfism-inspired pain. Currently remodelling his family home which he recently inherited, he's now hosting Ultra Power Network's hit *Brotherfly for the Regular Guy*, featuring André dispensing superhero chic for the fashion-challenged ordinary citizen.

Omnipotent Man, Flying Squirrel, and Iron Lass unveiled their strategy for a revitalised F*O*O*Jification of global affairs. **The Prospects for a New Superheroic Century** calls for and maps out a vigilant stance against the new breed of super-menaces lurking beneath the illusion of peace like subtopical acne waiting to erupt on the face of an innocent adolescent.

Wally W. Watchtower has made astounding progress in overcoming his Crisis of Infinite Dearths, Mission-Identity Loss Disturbance, Icon Trap, Post-Power Stress Disorder, and Secret Identity Diffusion, integrating his manifold alters and powers into a unified, successful new identity. Like an eagle, Omnipotent Man has soared past his previous popularity to unexpected new heights, not only because of his triumphant return to superheroism and his victory in the July 16th attacks, but because of a new development sweeping the nation. Piltdown Psychotronics has developed and mass-marketed a home consumer OM-meter, one which in these uncertain times allows ordinary Americans to connect empathically with one of their greatest leaders, one whom they feel confident is in direct, daily connection with the *Ka* of Hawk King himself. After only a few months of retail sales of the OM-pathy Box, it's estimated that half of all Americans own or regularly use one and pay monthly subscription fees. Sales of OM-pathy Boxes show no sign of slowing down.

Hnossi Icegaard and Wally W. Watchtower are now happily married, and Hnossi has given birth to a baby boy. The product of combined Aesirian and Argonian genes, the fast-forming foetus gestated to full term in less than a month, with a birthday of September 12th. Eager to celebrate their union in numerous ways, the couple toyed with the names "Hnally" and "Wossi," but arrived at a happy third option by naming their child "Freedom."

Professor Icegaard has overcome her Saviour Complex, removed herself from her Id Crisis of scripted behaviour loops, deactivated her narcissistic tendencies and Uranus Conflict with her daughter, countered her Mortiquaeroticism, and successfully disassembled her Icon Trap. In doing so, she's found a new life and new love, and has gone past mere consultation with Piltdown Dynamics to become its Chief Research + Design Officer as Piltdyne's vanguard in the development of all new peace-delivery technology systems including the new B10 ballistic-pacification flight vehicle currently under construction.

Mr. Piltdown, still unmarried, remains saddened by the loss of his former protégé, whom he still remembers as the happy, smiling child he'd once been. More pleasantly, he's processed his way through his own Icon Trap. Because of his rôle in protecting the public safety, he's been able to reduce his Mission-Identity Loss Disturbance, and he's made great strides in minimising his Id Confrontational tendencies, his Obsessive Defensive-Ideation, and compulsive fight-or-flight behaviours, and has addressed his own case of the Achilles Three-Fold Folly of Superior Ability.

Buoyed by his newfound mental clarity and public acclaim for his heroic rôle in the July 16 Attacks, the Flying Squirrel was elevated by an overwhelming margin to the F*L*A*C as Director of Operations in the F*O*O*J election of September 12th. Awarded the contract to build the Asteroid Omega lunar-orbital penitentiary, Piltdown Dynamics is also constructing and will be operating a new network of high-tech criminal containment facilities around the United States, providing jobs and safety for the nation.

Festus Piltdown was perhaps my most reluctant sanity-supplicant, beginning as an angry, confrontational, embittered, and lonely man who was suffocating under the weight of his own past. Yet he employed our psychemotional processing more successfully than any of his comrades to undertake the greatest degree of self-actualisation into the humble, correctly-confident, serene, and wise leader he is today.

Because of that success, I'm going to give him the last word in *Unmasked! When Being a Superhero Can't Save You From Yourself*, quoting his final answer to my repeated question about how to face life if the glory days never returned. And because I'm giving him the last word, I'll even spot him a few more words than the allotted ten:

> *"New days are upon us. We have no need for personal rewards or individual glory. We, a new F*O*O*J for a new century, have only one mission, and we'll honour that mission to our highest capacity: to serve Man."*

> *—Festus Piltdown III*
> *HKA The Flying Squirrel*

THANKS

To **Bill Mantlo**, the phenomenal comic book writer whose work on *The Micronauts* inspired my lifelong devotion to the comic book medium and changed my life as much as if not more than any other writer.

To the late **Darren Zenko** for indispensable advice on revisions.

To amazing poet, author, and friend **Mark Kozub** for his encouragement on this project.

To **Elizabeth Sumamo** for use of her line "punched him in the soul."

To Figgy Yates for proofreading the manuscript, and for her kind encouragement.

To authors **John Gottman** (*The Relationship Fix*), **Sandy Hotchkiss**, LSCW (*Why Is It Always About You? Saving Yourself from the Narcissists in Your Life*), **Elizabeth Loftus** and **Katherine Ketcham** (*The Myth of Repressed Memory*), and **Nafeez Mosaddeq Ahmed** (*The War on Freedom: How and Why America was Attacked September 11, 2001*) for their often electrifying insights and case studies.

To **my wife Michelle,** my best friend and truly a blessing from the Divine, and to our daughters, who are our very own superhero (and occasionally supervillain) team.

And finally, to **the Supreme.**

READING GROUP QUESTIONS

CONTENT

1. The novel employs an unreliable narrator who frequently spouts nonsense. Nevertheless, at times the narrator seems to make sense. Is this inconsistency a flaw? If not, what purposes does it serve?

2. What various elements of North American culture does *Shrinking the Heroes* seek to satirise? Why?

3. What other works of satire bear similarities to *Shrinking the Heroes?*

4. *Shrinking the Heroes* makes numerous allusions to pop culture, literature, famous people, and historic and cultural events. How, and for what purposes, does the novel engage the following?

- Prescott Bush's WWII trading practices
- Ralph Nader
- Conrad Black
- Aaron McGruder
- Dick Cheney
- George H. W. Bush
- George W. Bush
- Condoleezza Rice
- X-Clan
- The Baltimore inner-city housing facility protected by a Nation of Islam-affiliated security agency

- The destruction of the MOVE house in Philadelphia
- The September 11, 2001 attacks

5. How, and for what purposes, does the novel engage issues of class, race, gender, sexual orientation, and sex?

6. How does the novel engage Africentricity, especially as it relates to Ancient Egypt? For what reasons does it do so?

STYLE

7. What are the purposes of formatting the novel as a book within a book?

8. When does the book provide burlesque, and when does it move into psychological realism? Why does it do either one?

9. The book contains numerous passages of intentionally bad writing, but also other sequences featuring unironic prose *style* (even if the *content* is ironic). What are the effects of that inconsistency? Is it a flaw?

ENTERTAINMENT

10. The book features of a range of comedic devices, from bawdy humour to wit. Which provoked the strongest reactions from you?

11. The book contains numerous passages and sections designed to evoke unhumourous responses. When? Why? Which provoked the strongest reactions from you?

12. Which characters do you find most engaging? Why? When?

13. Which characters inspire conflicting responses from you? When? Why?

14, What feelings does the end provoke from you? For what reasons?

ABOUT THE REAL AUTHOR

(Photo credit: Pink Sugar Photography)

The critically-acclaimed author of *The Alchemists of Kush* and the Kindred Award-winning and Philip K. Dick runner-up *Shrinking the Heroes*, Minister Faust first achieved literary accolades for his debut novel, *The Coyote Kings of the Space-Age Bachelor Pa*d, which was shortlisted for the Locus Best First Novel, Philip K. Dick, and Compton-Crook awards.

According to The Routledge Companion to Literature and Science, "Since 1960s, Afrodiasporic authors including Samuel R. Delany, Octavia E. Butler, Nalo Hopkinson, and Minister Faust have become luminaries within the SF community." Minister Faust refers to his sub-genre of writing as Imhotep-Hop, an Africentric literature that draws from myriad ancient African civilisations, explores present realities, and imagines a future in which people struggle not only for justice, but for the stars.

A lifelong fan of science fiction, his earliest memories of the genre were watching *Star Trek: The Original Series* in black & white and having his mother read to him from Robert Heinlein's *Red Planet*. After deciding to become a comic book writer and artist when he was ten, he secretly changed his ambition to science fiction novelist after glancing through the glossary to Frank Herbert's *Dune*. He'd planned to become an ecologist so as to gain Herbert's ecological depth, but before his first university class switched his entire enrolment to English Literature, having concluded that learning to write was more relevant than the hell on earth of four years of 7 am lab classes.

He took his English and Education degrees in the previous millennium at the University of Alberta with a focus on creative writing. After teaching English literature and composition in Edmonton junior high and high schools for a decade, Minister Faust worked as mentor and trainer for the Keshotu Leadership Academy, an Africentric organisation whose manual he also wrote. He later taught at creative writing at Shared Worlds and Clarion West, and presented at the Science Fiction Research Association Conference in Detroit, at Georgia Tech on the topic of Afrofuturism, Imhotep-Hop, and Canada's national journey of multiculturalism; at the University of Illinois at Urbana-Champaign on Afrofuturism and the meaning of Funkadelic's Mothership; and "The Cure for Death by Smalltalk" at TEDx Edmonton on the importance of questions and stories in genuine conversation.

He wrote the children's play *The Wonderful World of Wangari* about the Kenyan scientist, feminist, pro-democracy activist and Nobel Peace Laureate Dr. Wangari Maathai for the Edmonton Sprouts Festival, wrote and performed sketch comedy for Edmonton's 11:02 Show and Gordon's Big Bald Head, and wrote and directed the science fiction play *The Undiscovered Country* for Montreal's Creations, Etc. when he was 17. He contributed to BioWare's Mass Effect 2, co-wrote the Kasumi DLC for Mass Effect 2, and wrote BioWare's Gift of the Yeti and Maxis's DarkSpore.

Minister Faust's articles have appeared in numerous magazines, newspapers, and websites, including on *iO9*, and in *Alberta Views, Adventure Rocketship: Let's All Go to the Science Fiction Disco*, the ACSW *Advocate, Canada 150: Stories of Reconciliation Connecting Us All*, the Del Rey Internet Newsletter, *Engineer Magazine, Food for Thought, The Globe & Mail*, Greg Tate's *Coon Bidness, SEE Magazine, Unlimited, Vue Weekly*, and *Your Health*.

His short stories and poetry have appeared in anthologies including *Cyber World, Edmonton on Location: River City Chronicles, Fiery Spirits and Voices, Griots: A Sword and Soul Anthology, High Level Lit Anthology, Mothership: Tales from Afrofuturism and Beyond*, and *Poetry Nation*.

A former national television host and associate producer, Minister Faust also hosted and produced Canada's longest-running global African news and public affairs programme, *Africentric Radio* (originally *The Terrordome*) between 1991 and 2012, for which he interviewed luminaries such as Tariq Ali, Molefi Kete Asante, Martin Bernal, Noam Chomsky, Chuck D., Austin Clarke, Angela Davis, Karl Evanzz, Tom Fontana, Glen Ford, Nalo Hopkinson, Reginald Hudlin, Ice-T, Janine Jackson, Michael Parenti, Ishmael Reed, Gil Scott-Heron, Vandana Shiva, David Simon, Scott Taylor, and many more. He now hosts *MF GALAXY*, a podcast focusing on the craft and business of writing.

As a radio and print journalist, he has gone as far as the 1995 Million Man March in Washington, DC, and to the Ain-al-Hilweh Palestinian refugee camp in southern Lebanon, to collect stories and hear directly from people living and making history. In 2007-8, he hosted and associate produced *HelpTV*, Canada's highest-rated live national daily programme produced outside Toronto, and for two seasons was a celebrity judge on Book TV's *3 Day Novel Contest*. He also freelanced for CBC's *OutFront* and *DNTO*.

He lives in Edmonton with his wife and daughters inside a refurbished, abandoned planetarium outfitted with a rooftop gravity beam and a helipad. It's the one at the end of the block with a big butterfly on the dome.

The Music of
Shrinking the Heroes

Music always plays an indispensable role for me in creating any novel. It inspires and focuses me while I write, and in many cases certain songs serve as my sound track for select chapters, or moments within chapters.

Please visit the *Shrinking the Heroes* page of ministerfaust.com and click on the music link for the complete music listings for this novel (and for my others, in progress). You'll find links there to buy the albums online, but I encourage you to support your local independent record stores.

Don't call fanboys Hamza and Yehat *slackers*. They're just way too smart for a job market that has beaten their space-age asses into space *dust*. But when rich old enemies from high school, an ex-CFL leg-breaker turned health food kingpin, a van full of mind-enslaving, thanatodelic drug dealers, and a mysterious Ethiopian woman named Sherem with a centuries-old secret, all combine to crush them like the walls of a Death Star trash compactor, Hamza and Yehat haveonly two options:
Be awesome. Or die.

THE COYOTE KINGS
OF THE SPACE-AGE BACHELOR PAD
by Minister Faust

**THE PHILIP K. DICK AWARD FINALIST
THE LOCUS BEST FIRST NOVEL AWARD FINALIST
THE COMPTON-CROOK AWARD FINALIST**

A LOCUS NOTABLE BOOK

A searing novel fusing modern realities with ancient yearning, struggle, and triumph.

Two Sudanese "lost boys." Both lost fathers to civil war, and mothers TO the path of escape. Both were hunted and fell into violence to survive. Both fell beneath the sway of mystic madmen who promised to transform them. And both vowed to transform their worlds, or die trying.

One is Raphael Garang, known to the streets of E-Town as the Supreme Raptor.

The other lost boy is Hru-sa-Usir, who lived 7,000 years ago in the Savage Lands of the Lower Nile, and known to the Greeks as Horus, son of Osiris.

THE ALCHEMISTS
OF KUSH

When Taharqa "Harq" Douglass injures his eye in a freak accident, he discovers that his bizarre immigrant doctor friend Thago is more than a mere muckle-mouthed fish-out-of-water, but an interplanetary "Warmunk" investigating a cosmic mystery and fighting a war across this solar system.

Learning that he possesses of the visionary capacity of chronosis, Harq finds himself drafted into Thago's mission to rescue a princess, free an enslaved boy, and transform an age-old conflict that could claim millions of lives. Fighting fanatics and sheltering inside the doomed Soviet space station Mir, Harq faces the starkest stakes of his life: evolve or die.

WAR & MIR
Volume I: Ascension

After the chaos in Naayt, Harq and Ti-Joto are forced into the dangers of Shr-Koioon, a savage land where the only laws are greed and violence.

While fighting against cruel and vindictive new enemies, Harq and his young charge face new obstacles and new breakthroughs along their path to becoming chronostics.

And while Kaiabreen gears up for a devastating war, Thagó and MarAset engage a top-secret mission that will tear the four of them away from Qorodis and into the terrors of the Darkold. If they succeed, they will transform civilisation itself. But if they fail... will they destroy it?

WAR & MIR
Volume II: The Darkold

Contact
Minister Faust

ministerfaust.com/contacts
Twitter @MinisterFaust

To purchase other fine books
by Minister Faust, visit

ministerfaust.com

Music, videos,
book trailers, speeches:
ministerfaust.com/audio_interviews_talks

MF GALAXY Podcast

Are you a writer who'd like to learn more about the craft
and business of writing? And maybe while you're at it,
gain insights from pop culture, progressive politics, and
Africentricity?

Then enjoy Minister Faust's podcast MF GALAXY!
And it's all free!

patreon.com/mfgalaxy
mfgalaxy.org